DAN LORD
FROM A DARK WAYOVER

BOOK TWO OF THE
VON KOPPERSMITH SAGA

From a Dark Wayover

Copyright © 2016 by Dan Lord. Published 2016.

All rights reserved. Contact: Salvo Publishing, P.O. Box 568, Mount Pleasant, SC 29465; thatstrangestofwars@gmail.com

From a Dark Wayover is a work of fiction. Names, characters, places, and incidents are the products of the author's imagination or are used fictitiously. Any resemblance to actual events, locales, or persons, living or dead, is entirely coincidental.

Works cited:
A Complete Illustrated History of the Crusades and the Crusader Knights by Charles Phillips, Anness Publishing: London, 2010
The Song of Roland Transl. by W.S. Merwin, Modern Library: New York, 2001

ISBN 10: 0-692-79680-0
ISBN 13: 978-0-692-79680-1
Interior maps & images by Dan Lord
Book design by John Herreid

Printed in the United States of America

SALVO
PUBLISHING

From a Dark Wayover

Thanks to my sister Jenny, for her plentiful anecdotes and acumen
And extra-special thanks to the superb efforts of my editorial team, Daniel and Jack

This book is for Hallie, the One for Me

From a Dark Wayover

From a Dark Wayover

Contents

Part 1 – Death Looks for Leo. A Mysterious Superhero and a Man Named Max. Melvin Keystack Makes a Proposal…**0**

Part 2 – Back to the Island, Which Is Behaving Strangely. To Mount Highpalace. A Dire Balloon Adventure. Chasing Mealworm, and Vice Versa…**168**

Part 3 – Ms. Winnipeg's Sword Search. Darkshot Is Born. Max and Walter Hatch a Plan, and Leo Hatches a Borrowing, But None of It Goes Very Well…**432**

From a Dark Wayover

Part 1 - Death Looks for Leo. A Mysterious Superhero and a Man Named Max. Melvin Keystack Makes a Proposal.

Excerpt from *A Complete Illustrated History of the Crusades and the Crusader Knights*:

"There were two waves to the Children's Crusade, one issuing from northern France and one beginning in Germany. The story goes that in May 1212 a shepherd boy named Stephen from Cloyes-sur-le-Loir (near Châteaudun in the Vermandois)...embarked on a preaching tour of the countryside and gathered many followers among the youth and children of the area...

The French group headed southwards towards the Mediterranean coast under Stephen's leadership...Many died of exhaustion, illness or starvation on the way, and others simply drifted away, but when they reached Marseilles they were still as many as 30,000 in number...

They were never seen again in France..."

From a Dark Wayover

One

There was some snow, but mostly ice, clean and glittering. The twigs on every tree were sealed in tiny crystal coats, and showers of slush and grains of hail rattled through the branches and down the wide, shimmery slopes of the Von Koppersmith mansion.

The boys, all four hundred fifty of them, were already out in it, even though it was only eight o'clock in the morning. This kind of weather was a rare and aggravating phenomenon for most of South Carolina's Lowcountry denizens, but for the boys it brought back bittersweet memories of the snowier places of the German countryside from which they had come, far away and many centuries in the past.

Mrs. Von Koppersmith watched them from a wraparound screened-in porch. Past the fluff of her sky-

From a Dark Wayover

blue slippers and under the fringes of the azure-colored wool blanket in which she had cocooned herself, wintry air was sneaking in and beginning to prickle her with invisible fingernails. She didn't mind. The boys' cacophonous squeals seemed to add lining to her blanket. She was warmed by their unpolluted delight over the ordinary magic of icicles hanging like diamond necklaces from the bushes and the fences, and of the gold, emerald and vermillion Christmas lights on green strands which spread like kudzu vines around the majestic house. The two years since the boys arrived had simply been the best of her adult life.

At last the cold gave her a ruder pinch, and with a good-natured yelp she scurried back indoors. She laughed at herself, but the sound ran away when she heard Anselm calling for her.

Her faithful old head of housekeeping had a peculiar tone in his voice that drew her quickly, through an oak-floored study with a crackling fireplace and down a spacious hall, to the kitchen.

Anselm was leaning against the stainless steel counter, staring at a mounted television. Without glancing at Mrs. Von Koppersmith, he said bluntly, "You ought to see this, ma'am."

Recorded news footage played upon the T.V. screen. Multiple versions of the same scene looped above bright headlines and earnestly scrolling text, while reporters jabbered back and forth to one another like macaws.

"...*filmed less than twenty minutes ago here in Manhattan...*"

One video loop, recorded by some quivering amateur with a digital camera, showed the Empire State Building...

"...*attempted terrorist attack...eerie similarities to 9/11...*"

From a Dark Wayover

Mrs. Von Koppersmith watched in dread as another camera showed a shadowy passenger airliner sweeping across the New York sky like a gray claw…

"Oh no…" She clutched Anselm's forearm. "Oh no, not again…"

"No, ma'am," Anselm replied gravely, "Just watch…"

The pitch of the news reporter's voice rose with anticipation as the recorded footage showed the Empire State Building again, its terraced walls like white gold, and the airplane speeding towards it with lethal certainty…

"…*travelling at more than 400 miles per hour, and yet…*"

Coming in like a dart from another angle lower on the screen, a blurry figure appeared, surrounded by a clean, white halo that had been added in by the news network's editors to help distinguish it from its surroundings. To a chorus of squawking newscasters, a

From a Dark Wayover

montage of recorded perspectives showed the figure intercepting the huge, rushing aircraft and driving its nose away from the Empire State Building...

"...*we cannot at this time say exactly what has happened, but, as you can see here, it appears a...a man has diverted the terrorists from their attack trajectory, avoiding collision with the Empire State Building by less than a hundred yards...*"

Mrs. Von Koppersmith gasped. "A flying man..."

Anselm smiled. "The passengers are all safe! The terrorists have been apprehended. And they aren't even from the Middle East. They're some international group, calling themselves 'the Hitbacks'..."

The news network had now cut to a pretty reporter bundled up in a thick coat and a wool cap, standing on a regional airport tarmac in real time, with the rescued airliner and a jumble of police lights and emergency vehicles in the background: "...taken into custody by federal authorities, while the man responsible for the prevention of this disaster is no longer on scene. We do have several eyewitnesses with some more spectacular details concerning what is truly a spectacular event…"

She pushed her microphone in front of a jovial ambulance driver with thick facial hair and a thicker New York accent who had been eagerly awaiting his cue to speak: "Yeah, dat's right, he, like, gently put dat whole entire plane on the ground right here like he was frickin' Superman or somethin', then he pulled off the door and tossed out the terrorists like dey was nothin', and as soon as the authorities had 'em he just flew off…"

"…he flew off," parroted the reporter, nodding solemnly. "Into the sky?"

The ambulance driver couldn't suppress a throaty laugh. " 'Into da sky' is right! Like a boid, like a plane…I don't even *know*, y'know?"

From a Dark Wayover

"And can you describe him?"

"Yeah, he was in dis gold and white outfit, wit' a gold cape, and a gold helmet that, like, covered da' top half of his head, wit' a 'I' on it. Big, tall guy. Long, black hair. Real superstar-lookin', y'know?"

"And, just before he departed, he said something to the onlookers, isn't that right?"

"Yeah, he told us his name! It's 'Invictus'."

"Invictus…"

Mrs. Von Koppersmith stared at Anselm. "What is this? What in the world is happening?"

Anselm let out a laugh, and then stifled it just as quickly, slowly shaking his head in bewilderment. "Does Leo know, I wonder?"

"Today was his last day on shift at the fire station. He should be leaving…" She looked at a clock on a far wall. "…Right about now…"

From a Dark Wayover

Outside, the sleet had transformed into fat snowflakes. Across the sprawling estate, patches of white had begun to accumulate here and there, and down Highway 12 southerners drove cautiously, perplexed by the unusual precipitation. Outside Charleston, at Fire Department Station 7, the resident emergency responders were briskly reminded by their superior to stay alert for weather-related mayhem.

"Aw, it's just a lil' bit a' snow," drawled Macmullin as he leaned back comfortably in a La-Z-Boy in the break room. "That ain't nuthin'. But that right there…," he stabbed a finger in the direction of the big Vizio in the corner of the room, upon which the footage of the attempted terrorist attack and the mysterious Invictus was being replayed and commented upon incessantly. "*That's* somethin'!"

His fellow firemen on duty, their eyes fixed on the Vizio, all eagerly concurred. Macmullin gave an appreciative whistle, watching for the sixth time as the airborne figure diverted the airplane from its fearful course. "Man, that is <u>unbelievable</u>. Wutchoo think, Von Koppersmith?"

Leo was on one knee, tying the laces of his shoes. His hair was still damp from the shower, and he brushed off a plump drop of water that had rolled past his eye and into his brown, closely trimmed beard. "It's not unbelievable. I believe. I just don't know what it all means yet." He stood, and gave Macmullin a gentle punch in the shoulder. "I'm going home. You fellas take care."

It was a forty-five minute drive back to the estate. Highway 12 was only two lanes meandering sleepily through shady forests of mossy cypress trees and, as he followed it, Leo contemplated the amiable crew back at the fire station.

From a Dark Wayover

They didn't really know him. They knew he was a Von Koppersmith, and everything that entailed: a huge inheritance, a gigantic secluded mansion, and a colorful family history. They knew he didn't have to work—they themselves were workingmen, so it was a mystery to them that Leo had chosen to become a firefighter. "I wanted to give something," Leo had once said, when pressed about it. "And not just write a check, but put my *hands* into something. And I wanted to show the boys that that was important."

Most every local knew about the high population of children now inhabiting the Von Koppersmith mansion. On the other hand, no one knew that those same children were originally from the thirteenth century, or that they had been part of the Children's Crusade, or that the legendary Pied Piper had captured and transported them to a hidden island where they had lived without aging for eight centuries. Those weren't the sorts

From a Dark Wayover

of details one revealed to federal, state and county authorities when applying to establish a domestic orphanage and fill it with what were essentially hundreds of undocumented illegal aliens. Fortunately for Leo, a surprisingly miniscule amount of information was required once massive amounts of money had surreptitiously been awarded to the right people.

Leo tapped the remote on his dashboard, and the huge, black, wrought iron gates at the entrance to the Von Koppersmith estate parted for him.

Whisking down a blacktop lane towards the mansion, he began to feel the hallowed thrill of returning home. Gray and yellow warblers hopped among his nets of Christmas lights glowing warmly against the white snow. A hundred yards out from the venerable old house, he began passing the unmistakable signs of multitudinous young boys: entire suburbs of tree houses…copious and sundry bicycles lying around in the fields in spite of all stern instructions to not leave them lying around in the fields…a sporting goods store's worth of soccer balls, footballs and boomerangs…discarded shoes—what were likely hundreds of them—dotting the landscape like a vast crop of some new kind of leather-bound cabbages. This was the world he lived in now. He shook his head and grinned.

The boys had already spotted his familiar brown and yellow Ford pick-up. Prior to that, they had been widely scattered (though concentrated on the south side of the mansion engaged in a make-believe battle of robots), but with Leo's advent they now began to unify like a flock of migrating birds. They wheeled across the lawn, flapping their arms, rushing past slides and monkey bars, cheering and shouting. Leo, the man who had become, for all practical purposes, their dad, had been away on a week-and-a-half shift, but now he was home, at last.

From a Dark Wayover

They knew not to climb on the truck. That was about as much discipline as could be expected at times like these. They crashed into him like human whitewater, hollering and waving, smothering him in hugs. As he tried to make it from the truck to the mansion, they moved with him, but also propelled him.

Stumbling in through the massive front doors, Leo fielded innumerable questions and did his best to attend to the plentiful parallel tales being told to him, even as he almost helplessly followed the savory aroma of beef and carrot stew to the kitchen.

Four cooks were busy preparing dinner, which—these days—was always a mighty affair. Anselm and a servant stood polishing silverware.

The head of housekeeping gave Leo a welcoming smile. "I imagine you've seen this already?" He pointed towards the breaking headlines on the television.

Before responding, Leo convinced the boys to go find other things to do until dinnertime. Once he pushed the last few shaved heads through the swinging doors, he nodded gravely. "Yep, at the station, as I was leaving."

"A flying man. Do you suppose it could be him?"

"The description sounds awfully close to Zechariah, if what the eyewitnesses are saying is right. But, why would he do this? Not that it isn't a great thing, but he could have been rescuing people from disasters a long time ago. Why start now?"

"Indeed. But who other than Zechariah possesses these sorts of powers?"

Just then, Oddo burst in and reminded Leo that he had promised to move a hefty toy chest up to the den. Leo glanced at Anselm. "We'll talk more about this later."

The toy chest was wide and made of a dense wood, but Leo was pleased at the relative ease with which he was able to transport it to the second floor. He had been exercising almost every day for the past eighteen months, and had increased his physical strength dramatically.

    His beloved old den already had a cheerful fire in the fireplace. The curtains were drawn back from the big picture window, showing the gray sky and the light snowfall. Most of the boys were now tramping around downstairs or outside, and after Leo put down the toy chest he paused to soak in the calm.

    He listened to the tiny pops of the fire, and to the low, freezing wind moaning softly outside. Stretching his arms casually, he turned and spied a skinny, diminutive figure crouching in a dim corner of the den.

    One of the boys, Leo thought at first, until it stepped onto the wall and stuck there on all fours, like a tree frog.

    "Gollyplox!" Leo exclaimed with a grin. He could not imagine how the Cheevilnid had made it here from the Island without Leo's Flute to open the Wayover, but here he was!

Leo took two steps towards him, but some indistinct misgiving made him stop again. "Gollyplox?"

The Cheevilnid did not make a sound. He just hung upon the wall in the shadows, and his bulbous eyes barely caught a few glimmers of light from the fire. Without taking his gaze off of Leo, he reached into a small black shoulder bag and withdrew something silvery.

Leo peered into the darkness. "Gollyplox, what's wrong?"

There was a small, sticky wet sound as the Cheevilnid opened his mouth and let the end of his tongue slide out. Onto the tip he slipped a metallic cap with several two-inch long spikes jutting out at clumsy angles.

This was not Gollyplox, Leo suddenly realized. It was some other Cheevilnid, gray-skinned, with a different shape to the head, and a shorter neck. As Leo took one more step, the Cheevilnid leaned his head slightly forward, and his face caught some of the light from the window. Above the globular eyes, upon the smooth, gray forehead, dark glyphs showed:

3̃3̃3̃
3̃3̃3̃

Leo stepped back, confused. The Cheevilnid opened his mouth, firing his tongue, and the spiked metal cap sped towards Leo's face.

Some grace or instinct moved Leo's body for him, twisting it out of the way at the last instant. He fell backwards over the leather couch.

The Cheevilnid leapt to another wall and spit his tongue out just as Leo stood back up. This time the spikes caught him squarely in the left clavicle, sticking in the bone for a second before he pulled away with a shout.

From a Dark Wayover

"*Rakraaaaakkkcriktu,*" cried the Cheevilnid, firing again. Already in mid-leap, Leo avoided the strike. The spiked cap smashed through the fireplace tools, retracted, then fired again, and again. Leo whirled and bent wildly, barely avoiding the deadly cap, hearing it buzz by his face over and over. As lamps shattered around him and framed paintings were knocked from their hangers, all he could do was just keep dodging, moving around the room, hoping to somehow make a break for the doorway…

He stumbled, feeling the cap whir over his head. When he stood again, he found himself against the wintery, gray light of the picture window.

The spiked cap snapped across the room in a sprinkle of saliva, striking Leo dead on the chin. It hit like a boxer's fist. Leo's head rocked back, and his upper body smashed through the window glass and into the icy air.

From a Dark Wayover

The Cheevilnid bounced nimbly over the top of the leather couch and onto the windowsill. Flakes of snow wafted through the shattered picture window, landing upon his tombstone-colored skin.

He recoiled. He had never experienced snow before, and the coldness of it was hateful to him.

He looked down. Almost forty feet below, Leo's body lay upon a thin rug of snow and dead yellow grass. Some of the boys were running to him now, shouting for help. Blood trickled out from Leo's scalp and turned the icy white ground to red.

The Cheevilnid plucked the spiked cap off of his tongue. As he placed it back in his black shoulder bag, he drew out a brown, wooden flute. It had spikes, too, shorter and duller, covering its length and the outside of its bell like a skin disease. The Cheevilnid put his thin lips to the mouth hole and breathed. Out came an off-key, serpentine melody, a morose song for an evil dream.

From a Dark Wayover

The air around the couch and the fireplace tore apart. Wind whistled through the dark opening of a Wayover, and reality vibrated around the edges.

Three of the boys burst into the room, but they were immediately paralyzed by what they saw. The Cheevilnid, giving them a look of bated loathing, nonchalantly put his instrument back into his bag. He stepped into the Wayover, and the aperture closed behind him with a gulping sound.

The fire crackled. Wind and snow blew through the window. Outside and throughout the mansion, the boys screamed for help.

From a Dark Wayover

Two

Twenty-five years ago,

Cincinnati, Ohio...

Maximilian Bosco resolutely guarded a partly demolished ant bed.

He stood in the grassy, fenced-in schoolyard of Little Flower Catholic School (which stood across from the eponymous church), his little hands hovering a few inches from his waistline in the closest thing to a pugilistic stance that a four-year-old can strike. Around the ant bed was a ring of round, diminutive gnome heads. The sun glowed dully on the backs of their necks and ears.

"Look at 'em wunning awound!" giggled portly Franklin, leering down at the ant bed. "Let's put a bug on 'em!"

Max frowned severely at the suggestion. He balled up his fists and made a statue out of himself.

"Leave 'em alone. You already messed up their house. They worked really hard on that…"

Another boy—Jimmy—poked his head farther into the center of the circle and snorted. "Dumb anth! They can't even thee where they goin'!" The ants did indeed seem to be scuttling randomly in all directions.

Jimmy grabbed a stick and stabbed the part of the mound that was still intact.

"Cut it out!" Max grabbed the stick out of Jimmy's hand and threw it into an azalea bush.

"Max likes ants!" shouted Thomas with scornful glee.

From a Dark Wayover

Jimmy made a goggle-eye look at Max. "Yeah, he wanth ta kith 'em!"

"He wants to *marry* 'em!"

Max just stood there, fists clenched, face frowning. The fusillade of tiny insults flew at him and bounced off like nerf darts against a bronze shield.

Not getting the desired reaction, Franklin got bored, and Jimmy and the others flitted away to the monkey bars. Max remained, his shadow lying over the ant bed. A breeze blew his pumice blond hair.

He crouched and examined the sandy debris. The ants were slowing down, as if an invisible switch had been thrown that downgraded the whole crisis from red alert to yellow, but they continued to nervously patrol their borders.

Max gently reached down and extended a finger, inviting one of the ants on board. His nail burrowed into the ground slightly, and it crept up the pale bridge to his knuckle.

With his eyes forming a blue sky over the insect, Max watched the ant scamper around his hand, from the back to the palm and back up the forefinger. The boy turned his hand in careful synchronicity with it, whispering lovingly, calming its fears, letting it know that the danger was over now, the threat had passed…

The ant reached his middle knuckle and stopped. Max admired its gossamer legs and its trembling antennae.

It bit him. Max did not make a sound, but instinctively he grabbed his finger with his other hand and obliterated the creature with his thumb, grinding it into ragged specks. He had not meant to kill it; it was just a blind act of self-preservation.

His finger ached. He held it and looked around to see if there had been any witnesses. No one had noticed.

From a Dark Wayover

Max walked to the water fountain to soak the stinging bite.

⋯✦⋅✦⋅✦⋅✦⋅✦⋅✦

Years later, in sixth grade, he was still very small for his age. His peers often referred to him as "Pee Wee" and "Little Bit." The girls thought he was cute, and most everyone regarded him as likeable.

His best friend was Walter Wallace, one of the tallest boys in class. When Walter and Max stood together they looked like an upper case "I" and a lower case "i." Walter was slow-moving and congenial, and his height made him (if nothing else) an ideal center for the basketball team. Max, being small and quick, was better suited as a forward. During games, they occasionally accomplished some good plays together, such as when Walter managed to block a shot with one of his big, swaying arms so that Max could snatch up the ball and dribble it down the court to score a basket. On Fridays, every once in a while, Max's mother might let him spend the night at the Wallaces'. Walter's mom would order pizza, and a few other kids would show up for an after-dusk game of 'Flashlight,' or they would pretend to be *Star Trek* characters or medieval knights.

One evening, during basketball practice, some of the other players were making fun of Walter. They were bouncing basketballs off of his soft belly and calling him derogatory names related to his height.

Max had not yet noticed. He was on the opposite side of the gym at the time, small and pale in his shiny red baggy shorts and jersey, drinking ice water from a paper cup. Something—some sound or sense—made him turn, and there he saw his good friend being persecuted.

His paper cup dropped to the glossy gym floor with a hollow "thok."

From a Dark Wayover

Like a shimmering crimson dart he flew across the gym. He planted himself firmly between Walter and the bullies and shouted in a shrill voice, "Why don't you pick on someone your own size!" Max had picked up that line from a movie he had recently seen, and he thought it sounded bold.

"Max," Walter mumbled uncomfortably. "They *are* my size."

That was true. Worse, Max was definitely not their size by at least two feet.

Thankfully, Coach Simmons broke the whole thing up and sent the bullies to clean up basketballs. They gave Max several scowls as they retreated.

Later, when Max was walking out to his mom's waiting car under a purple floodlight, he heard a shout: "Hey, Pee Wee!" When he turned to see who was calling him, a basketball struck him flat in the nose like a round, brown boxing glove. Instantly, warm red blood began to flow from his nostrils.

Max's mother leapt out of the car and shouted angrily at the bullies as they scampered like gibbering Morlocks into the darkness behind the gym. She gathered her son up and began carefully inspecting his nose, vowing vengeance upon the attackers and their parents and their relatives and the city and the nation, in general. She led him by the shoulders to the passenger seat of the car, buckled him in, and closed the door.

Holding his nose and staring disinterestedly out of the windshield at a couple of moths flitting around a floodlight, Max earnestly hoped Walter was safe, and that the bullies had not done anything to him similar to what they had done to Max.

⋯⇥⋅⇥⋅⇥⋅⇥⋅⇥⋅⇥

By the time he was a senior in high school, Max was six feet tall, and no one called him "Pee Wee"

From a Dark Wayover

anymore. He had begun lifting weights his freshman year, and now he had a lean, strong body with a rack of abdominal muscles that looked like two rows of young turtle shells. He was painfully shy, although he remained as affable as always. He did not care for school very much, but managed to maintain a row of modest little 'C's on his report card.

One thing that Max particularly hated was any kind of disrespect towards women. His mother was sweet and devoted, and his two older sisters had doted on him all of his life. Females were therefore considered by him to be lofty, irreproachable beings against whom any insult was tantamount to blasphemy. So, when pubescent cads inappropriately accosted Suzilu Milligan at a cafeteria table during lunch one day, Max felt compelled by every molecule in his body to defend her sanctity.

In fact, she was defending it herself, in her own way, with carefully chosen expletives and, as a final measure, a handful of French fries thrown in the faces of the three offenders. When they responded to that with a round of simian hoots and gesticulations, Suzilu became exasperated and hopped to her feet. Her circle of friends mimicked her. They all yanked their purses around their shoulders and were about to march out with chins held high when Max appeared before the three lascivious scoundrels.

"Why don't you pick on someone your own size?" It was the only thing Max could think of to say; he was not a witty fellow. His talent, so to speak, was justice, not clever banter.

The cads all burst into laughter and spent some time mocking Max's catchphrase. Half of Suzilu's friends, making cracks about "boys always fighting," abandoned the scene, but the other half (including Suzilu) stepped back and waited to see what would happen.

From a Dark Wayover

Max stood his ground, his fists balled up and his body a rigid statue. Having gone through a cycle of caustic jibes at Max, at his catchphrase, at his manhood, and at his mother, the three bullies realized that Max was still just standing there, staring down at them. Their leader, another senior named Kurt Vank, snorted and began to ease out of his chair like a hunting reptile. This naturally involved having to lean forward some as he pushed his chair back. Max took advantage of the opportunity.

With a quick, deft move he grabbed the top of Kurt's disheveled brown hair and smashed the boy's face into the surface of the cafeteria table. Kurt howled and toppled over holding a broken nose.

Mr. Blaine, the biology teacher, and Mr. Goyen, the janitor, were suddenly among them all, holding back the bullies, who were now ready for war. The girls began a shrill tirade, telling the adults all the insults they had endured. Suzilu, in particular, was quite vocal in defending Max Bosco's chivalry. More teachers arrived. Max and his three opponents were hauled to the principal's office; all of their parents were called to come pick them up.

Neither Mrs. nor Mr. Bosco were angry with their son. After hearing the whole story, they expressed pride in his action, though they made him understand that he would have to pay, in a spirit of meekness, the school's penalties for breaking its rules against fighting, which included two weeks' suspension and summer school. "That's how the world is," his father told him. "Sometimes good things are punishable by law."

Regardless, they gave him hugs and told him he did the right thing. "If it had been one of your sisters they were talking to like that," blurted Mrs. Bosco, "I would have punched those rascals myself!"

From a Dark Wayover

There was buzz at school for some time afterwards that Max had a crush on Suzilu Milligan. Suzilu enjoyed the gossip, and she *did* think Max was cute and she thought she might even fall in love with him for a few weeks, if only because it rounded off the entire dramatic episode so romantically, like the end of a good movie.

Max did not really have much interest in Suzilu, and he bashfully avoided her. There were other girls at school who were more attractive to him (not that he was confident enough to talk to them). He finally decided to simply avoid her or any conversations about the fight and just get on with the school year, which would mercifully end in about three months. After a few weeks it really did seem like the uproar was dying away.

It was on a warm April afternoon while walking home from school that the entire episode came vividly back to life. He had just crossed the railroad tracks and was starting off across a small, decrepit parking lot that for years had stood in need of repaving. He often followed this lonely route, which took him to a spot behind a dingy plumbing parts store and a palm reader's shop. From there he could ford the shallow waters of a deep, wide drainage ditch and be home in five minutes.

    As he tramped along, idly watching chunks of dirty gray asphalt crumble beneath his shoes, a 1985 flame-colored Oldsmobile swept up beside him in a spray of leaves and trash. It was Kurt Vank's car.

    There were five riders in all, and Max recognized each from school. Two of them leapt out before the Oldsmobile came to a full stop, cutting him off from any possible escape across the drainage ditch. The other three, including Kurt himself, slinked out of the vehicle, grinning maliciously.

    With fists raised, Max stood glancing at each of them, thinking how he could get away. The boys circled him. They cackled and called out moronic insults. Three of them produced thick, black, plastic trash bags, each of which was filled with five pounds of broken glass.

Max went on the offensive. He ran straight for Kurt Vank, but before he got within two yards the others were piling on like army ants. Max caught one's chin with a desperate right hook, but then he was crushed chest-down by sheer weight. With a strange, girlish shriek, one of the boys brought his bag full of jagged glass smashing down on Max's back.

Max was so shocked by the pain that he shuddered wildly and nearly broke free. The assailants flung themselves on him again, and Kurt Vank caught Max's left jaw line with a bag of glass. Skin tore free. Another boy slammed Max's back again, and then another. The unarmed ones shouted with glee and kept Max pinned down, while Kurt and the other two went at him like crazed drummers.

From a Dark Wayover

It was the owner of the plumbing parts store who broke it up, a middle-aged army veteran waving a dirty Louisville Slugger in one hand and a Taser gun in the other.

The boys fled with their torn, black bags back to the flame-colored Oldsmobile, leaving trails of twinkling glass shards behind them.

What the plumbing parts storeowner found lying on the ground made his guts clench up. He saw a tattered shirt and a red, flayed back, dark blood and bits of glass. The body shivered, as if cold.

Max spent three full days in the hospital. He needed fifteen stitches for his jaw line and skin grafts for his back. Kurt Vank and his cohorts were sent to Cincinnati Juvenile for the rest of the school year, where they bragged to everyone about what they had done. Mr. Bosco filed suit against their parents, but eventually dropped the charges at Max's impassioned request. He just wanted to forget the whole thing and move on.

One night, at the hospital, her eyes welling up with tears, Mrs. Bosco, with trembling voice, asked her son about that day in the cafeteria when he defended the honor of Suzilu Milligan.

"Would you still have done it, son, if you had known what was coming?"

She knew the answer before he said it. She knew her son.

Three

Present day,

South Carolina…

Sounds spilled into Leo's mind slowly, as if flowing over a rim and into a sink.

Sounds of a machine-driven beeping; of breathing; of someone talking as they passed near and then faded away.

Now a smell: like a cleanser, something antiseptic.

Leo's eyes fluttered open. He was in a hospital room.

An oxygen tube was in his nose. He was dressed in a teal green gown, his feet in white socks. He felt cold and uncomfortable…but it was not simply because of the cold…what else?

The side of his head. It ached…

His eyes opened more widely now as he remembered: he had fallen out of the window…no, not just fallen—he had been <u>knocked</u> out…

The boys! Mom! Were they safe?

Leo turned left and right, looking for some way to call a nurse, but the movements made his neck hurt.

"Hey…" The summons came out like a frog's croak.

A frog…that Cheevilnid! Not Gollyplox. Who was he? Why did he attack me?

Leo's fingers found a dingy white call button at the end of a thick, soft cord and he repeatedly squashed it with his thumb as his imagination showed him visions of the mysterious gray Cheevilnid chasing the boys around the mansion and stabbing them with its spike-tongue…

"HEY!" His voice sounded raw.

A thin, pale, mousy nurse scurried into the room. "Oh! Mr. Von Koppersmith!" She spoke with a thick southern drawl. "Welcome back!" She reached up to a panel near Leo's head and turned a switch. "How you feelin'?"

"The boys…" Leo's heart rate had gone up quickly, and his breathing was shallow. "The boys…Mama…"

"Alright, alright," cooed the nurse, "Everything's fine, Mr. Von Koppersmith. Right, Debbie?"

A second nurse, as pale as the first but with blotches of pink, had appeared at the doorway. Debbie was heavyset, with dirty blond ringlets and a chubby chin that wobbled as she nodded enthusiastically. "Everything's fine. You just took a little spill, is all!"

Leo stared from one nurse to the other. "What? What do you mean?"

From a Dark Wayover

The thin, mousy nurse giggled and she bent closer to him to adjust some wires that were pasted to his chest and arms. "A little tumble-bumble! Got 'im a little bonkeroo on the head, didn't he, Deb'?"

Debbie snorted. "I'll say! A three-inch long one. Needed seventeen stitches! Five more on the chin. That, plus a concussion, four broken ribs, and a cracked right arm. The humerus, to be exact.'"

The mousy nurse stood erect and gave a look of faux outrage. "Oh, there's nothing humorous about it, Debbie Deb!"

Both women squealed with laughter while Leo breathed open-mouthed and stared in confusion.

Suddenly leaning in very closely, the mousy nurse frowned as part of an exaggerated show of maternal concern. "So, how you feelin', honey? What's hurtin'? My name is Janet, by the way."

The pain in the side of Leo's head seemed to intensify, and he felt dizzy. "The boys…is everybody safe back home?"

Janet straightened up and exchanged a long, sympathetic look with Debbie. "That is so su-weeet. Goes and takes a tumble-bumble like that and all he can think about is his kids. Now that's a good daddy…"

Debbie nodded profoundly, causing more wobbles to the chub of her chin. "A very good daddy. But they're fine, sugar. They're not the ones who took a spill!"

Janet giggled. "*You're* the one who took a spill, silly-billy! Your mama called the ambulance, and yer butler rode with you. He's been here for hours…just stepped out about fifteen minutes ago to go get some dinner, but he said he'll be back…"

Leo suddenly felt hypersensitive to the oxygen tube and the various wires that were attached to him. He

From a Dark Wayover

saw a y-shaped plastic plug protruding from his left wrist; into one side of the 'y' was connected a tube, which was receiving fluid from an IV bag on a metal stand next to the bed. It all made him feel queasy and claustrophobic; he forced himself to concentrate on the information the nurses were giving him. "My 'butler'? You mean Anselm? He's O.K.? He's safe?"

Debbie snickered. "He's good to go, honey. You just fell out of your window. What were you doin'…cleanin' the glass, and lost your balance?"

"That happened to a cousin of mine once," offered Janet with a grave expression.

"No…" Leo still couldn't catch his breath. "No…I didn't fall…I was pushed!"

Janet and Debbie stiffened and looked at each other.

Leo was sweating, and his eyesight had become blurry. "A Cheevilnid…!"

From a Dark Wayover

Janet frowned and leaned in again. "A what, honey?"

Leo shook his head impatiently, closing his eyes in the hope of ridding himself of the blurriness. He tried to explain, but only two words came out: "A frogman...!"

Nodding to each other, Janet and Debbie both sighed deeply and began to move about the room with heightened purpose. "O.K. now, honey," said Janet, "I think you've gotten yourself a *little* overexcited, sugar..."

"A *little* overexcited, that's right." Debbie had positioned herself next to the bed and was ready to employ her corpulent arms as stabilizers upon Leo's squirming body if the need arose.

Janet quickly hung a second IV bag upon the metal stand and took its tube in her fingers. The tip of the tube, Leo could see, was equipped with a sharp needle. "We're just gonna give you a nice little somethin'-

somethin' to help you relax a bitty-bit…gimme just a second now…"

Leo suddenly hoisted himself up so that he was propped on his elbows. His eyes were wide and staring. "No! You don't understand! The boys aren't safe!"

"Now, sugar," said Debbie firmly, reaching over and placing her hands on his shoulders. "Your family's fine. Everybody's O.K…"

Leo gripped her blubbery wrist imploringly. "I was attacked! I didn't fall!"

Debbie kept reassuring him in gentle tones.

"Almost got it," cooed Janet as she began to slide the needle into the other side of the y-shaped plastic plug sticking out of his wrist.

"And don't do THAT!" Leo swung his arm and swatted the metal stand over on its side with a loud clatter, yanking the needle and tube out of Janet's hand. The mousy nurse squeaked.

From a Dark Wayover

"Mr. Von Koppersmith!" grunted Debbie as she tried to hold Leo down. "Relax, now! Your family is fine!"

Ripping the tubes out of his nose and wrist, Leo pitched forward, right out of nurse Debbie's grip.

"Ohh!!" yelled Janet. She reached for him, but he threw himself towards the foot of the bed and toppled onto the floor.

"Harriet!" Debbie was shouting through the door even as she and Janet tried to grab hold of Leo. "Harriet, call a Code 27 *quick!*"

All the wires that had been pasted to Leo popped loose as he scrambled to his feet and lurched to the doorway. He was still dizzy, and his head and neck were throbbing with pain, yet he felt strangely energized. "The boys are in danger!" he shouted, as if he was officially declaring war. "I've got to save them!" He charged down a white hallway, while over the intercom a female voice said, "Code 27, Room 322…Code 27, Room 322…"

Leo considered the elevator but, hearing the patter of many footsteps behind him, he thought better of it and ran for the stairs.

His explosive burst through the door on the first floor turned the heads of various nurses, hospital staff members, and visitors. Knowing how suspicious he must look, standing there in his teal hospital gown and white ankle socks, he decided to stand suddenly in place and gaze around with tranquil inquisitiveness, as if he were waiting to meet someone. He took a few short steps forward, rubbing his arm for lack of anything else he could do that was normal looking. Just then the intercom system hiccupped and a robotic voice announced: "Security Code 6…Security Code 6…white male…Code 6…"

From a Dark Wayover

The monotone voice and the mysterious numbers had no effect on most of the people present, but the nurses jumped to their feet instantly. They now knew there was a patient who had gone roaming, and right away it became clear to all of them that Leo was that patient.

Leo ran for the big, sunny glass doors that led outside. The nurses pursued; there were twelve in all. At that same moment, from out of the stairwell, many more nurses poured out onto the first floor from the upper levels of the hospital. By the time Leo reached the glass front doors there were more than thirty female medical professionals racing after him, in white scrubs, or lavender scrubs, or scrubs printed with cartoon bunnies and monkeys and large-print friendly expressions such as "Hello friend!" and "You're fun!" Stethoscopes and blood monitors and little bottles of hand sanitizer dropped loose from their pockets, but there was no time to recover them, for this was a Code 6, an unauthorized self-removal of a patient from Charleston Medical College Hospital, and he must be stopped at all costs…

The back of his green shamrock-print boxers peeked at the pursuing throng from between the thin flaps of his hospital gown as Leo scampered along a shaded emergency lane and around a corner toward a vast parking lot.

"Oh, Mr. Von Koppersmith!" shrieked Janet. "You must stop! You must stop this instant!"

The entire mob of nurses hollered and called to him, losing more medical trinkets as their arms flapped desperately, but Leo had gone too far to stop now. He felt feverish, and his eyes still couldn't focus very well, but all he could think about was that gray Cheevilnid leaping throughout the mansion, hunting the screaming children from room to room.

From a Dark Wayover

A white and orange ambulance had pulled up, and two EMT men were bringing a gurney out from the back doors. Lying upon the thin mattress was Mr. Lloyd Buggins, a ninety-three year old retired accountant who had slipped and broken his ankle earlier while cleaning his cockatoo's birdcage. He gave out a dry, startled squawk at the sudden appearance of Leo, who barely noticed anything other than the fact that this ambulance could transport him back to the mansion in minutes, and the back doors were wide open, and the keys were twinkling in the ignition.

"Woah there, buddy!" shouted one of the EMT men, letting go of the gurney and snatching Leo by the arm as he tried to crawl into the back of the van. "Where you goin'?"

Leo didn't respond, but he didn't have the strength to resist as the EMT men forcibly maneuvered him out of and away from the ambulance.

From a Dark Wayover

They sternly instructed Leo to stand to the side, but they were forced to take their attention off of him because they had not yet stabilized Mr. Buggins' gurney. No sooner had they locked it down, the panic-stricken mob of hospital nurses spilled around the corner. Spotting Leo, their wails and shrieks were reinvigorated. The EMT men were momentarily stunned, and Leo took the opportunity to crawl sneakily back into the van.

Mr. Buggins squawked again when he saw the yammering horde of nurses falling down upon him, as if a dam that held back a lake of nurses had collapsed. "It's just a broken ankle!"

The van's engine sprung to life and its tires screeched furiously as Leo left the EMT men, the nurses, and Mr. Lloyd Buggins behind. He roared out of the parking lot and headed in the direction of Highway 12. The open back doors banged together moronically as the ambulance swerved in and out of lanes.

From a Dark Wayover

What am I doing? The question was beginning to penetrate the borderlands of his consciousness, but he drove it back. Desperate times called for desperate measures...

By the time Leo was nearing the black gates of the Von Koppersmith estate, Police Officer Randall Dowd (known to his fellow law enforcement professionals as "Cheeks") was in pursuit; as was Officer Marty Pane in a second patrol car. Both men had called for back up, but neither felt it was in accordance with the high standards of Charleston County law enforcement practices to wait for assistance while whoever it was who had stolen this emergency vehicle put lives at risk. Therefore, Cheeks and Marty had been trying to shoot out Leo's tires for nearly two miles. Many, many bullets had been spent in the effort, ricocheting off of the asphalt or punching little holes in the ambulance's rims.

From a Dark Wayover

Cheeks had already reloaded once; Marty would soon have to, as well.

Leo did not have his remote control gate opener, of course; he did not even have any pants. He crushed the brakes and brought the ambulance to a squealing stop a few feet from his estate walls. He toppled out of the driver's seat, lurched to the gates, and began climbing, even though his right arm was nearly useless and his ribs burned like fire. He had already made it over the side by the time Cheeks and Marty rushed up behind the ambulance.

The two policemen had fully reloaded their service revolvers. They leapt out of their patrol cars, remaining behind the safety of their doors. With frustrated screams they aimed their pistols and fired repeatedly.

Their accuracy was unerring. Even after they had discharged every bullet in their pistols, they continued screaming and squeezing their triggers. At last, Cheeks shouted, "Cease fire! Cease fire!" Marty stopped pulling his trigger. Both policemen surveyed their handiwork with calm self-satisfaction: all four tires of the ambulance were now thoroughly flat.

"O.K. Marty," said Cheeks. "Now let's go find that guy."

⋯✦⋅✦⋅✦⋅✦⋅✦⋅✦⋅✦

Leo stumbled over the frozen, yellow grass, feeling ice bite into his toes. The mansion was quiet. None of the boys were in the yard; there was no movement in the windows or on the verandas. Leo felt sick; a coldness that was colder than the weather was welling up in his heart.

His bare feet made a padding sound upon the stone steps of his front door. Air rushed out of his mouth in clouds of steam. He put his hand on the brass doorknob, but for a moment he did not dare to turn it.

"Please," he whispered. "Please, no…"

He turned the knob, and pushed open the door.

Coming down the stairs at that moment were his mother and the children's head tutor, Ms. Winnipeg. A few boys were chasing each other across the foyer. Wilwell was on a fluffy chair, reading Howard Pyle's *King Arthur and the Knights of the Round Table*. The air of the mansion was warm, and smelled like Christmas.

"Leo!" gasped Mrs. Von Koppersmith. The boys all shouted with glee.

Leo's shoulders slumped as he looked around at all of them. "You're…you're O.K.…." They all began to quiver and melt. Leo's eyes rolled up into his head, and he collapsed to the floor.

⋯✦·✦·✦·✦·✦·✦·✦

Two days later, the world was still wintery, but bright, and the snow and ice had melted. Anselm strode down a carpeted corridor, in his usual brown-and-green checkered jacket and pressed trousers, carrying a coffee tray.

He arrived at the doorway of a little reading room where Leo, bundled in clean white bandages and a red tartan robe, sat in the Conambulator by a large, sunny window. The Walkchair's back two legs were folded comfortably beneath him, allowing both he and Leo to recline. An e-reader was positioned on top of a black tripod in front of them. Leo stared through the window glass, restlessly chewing his bottom lip.

Anselm lightly tapped the doorjamb with his knuckles. Leo flinched.

The head of housekeeping frowned at himself. "I'm sorry, Leo—I didn't mean to startle you." He entered the room and began arranging a little table for Leo's coffee.

From a Dark Wayover

"Oh, not at all, Anselm, it's alright. I was just thinking."

Anselm poured steaming black coffee into a green cup. "It looked a bit more like worrying, than thinking."

Leo smiled uncomfortably. "Well...yeah."

Anselm took a quick glance at the e-reader, and then a longer one, after he realized that it was there not for Leo, but for the Conambulator. For a few moments, Anselm stood watching the black dot eyes at the front of the Walkchair's seat move back and forth across the e-reader screen. Periodically, the right front leg would lift and scoot the screen leftwards to advance to the next page.

"I've gotten used to—and quite fond of—having a noisy swarm of children around the place," Anselm muttered. "But I don't think I will ever get used to that..."

From a Dark Wayover

Leo chuckled. "It's Arthur Conan Doyle. Our Walkchair has become a big Sherlock Holmes fan, haven't you, man?" The Conambulator glanced up at them and rocked back and forth. Leo affectionately patted the Chair's arm. "And he's a big help—carting me around like this until I'm better. Did you get everything smoothed out with the hospital and…the police?"

"Everyone has been very understanding. No charges are being pressed. We've paid all damages, and thrown in some goodwill offerings here and there, as well."

Leo closed his eyes and tilted his head back, letting out a sigh that was partly contentment and partly the usual pain of a confined man trying to recover from injuries. "Great. Everybody's happy."

"Almost everybody. You're troubled. About that frogman invader, that…well, let's simply say it: that assassin…"

From a Dark Wayover

" 'Assassin' is right. And 'troubled' is right. It's going to take me months to recover from my injuries, Anselm. In the meantime, that Cheevilnid, whoever he is, could come back any time. We're not safe."

Anselm thought for a few seconds and nodded. "My rifle is loaded and in its usual spot. I'll contact a security company immediately and arrange for armed guards…"

Leo shook his head. "That's good, but they won't be able to help much. This Cheevilnid has a Flute—I don't know where he got it. But with it, he can appear anywhere in the mansion he wants, at any time. He could kill somebody and be gone before anybody even knows it!"

Anselm clasped his hands behind his back and gazed through the window at the cloudless blue sky. "I know what you're thinking. You'll have to go back to the Island. To investigate."

"Right. I need to know what's going on. And, look, in the meantime, you've got to find some temporary living arrangements for the kids…"

"What?"

"Of course. We can't risk keeping them here!"

"Leo…this is their home. This is your home."

"But…they aren't safe…I told you, that Cheevilnid can come and go however he pleases…we have to leave…"

Anselm stared down at him. "Leo. You are in no condition to go anywhere…"

"Forget about me! I have to make sure the boys are all out of danger…"

Anselm smiled and frowned at the same time. "Well, frankly, no you don't."

"What…?!"

"Leo, you are now their father. And it's true that you have a responsibility to care for them. But your primary duty is not merely to keep them out of danger. They aren't livestock—they're boys! Your job is to make them men. And you won't be doing that job very well if you teach them that, under any threat of danger, they should simply run away and abandon their home. You must show them what it means to defend home."

Leo thought of several retorts, but somehow none of them reached his lips. He stared, with an incredulity that steadily melted into reluctant acceptance. "But look at me." He gestured at the white bandages wrapped around his chest and arm. "I'm a mummy. I have *got* to get better, and quickly…"

Feeling a surge of frustration, Leo clinched his fists and cursed under his breath.

Anselm patted him gently on the shoulder. "Your body needs time, Leo. Don't be so hard on yourself."

Leo exhaled loudly. "You're right, I know. I just hate it: thinking that the boys need me, are in danger, and I'm…useless…"

Anselm waved Leo's pathos away as if it was no more than a small, lingering bad smell. "Just drink your coffee, son."

Leo obeyed, out of a decades-long habit: the aged housekeeper's familiar jutting chin and large nose reaching out as if to grab hold of one another, along with the warm, level voice and the smell of Old Spice, tended to tranquilize Leo. For a few minutes there was only silence.

"Hey," he said offhandedly, after a few sips of hot coffee, "What's going on with that flying man? 'Invictus'. Do we know any more about him?"

"Indeed we do," replied Anselm as he went through the room fluffing pillows and picking up out-of-place items. "He presented himself to President

Holloway this morning, and the meeting has been reported on relentlessly ever since."

"No kidding? Well, did you see what he looks like? Is it Zechariah?"

"He still hasn't taken off that gold helmet—you should see it. It has engraved wings on the side and a thick visor over the bridge of his nose. With that, and the gold and white costume, and that shining cape, he looks like he just flew down from Mount Olympus. But, no, he isn't Zechariah. Right then and there at that meeting with the president he revealed his true name: Conrad Garrison. He's from Cincinnati, of all places! Born and raised there. The press instantly stampeded to Ohio, of course, as soon as they found out. They've camped out in front of his parents' house. They're swarming every restaurant where he might have had lunch and every city park where he might have once swung on a swing set.

From a Dark Wayover

The principal from his old high school was on T.V. being interviewed thirty minutes ago."

Leo grunted. "Well, how does he have all these powers?"

"That is the sixty-four thousand dollar question, isn't it? All that Invictus would reveal to the president is that he was 'granted' them 'by destiny.' 'An ordinary, average citizen, who has been chosen to protect us'…"

"From what?"

"From these new lunatic terrorists. The Hitbacks. The ones who tried to crash that plane into the Empire State building. They dye the tips of their fingers green—it's their trademark, or some such nonsense. They are a 'new scourge,' says Invictus, and 'the whole world is in danger because of them'. In fact, only one hour ago Invictus rescued a tourist boat rigged with explosives in New York Harbor, courtesy of the Hit Back Harder Society."

"New York again. He likes New York. So do the Hitbacks, I guess."

Anselm mumbled a confirmation as he adjusted the room's thermostat.

Leo drank more coffee, already feelings its pleasant effects. "An international terrorist network…a real life comic book superhero…a Cheevilnid assassin. A lot of bizarre things all going on at the same time, huh, Anselm?"

Anselm shrugged again. "Yep. So it would seem."

"I've got the distinct feeling it's no coincidence."

Anselm took a last glance at the coffee tray to make sure there was nothing else Leo needed, and then he started towards the door. "Heal away, my boy, heal away. I'll go hire some well-armed security right now, and then I'll be back to check on you…"

"Anselm…" Leo rubbed the black stitches on his chin, staring out of the window again. "One more thing

From a Dark Wayover

is really bothering me about this Cheevilnid. I've learned a few things in the past couple of years, about Wayovers and how the Flutes that open them actually work. The Wayover we know has one end connected to a specific location: the Island. The portal on the far end is always open, and it always sits in the same place: thousands of feet over the Island, and just above Mount Hollowchest. That sky portal is also the only way you can leave the Island. But the <u>other</u> end of the Wayover is where you play the Flute so you can exit and go somewhere else—but not just *anywhere* you like. It has to be someplace you've physically been to before. So, for instance, I could go into the Wayover, turn right around, play the Flute and go to Peru if I wanted, because I've actually been to Peru. But I couldn't go to the Himalayas, because I've never been there. Get it? So, I can see this Cheevilnid somehow getting a Flute, climbing up to the Wayover above Hollowchest, and opening a portal. But how could

From a Dark Wayover

he come <u>here</u>? He's never been here, to the mansion. I'm wondering: do you think there was someone else who opened it for him? Someone who *has* been here before?"

Anselm clasped his hands behind his back again and considered the question for a few seconds. "I'm afraid you are only talking to a simple old soldier. I know the things I have to do, and I understand their place in the scheme of things. But magic flutes…magic islands…frog-people. I have a little trouble dealing with the fantastic. And it troubles me that the fantastic and the normal now suddenly seem to be on the verge of becoming…the *same*…"

Anselm turned and left, shaking his head.

From a Dark Wayover

Four

Months later,

Washington D.C....

There was a knock on Gregory Holloway's door.

The president did not look up from the legislation over which he was poring. "Come."

The thick mahogany office door swept open without the slightest sound from the oiled brass hinges. "Mr. President, sir? Sorry to interrupt."

"That's O.K., Bill. What's up?"

"It's Jhya Magán, sir. She nee…" Bill Owens caught 'needs' before it fully left his mouth, disliking the inappropriateness of it, "…would like to see you."

Holloway glanced up and exchanged a brief, silent look with his office coordinator which, if put into words, would have sounded something like this: *Why? She never comes to see me, which is a good thing, because she has to do with strange goings-on for which I have little interest or time. But I can see there's no getting out of this, so…*

"Send her in."

A haunted ten seconds went by before a sleek young Asian woman melted in, wearing a high-collared scarlet dress that flowed behind her in tongues of cold red flame.

Attempting to greet her, Holloway rose too quickly, scraping his thigh painfully against his desk and rattling all the items on the desktop.

"Madame Magán, what a pleasant surprise. It has been…my goodness, months, I suppose, hasn't it?"

"Four months, Mr. President." Her hands stayed beneath the folds of her long, red sleeves. Her dark eyes were inscrutable. "That is as it should be, wouldn't you agree?"

She did not smile, so Holloway smiled big enough for the both of them. "Well, I suppose it's no secret that I'm not really a spiritual kind of person like you and your boss. I'd rather leave all that to the experts. Water?" He pulled a chilled plastic water bottle from a small black refrigerator and extended it to Magán. He had meant to flatter her with the reference to spiritual 'experts,' but she was no more interested in it than she was in the bottle of water.

Holloway shrugged and opened it for himself. He took a short drink and chortled uncomfortably. "To be honest, the Vision Chamber has always given me the creeps."

One corner of Magán's thin lips quivered slightly in an upward direction. "That is unfortunate, Mr. President."

⸺✦✦✦✦✦✦⸺

From a Dark Wayover

Before twenty minutes passed, they were in a black sedan with opaque tinted windows.

Owens accompanied them. Although the office coordinator was well practiced at keeping his curiosity hidden beneath a flat expression, an unscheduled meeting with world-renowned clairvoyant, Jondas Molding, at the Augororium was an undeniably thrilling break from the usual business of the White House. Molding's unique, privileged relationship with the United States government was a well-known fact, but almost no one was allowed details about it, and the Visionary was extremely reclusive. One thing was certain: if Molding needed to speak privately with the president, it must be of paramount importance.

Owens took a thin card of what looked like transparent plastic from the inside pocket of his jacket. Unfolding it several times until it lay smoothly in his hands, he pushed a softly lit glyph on the bottom right hand section. A light blue screen came to life and he began manipulating the day's appointments electronically to accommodate this unforeseen visit from the Vision Chamber's beautiful and mysterious chief liaison.

"As you can see," Holloway gestured complaisantly towards the veil-thin computer, "Our Mr. Owens is thoroughly enjoying the new toy that Jondas designed for him!"

Magán, sitting across from the two men, stared through the window glass like an Asian mannequin, and nodded once in acknowledgement.

The president stifled his conviviality, but remaining silent in the company of others was almost physically impossible for him. "So, I hear that your boss has arranged a little meeting with Invictus! How exciting!"

Getting no reply, he soldiered on. "And how is his health—our irreplaceable Visionary?"

From a Dark Wayover

Bands of sunlight filtering through the shaded windows swept Magán's face. "He is well."

"No change in his condition, I suppose? Blood cancer, correct? It's a pity."

"He would not agree. The state of his body is of little concern to him, as long as it does not interfere with his mind."

"And does it?"

Again Magán's mouth seemed almost to smile. "It does not."

Turning left and skimming down 17th Street Northwest, the glossy black sedan was a sinister contradiction to the smiling D.C. tourists in colorful vacation clothes moseying along the sunny sidewalks. The incongruity disappeared once it reached the gray, monolithic FDIC building. Its black windows stared over the street like hundreds of rectangular eyes, and when the sedan swerved into a guarded side entrance it was as if a monstrous alien mother was sheltering its ugly hatchling.

⋯→⋅→⋅→⋅→⋅→⋅→

The cement walls of the foyer beneath this section of the FDIC building were still clean and light gray, having only been constructed two years before. The little room looked like a dead end, or an unfinished storage closet, except for a black panel set into one wall.

Magán, Holloway and Owens approached the box, and green fingers of light probed their eyes one after the other. One of the walls slid open and Magán led them into another room, similarly plain but with wood paneling, and filled with a light white mist. The wall closed behind them, and the mist began to shimmer with soft tones of alternating blue and yellow.

"It's called a scancloud," said Holloway to Owens, whose eyebrows had pinched together nervously. "Retinal scans are kind of passé, didn't you know? Guys like Jondas Molding feel the need to scan our DNA, as well."

"He invented it?" Owens said, with a star struck expression. "Is there anything this guy can't do? He's like Leonardo da Vinci times twenty."

At last there was a pulse from a green light on the wall across from them. A recorded greeting from a gentle, young, male voice said: "Peace be with you. Welcome to the Augurorium."

Another doorway opened, leading to a third room, this one furnished like a scene from a play about an 18th century funeral parlor. A lavish gush of purple larkspur crowned the top of a carved mahogany drop-leaf table, and across from it the three visitors all took a seat on a softly cushioned rose-colored couch. Owens clutched the upholstery frantically when a dark passage opened and the entire couch was silently whisked away on a sleek, silvery rail.

From a Dark Wayover

The passage was lit by a series of amber lights that streaked by as the couch rode its rail at what both Holloway and Owens felt was an alarming rate of speed. Magán seemed to take no notice, even as the rush of air set free a few strands of polished black hair from her ornate bouquet of hairpins. Holloway watched as she reached up casually from the blood red folds of her cloak to brush the hairs out of her eyes.

He did a small double take when he saw that she had no right hand.

Her arm was tipped with a disc of rubbery synthetic tissue from which extended several ghost-white tendrils. The little serpentine appendages deftly smoothed Magán's hair back into place and adjusted the hairpins.

Holloway cleared his throat. "I never knew about that." He would normally have been too polite to say anything, but he was feeling put out by the mysterious summons to the Vision Chamber and he was growing irritated and unsettled by Magán's manner. Thank goodness, in the four years he had been in office, he had never really needed to spend much time with her or with the celebrated Visionary whom she served. "Did Jondas design it?"

"Of course."

"May I ask how it…happened?"

"My mother and I were working in a textile factory in Myanmar. I was nine years old. I wasn't paying attention—one of the machines pulled my hand off so quickly that for a few seconds I did not realize what had happened. My mother and I were fired immediately, of course. We were escorted out of the building and left alone. Jondas Molding happened to be touring the facility that day to see what improvements could be made to the machinery. He found me lying there, bleeding to death between the factory wall and the jungle. He rescued me, had me flown back here to the United States. He restored me."

Holloway watched the tentacular hand disappear again beneath Magán's cloak. "Quite a story. What about your mother?"

"He had no need of her."

The couch hissed to a gentle stop. The three riders disembarked and followed a short paneled hall to a pair of stout cherry wood doors that looked as if they were designed for a dwarf. Magán extended her false hand to the round, polished doorknob and one of her twisting white fingers tightened into the shape of a key. She inserted it into the lock, gave it a quick twist, and the doors swung wide. Her hand slipped back inside her flowing red cloak and, ducking down, she led them all into the Vision Chamber.

From a Dark Wayover

Holloway had not forgotten what the room looked like, principally because there was not much to remember. For Owens, it was all-new.

Everything was the color of acid-washed bone. The floor was smooth; the high walls were of rough, porous unevenly spaced bricks, as if the place had been designed to appear ancient. Vents at the tops of the walls incessantly breathed floral air into the room in barely audible tones. On either side of the chamber was a Greco-Roman statue of a robed, hooded figure. Only the lower halves of the smooth, classical faces were showing. Both statues held a stone vase containing a majestic bouquet of stargazer lilies with huge, creamy petals and fragrant, vanilla colored stamen—more shades of white to match the eggshell color of the statues and the floor and the walls.

A few yards farther in, beyond a rugged, corbelled arch, was a lower, narrower space. Past that, the chamber opened up again. It would have seemed at first as if the smaller space functioned only as an odd little hallway, but it was, in fact, the focal point: within it sat a solid, rectangular stone dais, approximately the length of a man's body.

"Wait here, please."

Magán left them standing uncomfortably between the two statues. She bent under the arch, turning sideways to move past the dais. Beyond it she straightened again and disappeared around a corner.

Owens barely allowed himself to breathe. Without taking a step from the spot where Magán told him to wait, he gestured with his head towards the dais. "Is that...*it?*"

Having been here before, the president was more at ease than Owens, if not very comfortable. He slowly approached the dais. "That's it...where he has his visions."

"American taxpayer dollars at work, eh, sir?"

"The Fed pays pennies for his work, comparatively speaking. We maintain the Augurorium, and the Vision Chamber here, but that's all. He doesn't ask for anything else."

Owens' forehead wrinkled up. "But all that research he does? All those overseas projects? How does he pay for all that?"

"I know he's received substantial recompense for telling the futures of various foreign big shots, an Arab sheik or two. But there's also a steady stream of private donations. From everywhere. Remember: Molding's a mega-celebrity. A lot of people practically think he keeps the planet turning."

Magán returned. She unintentionally provided two separate contrasts. The first was in the startling red of her flowing gown against the stark white walls. The second was in her physicality: she was elegant and lissome, moving with long, youthful strides and a gaze that was a cold laser beam of confident scrutiny, while following her was decrepitude itself.

"Mr. President, how good of you to respond so quickly to my request!" The voice was a bloodless croak, like the whir of a locust.

Holloway and Owens stepped forward and shook hands with the famous Visionary. His diminutive stature forced them to stoop, and they knew instinctively to decrease the strength of their grip to accommodate the feeble claw pinching at them from beneath gray, padded gloves, which he never took off in public because of the danger of infection. His clothes were in the style of a wealthy upper-caste Indian on holiday: a type of khalat, loose, hanging to the ankles, long sleeves with shiny red embroidery, and an overall pattern of tiny red stars over pale silk. Their exotic sumptuousness did very little to offset the deathly face of the Visionary, with its spider's web of deep wrinkles, and brown liver spots spattering the upper cheeks, bridge of the nose, and patches of scalp showing through a wild, wispy mane of white, musty-smelling hair.

    Holloway, distressed as always by Molding's decaying appearance, unconsciously became overly formal, as if he was an ambassador visiting a foreign country. "Thank you for seeing me, Jondas. It is a real privilege. I am very eager to find out the reason you sent for me."

    After greeting Owens and exchanging a few enthusiastic but vapid pleasantries, Molding craned his neck and fixed the President with an intense stare. His eyes were small but penetrating, with bright ochre irises that flashed like two tiny sunsets in a lonely desert of crumpled, white skin. "Mr. President, an extraordinary thing has occurred! You must see for yourself."

Molding shuffled over to the bare, stone slab and leaned against it with a grunt of discomfort. He let out a portentous sigh and looked up at Holloway.

"Death is coming, Mr. President."

Holloway matched his stare, but uncertainty darted beneath the surface of his eyes like wary fish in a shallow pond. "Death?"

"And salvation."

Holloway almost responded, but only chortled moronically. Jondas continued to stare, until the President stifled the laugh and swallowed it back down.

"Shall I show you?"

Holloway understood now. He did not want to be shown, because he knew very well the way that Molding's visions worked. Yet it was not really possible to refuse. He cleared his throat and agreed, the way that people agree to be led into a room where they know an open casket awaits.

From a Dark Wayover

Jhya Magán held Molding by the shoulders and helped him crawl onto the slab. She reached beneath it and tapped a few buttons, which caused recessed bulbs to light up, softly illuminating the space, and the slab to sink several inches and then tilt like a hospital bed. Both she and Owens, and then even Holloway, carefully helped the Visionary lie back.

Jhya reached out with her left hand, the one she had been born with, and it was soft and brown and beautiful. The nails were like polished seashells, and they found the edges of Jondas' coat and pulled it back. He wore no shirt beneath; the flaps of the khalat fell away to show a hairless, sickly pale chest and torso. The nipples were like gray coins, and the ribs quivered as they rose and fell to the rhythm of Molding's papery lungs.

Holloway felt nauseous, but strove not to let it show. He avoided looking at Molding's body by exchanging long, pointless looks with Owens.

"It's about to happen, Mr. President," croaked Molding. His breathing was erratic; his rib cage expanded like a bleached lizard egg slowly beginning to hatch. The Visionary arched his back, and it seemed like it must certainly break, for no man in his condition could bend so severely, and yet the groans that rattled out of his gaping mouth did not sound like agony, but like carnal pleasure. Owens winced with disgust; Holloway waited.

Molding's chest rippled.

Owens gaped and he glanced at the President, who remained somber.

The two men watched as Molding's chest rippled again, as if a strong jet of air had swept across it. The flesh of his torso tightened up, and the nipples moved slightly as if they were being caressed.

"It's happening," Molding grunted. "Watch! See!"

Magán kept her good hand on his shoulder, steadying him as he occasionally jerked. He breathed out loudly, with pain, or pleasure, or both, and on his chest a line formed.

It seemed, at first, as if an invisible knife was cutting across the Visionary's chest, but there was no blood. Daring to look closer, Owens saw that the flesh was actually being pinched tightly in specific ways, rising in little hard, white rows to slowly, steadily form recognizable shapes.

"Do you see it, Mr. President?" Jondas was looking down at himself, smiling with satisfaction.

There were now two humanoid figures on his chest, their outlines made of Molding's own skin. They were in hierarchical proportion, similar to ancient Mesopotamian carvings, with the more important one noticeably larger.

Holloway had pulled a handkerchief out of his pocket and was holding it against his mouth, in a dignified effort to not throw up. "Well, this is interesting, Jondas…who…what am I looking at?"

Molding grinned with jagged yellow teeth. "Heroes. Two heroes. One will follow the other. The first will fight, but will fail. The second will save the world."

Holloway stared at Molding's leering face, waiting with consternation for more details. When none came, he blinked and gave a quick, impatient shake of his head.

"From what, Jondas? Save the world from what?"

Molding pointed with one bony finger to an area of his chest near the left shoulder, and indicated a single raised bump, towards which the Two Heroes were facing. It looked like a large, tear-shaped blister. To Holloway it seemed to represent…a cloud? The moon, maybe?

Owens leaned in for a closer look. "What is it?"

Molding sat up suddenly and grabbed Owens by the arm, his brittle fingers closing with surprising force.

His eyes were lit up with an almost maniacal jubilation. A smile peeled open on his face, showing every ragged tooth that was left in his mouth.

"A comet! It is going to crash into the earth!"

···✦··✦··✦··✦··✦··✦·✦

Two days later, the news of Jondas Molding's vision had still not been released, nor would it be anytime soon, by strict order of the President. He did not want to spark an international panic. As yet, no telescope had spotted what Molding was predicting, and for that Holloway was deeply grateful. There was time. Time to decide what to do.

Though he was fairly sure he already knew. Molding himself stated it at the Augurorium: "*Invictus*, Mr. President. Only he has the ability to stop this. Certainly, he must be the Second Hero from my vision, the one who has appeared at exactly the right time in human history—in the very fullness of time—to save us from global annihilation!"

"I wonder," said Owens later, as he and the President sat alone in a stately sitting room of the White House. "Who is the First Hero?"

"Does it matter? Whoever he is, he's just going to fail. All we care about is the Second Hero. It's time to call Invictus."

It could not be the president who would send the message; it would imply that national security was involved in some way (which, of course, it was, and that was exactly what Holloway wanted to keep secret). Magán proposed, in her usual way that seemed more like a command than a suggestion, that Molding be the one to contact Invictus, via the press, and invite him to meet at a neutral location. From there, they could move to a secret site where Molding could reveal the vision to Invictus.

From a Dark Wayover

"For that, the Augurorium will be appropriate." She stared at Holloway with no indication of compromise, and the president found himself nodding in agreement, while privately noting the use of the word 'appropriate', and how *in*appropriate it was for a president of the United States to be manipulated by non-elected agents... *but the future of the planet is at stake here*, he thought. *Molding knows what he's doing. Sometimes the best way to lead is to just get out of the way...*

Five

Cincinnati…

Walter Wallace burst out laughing and sat down across from his oldest and best friend, Max Bosco, fixing him with a jester's gaze. "So, tell me again: *what* happened?"

Max sighed, smiling patiently. "I lost my job."

"No…I know. I mean: tell me again *how* you lost your job? You were the Superintendent of an apartment building, the Wellington. Low stress job…you do light repairs, you keep an eye on things, you help Granny in Room 235-whatever get her false teeth out of the garbage disposal, and for that you get $15,000 a year and free rent. Then you LOSE that job because…" Walter cupped his hands over his mouth, waiting.

"I tried to stop a burglar…"

"Wait! Did you first say to him: 'why don't you pick on someone your own size'?"

"Can I just tell this story?"

"But did you say it?"

Max frowned. "Yes."

Walter's face turned red and a tight-lipped smile stretched from earlobe to earlobe, but out of respect for his friend he refrained from commenting further.

"He had broken into Ms. Brekelbaum's apartment, with her there and everything. He had her money, her jewelry…her wedding ring. I caught him just as he was trying to leave. I chased him down, I shot at him…"

Walter let out a blast of laughter. "You shot at him! With a gun! Your shotgun, right?"

"Just warning shots."

Walter began to chortle, but he slapped his hands back over his mouth so that Max could continue.

"I got Ms. Brekelbaum's stuff back. I tore the burglar's bag off of his shoulder while he was escaping. The burglar got away. But the building manager fired me. For discharging an unauthorized weapon on the premises."

Walter's body had been quivering with delight, but once the story's conclusion was reached he collapsed with mirth and engulfed Max in a bear hug.

"Only you, Max! Only you would do such an awesome thing and end up getting fired for it! Man, you are *cursed!* You're like…Job!"

Max smiled, but his face wrinkled. "Who's Job?"

"Job! *You* know…Job from the Bible…lost everything, his kids all died, crops withered, everybody abandoned him…"

"Thanks, Walter."

From a Dark Wayover

Max's coffeemaker, the same Black and Decker he'd had for three years, wheezed and sent steam into the Saturday morning sunlight. Hearing the sound, Walter rose quickly. "Coffee's ready!" He was still taller than Max, as he had been since he played center for their grade school basketball team so many years ago. He was still pudgy, too. The belly area of his gray sweatshirt was like a soft throw pillow.

"I like the new place," he said offhandedly as he poured a cup for Max and then for himself. "And it's ground level, too—and in kind of a neighborhood, instead of that concrete maze surrounding the Wellington."

Max looked around, shrugging. The new apartment was smaller than his last one, with a foldout bed hidden in one wall. Boxes were stacked on one side of the kitchen, yet to be unpacked. "How's New York, and the seminary? How far along are you?"

From a Dark Wayover

Walter took a sip of black coffee. "Outstanding. About one more year—maybe less. Father Brooks—you remember him, the Vocations Director for the Archdiocese—he asked me if I'd want to take a couple of classes this summer instead of working. So I can graduate sooner."

"Are you going to?"

"I think I might. Even then, I'll still have to do about three more years of pastoral training before I'm officially ordained."

Max poured his second cup. "A priest. Are you ready?"

Walter smiled, staring down at his coffee, weighing the deceptively simple question. "Yes." It wasn't confident, and a moment later he seemed to realize it. "Yeah, I'm ready. I mean, I will be…in four years! But I'm ready now, too."

From a Dark Wayover

"You were ready in high school, I think," Max said with a chortle. "I always thought that."

Walter breathed out heavily. "I didn't! It's crazy what happens to people—they turn into things you'd never expect."

"Like Conrad." Max idly scratched away a tiny blotch of dried goo from the tabletop.

Walter guffawed. "*Conrad Garrison!* That's *completely* bonkers! He's a *superhero*! And we're supposed to call him Invictus now, I guess. I mean, I've heard of people going to high school with guys who go off and end up becoming big movie stars or, like, a U.S. Senator or something, but *this*. This is excessive."

"Did you hear about him and Molding? They're supposed to meet."

Headlines everywhere had proclaimed it: Jondas Molding himself had issued a press release inviting Invictus—Conrad—to a private meeting in Washington,

From a Dark Wayover

D.C., where Molding resided. Although the meeting's agenda (if there was one) remained undisclosed, it was considered by pundits to be no more than a friendly gesture, an opening of relations between two embassies who shared a common love for the welfare of the people.

"Yeah, I just found out. I don't know the details but, to be honest, I don't like it."

"What do you mean? I almost expected it. A man with powers like Conrad has big responsibilities now; he <u>should</u> meet with Molding, and other influential leaders, right?"

"I guess. I don't know. Molding gives me the creeps."

Max laughed at Walter's disapproval. "What's wrong with him?"

"He has that weird, reptilian, snaggletooth smile—and he's <u>always</u> smiling. That time he got on that talk show—whatever it's called—and predicted the faulty brake system for that line of SUVs, the Exploit. People had already begun to die in car accidents because of that bad brake system, before anyone knew why. Molding had seen it in a vision, and he sat there on T.V. and described it and just…*smiled* the whole time…"

"I remember. I just thought he was being optimistic, or something. It did lead to a quick recall. He saved a lot of lives."

"Well, I don't care, he's always seemed weird to me. And the way he gets his visions, appearing on his skin like that…" Walter made an exaggerated facial expression.

"Hey, you're going to be a priest! Aren't you supposed to be comfortable with crazy stuff like that?"

Walter harrumphed. "Yes and no. Anyway, Conrad Garrison is going to meet him?"

"Yep. I read about it this morning."

From a Dark Wayover

"Bonkers. Out of everybody on the planet, Conrad ends up with super powers."

"Still no explanation of how he got them?"

"Nope! They were 'granted by destiny,' says Conrad. That's all anybody knows. I'll tell you, if *I* was destiny, Conrad wouldn't have been at the top of my super power-granting list. I never talked to him much back in the day, but I always thought he was kind of a…" Walter paused, searching carefully for the right word. "Kind of a tallywacker."

Max found himself reluctantly agreeing. "He cheated on tests. All the time. He would make these tiny little cheat sheets and keep them under his hand."

"And, magically, he got all A's. And was on the honor roll all the time."

"And he was always showing off. And remember that kid, Kirby?"

"Kirby Derby? (What a name!)"

From a Dark Wayover

"Remember that day after school, Kirby was in the port-o-let by the soccer field, and somebody knocked the whole thing over?"

"Yeah, he came out with waste product all over him. That was pretty cruel. I heard that it was Conrad who did it."

Max nodded. "I'm pretty sure it was." Unconsciously, his clenched his fists. "I wish I'd been there…"

"See? It should be you with the super powers, my brother. You actually deserve them! The way you stood up for goofy old Suzilu Mulligan our senior year, only to get ganged up on by Kurt Vank and his evil minions. That took a lot of guts, man. And when Dylan Cooper ripped up those trees, those little whatever trees, out in front of the principal's office, as a practical joke—you were the one who put them all back! You were all dirty, and covered in bits of mulch. The principal thought you were the one who ripped them up in the first place! He was all set to expel you. Then Dylan felt so guilty he confessed, that little monkey. But you were prepared to accept the consequences either way, weren't you? All you want is for the right thing to win…and everybody should get what they deserve, right? You're a good man, dude. <u>You</u> should be the ones with the powers, not Tallywacker Conrad."

    Max didn't respond, except by staring down at the floor. For a minute they both sat, drinking coffee, not speaking, until Walter set his cup down with a dramatic finality. "'Hey look, man, I need to get over to my parents' house and check on everybody. Easter break's almost over and I want to spend more time with them before I have to head back to New York."

    Max, saying nothing, nodded and stood.

    "You should come over tonight. Eat dinner with us. You're by yourself too much."

From a Dark Wayover

"You're going to spend the rest of your life with no wife or kids and you're telling *me* I'm by myself too much?"

"At this rate *you're* not gonna have a wife or kids, either. Come on, loser...tonight, yeah?"

"O.K....thanks."

"Yep. Hey, so what are you going to do for employment?"

"Oh, I got a new job. Not far from here...walking distance. It's a new military surplus store called *Keystack's*. It's good. I've only been there a few days, of course. You should stop by and visit. The owner's an interesting guy. He has some disabilities: a speech impediment, and a bad leg. He has trouble getting around..."

"That's great! I bet he'll really appreciate having you there to shoot at people."

"Thanks, Walter."

The tall, plumpish seminarian plucked his keys from the top of the stack of boxes where he had left them, cheerfully jangling them as he opened the door. He had only just stepped onto the front step when Max suddenly stopped him again.

"Why him?"

"Why who what?"

"Conrad. Why <u>does</u> he get to have all those powers? And not…someone else?"

Walter sighed and thought for a few seconds. "Hmm, that sounds vaguely like a theological question, so I guess you were hoping I might have some awesome theological thing to say about that, but I don't think I do. I mean, on the other hand, there are also people who are totally power<u>less</u>, completely dependent on other people to survive. Why them?"

"Yeah…but there are already lots of those people out there. You kind of expect it. But then here comes this one guy, and…" Max caught his words in mid-sentence, taking a deep breath.

Walter patted his friend's shoulder. "You know, I can be kind of obtuse sometimes when people try to tell me things, but luckily I've known you long enough to know when something is agitating you. And I think I get it: this is envy, isn't it? I guess I didn't help much, with all my talk about how you should be the one with the special powers, to fight bad guys and protect people."

Max looked embarrassed. "Forget it…it's stupid."

"Nahh, it's not stupid. It's un<u>fair</u>. But, what are you gonna do, right?"

Max forced himself to smile. "What are you gonna do?"

Walter hopped in his car and left. Max went back inside and slowly began unpacking boxes, and his heart felt heavy.

From a Dark Wayover

Six

A creeping swarm of black and gray March clouds lay over the Von Koppersmith estate, from the old mill on the eastern side to the cemetery to the west.

Leo sat on his bed, with pillows stacked behind him and under his arms. Rinchwick and Frederick were curled up on either side, leaning against him but careful not to brush the bandages on their adoptive father's arms and ribs. William, Karl, Albert and big Benjamus sat on the floor tossing pennies at a huge toy battlefield, with every shot sending green plastic soldiers toppling off of watchtowers made from books and blocks and jars. Shaggy-haired Edward was sprawled on top of the blankets next to Leo's feet, reading aloud, slowly and clumsily, from a big, colorful collection of Robert Louis Stevenson poems:

"When I was sick and lay abed,

I had two pillows at my head,

And all my toys beside me lay

To keep me happy all the day…"

Leo listened, and made a show of listening, but thoughts wriggled through his mind like spiny centipedes: *My back hurts…I need to get up…the kids are not safe…how am I going to keep them safe if there is another attack…?*

"…I was the giant great and still

That sits upon the pillow-hill,

And sees before him, dale and plain,

The pleasant land of counterpane."

Having finished, Edward smiled shyly and looked at Leo.

Leo nudged the boy fondly with his foot. "Great reading, Ed! Wow, what happened? You could hardly have read any of that two months ago."

"Ms. Winnipeg has been working with me. I've been practicing a lot."

"I can tell!"

Rinchwick, warm and sleepy on Leo's right side and staring aimlessly out the window, murmured, "Leo? Is that Evilnid going to come back in our house?"

Leo winced slightly at the resurfacing of this sensitive topic, and immediately he felt a gravity tugging on the other children's spirits. Naturally, the boys had all been flabbergasted to learn that one of their beloved Cheevilnids had taken the unthinkable step of aligning himself with the Corpse, their ultimate enemy, even to the point of accepting the Double 333 forehead mark. Oddo had been the first to refer to him (whatever his actual name was) as 'the Evilnid'.

"Leo will stomp on his head if he does," admonished Albert from the floor as he fired a copper penny through a Lego bunker filled with green soldiers.

"But he hurt you before," protested Rinchwick, staring up at Leo. "What if he does it again?"

Leo felt a sting of emotions, but refused them access to his face. "I'll stomp on his head. He just caught me by surprise at first, that's all…I thought he was Gollyplox…"

"Besides," chirped Edward matter-of-factly, "we have security guards all over the place now! Even inside, during the day. Leo really is like the giant, and they are our leaden soldiers, and the whole estate is like our own pleasant land of counterpane."

Edward's image had a palliative effect, more or less, on everyone's mood, and Leo was gratified to know that, in spite of the nearly successful assassination attempt, he could still be seen as a vigilant, majestic giant. He was even more relieved when a distraction presented itself, in the form of eight-year old Joseph, carefully transporting a wooden tray with various breakfast items wobbling upon it.

Benjamus cheered dopily. "Bagel! Can I have some?"

"No, Benjamus," growled Joseph. "It's for *Dad*."

Leo smiled, clearing a space upon the covers for the tray. "Thanks, Joseph. Looks good." He petted Rinchwick's thin, prickly cap of reddish-brown hair. "It's O.K. Don't worry about the Evilnid…" The boy nodded and smiled, but without conviction.

Mrs. Von Koppersmith appeared, wearing a long cornflower blue dress dotted with small, printed roses. "It's time, boys! Group 27: Ms. Winnipeg is ready for you in the south parlor. Off you go!"

Expressing reluctance and acclaim, the boys roused themselves and shuffled towards the door.

"You, too, Albert," cooed Mrs. Von Koppersmith.

"I'm not in Group 27. I'm in Group 9."

"Well, take off, anyway," said Leo. "Go run around outside, O.K.?"

"Awww…" Albert launched one final assault, three pennies at once, toppling a plastic bridge, along with a tank, four soldiers and a velociraptor. Making an explosion sound and some appropriate tiny screams of death, Albert hustled to his feet and scurried cheerfully out the door. "Bye, Grandma! Bye, Leo!"

The cackles and blather of boys receded into other halls and passages of the mansion, leaving Leo's room in quietude.

Mrs. Von Koppersmith sat on the edge of the bed and stroked her son's forearm. "Do you miss the fire station?"

Leo spread cream cheese on his Everything bagel and wrinkled up one side of his nose. "Nah…not really. They're good guys, and I liked for the boys to see me go off and be a fireman. But it was time to take a break from it, anyway."

His mother laughed. "Well, I bet they miss you! Not many fire departments can say they had a man who rescued three people—one at a time—from a blazing office building, and no one was burned!"

Leo chortled. "Well, I had a secret fire-proof Hair Shirt. I cheated."

"Those nice people you saved wouldn't think so."

Sighing contentedly, Mrs. Von Koppersmith rubbed her son's unkempt hair. Watching his pecan-shell-colored eyes, she could see that he was steadily working his way up to discussing a more serious matter.

At last he spoke. "Albert still calls me 'Leo'. So does Rinchwick. Most of the boys call me 'Dad' now—Joseph just did…for the first time, I think. But some still don't. I just don't think they can quite bring themselves to say it. It's trust, I guess…"

His mother gave him a look of sympathy. "They've had a hard-knock life. Trust can take a little time."

Leo nodded, taking a hearty bite from his bagel. He breathed out heavily through his nostrils as he chewed. "I know a lot of them are worried about that gray Cheevilnid. 'The Evilnid', they call him. Rinchwick just asked me about him; he asks every day."

Mrs. Von Koppersmith pursed her lips and sighed.

Leo took a gulp of orange juice. "I'm going to have to check it out."

"I know. You've talked about that before. You're going to use that calling thing on Zechariah's mountain, right? To contact him?"

"Yes. The boys tell me it's actually his own Sleeping Pool…the Pool he used for his annual sleeping cycle. That's how we contact him, somehow. Zechariah

From a Dark Wayover

once told me I should call on him if there was ever a serious need, and if this isn't that time then I don't know what is. Hopefully, he can tell me who this gray Cheevilnid is and why he wanted to kill me."

His mother's eyes had gone misty. "You know that Island; I don't. But, still—that will be a hard trip. Are you sure you're feeling up to it?"

Leo looked down at his bandages. "The bones are healed. I have some aches and pains, but it's not that bad."

"There's no doubt you've healed awfully fast. Doctor Higgins is duly impressed. You were supposed to take a good five months to heal—but I guess you're determined to do it in three!"

"Yeah, I really am starting to feel pretty good. I even did a little exercise yesterday."

His mother frowned. "Well, you still have to take it easy. Those are doctor's orders; otherwise, you might break something again. You have to give it two more months."

"Mom, that's two more months of worrying if someone's about to sneak through a secret portal and kill us in our sleep."

His mother made a groan of exasperation. "Well, you'll be doing their work for them if you try to go now! Just slow it down, *please*. Don't overdo it."

Leo nodded silently, tearing off another piece of his bagel.

"Right…of *course*," said Mrs. Von Koppersmith, rising to her feet with a smile, "You would *never* overdo it. Well, I should get downstairs. Ms. Winnipeg likes it if I can help her get materials passed out."

Leo swallowed, rolling his eyes.

Mrs. Von Koppersmith made a clucking sound of playful umbrage. "Well, what is that look all about? Ms.

From a Dark Wayover

Winnipeg is sweet, and the boys adore her. Don't you like her?"

"I liked her mom—*my* teacher—Mrs. Winnipeg." With an incline of his head, Leo acknowledged that he was being too harsh. "She's fine. She's great, actually. We have four hundred and fifty boys who have to be educated, and we can't just have any tutor here, because if they learn anything at all about where these boys come from they are going to think we're all crazy and report us to the state."

"We have a good arrangement, honey," his mother reminded him. "Of all the tutors we have, only Ms. Winnipeg knows the truth! We can trust her, like we can trust her mother—who, as you know, was a very dear friend to me, especially after your father passed. And Ms. Winnipeg has those boys <u>reading</u>. None of them could read a word of English when they first got here. Now they can all read! Her rotating system of thirty groups of fifteen taking their different classes throughout the week is working wonderfully…"

"I know, Mom, I know…" Leo drank more orange juice. "She's great." He snickered, and then grimaced. "How come she never says anything to me?"

"Ohhh, she does say things to you…"

"Not really. I pass by and ask her about something and she hardly says a word. And what's with this whole '*Ms.* Winnipeg' thing?"

"Well, that's her name, silly!"

"Yeah, but 'Mizzz' Winnipeg…" Leo twisted his face up to resemble an eighteenth century English aristocrat. "*Mizzz* Winnipeg. I know perfectly well that her first name is Waldhurga…*she* knows I know…and she's been teaching the boys in the mansion here for two years. Why all of this formality?"

"Well, she has good, classic manners. You know, it wasn't that long ago that all young ladies would insist on being called by their last name in polite society."

Leo guffawed and shook his head. "That girl's wound way too tight."

"Tight-*ly*," his mother said with a mischievous grin. "That's an adverb, as *Mizzz* Winnipeg would remind you." She leaned over and kissed her son's cheek. "I'll send Anselm up soon to collect your dishes and bring you some aspirin and ibuprofen, O.K.?"

Leo patted her arm as she walked away. "Thanks, Mama."

"Ouch!" She threw a look of disapproval at the plastic tank she had just accidentally trod upon, but quickly giggled at herself. "I'm going to end up like you if I'm not more careful…" Pausing in the doorway, she looked back at Leo. "She is a nice girl, though. You should try and talk to her again."

From a Dark Wayover

She left the room and disappeared down the hallway.

For a few seconds, Leo thought about what she said, and then he snorted and went back to his bagel.

He swallowed a mouthful. He took a drink.

And the terrifying scream of a child shattered the calm.

A subzero coldness, the same sensation that had periodically visited Leo since his breakout from the hospital, overcame him again. "The Cheevilnid…"

His legs left the bed almost without him willing it, and he charged down the hall. He could not ignore the tiny threads of pain in his arm and ribcage, but he broke into a dead sprint, regardless. He heard a whining sound ahead of him, near the west stairwell.

"Who is it?!" Leo bellowed, his heart pounding. "Are you O.K.?"

He heard his mother calling out from somewhere else. "Leo! What was that?"

He reached the top of the stairwell, just as his mother came running up from the bottom. Towards the middle, lying on the carpeted stairs, was Oddo. Albert lay across from him.

Oddo saw the look of horror on Leo's face and realized that a speedy explanation was in order. "It was Albert! All I was doing was just coming up the stairs and Albert popped out like a devil and scared me!"

Albert snickered and gave everybody his trademark toothy grin.

Oddo kicked him hard with one, long bony leg. "It's not funny, Albert!"

The younger boy finally accepted that his antic had not produced the mirth for which he had hoped, and his face dropped.

From a Dark Wayover

A security guard in black came bounding up the stairs at that moment, his hand on the grip of his holstered Beretta 9mm. "I heard noises. Everything alright, Mr. Von Koppersmith?"

Leo leaned against the stairwell banister with his chest heaving, trying to recover from the fright and from his sudden physical exertion. He glared at the boys. He thought about punishing Albert for his prank, or Oddo for his blood-curdling overreaction, but he knew in an instant that it would be an action that was more vengeful than punitive, so, with some difficulty, he suppressed the impulse.

"Everything's fine, Joe," he mumbled to the security guard. "False alarm. Sorry about that."

The guard nodded and returned downstairs.

Without saying anything else, Leo turned to go back to his room. There stood Rinchwick, with his little arms drawn close around his chest, standing close to the wall as if it provided him protection. His eyes were filled with dread, and his face was pale. "The Evilnid?" he whimpered.

Leo wheeled around again with his face full of hot blood and he shot a look at his mother, almost as though the whole incident were her fault. "That! Right there! This is the kind of thing that is going to drive me completely crazy! I can't live like this anymore—I have to know what's going on, or I will never know if everybody around here is safe or not!" He let out a big breath and took in another one. "Two weeks. Not two months. I'm going to get myself back into shape and I am going back to that Island in two weeks."

Turning again, he marched back towards his bedroom. All of a sudden he realized that he was still too agitated to go to a place of soft pillows and rest, so he changed course and stomped downstairs.

From a Dark Wayover

His mother nudged Oddo and Albert down the hall. She sent Rinchwick with one of the part-time tutors to the kitchen for a glass of warm milk to calm his nerves. Then she followed her son.

She found him in the exercise room. He was batting at a red speed bag, trying to attain a rhythm of punches, but he was sore and out of practice and it was obviously frustrating him. Finally, he gave the bag one last, big, rancorous hit and abandoned it. He was surprised when he saw his mother standing in the door.

"Hi, honey. I know you're upset—and I know it's not about Albert's foolishness, of course. I understand what's weighing on you. You have to go to the Island to find out where that awful Cheevilnid came from. I don't like it; it scares me. But I know you have to do it, in order to protect all of us. All I want to know now is: who are you going to take with you?"

Leo relaxed a little. He picked up a small dumbbell to see how his right arm would react to it. "Well…I don't know. I mean: I can't take anybody with me, can I?"

His mother clasped her hands together instinctively. "Leo, you can't go alone!"

"Who am I supposed to take with me? Anselm's too old, as tough as he is…"

"But you don't even know how to get to that Pool, or how to use it! Take Wilwell…he's old enough. And so dependable."

"Wilwell? He's a ten-year-old boy! What kind of a dad would I be to take him into a situation like this?"

"Oh, hogwash. When I was a girl, ten year old boys were going off to work with their dads, they were learning how to handle hunting rifles, and how to gut and clean fish…there's no reason ten-year-olds can't do the same things today…"

From a Dark Wayover

"Mom, we're not talking about him going down to the garage to help his old man fix a flat tire. We're talking about homicidal frog-people shooting at him with tongue spikes. In fact, I don't even know what we're talking about—that's the problem. There could be a whole battalion of monsters waiting for us on the Island. I can just have Wilwell describe to me where exactly the Pool is in the palace, and how to use it, and I'll take it from there. I'm not taking a kid into a hostile situation."

"But, honey, that same boy survived in a hostile situation for a long time before you ever came along. He's smart, resourceful, he knows the Island backwards and forwards, and you can't do this alone! And one more thing: he needs to do this. He's growing into a young man! He can't sit around like a baby forever letting you do everything for him."

He almost fired back with a sarcastic retort along the lines of: "Mom, come *on*…this isn't the time for some kind of wackobrain rite-of-passage experience. If that's what he needs, then I can take him camping for the weekend and we can shoot b.b.'s at squirrels and then skin them with our bare teeth." Then he realized he was being obstinate, not to mention disrespectful. He began to hear Anselm's words again: *They aren't livestock—they're boys! Your job is to make them men.* On top of it all, Leo felt the twinges and stings of his own damaged body. There was no denying it: he needed help.

"O.K.," he said at last. "I'll take Wilwell. And Oddo. But no one else. And if we get there and find out something terrible is going on, I'm going to turn right back around and bring them home."

"Woo-hooooo!" Oddo crowed, marching victoriously into the exercise room from around the corner where he had been hiding. Albert appeared, as well, shrugging his shoulders and glowering at Leo. "What?! What?! What about me? I want to go!"

From a Dark Wayover

Leo groaned. "No, Albert! Wilwell and Oddo are a lot older than you—although, to be fair, nobody knows when any of your birthdays are, so I'll never really know any of your actual ages. But I know Wilwell and Oddo are older than you by three or four years, and they are bigger than you. It would be too dangerous to bring you with me."

"And," said Oddo, rubbing his chin intellectually. "Albert, you would probably destroy something. Or die."

The younger boy made a chirp of protest. "I won't!"

Leo knelt down in front of him. "Quiet, Oddo. Look, Albert, you just can't come this time, O.K.? As soon as we check things out and make sure there's no danger, I'll take you back on a special trip…we can all go visit. But, this time, it has to be just Wilwell and Oddo."

Albert's dark olive eyes had plump, trembling tears in the corners. Shrugging his shoulders, he said weakly, "But…I'm a boy, too…"

"You *are*, little man, you are. But this time, stay here. Protect the house, alright? We'll only be gone for a day."

Leo took the little boy in an embrace, wishing he had never agreed to take anyone in the first place.

Seven

"Is that…*jungle* camouflage?"

The tall man with the green and yellow baseball cap had come in to Keystack's Surplus and Ammo while Walter and Max were chatting beside the front counter. Walter wanted to see his friend's new workplace before returning to New York, and had been in the middle of a humorous anecdote from seminary life involving a ridiculous fishing accident, when the tall man interrupted them. Striding slowly but deliberately up to the counter, he reached between the two young men and grabbed hold of several green camouflage ponchos hanging beside the cash register.

"Why do you guys even bother to sell this stuff anymore?"

From a Dark Wayover

Walter gave Max a look that said, *Is this a normal question here at the surplus store? What do you say to that?*

Max stood straight, awkwardly clearing his throat. "Um…those are for hunting…"

The tall man sniffed loudly and looked the ponchos up and down like he was examining an archaic religious relic. "Jungle warfare is a thing of the past, gentlemen. There has been a paradigm shift."

Walter stared at the man blankly. "Those are for hunting."

Adjusting his green and yellow baseball hat, the tall man let out a long, self-important sigh.

"Sure, jungle camouflage is useful—in a *jungle*. Just like desert camo is what you use for combat *in the desert*. But with this new Hit Back Harder Society, as they call themselves, modern warfare has now officially shifted to urban centers. The norm will be house-to-house combat, even here in Cincinnati. The town square is the new battlefield. Make no mistake: today's soldier will have to adjust to the asphalt jungle, to coin a phrase."

Walter continued to stare blankly, but couldn't suppress a snort of laughter. " 'The asphalt jungle'? Isn't that an old movie about a public school or something?"

The tall man gave no indication that he valued Walter or his comment in any way. "As I was saying: urban warfare. No more 'take that hill, men'! No charge of the light brigade up San Juan Hill…"

Walter did a small double take. "Wha…?"

"As I was saying: none of that Hamburger Hill stuff anymore…"

"That's another movie…"

The tall man finally looked at Walter, and leaned in slowly until the brim of his cap nearly touched Walter's forehead. "Urban. Combat."

Without responding, Walter stood motionless.

The tall man straightened up again and turned his attention back to the ponchos. "This jungle camo will be obsolete."

Walter exchanged another cautious look with Max. "So, will the new camo be, like, pictures of houses and banks? Florist shops? Those little hot dog vendors, with the red and white striped umbrellas?"

The tall man stared down through a glass display case at rows of pocketknives and pretended as if he had not heard.

Max refused to look at Walter anymore, so Walter just began talking to no one in particular. "Maybe just a picture of a *road*. So enemy soldiers on the real road would never see you coming. You know, like in those old Road Runner cartoons, when Wiley Coyote would paint a picture of a road on the side of a mountain, hoping that the Road Runner would run into it…"

From a Dark Wayover

The tall man suddenly whirled towards Walter and pointed one long finger at him. "Now you listen here—I know you think you're real funny, 'ha ha ha', but I can assure you that future battlefields won't have need of any court jesters…"

Walter opened his mouth to protest, but another voice overwhelmed his efforts. It was electronic, like dialogue from a 1990's video game.

"Humans will always fight each other, and there is no place on earth that is safe."

Relying heavily on a smooth, black cane, a man had trudged out from the back office behind the counter. He had one hand upon a thick, gray box hanging across his chest by a thick canvas strap. Alphanumeric keys lined the front of the box, under an LED screen, across which were scrolling the words everyone had just heard.

Although Walter, who, until this moment, had never met Melvin Keystack, caught himself staring too long at the storeowner's heavy club foot, there was no lack of other attention-drawing eccentricities. Keystack was tall, taller even than the man in the green and yellow cap, and large—overweight, probably, by medical standards, but robustly so. His plump head was close-shaved, almost bald. He wore a long-sleeved shirt and trousers, with a dark, gray rayon vest and a black tie, but they were all threadbare, their colors faded, their style antiquated.

Keystack's right hand played deftly over the gray box's buttons again and, as he typed, the words were spoken by the outdated electronic voice through a circular speaker at the top of the box: "`If they fight in the city, and the city is destroyed, will they not fight in the jungle after that?`"

The man in the green and yellow cap stared uncomfortably, acknowledging Keystack with an awkward nod.

From a Dark Wayover

Keystack looked over placidly towards the hanging ponchos, and his fingers typed quickly upon his box. "These are for hunting."

"Right," grumbled the tall man, "I just…"

"Is there anything we can help you find?"

"No…no, sir. I was just browsing." The man stuffed his hands in his pockets and walked sheepishly to the front door.

Under his breath, Walter mumbled, "Have a super great day…"

The man exited the store and stepped onto the sidewalk, only to be slammed to the ground by two scruffy white men, one in a gray hoodie, and the other, shorter in stature, wearing a red skull cap. They threw open the door and charged into the surplus store. The one in the red cap produced a handgun and loudly announced, "It's fun time!"

Walter glanced at Keystack, who was already typing on his gray box.

"What do you want?"

The taller man in the gray hoodie withdrew a black billy club. "What you owe us. What you owe everybody, for opening up your big shot capitalist store and keeping all the money for yourself! So, let's have it—we want our piece of the pie."

"This is a small business. There are no hidden reserves of wealth here. When you steal from us, you hurt the entire community, including yourselves."

Gray Hood smirked. "Small business, big business, banks, governments…it's all the same, Clubfoot. All of you deserve to be hit, because you been hittin' on everybody else for way too long. You're the enemy!" He paused to take a breath, and his next words rolled out as though rehearsed, and his red-capped compatriot joined in: "When life hits you, hit back harder!"

Hitbacks! thought Walter. He saw now that their fingertips had the notorious signature green dye upon them.

"`Ridiculous`," responded Keystack, typing on his box without taking his eyes off of them. "`Who fills your heads with this nonsense?`"

Gray Hood looked pleased to have an opportunity to proclaim his organization's philosophy. "Nobody knows him—and *that's* why we know we can trust him: because he isn't tryin' to fool people into letting him be the boss. He funds us, let's us elect our own local leaders; takes the leash off our necks. He just wants us to be free…"

"Free from the shackles of society," growled Red Cap.

"And free from big shot business owners like you. Now open that cash register, and give us our piece of the pie. *Now*."

Walter's legs felt frozen in place by fear. He cast a fleeting look at Max, only to discover that his friend had disappeared.

Keystack leaned on his black cane and stared defiantly at the thieves. He made no further effort to communicate, but neither did he make any move to comply with their demands.

Red Cap took a step towards the man, his gun unwavering. "You don't know what you're getting into, freak…"

A flash of movement drew Walter's attention. Max had reappeared from behind the far end of the counter with a gray and black sport slingshot. Without making a sound he drew back the bands and fired, sending a .44 caliber lead ball bearing at two hundred twenty feet per second into Red Cap's trigger finger. The gun twirled away, while Red Cap held his hand and howled in agony, his face now almost precisely the same color as his headgear.

Gray Hood spun and, with his club raised, he ran at Max, who fumbled behind the counter for another projectile. Loading it, he aimed for the thief's forehead, but he pulled back the pouch only part way, knowing that too much force would kill the man instantly. He fired. Gray Hood dropped his club and fell to the ground, clutching his forehead and groaning.

"May I suggest these, to detain them?" Keystack handed several long, thick zip ties to Walter, who was so stunned by all that had happened that he was speechless. "Around their wrists and ankles. Meanwhile, I will call the police."

From a Dark Wayover

Within the next half-hour the two Hitbacks were having Keystack's zip ties replaced by official handcuffs, and their Miranda rights sternly read to them by a stony-faced CPD officer. Walter stayed to help clean up, though there was little for him to do, and his impending return flight to the seminary made it impossible for him to stay very long. The whole experience had left him feeling badly shaken up, so Melvin made him a cup of hot chamomile tea to calm his nerves.

Max, on the other hand, was unperturbed. He remained excited and charged with adrenaline for a little while after they apprehended the Hitbacks, but it soon subsided to a current of warm confidence and glowing peacefulness. Observing it, Walter laughed and recommended that Keystack give Max a substantial raise.

Having finished his tea, he sighed and announced that it was time for him to leave. He gave his friend a powerful embrace, shook Keystack's hand, and departed.

From a Dark Wayover

Melvin had closed the store after the police left, and now, having locked up behind Walter, he thumped with his cane over to a stool near the counter and sat down. A deep stillness filled up the place, disturbed only by the low click of an oscillating fan next to the cash register. Max began to clean up the rest of the lead ball bearings and put them back behind the counter.

"That was quick thinking, Max. Thank you for your bravery."

"Thanks, Mr. Keystack."

"You didn't mention, during your job interview, that you were an expert slingshot marksman."

Max smiled. "I'm not. I mean, I had one when I was a kid, but it's been that long since I fired one."

Keystack paused a second or two before typing on his keyboard again. "That is impressive.

Surely, you must have extensive training in projectile weapons?"

"Oh, no. I'm just naturally a pretty good shot."

Melvin was silent again, leaving Max unsure of what he should do or say next. He decided to sweep; he grabbed a broom from a corner and went to work on the area near the front entrance.

"Remind me: do you have family here in the city?"

"My parents aren't alive anymore. When I was twenty-one my mother died of pulmonary hypertension, and cancer took my dad a year and a half after that. I have two sisters. They both married naval officers. One is living in Hawaii, the other in San Diego."

"But you are not married?"

Max shook his head.

"And how old are you, Max?"

"Twenty-nine."

"Twenty-nine years old. Many men your age have already married and begun raising children. And they have professional careers."

Max smiled without looking up from the dirt he was sweeping. "You're politely telling me I'm a loser, aren't you, sir?"

"Not remotely. But it would seem you are stuck."

Max kept sweeping, slowly now, without direction. "I'm stuck."

"Yet you are a capable person. Don't you have aspirations?"

"Sure…I mean, yeah. I guess. I've tried a few things. Nothing seems right, though."

"What do you want to do?"

"I thought about the army. Talked to a recruiter, took a test."

"You like the idea of defending people, don't you?"

"Yeah. I do. A lot. But then, I didn't join the army, after all. So, then I almost became a cop. I was thinking I could be a detective, eventually. Track down murderers, and stuff. You know."

"These are all very noble pursuits. What stopped you?"

Max stopped sweeping, and stood holding the broom as if it was a quarterstaff. He looked carefully at Melvin. "I thought: what if the army goes to fight a war that I don't believe is right? How could I do that? Or, what if, as a policeman, I'm expected to arrest someone I know is innocent? There's no *way* I could do that. So, I would just end up letting everyone down. No. Those things weren't right for me."

Melvin arose from his seat, leaning his cane against the counter. Awkwardly, he shuffled over to Max, the thick black rubber of the shoe on his clubfoot dragging the linoleum floor, until he was so close that the raggedy ticking along the edges of his gray rayon vest was plain to see. Max straightened his shoulders, feeling confused about how he should react.

Reaching out and taking the broom from his employee's hands, Melvin typed upon his gray box.

"Max, what do you *want* to do?"

The two men looked into each other's eyes, and it was as if any excuse for not speaking in the most blunt, honest terms suddenly evaporated.

"I want to fight crime. I want to stop people, like those Hitbacks, from doing bad things."

"I see. Why don't you do that, then?"

"Well, I told you, I just don't think I could be a cop, at least not the cop they would want me to be…"

"Not as a policeman. Just you."

"You mean, organize rallies and that kind of thing? Letter-writing campaigns? Or be a politician?"

"Not at all. You're a man who fights, Max. You have physical gifts, and toughness of mind. What I mean is: fight crime. Yourself."

Max began to reply, but had to laugh first. "I don't know…wow, Mr. Keystack, I'm surprised to hear you make a suggestion like this…encouraging me to break the law, be a vigilante and all that. Aren't we supposed to let the police fight the bad guys?"

"That is a very good policy. But if someone fell into a pit would you not go and get that person out? Even if the law said that only authorized men could enter the pit?"

"Well, yes, when you put it that way, you're right."

"Then I am right."

Max laughed again. "How would I…? How would I do that?"

"You work at a store that can supply you with everything you need, and you have the blessing of your employer."

Max was tongue-tied.

"Meditate on these things before you take any action. There is no urgency here. It is simply an idea. A possibility. Consider the reality of you as this crime-fighting person whom, in your heart, you want to be."

Keystack smiled warmly, and gave him back the broom. He turned and clumsily made his way around the counter towards the store's back exit. `"Finish cleaning up, please. Don't forget to set the alarm."`

Lightly stunned by the conversation, Max just watched as the disabled, shuffling man reclaimed his cane and slowly toddled around the corner and out of sight. Then his large, round head reappeared, as if he was leaning back.

`"And think about what weapon you would use. That's important. And one caveat, if I may: you cannot really 'stop people from doing bad things.' They all seek the bad in their hearts, and you have no power to enter there. You can only work to ensure that people receive what rightfully belongs to` them. That is justice. The world is in bad need of justice, wouldn't you say? Good night, Max."

The sun drifted westwards, and Cincinnati steadily began to glow and gleam with electric light, from Over-the-Rhine to the idle, shady streets around St. Gertrude in Madeira. As Max brushed his teeth for the night, he could think of little else other than his last conversation with Melvin Keystack. He weighed the old man's every insight and suggestion like they were newly recovered antiques—peculiar and fascinating, but of unknown value. Fight crime, all by himself? Was this really a rational idea?

It would be several days before Max would reach a conclusion.

Eight

Leo did not want to have the meeting. He just wanted Mom to tell Ms. Winnipeg that there was a minor ongoing threat to everyone at the house (which, surely, had already been surmised by the overeducated Mizzzz Winnipeg, owing to the presence of patrolling security guards); that the threat originated from the Island; that Leo was going there to investigate, and he would be taking Wilwell and Oddo, and so they would be absent from their classes for a day and would she please save their assignments for when they return…Leo saw no particular reason that he should have to be the one to tell Ms. Winnipeg all that. Unfortunately, his mother, employing her usual mix of cloud-like gentleness and glacier-like pertinacity, reminded him that he was the man of the house and as such was duty-bound to personally handle this matter. He suspected that she had a secret agenda, and he was fairly certain he knew what it was, but he capitulated, anyway.

The three of them—Leo, his mother, and Ms. Winnipeg—were supposed to meet in the east parlor at eleven o'clock. The time had come, but when Leo strode into the room he saw that the young tutor was sitting by herself.

Leo made efforts to hide his discomfort. "Hello! Oh no, please don't get up…"

Ms. Winnipeg stopped midway between standing and sitting, her flamingo legs stuck together tightly. She smiled awkwardly, pushed her glasses back to the top of her nose, and sat. *Her glasses*, Leo thought with an interior smirk. Thick, indigo frames with chunky bifocal lenses that made her hazel eyes look cartoonish-ly large. *Pretty eyes, though…*

"Sorry, I guess my mother isn't here yet…"

Ms. Winnipeg nodded, but it was overly energetic, like the flapping of a cream-colored wren's wing. "Yes, she isn't…I mean: no, she isn't. Well….." She snorted and gestured dramatically around the room. "Obviously."

Leo followed her gesture with his eyes, and then felt strangely stupid all of a sudden. "She should be here any minute."

Ms. Winnipeg cleared her throat.

Leo cleared his throat, too. "Oh, do you like to do crossword puzzles?" He was looking at a thick purple book lying beside her, entitled *Crackerjack Crosswords: 200 Word Puzzles Designed to Melt Your Brain*. "Those look a little out of my league."

She chuckled in response and brushed off his assessment. "No, no…they aren't…well, they *are* supposed to be rather challenging, naturally, but…yes, I do enjoy them…"

From a Dark Wayover

She held the book in her hands and turned it over aimlessly, as if she was demonstrating something, but then she put it back down and stared in its direction. With her head down, Leo could see that she had a bright red and blue oriental hair pen stuck through the back of her dark blond hair. It provided the only flash of vivid color to her entire appearance—it and the indigo frames of her glasses. Otherwise, her clothes were a montage of grays and drab yellows; her skin, although smooth and clean, was that of a young lady who infinitely preferred complex crossword puzzles to bicycling; her nails were short and treated only with a thin, aged layer of clear polish; the only make-up evident was a single application of very average lipstick. Leo detected no perfume…just a soap smell…lavender, with a hint of lemon, maybe…

He found himself highly relieved when his mother arrived, at last.

"Hello! Sorry I'm a bit late!"

From a Dark Wayover

"Oh, Mrs. Von Koppersmith, that's a lovely dress." Ms. Winnipeg smiled appreciatively at the older woman's long orange gown with a pattern of red roses across the front. "You like roses, don't you?"

Mrs. Von Koppersmith bowed her head demurely as she seated herself. "I do! They're my favorite. Do you have a favorite flower, sweetheart?"

Ms. Winnipeg smoothed out the front of her skirt and let her small hands rest in her lap. "The grapeleaf anemone."

Leo's eyebrows rose. "The what? I don't know that one."

"Yes, they grow well in Zone 4, and Zone 5…even down here in Zone 8."

"Zones?"

"Oh…I mean, plants are classified according to where they can grow properly…according to the USDA Plant Hardiness Zone Map…"

"Uhh…oh. Are we in Zone 8?"

"Of course."

Leo looked at his mother and spread his hands disingenuously. "Of course."

"Mrs. Von Koppersmith gave her son a subtle frown and turned back to Ms. Winnipeg. "What do they *look* like, honey?"

"Oh. A pretty pink, with bright yellow centers. They grow three to four feet tall."

"My! That's tall!" Mrs. Von Koppersmith stared with wide eyes at Leo. "Isn't that tall for a flower, Leo?"

"Yeah, that's real tall. Look, Ms. Winnipeg, I just wanted to talk to you for a few minutes and let you know about something kind of unusual that's going to happen soon, which you need to know about…"

This was the second time Leo had a frank conversation about the Island with Ms. Winnipeg.

From a Dark Wayover

The first was nearly two years before, not long after she began tutoring full-time at the mansion. Individually, in private, the children had already divulged to her anecdotes from their past, everything from misadventures on the streets of medieval European villages to "Ms. Winnipeg! Did you know that I was almost eaten by a Throtrex?" With good-natured indulgence, their tutor at first dismissed these disclosures as typical childhood flights of fancy, but soon she was being told long, detailed stories by entire groups of boys at one time. Perplexed, she brought it to the attention of Mrs. Von Koppersmith, who then urged Leo to let the young lady in on the whole thing.

Since then, Leo just accepted that she was a part of their lives and of their conspiracy to keep the world from discovering the boys' extraordinary origins. Even as she was educating the children, they simultaneously educated her about all things related to the Island, the

From a Dark Wayover

Protector, Throtrex, Kak, the Wayover, and how they met Leo and finally ended up in the United States.

Even so, it felt strange for Leo to be talking about these bizarre realities with another adult besides his mother or Anselm. He was not sure that he liked it; by habit he resisted anything that might threaten the boys' new stable lives at the mansion, and he strictly forbade everyone to discuss the past with any of the part-time tutors (or anybody at all, for that matter).

"So," he said, having divulged his intentions, "Wilwell, Oddo and I will leave next Thursday morning and we'll return by dinnertime on Friday. Anselm and Mom will keep things running smoothly, but, of course, it would be a huge help if you just make sure the other tutors do what they're supposed to and, basically, just treat it like a normal day, alright?"

Ms. Winnipeg had been listening carefully and with an expression of nearly Rhadamanthine sobriety, but in response to Leo's final directives she let out a small, breathy squawk, followed by a quick series of musical titters. " A 'normal day'…that's funny…I teach children who are eight hundred years old…normal, hm!…oh, look, kids! A homicidal tree frog!"

Leo and his mother smiled agreeably, but Ms. Winnipeg abruptly showed regret for appearing flippant. "But, yes, of course…on me you *can* rely! I'll make sure the children are occupied."

⋯✢⋅✢⋅✢⋅✢⋅✢⋅✢⋅✢

The day before they were to leave, Leo showed up in Wilwell and Oddo's room with supplies for what the boys had affectionately begun referring to as 'the Expedition.'

The boys cheered. "New backpacks!"

They were made of heavy-duty polyester. There was a gray one for Leo, a black one for Wilwell, and a camouflage one for Oddo. Together, they began filling the compartments with matches, flashlights, water bottles, pocketknives, snacks, even fishing line and tackle.

The two boys babbled joyfully as they packed, wondering aloud what exciting challenges they might face on the Island.

Leo remained sober. "Look, guys, I know this all may seem really cool, but it's not. It's scary and dangerous, and I wish I didn't have to take you at all."

Wilwell frowned, but he didn't want to be disrespectful. "It'll be *fine*, Dad," he murmured uncertainly. "*Really*."

"Oh, and here…pack these, too…your grandma made sure we all have extra pairs of socks, and fresh underwear, too…"

"I don't know why," chirped Oddo innocently. "I never change my underwear."

"That's nasty, Oddo. You're supposed to."

"I just meant: almost never."

From a Dark Wayover

Wilwell laughed. Then he grew serious again, and he touched Leo's arm. "Everything's going to be fine, Dad. I don't want you to worry. And you've been working really hard these past two weeks, getting in shape...running...you can hit your speed bag really fast now. You're ready to go!"

Leo's heart became fluid, and he strove to knit a thin layer of fake joy over his face to cover his months-old snake pit of dread and its slithery thoughts: *something bad is going to happen to one of my boys...I can't protect them...it's supposed to be my job to take care of them, but I don't have what it takes, and they're going to suffer because of it...it could happen any day...* "Thanks, Wilwell. I know it'll be O.K. We'll be fine...you're right. What about you...are you ready?"

Wilwell stood up, proudly displaying his new black backpack. "Yep! Ready!"

From a Dark Wayover

"Wait one second," said Oddo, who was turned away, concealing something from Leo. "I'm not ready! Don't look!"

Wilwell held up one finger, abruptly recalling something. "Did you pack the Hair Shirt, Dad?"

"I'll just wear it. Under a tee shirt. It's scratchy, but you never know."

"Alright, Dad," said Oddo. "You can look now!" He turned around, standing with his knuckles on his hips. He had on his camouflage backpack, but that was only part of what he wanted Leo to see. "Can Fredlegs come? Please?"

Standing on Oddo's shoulder, striking the same pose as the boy, was the tiny Acorn Man who had been created in Kak's jail cell two years ago. His dot eyes blinked proudly upon his glossy, green-brown acorn face.

Leo smiled. "Sure. Of course. Just keep him safe, O.K.?"

Oddo hooted happily. "Definitely! He can ride along here in my pocket. There's plenty of room…"

Leo leaned in close and used his forefinger to affectionately rub Fredlegs' stick chest. "We're glad to have you with us! Hey, what's this?"

Under one of the little creature's arms was another acorn. A black permanent marker had been used to create eyes upon it, and tiny lengths of red string were clumsily glued on for arms and legs.

"That's Cap," replied Oddo. "Fredlegs made him! It's kind of like his teddy bear."

"Oh!" Leo grinned at Fredlegs. "Nice! I like Cap!"

"I have some string to tie it to his back," said Oddo. "So it doesn't get lost."

Fredlegs' eyes twinkled as he cheerfully displayed his creation and gave it a miniscule hug.

From a Dark Wayover

Leo drew Wilwell and Oddo close, holding his forehead against theirs. "I know you're excited about all this, but, as you probably noticed, I'm a little anxious."

"We know, Dad," said Oddo, sliding his thin, white fingers around the back of Leo's neck. "It's alright."

"I just want you to be safe. So, remember: it isn't a 'fun' trip. There's a lot of danger. Stay close to me, and do as I tell you. I don't know what to expect, but I'm not going to let anything bad happen to you."

They all embraced.

"I love you, boys."

"We love you, too, Dad."

In the hallway, Albert crept away from their doorway to return to his own room.

···✦·✦·✦·✦·✦·✦

On a hill covered in golden-green grass there stood a short, fat man. He faced south. Mount

From a Dark Wayover

Hollowchest rose up before him, still miles away, but his eyes were so large that he didn't even need to squint to see each stone stair that was cut into the mountain's shoulders and every notch and crag that lined its sides like wrinkles on a leathery face. His pupils, already as big as black saucers, waxed and focused on the taller mountain beyond Hollowchest, the one Zechariah had once called his home. White clouds concealed its peak.

Breezes blew sporadically, making the grass on the hill shiver, and the hem of the fat man's dark brown robe jump.

"No time to sthpare, sthad to sthay…" His voice was a slow, dreary whine. The lisp-y words were carried away on the wind like pieces of old, flaky skin.

From a nearby grove of trees that had been used as a natural shelter for a campsite, two figures emerged.

One of them was a gray, sour-faced Cheevilnid.

From a Dark Wayover

The other was an unusually tall, broad-shouldered man with pale, yellow skin and a hairless scalp. He had no mouth. His feet were many times larger than an ordinary man's, and clad in heavy boots with iron soles. In his left hand he held a woodcutter's ax; in his right hand, a rusty sword; and in the huge, misshapen hand of the arm that grew from out of the middle of his back, an oversized hammer.

The sudden anxious twittering of birds caught the three-armed man's attention. He turned and, with no great interest, watched a sparrow and a thrush flap their wings frenziedly inside a net bag made of thick coils of rope. The bag lay over the shoulder of the fat man; he held onto it firmly with one hand. Beneath the two fluttering birds were dozens more, of various species, crammed together in a sad pile, kicking their legs weakly and making occasional thin peeps. Beneath them was another layer of birds, but they were all quite dead.

Beneath them, another layer, putrid and rotting. A final layer, at the bottom, was comprised of just bird bones and old, dirty feathers.

"He'll be there sthoon." The words floated away, sounding nearly melancholy. "It'sth bestht if we arrive before he doesth. To give him a sthweet sthurpristhe."

With a soft clapping together of his giant eyelids, the fat man gingerly made his way down the golden-green hill. Sheathing his weapons in a brown leather back harness, the three-armed man followed, with the Cheevilnid not far behind.

Mount Hollowchest rumbled. A brief tremor of horrendous force rose from deep under the Island and shook fragments of stone loose from the spindly peak. The vibrations shot quickly across the grassy hills, making two of the three travelers stop in mid-stride and nervously glance up at Hollowchest. The short man in

From a Dark Wayover

the dark brown robe did not even pause. It was as if he had not heard; or had already known it was coming.

"No time to sthpare," he said again.

From a Dark Wayover

Part 2 - Back to the Island, Which Is Behaving Strangely. To Mount Highpalace. A Dire Balloon Adventure. Chasing Mealworm, and Vice Versa.

From a Dark Wayover

Nine

Zechariah's Island…

Like most Cheevilnids, Strum once lived in a cave that could only be reached by swimming through a short underwater tunnel along the banks of the Fillwishing. Strum's cave had fresh worms, soft sand, moss for storing things, lampflowers—in short, it had everything any Cheevilnid could ask for. Until Strum woke up one day and realized, without knowing why, that everything was no longer enough.

Other Cheevilnids up and down the Fillwishing were simultaneously coming to the same awareness. One result was that Relm, the boys' abandoned village in the valley, had become an irresistible attraction. Like his brother Cheevilnids, Strum began to explore the houses:

they were cozy, made of smooth, sunbaked grayish white clay topped by light pink and green thatch.

Each one came with a small fire pit. All the Cheevilnids had the fondest memories of their boys preparing delectable meals over warm, crackling fires! The very idea of cooking food bordered on the miraculous, and after the boys migrated to the Rest-of-the-World it quickly turned into a cherished tradition. The disc-shaped, silver-shelled Medallion bugs were a tasty treat anytime, snatched up raw with the tongue from the side of the river, but seasoned and roasted on a spit over open flame and served with warm riverbeans? That was something so delicious that it seemed to have fallen from heaven.

That was only one of the benefits of inheriting an advanced civilization. On one of their return visits, the boys themselves had shown everyone simple techniques for shepherding and raising the round, rolling Waywobs, and how to harvest their milk and wool. The Cheevilnids had learned how to operate and maintain the millwheel, and use it to irrigate crops. The planting of flowers throughout the village for no other reason than the joy and peace it stirred in all had become a Cheevilnid passion.

Strum was happy here. All he needed now was a female to share his life with, and a wiggling little catch of podnids…he had already made the acquaintance of a certain lovely little green bean named Moing, who lived along the jungle on the northeastern side of the village. It was for her that he was even now gathering a bouquet of purple and yellow Breezebreathers from along the Fillwishing (all females loved the way they gently inhaled and exhaled, like sleeping podnids…)

What was that noise?

Was it another one of those rumblings from Mount Hollowchest? There had been three of those today, snarling and angry. But no, this wasn't coming from the mountain…

His fellow Cheevilnids nearby stood at attention, facing towards the north end of the village. Another smashing sound shot over the roofs of the clay houses, followed by what might have been a distant, alarmed croak.

Strum and his brother villagers cautiously began to waddle on their long, broad amphibian feet towards the clamor, their globular eyes unblinking, searching for danger.

The noises, whatever their origin, were still on the far end of the village, past the watchtower that the boys had helped them build last year, with its immense clay Cheevilnid head at the top. As Strum watched, a villager scampered up the tower's ladders and began to frantically ring the multiple sets of bamboo bells that hung inside the head, sending a riotous chorus of airy tones clattering across the valley.

Strum bent his knees to leap, but he froze in place when the watchtower suddenly shook. One leg of it collapsed, making the entire structure keel to the side. As the bell-ringer leapt to safety, the watchtower shook again, as if something powerful were battering against it. A third strike brought it down completely, sending the clay head rolling.

Strum vaulted over a house, then down a black dirt lane lined with flowerbeds. He turned a corner, and came in full view of the remains of the watchtower. The head was split down the middle, with one eye looking at the clouds and the other staring at Strum. Houses had been demolished, too, and Cheevilnids were shrieking with terror, springing over one another to get away from that area of the village.

From a Dark Wayover

From the thick dust that billowed among the fallen structures, Strum watched a horrific figure emerge: a tall, powerful, yellow-skinned man with a smooth, hairless head. A third arm grew from his back, violently swinging a massive hammer in all directions.

A gray-skinned Cheevilnid followed behind him: old, hateful Flimp, who had rejected the boys and their society so many sunsets ago. Here he was, strangely energetic and youthful, leering at everyone, looking for any way to contribute to the mayhem.

Finally, a short, overweight man with a net bag over one shoulder shuffled out of the dust cloud. His eyes were absurdly large, like an owl's, with pupils scanning calculatingly from side to side.

Strum turned to flee with his fellow villagers…

Then he stopped. A female Cheevilnid stumbled out of the wreckage of one of the houses, disoriented and afraid. It was Moing…the secret object of Strum's affections. He realized he was still holding the purple and yellow blossoms he had picked for her.

Dropping the flowers, he leapt towards Moing.

She was beginning to recover her senses, but the hammer-wielding man had already spotted her. He turned, eagerly spinning his ponderous weapon in the palm of his hand.

Strum landed by her side and clutched her around the waist. Together they hopped out of the way just before the hammer came crashing down upon them.

"*Crikcriiiik!*" Strum firmly pushed Moing from behind, and she, now fully alert, catapulted over the nearest house and out of sight. Strum coiled his legs to go after her, but he paused when he felt something around his ankle.

It was brown rope. Strong and coarse, thick and supple as an eel, it held onto Strum's leg as if it *wanted to*. Strum's eyes followed it over piles of rubble and wooden beams to the bag carried on the shoulder of the fat, owl-eyed man. The bag itself was of the same rope, and from it had come the coil that had ensnared Strum. Even now more and more of it was slithering out of the bag, while the fat man stared intensely at it, guiding it with hypnotic waves of his other hand.

Strum jumped. The rope yanked him back down to the ground.

As if fending off a boa constrictor, he beat at the loop, but without effect. The three-armed man strode towards him confidently, and Strum could see now that beneath his nose, where a mouth should have been, there was only featureless skin.

Strum tried to escape again. The fat man sharply waved his hand, sending an undulation through the rope that snapped Strum against the side of a house.

The Cheevilnid was dazed. He stood, slowly turning towards his attackers. His legs felt wobbly, and there was a ringing inside his head. The shadow of the three-armed man melted over him, and the massive hammer fell with a low rush of air. The last thought Strum had was a sudden memory of being young and floating free on the river…

The fat man drew the rope back to his bag with swaying hand motions and inclinations of his head. It retracted, like a serpent on a spool, until the tip disappeared somewhere inside the heap of feathers and bird bones at the bottom of the bag.

A silence followed. The fat man stood, staring into nowhere as if a sudden thought had occurred to him. "Oh," he said at last, his voice slow and dreary. "Here it comesth. Better cover your earsth."

He cupped his free hand over his left ear, and hunched his shoulder so that it covered the right.

The valley suddenly jerked, like a living man having a heart attack. The spasm shot up through

From a Dark Wayover

Hollowchest, followed by an explosion that was so loud that the human with three arms and every Cheevilnid on the Island fell to the ground in terror.

The fat man remained standing, squinting his eyes, holding his ears. And smiling.

From a Dark Wayover

Ten

The next morning, the South Carolina sky was a vast, tilled field of pink and orange furrows, and by that evening it had sprouted a dark and wild crop of rain and lightning flashes. Whistling winds splashed sheets of water against the mansion's tall windows and Corinthian columns.

The tempestuous weather was nearly inaudible inside the huge home theater that Leo had constructed a few months ago. Gathered there, besides Anselm, Mrs. Von Koppersmith, and Ms. Winnipeg, were four hundred forty-seven crusader boys in rows of cushiony blue seats, with their legs drawn up almost to their ears and cold drinks in the cup holders, tossing popcorn into their mouths and laughing at Danny Kaye in *The Court Jester*.

From a Dark Wayover

In the east wing, in a small room that was the farthest one away from the theater, Leo, Wilwell and Oddo prepared to leave.

Oddo looked at Leo with a look of mild pain. "Can you help me tie my shoestrings?"

Leo smiled, knelt, and began tying double knots.

"I see you've got your pistol!" Oddo could see the brown grip of a Smith and Wesson in a black shoulder holster under Leo's jacket.

"Hopefully we won't even need it." Leo gave Oddo's shoestrings a last, firm tug and tapped the boy lovingly on the chin. "But just in case, right?"

He stood again, and Wilwell and Oddo drew close to him. "O.K. Here we go."

Out in the hallway, Albert crouched furtively behind a big, green, potted philodendron. In one sturdy little hand he clutched his favorite walking stick, which Anselm had cut for him from a river birch tree two months ago. Strapped to his back was his brown canvas pack, which was filled with half a roll of Ritz crackers, a Ziploc bag full of ham, his toothbrush, and a sock. And a toy car.

...+.+.+.+.+.+.→

Even amidst the blithe sounds and sights of *The Court Jester*, Ms. Winnipeg sensed that something was awry (and she was not someone who ascribed to herself the gift of intuition). Upon the giant flickering screen, as Mildred Natwick's witch character, Griselda, chanted:

> *Closer, closer…deeper, deeper…tails of lizards, ears of*
> *swine, chicken gizzards soaked in brine,*
> *now thine eyes and mine entwine, thy will is broken, thou*
> *art MINE!*

…lightning sparkled behind the window glass, and right then Ms. Winnipeg knew that there was a pressing need to go check on Leo, Wilwell and Oddo as they set about opening their trans-spatial portal to the faraway Island.

⋯♦·♦·♦·♦·♦·♦·♦

From his hiding spot, Albert secretly listened as Leo's sleek, silvery Flute played an impish tune. It sounded (though Albert would not have known to describe it this way) like a Claude Debussy composition, something like *Clair de Lune*. Following it was the tearing of space and time, and the inhalation of air.

Wilwell and Oddo stepped through the tattered aperture. Leo followed.

For a second there was only the black opening and the sounds of air being drawn into it. Albert felt a rush of panic, because his opportunity was about to be lost, and yet he knew he would get in horrible trouble if he tried to join the Expedition. But, oh, he didn't want to miss it!

From a Dark Wayover

Thunder rumbled outside. The aperture trembled and began to close.

Albert leapt out from behind the philodendron. He ran towards the portal, though it had already waned to the diameter of a hula-hoop. He held out his walking stick in front of him as if to stab a fencing opponent, but stumbled over a wrinkle in the room's green-and-vanilla area rug. The tip of his white and gray birch branch jabbed inside the portal as it shrunk to the size of a Frisbee…to a teacup saucer…to a poker chip…

And it stopped.

Albert lay upon the floor with his walking stick extended, staring wide-eyed. He had previously assumed that if something was in the portal when it closed that whatever it was would just be severed, an idea that had always made him nervous, especially when he imagined that his own arm was that something. Instead, the aperture settled gently around his birch branch; it even expanded a little bit whenever he moved the stick around.

    Albert was intrigued. He waved the stick in wider arcs. This caused the aperture to open up in uneven, gelatinous ripples, even though it kept trying to close. Little rushing streams of wind, rushing in past the birch branch as it waved, made various high and low pitched whistles.

    Getting up on one knee, Albert took a firm hold of his walking stick and shook it left to right as hard as he could.

    This caused the aperture to give up its efforts to close. It expanded fully, the same as if someone had played a Wayover Flute.

    Albert grinned. He cautiously approached the portal. Without entering, he looked inside. He saw only darkness, but he could smell the familiar organic warmth of the Wayover. He clicked on a flashlight from his pack, half-expecting it to reveal Leo, frowning down at him, but no one was there.

"They must have already gone on ahead," he whispered. *They would have heard the portal closing behind them. No reason for them to wait. They've probably started the climb down to the Island by now!*

"Well," he said confidently to himself, "I better catch up! I can't wait to surprise them…" He took a step through the portal.

"Albert!"

Ms. Winnipeg stood in the doorway to the room, looking completely dismayed. She had only heard about the Wayover up until this point, but actually seeing with her own eyes a parallax puncture, hovering upon the surface of reality like a big hole in a painting, proved to be deeply disconcerting to her. Worse, seeing little Albert stepping boldly through this impossible opening and into windswept darkness made her want to scream. Which she did.

"Albert, NO!"

The boy only hurried into the Wayover faster. Ms. Winnipeg ran after him, but she blundered over the exact same wrinkle in the area rug that had previously arrested Albert. With arms waving wildly she tripped forward, catching the boy by his brown canvas backpack, and together they toppled into the Wayover.

The portal, now free of objects, squeezed closed with a loud draining-sink sound.

The silence that followed, within the confines of the Wayover, was eerie.

"Albert!"

It was too dark for Ms. Winnipeg to see anything. She felt wildly in front of her. The floor was like dough, and she almost rolled over on her side when she tried to stand.

"Albert! Albert, honey, where are you? I can't see!"

She could not hear anything, either. The air felt close, though not unpleasant. Her hand discovered a wall, and it seemed to be made of the same pliant material as the floor. She tried to take a step, but she felt too unsteady. Her heart beat rapidly in her throat, and she began to pant. She felt tears in her eyes.

"Albert! Anybody! Please help!"

Suddenly a flashlight switched on, shining up from beneath Albert's chin and making the boy's face look like a ghost's. "Welcome to the forbidden castle…"

Ms. Winnipeg shrieked and smacked him on the top of the head. "Stop that! What in the world are you doing here?!"

Albert looked crestfallen. "I'm sorry. You weren't supposed to get stuck here, too."

His teacher squeaked. "*Are* we stuck? We're stuck? How do we get out?"

"Well, my plan was to catch up to Leo, of course. He's the one with the Flute…we can't get back to the mansion without it…"

Ms. Winnipeg's thin arms fluttered with indignation. "You vexatious little simian scoundrel! You weren't supposed to be here at all!" She began digging her fingers into the mushy walls, searching deliriously for a seam that she could pry apart.

"That won't work, Ms. Winnipeg! You have to have a Flute. I'm sorry. We'll just have to catch up to Leo and Wilwell and Oddo."

The young tutor stopped her clawing. Her shoulders dropped. She pressed her forehead against the warm, elastic wall and let out a long, disheartened, capitulatory sigh.

From a Dark Wayover

At that moment, from deeper into the dark of the Wayover, there came a faint, low-pitched roar.

For a split second, Ms. Winnipeg assumed that it was the thunder of the storm over the mansion…until she remembered that they were no longer anywhere near the mansion.

She whirled to face the sound. "What was that?"

They heard it again: a dull bellow, as if a gigantic beast was warning them away from its nest.

Albert swallowed heavily. "That sounded closer…"

Almost five minutes crawled by. They did not hear the sound again.

"We can't stay here anymore, Ms. Winnipeg," Albert insisted.

"But that noise! What was it?"

"I don't know, but we have to find Leo! And I'm tired of just standing here. We haven't heard anything else…maybe we were just hearing things the first time…"

Ms. Winnipeg knew that explanation was ludicrous, but there was no denying that they had to press on. She thought she should lead the way forward, then decided that she was too afraid…but she also couldn't abide the thought of letting a little boy go first. At last, they decided to simply travel side by side.

As Albert's yellow flashlight beam crept along in front of them, it was not long before the passage began to narrow. Eventually, they were forced to go one in front of the other, and it was Ms. Winnipeg, with her heart trembling, who forced herself to go first. Albert lent her his flashlight.

The walls soon grew so close that she had to move sideways. She stopped altogether when the glutinous material of the Wayover began dragging on her hair and clothes.

Albert patted her hip. "You just have to push through, Ms. Winnipeg! Don't worry! Just push right through!"

She had never been a very daring person. Physical self-challenges simply held little interest for her. Now, though, there was no getting around it, and she knew it. She had a little boy to protect and, even though she wanted to throttle his neck for getting her into all this, she was going to get him back to Leo. *Wherever Leo is…if that roaring thing we heard hasn't eaten him…*

Albert punched her in the hip. "Ms. Winnipeg! Get going!"

She frowned, took a breath and shoved her head and upper torso between the compressed walls.

From a Dark Wayover

On the other side, her face met cold, refreshing air. She had only a moment to enjoy it before another rumbling, bellowing sound made her cry out.

Whatever the source of the noise, there was no sight of it. All she could see was a cave-like area that seemed to be the end of the Wayover. The floor sloped towards an oval opening, filled with the faintest glow, colored a midnight blue that occasionally pulsed a dim orange.

After she pushed through into the cave, Albert quickly followed. "Come on!" he exclaimed. "Here's the sky portal! Hey, it's nighttime on the Island…it's dark down there. And, see? Here's the ladder Leo installed!"

She had not seen it, at first: the tops of two aluminum stiles protruding through the oval-shaped opening. Without drawing another inch closer, she stretched her neck and spied the first few rungs.

From a Dark Wayover

Albert fearlessly grabbed the ladder and stared down. "Zoiks! Look at that, Ms. Winnipeg! What is it?"

She despised heights, and she knew that the top of a mountain called Hollowchest lay somewhere below, but she also knew that Albert wouldn't allow her to avoid his question. Squinting in the cold air that blasted her cheeks, she peeked into the opening.

"Hm. A glowing orange ribbon down there…I don't know what it is. But shouldn't you know? Didn't you ever see it when you lived here? Well, perhaps, if you brought a telescope or some binoculars, we could take a closer l…Albert? Albert!!"

The boy was already halfway down the ladder. She held her breath and, without looking, stepped onto the first rung. "Albert! Slow down, honey! I can't go as fast as you! Albert…"

She risked a glance in his direction, but she could not see the boy anymore.

She stepped on to the next rung. A cold cloud swept across her calf. "A *cloud*," she muttered, "I'm as high as a *cloud*!"

She took another step. Her arms trembled and her fingers clenched the ladder stiles.

"Stiles…," she mumbled. "Stiles…last week's New York Times crossword…12 down, six letters…'sides of a ladder'…" She steadily descended, counting the rungs with letters: "S…T…I…L…" Her foot slipped on a wet rung and, hanging only by her fingers, she cried "EEEEEEEE…!"

She dangled for a few moments, and the only sound was her own rapid breathing. Then came another roar that was so loud that it almost made her lose her grip completely. She instinctively drew her legs up, firmly planting her feet back on a rung.

That roar…that's no animal…

From a Dark Wayover

The sound reached a crescendo, causing the entire ladder to vibrate as if an ogre was drumming upon it. She clung to the metal stiles and shut her eyes, gritting her teeth, holding her breath…*it's like an earthquake…*

The drumming and the terrible thunderous sounds subsided. Her breath coming in rasps, she made herself look down. She caught sight of the distant orange band again: "Lava…"

A raincloud rolled over her position on the ladder, obscuring her view. She was thankful for it; not having to see anything made it easier to summon the courage to continue her descent.

"Albert? Can you hear me?"

There was no reply.

She began counting rungs again as she climbed: "3 Down, 7 letters…'Vesuvius was one'…V…O…L…C…A…Albert? Can you hear me? I'm coming, honey! Fico, does this ladder ever end? Where was I? V,o,l,c,…oh, right: A…N…OHHH!"

Albert was right below her, punching her ankle with his tiny, square fist. "Ms. Winnipeg, stop being such a sissy and get down here! Mount Hollowchest has turned into a volcano!"

Comforted by the boy's presence, she finished the climb. As she took her first step onto the flat, rocky peak of Mount Hollowchest, the ground shuddered beneath her feet, and she clutched Albert's shoulder.

"Is it supposed to be like this?"

Albert stared out at the night, seeing his beloved Island's stars sprawled out above like a ceiling of milky jewels. Aware that he was facing north, he looked down, following what he knew was the steep slope of the old mountain. Somewhere below, a huge gash had been blown open. Blazing brightly, a wide river of molten rock flowed off among the hills, separating into smaller rivers that drifted northwards or to the east until they rolled into the sea.

"No," said Albert. "It's not supposed to be like this. Do you think Leo and the others are alright?"

Without waiting for a response, he took his teacher's hand and led her to the first steps of the mountain's stone staircase. "Oh boy, it sure is a good thing it's nighttime, Ms. Winnipeg! If the sun was up you would see that you're on some stairs that are thousands of feet high with <u>no hand rail</u> winding along the outside of the mountain and if you take one wrong step you would fall wayyyyyyy far down and CRASH and probably explode."

Ms. Winnipeg pursed her lips. "Hm."

She felt the chilly, high altitude winds and sensed the broadness of space around her. Keeping her face turned towards the wall on her right, she followed the boy down the stairs.

From a Dark Wayover

She began to recall all the descriptions she had been given in the past few months of this mountain, and of its frightful staircase, designed by an immortal being and carved by his army of moon-colored minions, on an island that no passing sailor could detect. It was here that the children…her students…had lived, without aging, for over seven centuries.

It was all mind-boggling, and yet never, in all the months that had passed since she had been let in on these secrets, had she disbelieved. She had not even experienced a suspicion that all four hundred fifty children, plus Mrs. Von Koppersmith and her thirty-two year old son AND the head of housekeeping, were all conspiring in a gigantic hoax meant to fool just her. She was not an incredulous person. If a large group of people said they saw an alien spacecraft, she would believe in the existence of alien spacecraft, rather than take the far more convoluted approach of believing they were all

From a Dark Wayover

having the exact same hallucination, or the far more cynical approach of believing they were all liars. Yet, despite having not doubted the stories told to her at the Von Koppersmith mansion, to actually be on the Island, at last, breathing the air and smelling the distinctive scents of rock and beach and jungle and truly knowing that it was all real…

Her reveries crumbled when Hollowchest suddenly began another episode of shudders, more violent than any previous. Boulders snapped away, beneath them and from above. Out of the massive hole at the base of the mountain, half-melted chunks of stone soared high into the air and sprayed deadly lava upon the staircase. Albert, his usual spunk finally dissolving, grabbed hold of Ms. Winnipeg's waist and buried his face in her skirt.

After the quake tapered off, Ms. Winnipeg stroked the boy's copper-blond hair, feeling how oily with sweat it had become. "The mountain's eased down a little, Albert—for the moment. Let's keep going. Do you think it's much farther?"

Albert timidly stepped away from her and led her by the hand. "No, not much farther…"

They traveled a hundred more steps, with the mountain growling at them almost the entire way, before Albert happily squeezed his teacher's hand. "We're here!"

The boy flicked on his flashlight, revealing the end of the stairs and a cave entrance. Pieces of rubble lay on the ground, and thin clouds of steam swirled out of the opening.

"There used to be a door here. Chog broke through it, when he was chasing Leo and Zechariah. That story's famous. Ugh! It's really hot in here!"

Ms. Winnipeg had to duck her head as she followed him inside. She involuntarily peeped when another small tremor rattled the tunnel walls. "We really need to find Leo and the other boys. Where do you suppose they are?"

Albert found the top of the second flight of spiraling stairs that led down into the interior of Hollowchest.

"They *had* to have come this way. It's the only way down, unless you count falling from the top of the mountain as a way down. We just need to keep moving, and we'll catch up to them."

From a Dark Wayover

Eleven

Ms. Winnipeg struggled to appear self-controlled, even as she kept a white-knuckle grip on Albert's shoulder. As they descended, tendrils of ghostly steam wound through their flashlight's beam, making it difficult to see more than a few feet ahead. Their shoes upon the steps made ticking sounds, causing whispery echoes that either fluttered throughout the stairwell or were suddenly smothered by random snarling quakes.

Albert faltered. He looked up at Ms. Winnipeg, his olive eyes soft with fear. "Maybe I shouldn't have come, after all. I'm sorry I got you into this."

Ms. Winnipeg shook her head, quickly, like a bird's wing. "It's alright. It's alright. Let's just walk together, side by side, O.K.? Hold my hand…there, that's good. You know, I'll just bet that Leo and the boys are close now. Should we call out to them, do you think?"

"But, what if the Evilnid hears us? He could be hiding somewhere."

Fico! She had forgotten about the gray-skinned assassin.

"Well, I don't like it…but we should just try, once, calling out, and if we hear something we don't like we'll turn right around and race out of here, O.K.?"

At that moment they found themselves at the bottom of the stairs, in an anteroom with wet, stone walls. Shadows seemed to crowd in around their flashlight, and its ray was clogged by volcanic mist.

Ms. Winnipeg gulped, took a breath and timidly called out: "Leo?"

Light emblazoned her face and filled the stairwell, causing her to jerk back and scream.

From a Dark Wayover

Albert whirled around to face her. "Shhhh! They're just lampflowers!"

In front of them lay a broken doorway rimmed with chunks of jagged stone. Upon the debris grew thick green vines lined with flowers that radiated clean, white light. "They shine when they hear voices. Zoiks, Ms. Winnipeg. I guess everybody on the Island knows we're here now…" He frowned and led them through the doorway.

Ms. Winnipeg felt ridiculous. "You might warn me about such things…"

They strode out onto the wide, thick wooden platforms that clung to the interior walls far above the mountain's floor. Looking down, Albert was horrified at what he saw: the lovably unsightly and benign old Hollowchest that he remembered had become hellish, spewing poison steam and magma from a jagged vent.

From a Dark Wayover

Ms. Winnipeg shared his dismay, but she became especially appalled after the boy showed her the only way to continue their journey: an elevator, which she could plainly see was no more than a swaying, square base with spindly rails, held aloft by frayed ropes and pulleys.

It took several minutes to convince her to board, but at last she reluctantly acquiesced. Albert pulled the proper switch and started them sinking slowly towards the boiling, oozing, golden-orange lava swamp that filled the guts of the mountain.

The pulleys clacked, and the ropes hissed. Ms. Winnipeg whispered prayers, closing her eyes tightly. She dug her nails into the palms of her clenched fists when vibrations from the earth jangled the elevator. *We're going to fall…the ropes will break…*

There was a jarringly loud snap and a thunk.

They had reached the bottom, and the elevator had settled onto a low, flat landing stage.

From a Dark Wayover

The heat here was withering. Although there was still enough solid ground to walk upon, sludgy brooks of lava were uncomfortably close, almost forming a moat around the stage.

They now had a ground-level view of where the cavern had been blasted out. Most of the lava flowed in that direction, past black, shattered splinters of rock, and out to the rest of the Island under the cool night sky and its swarm of stars.

Near the southern interior, the river Fillwishing still flowed through the mountain as if nothing had changed. The bridge that spanned it remained intact, though sharply cracked along one edge. As they crossed, glimmers of lava light twitched upon the dark waters rushing by.

"There's a cave over there, where some of us used to play and spend the night," said Albert. "Inside is an entrance to an underground tunnel that leads out to the valley where our old village was. That would have to be the way that Leo...LEO!"

Ms. Winnipeg quailed at Albert's sudden shout. From out of the very cave towards which he had been pointing strode his foster-father, and the boy ran and hugged him tightly around the leg.

Wilwell and Oddo emerged from the cave and ran to join them. "Whew!" shouted Wilwell, smiling gratefully. "We heard the elevator land—we didn't know who that was!"

Leo stood with his fists upon his hips, looking perplexed. "What are you *doing* here?"

Ms. Winnipeg began to explain, but she stammered so much and issued so many disclaimers that Leo lost patience. "What are you doing here," he repeated, "on the Island? Why is Albert here? You're supposed to be with the other boys...taking care of them...are they alright? They aren't in trouble, are they?"

From a Dark Wayover

Ms. Winnipeg quickly rushed to explain that they were all fine, of course, and there was nothing to worry about…

"Nothing to worry about?! You and Albert are *here*, which is exactly where you aren't supposed to be. That's something to worry about. And you don't know if the other boys are safe right now or not—*that's* something to worry about. Can't you see the Island has become volcanic?!"

"Well, yes, of course, one doesn't need to be a vulcanologist to see that…"

"A what? Nevermind, don't define that, because I don't care, because my point is…wait—'vulcanologist'… 'vulcan'… 'volcano'…a person who studies volcanoes…I get it. Who cares? My point is that this trip is turning out to be ten times more dangerous than I thought, and I should have my brain examined for bringing Wilwell and Oddo, and now you've abandoned all the other boys, who I'm trying to protect, and brought Albert along with you…!!"

Ms. Winnipeg's face had turned red with embarrassment and indignation. "Now, wait! You don't understand…"

"It was my fault, Leo," announced Albert. "I was trying to sneak into the Wayover before it closed. Ms. Winnipeg tried to stop me, but she accidentally fell in!"

Leo glared at the boy. "Oh, yeah? Well, I…"

" 'Well' nothing!" Ms. Winnipeg's hands were pressed defiantly upon the backs of her hips. "It's not as if I meant to fall into that preposterous Wayover. Fico! I'm doing everything in the world that I can to help, while you're having a fine time blaming me for the entire mess, and in front of the children, like you're Captain Super Pants!"

Leo blinked. "Captain Su…"

"Oh, just stop it!" She turned away from all of them, and they realized she was trying to keep herself from bursting into tears. "This is difficult for me," she mumbled piteously. "I'm not an outdoors-y type, you know."

Leo rubbed his elbow and stared awkwardly at her back. "Well...you're no Captain Super Pants, that's for sure..."

The words hovered in the air for several seconds before Ms. Winnipeg's shoulders trembled, and she turned slowly, tears rolling down her cheeks but a goofy grin on her face. The boys all began to chuckle. Leo touched her arm and smiled. "I'm sorry. I'm acting like an idiot. Forgive me."

She rubbed the dampness from her face and let out a pleasant sigh. "Oh, of course. It's nothing. I'm sorry, too..."

From a Dark Wayover

She froze. Her voice came out in a ragged whisper: "Look! Something just moved over there, did you see?"

They all turned and faced upriver, peering into the darkness. "It's nothing, I'm sure," said Albert in a low, tremulous voice. "Probably just a chickenbat…?"

"No, not there! Over *there*! By the cave that you three just came out of. See? Look…it moved again…"

Oddo squinted, then his eyes widened fearfully when a nearby burst of lava briefly cast more light upon what Ms. Winnipeg had seen. "It's a…I think…a Cheevilnid…clinging to the wall…"

Ms. Winnipeg cried out and turned to run back to the bridge, dragging Albert by the collar. Leo shoved the other two boys behind him and ripped out his pistol, aiming its four-inch barrel at the lurking prowler.

"Not this time," growled Leo as he slowly advanced towards the cave. Wilwell and Oddo clicked on their flashlights, catching the slinking Cheevilnid in their beams as it padded along the wall like a green spider…

Green, thought Leo.

"Wait! Ms. Winnipeg! Albert! Come back! It isn't the Evilnid. Look! It's Gollyplox!"

Their old friend suddenly joined them all in a single, merry leap, giving them all hugs with his long, lime-green arms. They noticed a small, wool pouch strapped to his back—not a typical sight, since Cheevilnids always preferred their natural nakedness to any kind of clothing.

Having returned from her panicked flight, Ms. Winnipeg now went as stiff as a plank, her arms straight and locked against her sides, as she nervously appraised the Cheevilnid. "Oh! So…this is Gollyplox…I've heard so much about him…"

Gollyplox stared back at her with huge, goggle eyes. He rose up as high as he could on his long, skinny, back legs, exposing the dark yellow-with-red-splotches of his rubbery chest, bringing him face to face with Ms. Winnipeg. A slow, loud croak escaped his wide lips, and his breath smelled like a briny marsh.

"That's a 'hello', I guess," she clucked nervously to the boys. "I'm sure it must be."

From out of Oddo's pocket popped Fredlegs, waving his twig arms to get Gollyplox's attention. The Cheevilnid made a kind of purring sound. Against the Acorn Man's chest he affectionately placed the bulbous node of one long finger. Fredlegs hugged it, as if it was a puffy green pillow. He proudly showed off Cap, but Gollyplox didn't understand, and only stared blankly. Fredlegs was mildly insulted; to make Cap feel better, he gave the scribbled-on acorn a paternal squeeze and strapped it back on.

Leo clapped Gollyplox fondly on one scrawny shoulder. "This can't be a coincidence right? Did you know we would be here?"

The Cheevilnid nodded.

"How?"

Gollyplox stretched one cane-thin arm behind his back and pulled something out of the wool pouch. He opened his hand, and in the beams of the boys' flashlights they saw that he was holding two smooth, oval stones, made of something like quartz. One was black, and the other was white.

Bemused, Leo stared at the Cheevilnid. "What…don't tell me 'magic stones'"?

"*Criiiiiik*." Gollyplox shook his head. "*Speak me. Spoken.*"

No one understood what that meant. They let Gollyplox lead them back to the cave, which was the same one in which Leo had once tasted his first roasted chickenbat. The boys waited around the old campfire spot, guzzling water from the bottles they had packed.

Gollyplox gently tapped Leo's upper arm and led him a few feet away, where they began to converse in low tones. Ms. Winnipeg could see that the subject matter, whatever it was, was grave. She watched as Leo listened carefully for many minutes, a ponderous frown upon his face, while croaks and chirrups steadily percolated from the Cheevilnid's broad frog mouth.

At last, after a long *criiikkkkkk* and a reassuring pat on Leo's shoulder, Gollyplox stopped talking and crouched down vigilantly, as if waiting for a verdict.

Leo stared away into the dark of the mountain. Ms. Winnipeg approached him. "What's wrong?"

"Gollyplox says the Cheevilnids were attacked this morning."

"Oh! By the gray one?"

"Yes, he was part of it. They all know about him. It sounds like he left the other Cheevilnids a long time ago, because he hated the boys. Apparently they made him feel inferior, or something. He was called Flimp, originally, but now he has this crazy long name: Xylykynyxytyr. And there are two others with him. One was more like a human. They don't know his name. He has 'owl eyes,' Gollyplox kept saying. Owl eyes..."

Wilwell had drawn close. "What about the third one?"

"He sounds pretty bad...a man, I guess, or human-like, anyway. But taller, and very strong. And with three arms, right Gollyplox?"

A gurgling noise began deep in the Cheevilnid's throat and burbled out as a confirmation.

"The third arm grows right out of his back," Leo went on. "The owl eye guy called him 'Bludgeon.' He smashed up the village with a huge hammer."

He paused, and gave the boys a look of pity before continuing.

"He killed a Cheevilnid."

Everyone gasped. Oddo cried out. "What?! Who?"

They looked at Gollyplox, who nodded gravely. "*Strum.*"

The boys hung their heads heavily. Albert sniffed.

"A Cheevilnid has never died before," muttered Wilwell.

"When Zechariah was still here, the Cheevilnids enjoyed the same timeless existence as the boys," explained Leo to Ms. Winnipeg. "Even after the Protector left, the Cheevilnids were all still fairly young. None of them have died of old age, or for any other reason, for that matter. Not until now."

Oddo wiped his eyes. "Strum is the first."

Leo sighed, and considered other details that Gollyplox had related about the attack.

"The man with owl eyes gave them a message, to give to me. He said: Leo will be…" He looked at Gollyplox. "Am I translating this right? He said: 'Leo will be…no, must be…Leo must be dead, for the Living Ones to rest in peace.'"

Wilwell, rubbing away his tears for the murdered Cheevilnid, looked at Leo with his big, blue, red-rimmed eyes. "What does that mean?"

"I don't have the foggiest idea." Leo stared out across the Fillwishing. "The immediate problem is getting Ms. Winnipeg and Albert back home."

Albert drew his breath in sharply. "But we can't go back now!"

"The Cheevilnids, Leo," said Wilwell. "They need our help! We need to go investigate what happened to them…and we need to get them off the Island, right?"

"That's right," said Oddo. "They can't stay here. This Island might be about to explode! Hmmmm…" The lanky boy folded his hands behind his back as if he was trying to work out an algebra equation, even though it was obvious to everyone that he had already formed his conclusion: "They should probably all come live with us at the mansion, yes…"

"Now, look," grumbled Leo, raising a finger, "That's not for you to decide. I need to think about that! It was hard enough sneaking a bunch of kids into…"

"Wait!" Ms. Winnipeg looked at Leo. "It isn't safe at all to go back the way we came. This mountain is too unstable. I'm surprised that Albert and I made it this far."

Leo exhaled. He hated to admit it, but she was right. "A Balloon will get us safely back, then. We were going to borrow one from Relm, anyway, to get to Zechariah's palace. Once we're done there, we'll just fly across the valley back here to Hollowchest and straight to the peak. And, while we're in Relm, we can make a plan for how to save the Cheevilnids."

The boys began to cheer, but Gollyplox interrupted them with a dry croak and a series of monotone burbles.

Leo's face darkened. "What?! You're kidding me…"

Ms. Winnipeg was the only one who had not comprehended what the Cheevilnid had said.

"The house where they keep the Balloons," Leo explained. "The assassins hit it pretty hard, apparently. They stole one of the Balloons, and tore up the others. Wait! My gosh—they might have been going back to the Wayover, to attack the mansion…!"

Gollyplox quickly interjected. "*Crikcreeeekcrikcrik.*" *They did not come this way in the Balloon. Everyone saw them travel westwards, past Zechariah's mountain.*

From a Dark Wayover

Leo sighed, mildly relieved but not satisfied. "It's not possible for us to just climb Mount Highpalace. Without a way to fly up, we're stuck. We might as well go home. Except I'm not sure if Hollowchest is going to let us back up."

The craggy peak rumbled, as if to corroborate Leo's fears.

"Perhaps it would be best to just continue on to 'Relm'," said Ms. Winnipeg, trying the village's name for the first time. "Regardless, the inside of this mountain is the last place we should be!"

With a low, frustrated groan, Leo eyed the elevator, and the roiling lava twisting throughout the gargantuan cavern. He wanted to take the boys back to the mansion, and forget the Expedition entirely, but Hollowchest might very well collapse around them any minute. Even if they arrived safely home again, there would still be a trio of murderers at large out to destroy him. His family wasn't safe. He needed to figure out a way to contact Zechariah as soon as possible; of that, at least, Leo was certain. Only the Protector could rise to challenges of this magnitude.

He did not know why it agitated him so much to concede another point, or any point, made by Ms. Winnipeg, but it did. Nevertheless, he frowned and nodded.

The boys cheered.

"Don't get carried away! Once we're there, stay close to me. Don't wander off. Especially you, Albert."

Except I'm the one these three assassins are after, he thought. *The boys should probably stay as far away from me as possible. Then again, they might go after them just to get to me. Either way, if I don't get Zechariah's help soon things are going to take a turn for the worst…*

From a Dark Wayover

Twelve

Calling lampflowers to life as he went, Gollyplox led his human friends deeper under the mountain, into the narrow, wet tunnel that had once provided Leo with a much-needed escape from Throtrex.

Up and down the passage went the echoed sounds of their labored breathing, and of the slaps of their palms upon the tunnel floor. Ms. Winnipeg reminded everyone that she was not an 'outdoors-y type', but she only said it once, because she did not want to be a complainer. After the journey had continued for what was probably fifteen minutes but which felt to her like forty-nine hours, she began to think that she might want to be a complainer, after all. She breathed a deep sigh of relief when she heard Oddo, somewhere ahead, announce: "Sunlight! We're here!"

From a Dark Wayover

From the tunnel exit, a clear, recently made trail led them easily through the warm jungle. A morning time mist hovered among the trees and vines, making the sunlight into bouquets of lemon-colored beams. A school of Scumps crossed the path, looking no different than a cloud of large birthday party bubbles, except for the blue dot eyes on the underside and the tiny paddle-shaped feet that kept them bobbing along through the air. An amethyst-colored bird made a call like a loon and flew from one tree to another, trailing a single six-foot long leg beneath it like a big purple noodle. In and out of the jungle foliage scuttled Island insects: the beetle-ish Monchpibs traveling one on top of the other in little towers; the centipede-ish Uddles with organic catapults on their backs that fired beads of their own dried spit at predators; or the Tree-Going Lauds, black ants with comparatively huge, flat flapper-shaped limbs near their heads, which they used to catch mosquitos. The clapping sounds they made were like corn popping in a skillet.

Ms. Winnipeg couldn't stop letting out sighs of wonder, and even occasional laughter. "Now that we're out of that mountain, I can see what a spectacular place this is! Everything you told me about it is true! How long has it been since you've visited— the Christmas before last, I think?"

Though their moods were still damp from the news of Strum's death, the boys appreciated their tutor's excitement. "Yes, for three days," replied Wilwell.

"And once, before that, for Leo to install that ladder on Hollowchest," Oddo said. "We didn't stay long, though."

"And for a long time, last year," said Albert.

"That was last April," Leo clarified. "For an entire month. You had taken a few weeks off, so we did, too. Kind of an extended summer vacation. But we also helped the Cheevilnids improve the village. We showed them how to build things."

"And take care of Waywobs," said Oddo. "And other creatures. The whole valley really belongs to the Cheevilnids now."

The trail ended as the jungle seemed to pull apart almost like curtains on a stage, and the green, hilly meadows of Relm spread out before them. Flocks of Waywobs meandered some distance away, and the soft sounds of their bleats rode with the cool, flowery air of the valley.

Behind the travelers was Hollowchest, rising like a gigantic stalagmite. On this side, there was no visual evidence of its interior turmoil. Ahead was Zechariah's mountain—which the boys sometimes referred to as Highpalace—taller, broader, more majestic, with wintery-looking clouds dressing its peak like a royal crown.

From a Dark Wayover

Almost right away, Cheevilnids from across Relm began making their way towards the visitors. They did not hop and leap in the way to which the boys were accustomed, but approached slowly and shared weary hugs with everyone.

"Look at them," said Oddo. "They look so dejected…"

"They miss Strum," said Wilwell.

An earnest conversation began between Gollyplox and the rest of his people. Leo could see that they were consulting him. Gollyplox listened, then took a few moments to reflect, and finally called out, "*Igwish!*"

His slender, light-green wife toddled out of the assemblage and croaked affectionately. She and her husband exchanged a few *criks* and *creeks*, and she departed.

Ms. Winnipeg stood beside Leo. "I wonder what's happening?"

From a Dark Wayover

Leo admitted that he did not know, but he followed along with everyone else as Gollyplox led all of them to the banks of the Fillwishing.

The boys were distressed. Houses that they had helped build now lay in ruins. The watchtower was destroyed; the clay Cheevilnid head lay in two pieces, its eyes staring as if in shock.

Gollyplox took the group to a spot just downriver from the slow-churning millwheel. Strum's body had been laid upon a smooth, rock promontory bordered by bright red and yellow tropical flowers. Other Cheevilnids were already here, silent and somber, randomly placing white petals, green lily pads, or pink toadstool caps on their deceased friend.

Igwish returned. In her lime green hands was a robe.

"What's that for?" Ms. Winnipeg whispered to Leo, as Gollyplox let his wife place the robe across his knobby shoulders. The robe's material was of Waywob wool, roughly stitched, but into it had been woven egg-sized yellow or blue jewels gathered from around the Island.

"I don't know. I've never seen this before. I take it Gollyplox has turned into a kind of leader among his people. What's he doing now?"

Gollyplox had removed the black and white stones from his pouch. He rolled them around in one hand, then opened his fingers and let them rest upon his palm.

He stared at them for a half a minute. Tilting his head back, he closed his eyes, breathing slowly. He looked at the stones again. He rolled them gently in his hand, and nodded.

"*AmoAhsh'Qaya. Upaway.*" He turned to his people. "*Oolaronkas.*"

From a Dark Wayover

Several Cheevilnids left the promontory, and quickly returned carrying a spherical cage.

"I don't know what 'Upaway' is," whispered Leo to Ms. Winnipeg, "But Oolaronkas are just some funny bugs the boys invented a long time ago. The Cheevilnids domesticated them…that's what's inside that cage."

Gollyplox began to chant. The melody was simple—no more than four notes. He raised his long hands, and the jewels of his robe twinkled in the sunlight. The other Cheevilnids began to sing with him, arranging themselves spontaneously into groups, adding new layers to the hymn. Their voices were tremulous and pinched, but not unpleasant.

Gollyplox raised his hands high above him and wriggled his long, node-tipped fingers. He made a croak that rose above the chanting. The door on the spherical cage was opened, and the occupants were drawn out by special clicking, chirping calls made by the keepers.

From a Dark Wayover

The little honey-colored, oval-shaped Oolaronkas, carried by the propeller wings on the tops of their heads, flowed out of the cage with a soft, thick soundwave of coos. Guided by the calls of their Cheevilnid keepers, they swirled and swished like a waterspout above the heads of the mourners.

Gollyplox spread his arms wide, and the Oolaronkas descended. With their rigid, seedpod-type bodies crammed against each other, they all found a place beneath fallen Strum's arms or legs, back or head. Propeller wings buzzing, they pushed the body into the air and steadily lifted it higher and higher.

The chanting subsided. Everyone paid silent witness as the Oolaronkas, their cooing slowly fading away, carried their strange cargo beyond the valley and into the eastern sky.

Ms. Winnipeg brushed tears from her eyes. She was pleasantly surprised when Igwish waddled up and squeezed her waist pityingly. Smiling, she asked, "Where will he be taken?"

"*Big sea*," murmured Igwish.

"The ocean." She tried to smile again, but her mouth trembled. "I feel silly, because I didn't know him at all. But this just makes me so sad."

Wilwell, Oddo and Albert had gathered close to Leo, who draped his arms over them and held them tightly. His heart broke as he felt them sob into his shirt.

⋯✦⋅✦⋅✦⋅✦⋅✦⋅✦

The throng dispersed. Leo and Ms. Winnipeg left the boys with the Cheevilnids and strolled aimlessly over a stretch of bright green meadow grass.

Absorbed in their own thoughts, they didn't speak. Leo pondered what he had just observed: the Cheevilnids had extemporaneously invented their own funeral ceremony—an Upaway—led by Gollyplox, who had displayed some sort of mystical power using those white and black stones. It was as if he had become the village's official shaman or rabbi.

Leo's eyes were drawn to light playing upon the Fillwishing, and a breeze came rushing through the valley from the northwest. Just as he began to enjoy the moment, he detected the taint of ash in the air, while at the same time a low tremor rumbled out of Hollowchest, making the ground shiver.

He sighed heavily. "I don't understand what's happening. This is Zechariah's Island. With no Throtrex around, it shouldn't be dangerous. It's supposed to be a peaceful place; a haven. And to make things worse, it's all because of me, evidently! Why me? What is all this about me needing to be dead for the Living Ones to rest in peace? Who are these Living Ones?"

Ms. Winnipeg crossed her arms and thought about it, though she really had no idea how to respond.

She was grateful when Oddo, Wilwell, and Albert interrupted them.

"Igwish asked us to dinner!"

Leo looked pained. "Oh, gee…I don't know, fellas. We really need to keep moving…those assassins are still out there…"

Albert groaned like a phillip's head screwdriver was being driven into his belly, and his legs buckled. "But I'm sooo hunnnngry…"

Oddo thrust his hands out imploringly. "Igwish really wants to feed us! Please?"

Gollyplox and Igwish had ambled over to join them; his jeweled robe was draped over her arm. With her wriggling fingers, she enfolded Leo's forearm and pressed gently but insistently. "*Please?*"

Leo surrendered with a smile that faded quickly. "But I want to take a look at the Balloons, first. If there is a possibility that we can salvage one, then we can get to

Zechariah's palace and find out what to do about all this chaos. Otherwise, we should go back home as soon as possible."

...✦·✦·✦·✦·✦·✦·✦

Gollyplox led them to what used to be a long, one-story structure, like a bungalow. The roof was made of sections of thatch that could be easily lifted off. The walls had been painted with bright red, orange, and yellow pictures of balloons, with Oblates and Billodriffs soaring through the sky along with them. Bludgeon had crushed the walls into colored shards; he had torn away the roof and smashed the door off of its hinges.

"There were four Balloons here, in total," said Leo, sifting through the wreckage. "The invaders stole one. For travel, I guess…to get around the Island faster. Any ideas where they might have gone?"

Gollyplox and the boys all shrugged. Oddo clasped his hands behind his back and thought hard. "Maybe Kak's old palace?"

Wilwell scratched the back of his head. "Gollyplox said they went west. And why go to Kak's palace, anyway? The Oblates didn't leave one stone on top of the other. Could there be something else there, Leo?"

"Look!" Leo held up the fabric of one of the Balloons. "Am I going crazy, or is this Balloon undamaged? Help me get it out…"

They all reached their hands in to grab a part of the vehicle, but it took several minutes to remove it entirely from the barrow where it was normally stored.

Gollyplox spent a long time inspecting it, but finally made an approving purr-sound.

Albert cheered. "It's alright!"

"Thank goodness!" Oddo exclaimed. "We can make the journey to Highpalace!"

Leo chewed his bottom lip reflectively. "That's a little weird. They stole the one Balloon…they smashed two others to bits—you can see all the broken parts here. But the fourth they left intact. Why?"

Wilwell frowned at this puzzle. "Maybe they were in a hurry?"

"From what Gollyplox described, they weren't in a hurry. They had the Cheevilnids frightened to death; there was no threat to them…no reason to be in a hurry."

Ms. Winnipeg made her signature "hm" sound. "Maybe it doesn't mean anything, Leo. They were just randomly destroying things—see how they only wrecked some houses, but not others."

Leo continued chewing his bottom lip, but he exhaled in surrender. "I guess you're right. It still seems weird to me. Anyway, we should get the Balloon ready to go, boys. Then we can eat—is that alright, Igwish?" The light-lime-colored Cheevilnidress bowed sweetly and hopped off in the direction of her house to prepare her meal.

Everyone helped to place the Balloon's gondola on a low cart, and then roll it away from the bungalow and into the sun. The fabric of the Balloon was a vivid Lincoln green, and it was carefully spread out flat on the ground beside the gondola.

"We'll need torchtruffles!" said Oddo, and he led Wilwell and Albert to a warm, shady pen near the river. Two Cheevilnids with reed baskets ran along with them. After a few minutes they came trotting back.

Mushrooms, with wide caps and thick stems, filled their baskets. As the boys chattered to each other about movies they had recently seen and other unrelated items, they began scooping the mushrooms into the gondola's burner.

Leo idly picked one up, though, by now, he was familiar with them. Colored dark red and dull silver (inspired by the Oblates' metal fez-helmets), it had the same earthy, musky smell as most fungi. He snapped the stem, and there was a tiny crackling flare like a sparkler on Independence Day.

During Leo's entire first adventure on the Island, he never guessed the children's ingenious fuel source. Torchtruffles grew quickly and easily; once ignited, they burnt steadily for hours.

Igwish returned to call them all to dinner. Other Cheevilnids happily arrived to continue preparing the Balloon, so that the humans could, at last, rest and eat.

She led them through the simple, dark dirt paths of the village. Many of the Cheevilnids' domiciles along the way lay in various degrees of ruin; thatched roofs lay in tatters, and chunks of cobblestone walls were scattered helter skelter.

Gollyplox and Leo deliberated as they went. Ms. Winnipeg tried to listen, but it was hopeless, since Gollyplox's speech was, to her, a guttural hodgepodge of toady blurps and croaks. Finally, the frogman nodded at a statement of Leo's and leapt on ahead.

"It's amazing," Ms. Winnipeg remarked with a giggle, skipping forward to walk beside Leo. "How you can understand what the Cheevilnids are saying. I speak French, and some Italian. But I would certainly like to learn Cheevilnid!"

"I wish I could say that I worked hard at it and took a lot of long lessons, but that's not actually how it works."

"Oh?"

"Yeah, it's not a conventional language. I'd say it's more emotion-based, I guess. I mean, at first all you hear are a few combinations of the exact same handful of *criks*, croaks, and *creeks*. But the more time you spend with them, you begin to…I don't know…*absorb* what they want you to know. It goes the other way, too. You can just speak to them in English, and most of the time they comprehend."

    They reached Igwish and Gollyplox's house. A portion of the eastern wall had been demolished during Bludgeon's rampage, and the villagers had helped to cover the breach with a screen made of tree branches. Other than that, all remained intact. It retained the simple design it had originally been given by the boys: a central area with a fireplace, and a small, attached room, not much bigger than a closet, with a loft where the occupants slept. The one modification was a tunnel dug beneath the main room that led into a nursery for the podnids. After two years, the Cheevilnid children were no longer the polliwog-looking creatures they were. They were nidlings now, so (although still quite small) their tails were almost completely gone, and they had back legs, and they only spent about half their days in the murky pond created for them inside the subterranean nursery. The rest of the time they hopped, rolled, croaked, ate Medallion bugs, and tried to figure out how to escape the house and explore the Island. Sometimes they did escape, and they thought they were brave and ingenious, without realizing that Gollyplox and Igwish had only pretended not to see them leave.

    They all sat on the floor, in a circle, with wide, thick green leaves for plates. Igwish served her guests hot chickenbat fresh from a stone oven built around the fireplace. It was delicious, but it was served with the yellow riverbeans harvested from the bottom of the Fillwishing, which were nauseating to the humans. Albert nearly retched; Igwish smiled good-naturedly and plucked the beans off of his leafy plate using her tongue.

From a Dark Wayover

Oddo helped Fredlegs out of his pocket so that he could sit beside him on a tiny makeshift stool. The Acorn Man had no need of food, of course, since he absorbed energy by photosynthesis, like most any plant. A regular intake of water, however, was essential. He had no mouth for drinking, though. Instead, Oddo placed a little cup of water in front of him. Fredlegs, still sitting on his stool, placed his stick legs in the cup and happily absorbed the contents through his twiggy limbs. His eyes squinted with pleasure. He even dunked Cap in the cup, as if he was giving his artificial friend a bath.

Everyone chatted, enjoying the meal and each other's company, but twice Leo stood and looked out of the doorway.

Wilwell looked concerned. "What's wrong?"

"Just checking."

"You're worried about that Evilnid, aren't you? And the three-armed man?"

" 'Bludgeon'," Oddo reminded him.

"I'm not worried. Just checking, that's all." He was lying, of course. There was no way he could really allow himself to relax here; there were far too many threats to the boys. "We should get going soon, though. I want to contact Zechariah."

Ms. Winnipeg tentatively approached him, and her voice was a whisper. "Don't you think that the boys need some rest?"

"Aren't they resting now?"

"Well…I mean: sleep."

"Sleep? Here? Oh, no…it's too dangerous…"

She grimaced. "Look at them, Leo."

He gave them a careless glance, which soon became a more thoughtful gaze. All three boys had dark circles under their eyes. Their faces were smeared with soot, dried sweat, and dried tears. Their movements were sluggish—as Leo watched, the wood goblet of Waywob milk that Oddo was holding slipped right out of the boy's hand, spilling its contents down his left pants leg. The boy looked up towards the heavens and mumbled, "morrrrronn…"

Leo turned back to Ms. Winnipeg with a pained expression. "We can't stay here! Those assassins…"

"The boys are…just boys," she said, in as sweet a combination of sympathy and rigidity as Leo had ever heard. "They can't just keep going like this without rest."

"Ah ha!" Leo raised one finger as if to register a point scored. "And that's why I knew it was a bad idea to bring them…"

"Oh, not at all! They're wonderful boys. You should be proud of them. They're brave, and steadfast. Like their father."

Leo turned away. "Well…they aren't really related to me, of course. That's probably a good thing for them…"

"They have your daily example. That goes a long way."

Leo looked at her briefly, and she returned his stare. He looked away again, smiling awkwardly. "O.K., I give up. You're right. We all need rest." He shook his head, rubbing his eyes. "I need it, too, I guess. I'll talk to Gollyplox about a place for us."

He paused, as if regretting his decision. "But we'll need to get up extra early."

⋯✦·✦·✦·✦·✦·✦·✦

After dinner, they moved to a round beehive-shaped building that the villagers used as a meeting hall. A warm fire was made for them in the pit at the center of the hall, and everyone sat around it and chatted. The conversation would have trickled along for another half hour until it had run out like tea from a teapot and the boys would have drifted off to sleep on the straw mats that had been prepared for them, if it had not been for Gollyplox.

The Cheevilnid visited them one last time as the sunlight melted out of the western sky. He led Leo to a far corner of the meeting hall, and the ever-curious boys eagerly followed.

Gollyplox made a low croaking sound. He gestured towards a panel in the floor, which Leo slid to the side. The boys all drew in a breath, almost in unison.

"Potions!" They cheered.

There were eighteen in all: right away Leo spotted an opalescent bottle of *Fixmender*. There was a green bottle of *Smallsteam*, and four *Anti-Smallsteam Bigifiers*; there were others he recognized, and still more he didn't.

Leo looked down at Gollplox in wonder. "How are these here?"

The Cheevilnid explained that, during the past two years of slowly rebuilding the Island from the ruins that the Throtrex had left behind, they had discovered relics of the age when Zechariah and all the boys lived here in harmony. The Balloons were examples of these; so were the carefully preserved potions.

"Wow!" Albert shouted. "A *Snowball!*"

Wilwell nudged Oddo and pointed to a wooden flask. "And *Instant Jungle!* And there's a *Subtility.* And a *Fishbreath*…a *Niblung*…."

Oddo giggled. "And, look, Wilwell…" He picked up a cream-colored bottle shaped like a beaker. "*Vermiform.*"

Wilwell chortled. "*Vermiform.*" He and Oddo giggled together at a private joke. "So dumb."

"*Concretis!*" Albert exclaimed. "We can throw it at the Bludgeon-man and cover him in stone! It's mine! I'm putting it in my bag!"

He reached for the *Concretis,* but Leo barked in protest. "No, Albert! We're not bringing that!"

From a Dark Wayover

Albert looked shocked. "Whaaaa? But that's a really good weapon for us!"

"Yes, one that we could easily attack ourselves with. With our luck, that's exactly what would happen. You might trip, and drop it on yourself and—presto!—you're a garden gnome. It's good to know these are here, but we don't need to take them with us. They're too dangerous. Just leave them."

Wilwell and Oddo nodded reluctantly, but Albert was still nearly frozen in disbelief.

Leo reached for the opalescent bottle. "We'll take the *Fixmender*, just in case. And one of these *Smallsteams*. That could come in handy, maybe…"

Albert had a small convulsion of excitement. "Ooh! Yes! I'll put them in my bag…"

"No, Albert!" Leo's rebuke came out more forcefully than he had intended, and he forced himself to be calmer. "I'll carry them, Albert. You might lose them—accidentally, I mean. I know you wouldn't lose them on purpose, little man…"

Albert's face fell and his shoulders shrugged involuntarily. He turned away and shuffled back towards the fire. "I never get to do *anything*…"

"Albert…" Leo held out his hand towards the tiny boy, but it was ignored. "Alright, well, anyway, let's get to sleep, everybody. We have to get a really early start."

Some Cheevilnids from the village had happily offered to keep watch so the little band of humans could sleep, but Leo found himself needing almost an hour to relax. *The sooner I get these boys back home, the better…*

From a Dark Wayover

Thirteen

It was three o'clock in the morning when Gollyplox woke them up.

The fire was just a smoking, glimmering pile of red embers, which another Cheevilnid began to stoke.

Rubbing his eyes, Wilwell sat up, expressionless and not completely awake. Blearily he watched several pairs of froggish hands moving in the half-light. Around the flames, deftly and soundlessly, they assembled a simple, miniature kitchen: a rack of wooden stakes, overlaid with a thin, flat plate of smooth stone. Bulging Cheevilnid eyes glimmered in the firelight and the rounded tips of green fingers snapped open the purple and white striped eggs of the Hummingpelicans (pelicans that were the size of hummingbirds. Too small to catch fish, they used their tablespoon-shaped bills to scoop up

From a Dark Wayover

Fings, Poinks, and other wriggling water bugs from streams and ponds. Strangely, their eggs were almost as big as those laid by geese. It was a convulsive, spasmodic experience for a Hummingpelican to lay an egg, causing involuntary squawks and the loss of some feathers, but, thankfully, it was painless.) The Cheevilnids scrambled the eggs on the hot, flat stone, adding in dry herbs and chunks of island tomatoes and cooked crawfish, and served it all in wooden bowls. Leo brewed black coffee for himself and for Ms. Winnipeg, using a small aluminum kettle he'd brought along.

When breakfast was over, they put their shoes and packs on, and followed Gollyplox out under the vast dome of night with its endless glowing stars and its pale moon. Fredlegs rode along in Oddo's pocket with his arms and head peeking out, like an extremely tiny joey in a kangaroo pouch.

From a Dark Wayover

Thanks to the villagers, the Balloon was already fully inflated; the torchtruffles, loaded earlier by the boys, were now simmering in the cistern, illuminating the sturdy gondola with orange light. Only two strong ropes kept the craft from sailing away.

Shadowy Cheevilnids scurried back and forth, unmooring the Balloon and waving goodbye. From the south, a strong breeze, almost cold, blew across Leo's shoulders, and it smelled of jungle flowers and clean sea salt. It was deceptive. It was as if they were merely on an island paradise somewhere, except for the short, random earthquakes that sounded like hungry bears.

Wilwell was, as always, the pilot. Pushing pedals, he opened the cistern and sent powerful waves of heat into the Balloon's interior. As the vessel lumbered higher into the sky, its whirling wooden rotors propelled it. Wilwell spun the wide steering wheel and took them around the waist of Zechariah's mighty mountain.

From a Dark Wayover

"We won't be able to land in the palace itself," said Wilwell over his shoulder. "It's too dark to see, and I'm afraid I'll run into something. There's a wide clearing though, off of a path not far below the palace; we'll land there."

It was a slow ascent. Moonlight glowed upon the sides of Highpalace as they wound their way up. The flames purred in the cistern; the propellers sounded like fast clocks. They heard the call of a night bird somewhere, and another low rumble from Hollowchest's fiery insides.

Finally, they were close enough to the peak's cloudy covering that it hung above them like a black ceiling. In plain view was the clearing that Wilwell had mentioned, covered in thin grass, right on the edge of a broad spur.

"Remember, we're not going to be here long," Leo told everyone. "We'll use the Pool and then we'll need to get back home—so, leave the engine running, O.K.?"

Wilwell nodded, shutting off the propellers and reducing the flames in the cistern without snuffing them out entirely. The Balloon hovered a little over two yards above the clearing, and Leo leapt out with a rope in hand. Tying it to a nearby tree, he guided the craft to the ground.

They followed a rocky trail up a slope, through groves of short fir trees. The crunch and snap of their footsteps were the only sounds. The air was very cold and nearly still.

The path led them slowly to the eastern shoulder of the mountain, and through the trees they could spy the first, faintest radiance of dawn. A welcome sight after the oppressive darkness through which they had been travelling, it was nonetheless brief: the trail abruptly led them up into the thick clouds that circled the mountaintop.

"Just stay on the trail," said Wilwell, although no one could see him or anyone else anymore. "It's alright. But everybody should hold on to the shirt of the person in front of you!"

Leo, leading the way, stretched his arms out in front of him. His fingers felt branches to the side. His feet felt the smooth trail. His eyes saw nothing. The dense wetness of fog, cold and heavy, pushed against his face.

"Everyone O.K. back there?"

An ensemble of familiar voices responded, muted by the clouds and by the discomfort of uncertainty.

"What was that?" Oddo said, after a tremulous, high-pitched cry rang through the forest.

"It sounded like a ghost!" Albert said.

From a Dark Wayover

"It's just a bird," Wilwell said irritably. He was the only one of them who had ever visited the top of Zechariah's mountain before, having once been chosen to preside over the Protector's yearly Sleep. He felt he had a duty now to put everyone at ease. *But that didn't sound like any bird I've ever heard…*

Leo didn't like the thought of the group trudging along anxiously through the dark mist. "I can't wait to see Zechariah's palace," he declared, his voice coated in faux enthusiasm. "I bet it's amazing. How are you back there, Gollyplox?"

The Cheevilnid made a slimy-sounding croak in reply. It sounded to the boys like someone loudly passing gas, which brightened their moods considerably, until another ghostly, high-pitched wail filled the air.

Albert groaned miserably. "What is that horrible thing?"

Leo felt a fluttering of powerful wings near his face. He recoiled, unintentionally letting out a snarl.

"Leo!" Albert shouted. "Are you alright?"

Leo felt annoyed at himself. *It's just a bird.*

"Just keep hold of the person in front of you!"

He felt Wilwell's grip tighten on the back of his shirt. He slowly waved his arms in front of him and walked forward.

Air rushed around his eyes and another flapping of wings tossed his hair. Leo drew up his right hand to shield his head, keeping the left in front of him.

Albert cried out again.

Leo turned towards the boy, but of course he could not see him…then he realized that, for the first time, the mist itself was visible. It seemed lit from within by a pale glow. He could even see his arm reaching out.

From a Dark Wayover

All at once, he stepped out of the fog. By walking a few steps up the sloping path he brought Wilwell out of it, too, and then Ms. Winnipeg and the rest.

Early morning sunlight glittered upon the dew all around them. The strange, high-pitched sound filled the air again, but now they could all see what was making it: a creature, like an egret, with long, iridescent blue, white and gold feathers and a beak like a toucan's.

"It *was* a bird!" Wilwell laughed.

Oddo whooped. "A Tiara! I should have known! I forgot about those. Look, see the nest on its head, made from fresh fruit? That's where it keeps its eggs…and, look! They've hatched!"

They only had a few seconds to admire three tiny, fluffy hatchlings wriggling and peeping in the tightly knit fruit nest on the Tiara's head before the mother flew off through the trees. Wherever she ended up alighting, the hatchlings would have a breakfast of grapes and berries already waiting for them, since it was of such things that their head-mounted home was made.

The forest around them was nothing like what lay just below the clouds. Here, it was green and ancient and bursting with life and color.

Oddo gasped. "Ladygowns!"

Among the indigenous firs were trees that were, unmistakably, the inventions of Zechariah's beloved crusader children: the tops, though made of bark and leaf, suggested gentle mothers' faces with flowing hair, and the branches swept down like green dresses. Blue and orange fruit grew upon them.

Albert grabbed one of the fruits that had fallen to the ground and took a hearty bite. He smiled as he chewed and made a joyful sound. Reaching down, he seized another fruit and tossed it to Leo, who happily bit into his first Ladygown fruit and then offered it to Ms. Winnipeg. "Tastes kind of like a peach!"

From a Dark Wayover

"Mmmm…smells like chardonnay!" With a coquettishness that Leo would have previously considered uncharacteristic, she indicated that she had no intention of returning it to Leo, and she contentedly ate the rest.

Leo led them on through the lush woods. Damp ferns and vines lined the trail. Yellow wren-type birds flew before them in an ever-shifting flock, like a giant lemon suddenly made into a swirling mosaic. A Sodturtle slowly crossed their path, and from its shell grew earth and moss and three very long, skinny arms that gathered nuts and beetles from overhanging boughs. It gazed sleepily at the passersby, but did not seem remotely worried about them.

The path brought them near a jutting ridge that overlooked the valley. Far below, Relm looked like a baby nestled in a verdant cradle. Hollowchest was brown and hazy in the distance.

They had only a minute to gasp in wonder at the view, before the trail took them back into a grove of Ladygowns, then through lush pines. All at once, the trees broke and Zechariah's palace stood in plain view.

It was bafflingly huge. All of Relm would fit inside of it. Gleaming white towers soared above, and massive walls disappeared around the shoulders of the mountain peak. Vast tapestries of ivy clung to some portions, and yawning windows spangled the polished heights with perfect randomness, their sills flowing with red and purple flowers. Gold and white banners as big as ships' sails flew from the tops of the towers, each emblazoned with a silvery icon of the Protector's Spear.

A grand, arched entrance, with open gates, led into the palace.

Leo stopped, feeling suddenly self-conscious, not knowing why. For some reason, he decided to call out a greeting. Only the low winds sweeping the forests answered back.

Oddo giggled. "No one's home."

They passed beneath the arch and into a dim, polished hall lined with multicolored columns. The sheer quiet, and the immensity of the palace itself, drove them into a hush, and their movements now made rippling echoes. Chill bumps rose on their skin in the coldness of the sudden shade and polished granite.

The only way forward was a long flight of wide stairs. Lighting the way up were lanterns that were made of what looked like brass or new copper. Inside each, instead of flame, there floated a small yellow orb of light.

At the top of the stairs, they found an immense hall vaulting up to a round opening looking into the sky and burning with the golden rays of the rising sun. From there, Wilwell easily remembered the way to Zechariah's

Sleeping Pool, and he confidently took them all on a trek down massive corridors and up or down other staircases.

It was impossible for their eyes to take in everything there was to see. Leo had a sense of being in some European cathedral, except this was even larger, and filled with light and air. As they travelled through its majestic passages, they passed tall lancet windows through which they spotted more views of the Island spread out far below.

Wilwell led them up marble stairs and through a towering wooden door. "We're here! The Pool Chamber!"

Like most parts of the palace, the room had a lofty ceiling. At the far end was a curved area, like an apse, presided over by a round, red-and-green rose-shaped window, beneath which was what could only be the Sleeping Pool: a raised, rectangular basin, glowing softly with a variety of colors, filled with perfectly still water.

They walked between raised stands on either side that were like choir lofts, with many tiers rising up and back until they almost reached the ceiling. "That's where the Oblates stood," Wilwell said, like a tour guide. "They slept standing up, while the Protector was in the Pool."

They took off their packs and dropped them on the floor, breathing sighs of relief and stretching their backs. Leo stepped closer to the Pool, but stopped in midstride when something in Albert's pack caught his eye.

He knelt down, taking out a bottle, and showed it to Albert. "What's this?"

The boy shrugged and looked away.

Oddo examined the bottle's oval shape and silver-white color. "*Snowball.*"

Leo frowned. "You brought a *Snowball*? I told you we weren't going to bring any potions with us; just the *Fixmender*, just in case, and the *Smallsteam*. Why'd you do this, Albert?"

Albert stood rigidly, and his cheeks were flushed red. "Welllll….I thought we might get really hot from traveling…and snow would feel nice, and we could drink some if we got thirsty, 'cause snow turns to water…"

"Albert, what if you fell and broke the bottle? It could hurt you or one of us, all that snow suddenly bursting out…"

"I'm careful!"

"Accidentally, I mean—I know you wouldn't do it on purpose. Look, you can't have this. I'm going to put it in my pack…"

Albert's face dropped. "Awwwww!"

Leo held up one finger sharply. "Albert!"

From a Dark Wayover

"You know, Leo," Oddo offered cautiously, "I think he would probably be O.K. Those bottles really are safe…"

Wilwell nodded. "Yes, I don't think even Albert could accidentally break it. He would have to really be hitting it with a hammer, the way he did to your pick-up truck's headlight that time…"

Leo shook his head. "No, fellas. The Island's just a really dangerous place to be right now, because it's erupting, and because those killers are still out there somewhere…I don't want to take any chances." Leo put the *Snowball* into his pack. "Albert: this stays here now, O.K.? Don't take it out of my bag."

The boy's little shoulders wilted and he mumbled a "yes, sir" that was nearly unintelligible.

Leo surveyed the Sleeping Pool. The basin, over seven feet long and five feet wide, was smooth, gilded, and polished like the inside of a medieval chalice. The water that filled it was so clear that a deliveryman from a north Canadian artesian well might have placed it there five minutes before. The outside walls of the pool were thick and covered in a colorful, twinkling mosaic, made of tesserae like the ones used in various other spots around the Island.

"O.K. Wilwell," Leo said, staring down at the Pool. "How does it work?"

Fourteen

"Get into the water," said Wilwell. "All the way under. Picture Zechariah, and start talking to him in your mind."

"And he will talk back to me?"

"No, no, it isn't like making a cell phone call. While you're in the water, just think of a few things that you want to say—you know, like: 'Hello, Zechariah. How are things going? Are we all going to die?' Then, stop and wait. That batch of thoughts will go to him, like a package being delivered. After a few seconds, you will get a thought-batch from him."

"So, I won't be talking to him in real-time? It's like a telegraph machine…"

"What's a telegraph machine?"

"Forget it—bad example. It's like…texting."

Wilwell nodded appreciatively. "Sort of."

"Alright, I think I understand everything well enough. Let me give this a try."

Leo took off his shoes, socks, jacket and shoulder holster with his pistol in it. He would have taken off his shirt, but he felt self-conscious about doing it in front of Ms. Winnipeg. "I'm covered in dirt. I hope that Zechariah doesn't mind that I'm about to mess up his Sleeping Pool."

Oddo chuckled. "You won't. You can't."

Leo frowned in confusion, but the boy just shook his head and made a half-smile. "The water's special. You'll see."

Leo climbed over the glimmering edge. The Pool was stunningly frigid, causing Leo to breathe in quick, shallow gasps as he sat and reclined. He saw right away what Oddo had meant: the grime on his arms began to slowly disintegrate, but without clouding the Pool.

Taking a deep breath, he lay back. He felt the waters enfold him, and watched the faces of Wilwell and Ms. Winnipeg and the others transform into wriggling blobs as his head submerged and settled against the smooth, hard, shimmery floor.

He had expected magical phenomenon: colored lights, or a mysterious humming sound, or vibrations in the water; there were none. He might as well have been back home in his own bathtub. He stared up, hearing an occasional muffled voice from above. Two bubbles escaped his nose.

He closed his eyes. He pictured Zechariah: the spear's tip nose and the dark eyes. He remembered the Protector standing triumphantly with Kak impaled on the end of his Spear.

Zechariah? Can you hear me? This is Leo.

He waited for a response to occur in his mind, but there was nothing.

From a Dark Wayover

Zechariah?

His lungs were beginning to hurt. He frowned, and sat up.

"Nothing's happening," he announced, with water running down his face and out of his hair. "And I can't breathe. And it's freezing in here."

"Nothing we can do about the freezing-ness. But there used to be a bamboo tube for us humans to breathe through…"

They all glanced around, but there was no tube.

Ms. Winnipeg snapped her fingers. "Ooh! I know!" She reached up and pulled out her red and blue oriental hair pin. She pulled on one end, and a cap came off with a tiny pop, revealing the tip of a writing pen. Lifting it up for them all to see, she announced, with a tone of victory: "A tutor's secret weapon! My hair pin is a hair *pen*!" Seeing their apathetic response, she cleared her throat awkwardly and began taking the pen apart. "So you can breathe," she said, handing Leo the hollow red and blue tube.

"Oh," said Leo. "That's good. Thanks."

Leo lay back down in the water, holding the empty pen to his lips. He breathed evenly. He closed his eyes and envisioned the Protector waiting patiently for him to speak.

Zechariah? Hello? Look, I don't know if you can hear me or not, but we're in huge trouble. For one thing, the Island has become volcanic. I think it may be about to explode. It isn't safe. And there are three people out to assassinate me: one of them is a Cheevilnid, and there is a three-armed man, and a man with giant eyes…they have the Corpse tattoo, Zechariah—the double 333's. The Cheevilnid tried to kill me at our house, Zechariah. Somehow, he got a Flute, and came through the Wayover to our <u>house</u>! I don't know what to do. Are you there? We need your help!

Leo paused, listening to his own breath whistling in and out of the red and blue pen. His mind was dormant. He opened his eyes and sat up with a gush of water.

"Fellas, this just isn't working. Nothing is happening."

The boys all protested. "You have to stay down," whined Oddo.

"You have to be patient," Wilwell assured him, staring with his earnest blue eyes. "Trust him."

Leo scowled, but sighed resignedly. "It's still freezing in here. I need a Hair Shirt that blocks out the cold…" He lay back down in the water.

The moment the back of his head came to rest upon the Pool floor, thoughts from outside of his own mind fired through him. He felt no physical effect at all—*like a lightning bolt that doesn't hurt*, is how he described it afterwards. Yet it brought into his mind the voice of Zechariah as clearly as if through a pair of studio-quality headphones.

From a Dark Wayover

Leo Von Koppersmith! It is very, very good to hear from you. In fact, you are contacting me at exactly the time I was told you would! Please tell my boys that their old Zechariah misses them, and thinks of them often! In fact, I am close. Closer than you know. As for the assassins: you must be cautious, of course. But they do not act on their own. They have been sent. The Corpse is your real enemy. He knows about you. He knows he must destroy you in order for his plot to succeed. Have you gotten the sword yet?

The painless lightning bolt-sensation abated, and Leo realized that Zechariah's "thought-batch" was finished. He lay there blinking, breathing steadily through his tube. Above, the shadowy forms of the boys and Ms. Winnipeg were moving and making muffled sounds.

Sword?

He pictured Zechariah's face again and closed his eyes.

Sword? What sword? What do you mean 'the Corpse knows about me'? What's going on, Zechariah?

From a Dark Wayover

He waited. From above came the sound of Wilwell's voice, insistently repeating something, but Leo couldn't make out what it was. *Not now, boys*, Leo thought to himself. *Leave it to them: I finally get the Pool working and now they won't stop interrupting…*

Another painless lightning bolt; a new batch of Zechariah's thoughts streaked into Leo's mind:

Forgive me, Leo. I assumed that by now you would know more. You were chosen for an important mission in the war against the Corpse, and for that you have been granted the right to a sword that you will need. There is great peril coming, and danger that threatens the entire world. Obtaining the sword must be the focus of all your efforts, whatever happens. It is hardly more than a legend to me, because I was on the Island for so long and I missed so much of human history. But it is real; you will be able to find it. It is a sword of kings, a joyous sword! You will find it in the…

Right then Leo was torn from the water. A disproportionately large hand held the front of his shirt with all the force of an industrial machine, drawing him up and holding him suspended in the air. The red and blue pen tube fell and the Pool's water ran out of his clothes and splattered the floor as Leo swayed helplessly. Coughing out some water he had accidentally inhaled, Leo tried desperately to take in the grotesque things he was seeing.

The arm that held him was one of three; it grew out of the back of a twelve-foot tall yellow man with a smooth, round head. A mouth of any sort was conspicuously absent. Above dark green, lifeless eyes, a prominent mark lay in the center of the forehead:

3ψ3
333

His left hand held Wilwell by the neck. His right hand held Gollyplox. His huge, flat feet were shod with iron-soled boots, and the right one was propped on Oddo's back, holding the boy against the floor.

There could be no doubt that this was Bludgeon, and beside him stood the same gray Cheevilnid that had tried to murder Leo in the mansion, whose name, they now knew, was Xylykynyxytyr. Like Oddo, Ms. Winnipeg had been thrown to the floor, and Xylykynyxytyr sat upon her back, holding her tightly by the hair.

Albert was in the grip of a third person, a dumpy little man in a dark, brown robe, with a rope bag across one shoulder, filled with…Leo could not quite see what…were those birds? But Leo's attention was almost forcibly taken from the bag by the third person's eyes—eyes huge and bulging, outlandish, and terrible, somehow. Between them read the numbers:

ꒋΞꒋ
Ξꒋ Ξ

From a Dark Wayover

"Good morning, Misthter Von Koppersthmith," said the dumpy little man.

Fifteen

Bludgeon released his grip, and Leo fell helplessly. He hit the floor with a spray of droplets, but he recovered quickly and hopped to his feet, fists clenched and facial muscles twitching nervously. Cold water dripped down his back and his legs. His heart pounded against his chest.

The man with the gigantic eyes remained slightly behind his three-armed cohort as he continued speaking to Leo. "I sthee you found the Balloon we left you. You're welcome." He winked, attempting to convey a playful mischief, but the squashing together of the eye's wrinkly lids was repulsive.

He turned, and with pleasurable surprise he let out a long, low sigh. "What on earth isth *that*?"

From a Dark Wayover

Dragging Albert along with him, he shuffled towards Xylykynyxytyr, who, with wheezy grunts, was shoving Ms. Winnipeg into a sitting position. The dumpy man seemed to pass into a state of near-ecstasy, like a visitor to a museum seeing his favorite work of art in real life for the first time. Hunching over, he let his expansive gaze drink in the sight of Ms. Winnipeg, who could not escape from Xylykynyxytyr's strangely powerful grip. She squirmed as the enormous eyes drew closer, until they almost rested upon her, like two glistening pillows. "Ohhh, the lovelinessth…look at the cheekbonesth, the delicate limbsth, the eyesth, stho full of childlike unthertainty…"

He gave Leo a sidelong glance. "Oh, Misthter Von Koppersthmith. You're like me…you like collecting treasuresth, too. Like my birdiesth." He turned, letting Leo see his bag full of fowl in their various stages of death. "Don't you justht love them? Stho lovely and fragile…like little sthoulsth with featherth. But *thisth*…"

He turned back to Ms. Winnipeg, sighing again. "Stho rare and sthweet…Ohh, forgive me! I am a great lover of beauty, and I can be stho transthported when I encounter it that I quite forget mysthelf. Introductionsth are in order, aren't they? Meet Monsthieur Bludgeon…and Monsthieur Xth..xxthh…xthylyxthhh…"

Leo frowned. "Xylykynyxytyr?"

The man sighed with frustration. "Yesth. You'll have to exthcuthe my companion…" He gave the gray-skinned Cheevilnid a disapproving stare. "The new name he sthelected for himsthelf is very, very difficult for me to pronounth."

He turned back to Leo. "And I am Monsthieur Mealworm. Called 'the Ropemasthter' by many. Well…by nobody yet, to be honestht, but sthomeday, I will. We are the Living Onesth, aren't we, my friendsth? The firsthtborn. Imitatorsth of the Perfectusth, whosth name shall forevermore be Jean Dieu…"

"Look, I don't know what any of that means," replied Leo, raising one hand in a gesture of meekness. "We just came here to do something, and now we're done, so we're just going to leave, O.K.?"

"Oh, you shouldn't be here at all, *mon amie*." He glared again at Xylykynyxytyr. "<u>Sthomeone</u> was sthupposthed to sthee to that, but he <u>didn't…follow…through</u>."

Xylykynyxytyr scowled, looking away, and Mealworm turned back to Leo. "That'sth why Jean Dieu—at great costht to histh own health, it should be sthaid—woke up Msthr. Bludgeon and mysthelf from our long, long sthleep, there on the Brim of the Hateful Deep, down where the World King rulesth. Sthee, Jean Dieu sthaid he would call upon usth to help usher in the Age of the Living Onesth, and *voilà*! Asth sthoon as he sthent usth to find you, I could sthee what you were up to. I sthaw what you were coming here to do: contact the Protector. That'sth why we arrived here firstht—to catch you. And, stho we have. The Living Onesth cannot restht in peathe unlessth Leo Von Koppersthmith isth dead."

"What do you mean?! Why?! I don't even know you!"

"Well, Jean Dieu knowsth *you*. Do you know Jean Dieu? Ohhh, he'sth a geniusth. More than a geniusth, really, right Msthr. Bludgeon? Yesth. Jean Dieu found usth a long time ago—crusthader children, like theesth little fellowsth here."

Wilwell, Oddo and Albert were stunned. Wilwell haltingly protested, "We don't know you…"

Mealworm snickered, and it was a low, stuttering, nasal sound. "*Naturellement*! We are Françthais! You Germansth formed one group, led by that poor, poor Nicholasth…" His gigantic eyes shifted to Leo. "Your relative, wasth he not? But, sthee, in that sthame year, 1212 A.D., there wasth another group of crusthader children from our landsth. There were thousthandsth of us! Histhtory callth the leader of our group 'Sthephen'. And, it'sth true, that wasth histh name, onceth. He thought it wasth histh desthtiny to lead usth to the Holy Land and sthet it free. We were with him—Msr. Bludgeon and me, we believed! We believed! He led all of usth to the very bordersth of Consthtantinople."

Mealworm began slowly toddling around in a small circle as he described his past, and his left hand made small, agitated gestures. "But *thoseth people* wouldn't let usth continue, even though they were sthupposthed to be on our sthide. *Thoseth people* drove usth away. *Thoseth people* called us foolsth. And you know what Sthephen said, late one night while we all shivered in the cold, in the wildernessth, forsthaken by those people? He sthaid: we were foolsth! He sthaid he wasth being called to a new desthtiny, called by an ancient, mystherious forceth that called itsthelf the World King. *Be Sthephen no more*, it sthaid. *Be greater than any human! Become Jean Dieu!*"

As Leo listened, he stole a quick glance towards his black shoulder holster. It was still lying where he'd left it, next to his jacket, beside the Pool. *My gun…I could get it…*

"…And Jean Dieu, the Perfectusth, possthessthed of a new vision, achieved great powersth, powersth no ordinary human hasth! But he didn't sthtop there—he exthtended the World King'sth offer to usth! 'Choosthe your power', he sthaid! 'Follow me into an age where humansth will be justht old memoriesth, justht dead people…and <u>we</u> will be the Living Onesth…'"

Mealworm's raving had become bewildering, but Leo was thankful for it. He had decided he could make the leap towards his holster…Bludgeon would be too

From a Dark Wayover

slow to stop him. Grab the pistol...shoot this babbling lunatic, then make the other two let his people go...

Leo braced himself, bending his knees slightly. *On three, I jump...one...*

Mealworm paused in mid-step, staring at the floor as if he spied something.

...Two...

"Oh!" Mealworm spun towards Leo, but looked at Bludgeon. "A whizthbang, Msr. Bludgeon. He hasth one over there besthide his jacket."

Bludgeon, still clutching Wilwell and Gollyplox, tramped over to Leo's gear by the Pool and with his third hand he plucked the handgun from the holster. He dropped it to the floor, and drew out his woodcutter's axe. The blade whistled as it swept down and split the gun in half with a metallic crunch.

"*Au revoir*, whizthbang," said Mealworm gloomily. He frowned at Leo. "You ought to not try that again. I can sthee fearful thoughtsth when people have them. They danceth before my eyeths, like firefliesth." He used his foot to lazily kick open Leo's pack. "Anymore whizthbangs in here? Doesthn't look like it. Oh, but there'sth that Flute of yoursth. Niceth to know! We'll take good care of that for you, don't worry."

He gazed up at Bludgeon. "Now what wasth I sthaying? Oh, yesth! Stho, the World King gave Jean Dieu the power to change the world for the better, and Jean Dieu, in turn, offered all of usth crusthader boysth a sthpecial share in that power! Of courseth, asth it turned out, Msr. Bludgeon and I were the only individualsth who accthepted Jean Dieu'sth generousth offer. Hence, we became the demigodsth you sthee before you today."

Wilwell, with terrified tears trickling down his cheeks, sniffed and asked a question the answer to which he was not even sure he wanted: "What about the other crusader children, the ones who didn't accept his offer? What happened to them?"

Mealworm blinked, casually following a passing butterfly with his black saucer pupils. "He had no need of them."

Wilwell's breath caught in his throat. "You mean…he…"

"My goodnessth! He didn't murder them all, if that'sth what you're implying. But they wouldn't join usth. Stho he sthent them away."

"Without someone to take care of them?" Oddo whimpered. "He left thousands of children all alone? To starve? Or worse?"

Mealworm stared at the boy coldly. "He had no need of them. Asth he hasth no need of you."

He turned, gently, almost mechanically. "Msr. Bludgeon? If you pleasthe. Sthtart with the littlestht boy. The sthooner you are done, the sthooner we can return!

Ohh, but not thisth one…" he gestured towards Ms. Winnipeg. "It'sth coming with usth." He paused and looked over her face and neck, without quite letting his eyes meet hers. "Itsth sthuch a pretty one!"

Bludgeon sheathed his ax and drew out his hammer, spinning it in the palm of his hand as he strode towards Albert. Leo charged at him, but Bludgeon, tossing Wilwell aside, grabbed Leo deftly by the throat. Red-faced and desperate for breath, Leo punched at Bludgeon's thick yellow forearm, but was dragged along helplessly. The children and Ms. Winnipeg all began to squeal, which made Xylyktynyxytyr hiss with sick pleasure.

Mealworm threw Albert to the floor, and Bludgeon's shadow covered the boy. The hammer tilted back. Albert screamed and covered his face.

The hammer came down like a pile driver.

From a Dark Wayover

Bludgeon's dark green eyes stared, with the thick, leaden hammerhead frozen in the air an inch from little Albert's face. *A crusader boy.* Like he once was.

He lifted the hammer again, determined to strike this time. The muscles in his arm coiled tightly.

And uncoiled. He placed the hammerhead upon the floor and stared shyly towards his massive boots. He released Leo, who immediately stumbled forward, coughing and gasping, and collapsed upon Albert to shield the boy with his body.

Mealworm hummed pitifully from the back of his throat, looking around at his various captives as if he felt he owed them an apology. "Forgive Msthr. Bludgeon. He doesth have sthome sthlight trouble performing thertain tasthkth. He didn't mind stho much sthquashing that froggy down in the valley, but I guessth little human children are more difficult for him. Right, Msthr. Bludgeon?"

From a Dark Wayover

Mealworm sighed long and melancholically as he looked closely at Wilwell, Oddo and Albert. "I sthupposthe it isth easthier when you don't have to sthee them. Shall I justh have the Cheevilnid do it?"

Xylykynyxytyr gurgled gleefully and reached for his spiked tongue cap, but Bludgeon growled with indignation. He wasn't going to tolerate the embarrassment of having the Cheevilnid accomplish something he could not bring himself to do.

Mealworm signaled for Xylykynyxytyr to desist. Then, sighing again, he said, "Well, thatsth alright…" He began to make undulating motions with his free hand. From some inner recess of the bag draped across his shoulder, there slithered the end of a rope, as if a piece of the bag itself had suddenly popped loose. Like a serpent, it crawled to the floor and towards the captives. It nudged its way around Albert's hands, binding them as it went, then farther across the floor to tie Gollyplox's wrists, and on to the next captive. In a few minutes it had linked all of them.

It had grown impossibly long in the process. The bag was not large enough to have contained even half of the rope now stretched across the floor, and yet much more might have come forth if Mealworm had commanded it.

The giant-eyed man turned awkwardly towards the rope where it disappeared into the bag. "Sthay, Bludge…could you give me a little sthnip?"

With a small ringing sound Bludgeon unsheathed his sword and sliced the rope. The piece hanging from the bag quivered as if in pain.

"Oh, shush now," Mealworm said to it. "Back in you go." The dangling piece retreated.

The rope tying Albert, Gollyplox, Wilwell, Oddo and Leo now lay still, inanimate and ordinary and pulled tight around the captives' wrists.

From a Dark Wayover

"Sthplendid!" Mealworm began to lead them all out of the Pool Chamber, but, after a few steps, he stopped again. "Oh...Msthr. Bludgeon? Maybe you could do one more thing for usth? Desthroy that sthilly Pool. We don't want anyone elsthe trying to contact the Protector."

Although Leo and the boys shouted desperately for him to stop, Bludgeon did not hesitate. His hammer shattered the side of the Sleeping Pool with one hit; on the second, the wall collapsed and the clean, pure water rushed out like blood from a wound and spread across the chamber floor. As if disappointed that his chore had ended too quickly, Bludgeon smashed a hole in the other side of the basin, sending chunks of stone and colored glass spraying into the air.

Satisfied, Mealworm guided everyone out of the Pool Chamber and through the palace by labyrinthine routes: up sloping passages and narrow stairwells, through unlit hallways and creaking doors. He insisted on having Ms. Winnipeg, with hands bound, at his side, so Xylykynyxytyr regularly shoved her from behind to ensure that she kept up. As they walked, Mealworm gave her appreciative glances and let out breathy sighs. Behind them, Bludgeon used his third arm to drag the rope holding the rest of the captives, who stumbled along miserably.

At last there was a burst of cold sunlight, and they found themselves on a wide, smooth white balcony overlooking the Island. Billodriffs drifted by overhead, and wisps of cloud trolled across the blue morning sky. Near the edge of the balcony were two Balloons: the one Mealworm had stolen, rust red-colored, and the Lincoln green one Leo and his companions had used and left anchored just below the clouds.

Oddo groaned. "They stole our Balloon…"

From a Dark Wayover

Mealworm stopped, making a motion towards Bludgeon. The three-armed man took the end of the rope nearest Albert and tied it tightly to the railing of the boys' Balloon.

Mealworm turned and looked down at Xylykynyxytyr. "Stho here we are—ready to go! Msr. Thyx…Thzzylyxth…zth…." He stopped and let out a frustrated sigh. "Oh, you know your name. Anyway: it'sth easthy. Justht take them out over the valley, and then untie the rope. Make sure you are sthufficiently clear of the mountain'sth shoulder, or sthome of them may sthurvive the fall. Make sthense, little friend?"

Xylykynyxytyr hissed sourly, not liking Mealworm's condescension, but hopped away to do as he was told.

Bludgeon set about stowing all of the captives' packs on the other Balloon. While waiting for these preparations to be completed, Mealworm took a moment to stand near the edge of the balcony and gaze admiringly out over the Island. "You know sthomething? I think if more people had accthessth to an island like thisth, where they could bring their enemiesth and no one would ever be able to find them…I think that there would be a sthubsthtantial increasthe in murdersth, don't you?"

He smiled in a pleasant way at the thought of it, smacking his fleshy eyelids together, and then with a clumsy rocking motion he turned himself around and waddled to the rust-colored Balloon with Bludgeon and Ms. Winnipeg.

Xylykynyxytyr was already on board the green Balloon, and had begun to increase the flames and release the moorings. As it rose, it sluggishly tugged the boys, Gollyplox, and Leo closer to the rim of the balcony.

Helpless, the boys cried softly. Leo tried in vain to walk backwards against the pull of the Balloon. Panic rose in his guts. "Mealworm! You have to stop! You don't understand what you're dealing with! The Corpse is not your friend! He's lying to you…using you! He isn't leading you to some great, higher destiny, O.K.? He's a liar!"

Mealworm paused, turning with a look of almost parental sympathy, and returned to Leo. He opened his eyes as wide as he could, and Leo saw the tiny red veins at the edges and, through the blackness of the pupils, he seemed to perceive the depths not only of Mealworm's ambition, but of his desperation, as well, and of his fury.

"You ought to sthop calling him 'the Corpsthe'. He isth the World King! He isth no king of the dead, but of the living! All who follow the World King are the Living Onesth. Jean Dieu promisthesth that it'sth stho, and Jean Dieu would never lie. I'm proof of that! It'sth only becauseth of Jean Dieu"—he gestured at his own eyes, almost touching their bulbous curves—"that I can sthee!"

From a Dark Wayover

Mealworm boarded his Balloon and, without another look back, piloted it off the balcony. Bludgeon stood by his side, a stern statue of a monstrous man, with Ms. Winnipeg struggling in his grip. Tears flowed past the rims of her thick glasses and down her face. Without her red and blue hairpin, her hair had come loose and was flipping messily in the wind. She cried out to Leo to save her, but the sound soon became lost in the clouds.

Xylykynyxytyr's Balloon, weighed down with captives, moved more slowly than Mealworm's, and it swayed back and forth like a gigantic bumblebee. The propeller rattled loudly, and the fires in the cistern hissed and growled, but the Balloon finally began to gain momentum.

The gondola, though not rising very high yet, cleared the balcony and moved out into open air. All slack in the rope ran out, and Albert, at the front of the line, was dragged bodily across the smooth floor, followed quickly by the others.

"Leo!" cried Albert.

Oddo yowled something unintelligible.

"O.K.," called Leo, "Just hang on now…" He tried to sound level-headed and reassuring, almost as if this was only one of many times he and several of his loved ones had been tied to a rope and dragged off the side of a mountain, and if Gollyplox and the boys only had the rich benefit of his wisdom and experience then they, too, would see that there was nothing whatsoever to be concerned about…

"Leo!!" Albert shouted again.

Their shoes squealed against the floor and their clothes made hissing noises as the long, taut rope pulled them with increasing speed towards the precipice.

"Leo!" screamed Wilwell.

"Just hang on…!" Leo roared the words, knowing they were meaningless. The Balloon was now almost ten yards beyond the edge of the terrace; it's rotors beat the cold air of the open sky. Xylykynyxytr glanced over one shoulder, curiously watching his captives as they were forced to follow.

The boys and Gollyplox continued crying Leo's name, their voices rising in a crescendo until they just became a collective scream, drowning out the sounds of the rope buzzing after the Balloon.

"HANG ON!" Leo howled. Like a toy on a string Albert was swept across the edge of the mountain, and his scream caught in his throat. Gollyplox was next; and Wilwell, and Oddo; Leo dragged along after him, flat on his back, the heels of his shoes swishing the floor until there was no more floor left.

Sixteen

Everything turned into coldness, and driving winds, and thin wisps of cloud. Leo's wrists were pulled hard above him and his legs dangled like a puppet's. The valley sprawled far below.

Arms stretched over their heads, they all cried and shouted, bobbing upon the flapping rope like human bows hanging from a kite.

"Oddo!" Leo shouted upwards.

The boy couldn't hear him over the sound of his own screaming.

"ODDO!"

Oddo glanced down, looking perplexed.

"Y…Yes, Leo?"

From a Dark Wayover

"Fredlegs!" Leo had trouble getting words out with his arms drawn up so tightly by the thick rope. "Get...Fredlegs! S...send him up..."

Oddo was confused for another second, but quickly recovered. He pulled his legs up and yelled in the direction of his right pocket. A moment later, the little brown acorn hat and the tiny green head popped out, black dot eyes blinking curiously.

"What should he do?" Oddo shouted down to Leo.

"ANYTHING! A distraction! Do not let that Cheevilnid DROP US...!"

Oddo was about to repeat the instructions to Fredlegs, but with a wee salute the Acorn Man showed that he comprehended the situation perfectly. He wriggled the rest of the way out of Oddo's pocket, scampered up his shirt and up the length of one arm, and onto the long rope. With the deftness and quickness of a

From a Dark Wayover

figurine-sized spider monkey, he scuttled up the rope, past Wilwell, past Gollyplox…

⋯✦⋅✦⋅✦⋅✦⋅✦⋅✦

Xylykynyxytyr's fishbowl eyes stared over the edge of the gondola at the valley floor. A few more seconds were all he needed to fully clear the shoulder of the mountain, and then he would untie the rope and be done with Leopold Von Koppersmith at last. Afterwards, as promised, Jean Dieu would give Xylykynyxytyr rule over the Island, at which point he would promptly make it unlawful for humans to trespass here, <u>especially</u> any of those boys who had lived here so long. They had always irritated him to the point of fury, although he couldn't say exactly why. It was something about their smell, and their wildness, and their talk-talk-talking—he simply hated them.

It was a bitter concession, but the Cheevilnid had to admit: Jean Dieu's decision to raise Mealworm and

From a Dark Wayover

Bludgeon from the Brim of the Hateful Deep had been wise. They were turning out to be valuable allies, after all…

...+·+·+·+·+·+·→

Leo reached out with one shoe and hooked the rope, wrapping it once around his shin. Using his legs to push himself up, he was able to get hold of the rope with his hands and climb towards the gondola. He passed Oddo, and Wilwell after that; they were both connected to him, but there was nothing they could do to assist him. Leo had no choice but to drag them along with him as he ascended. His leg muscles began to burn, and his progress became sluggish…it was taking too long to get to the gondola…

...+·+·+·+·+·+·→

Xylykynyxytyr was satisfied that he was now at a distance from the slope of Zechariah's mountain sufficient to ensure the falling deaths of his captives.

From a Dark Wayover

Reaching over, he pulled a latch that locked the steering wheel in place. When he straightened again, he noticed a tiny creature scuttling up the rope. It dropped to the gondola floor and scampered to the big burner in the middle, where the torchtruffles flamed. At first he thought it was a misshapen dragonfly that had lost its wings. He bent low to take stock of the thing and, licking his thin lips, considered it for a quick snack.

Little stick arms and legs…an acorn head…this was no insect…

The Acorn Man turned abruptly and looked at Xylykynyxytyr with innocent black pinpoint eyes. Without changing his expression, he reached out with one twig arm and pushed a wooden tab at the base of the Balloon's burner.

A catch was released. Parallel slats snapped shut over the top of the burner, instantly snuffing out the torchtruffles. Xylykynyxytyr screeched with horror as the hot air from the cistern dissipated. The huge balloon above rippled, then became nothing more than an enormous blob of flapping material chasing after its plummeting gondola. The rope and all the people tied to it were dragged along, as if the gondola was a hand yanking a grape vine from the top of an arbor, causing all the little grapes to scream in terror.

Somehow, amid the cold hurricane-strength winds and the deafening chaos, Leo found the railing of the gondola; he was not sure how he had done it—it had been a combination of gravity and his own desperate flailing. He pulled himself closer, and, though his hands were still tightly tied, he finally got one elbow over the side of the rail…

Xylykynyxytyr, his wide hands and feet stuck fast to the gondola floor, spied him.

Von Koppersmith!

From a Dark Wayover

He wished he had his spiked cap on his tongue, but, then again, he wouldn't need it…just one sudden, sharp pop to the face would surely be enough to dislodge the human…

Fredlegs, seeing the danger, clicked the wooden tab again. The slats over the top of the burner opened wide and the smoldering embers among the torchtruffles were caught by the rushing air and instantly fanned into a hot, howling bonfire. Xylykynyxytyr recoiled, shutting his eyes against the aura of heat. The balloon inflated; the gondola's free-fall halted so suddenly that Xylykynyxytyr nearly broke his chin upon the floor, and was left dazed for a few precious seconds.

The rope swung back down below the gondola, leaving Gollyplox and the boys dangling again, like beetles caught on a strand of web.

Leo twisted the rope around the railing, and then lifted the loop that bound his wrists and held it against the whirling rotors of the propeller. The cords slowly split and began to come undone…

Recovering from his fall, Xylykynyxytyr thrust one spindly hand into his side-bag. Without taking his eyes off of Leo, he tore out his spiked cap and mounted the wicked appendage upon the tip of his tongue…

Fredlegs hopped in alarm. He pushed the tab at the base of the burner, and the slats over the flaming torchtruffles all clattered shut for the second time.

With no heat to keep it aloft, the gondola lurched and began to fall again; Xylykynyxytyr toppled over—so did Leo, but his bindings snapped in the same instant. The rest of the rope now drifted overhead; Leo grabbed hold of it and began hauling the boys and Gollyplox onboard.

Xylykynyxytyr hissed furiously and fired his tongue spikes at Fredlegs. The Acorn Man leapt aside, and the spikes brushed the tab at the base of the burner, throwing open the slats and sending out another rush of hot air to stop the fall.

Over a hundred yards away, beneath the rust-red Balloon, Mealworm and Bludgeon stared, stupefied by the bizarre series of deflations and inflations of the green Balloon.

On balance at last and hands free, Leo turned to face the gray Cheevilnid. He caught sight of the other Balloon, in the distance, slowly wheeling around and soaring towards them, but right then he was forced to dive for cover behind the burner as Xylykynyxytyr's silvery cap came buzzing after him.

Leo peeked around the side of the burner. The Cheevilnid was crouched on the rail at the front of the gondola, readying himself to fire his next shots at Gollyplox and the defenseless boys, who were all still trying to free themselves from their ties. At the same time, the other Balloon was approaching fast…it would not be long before Bludgeon would be close enough to board…

"Boys!" Leo shouted. "Grab hold of something and hold on TIGHT!"

He reached out with his left foot and smacked the wooden tab to close the burner slats. The flames were doused. The balloon shook, quickly deflating, and the gondola began to plummet a third time.

The boys all clung to the rail as the valley rushed up at them again. Gollyplox stuck himself reliably to the floorboards.

With whistling winds pushing his hair up, Leo scrabbled to the top of the burner and crouched upon the closed slats, earning Xylykynyxytyr's deadly attention. The tongue fired, but Leo evaded it. A second shot followed, and this time Leo felt the spikes puncture the flesh and bone of his shin, just above his right shoe. He doubled over, but refused to abandon his position.

From a Dark Wayover

As the human shifted his weight from foot to foot in the same spot on top of the closed burner, the gray Cheevilnid hatched an idea that was so very, very simple…

His gray-pink tongue launched, and the spikes cracked against the wooden tab to re-open the burner's slats. A bonfire blazed up, engulfing Leo, making a black blur out of him. The gondola's plunge was arrested, and the rotors put the vehicle back on a steady forward glide.

Xylykynyxytyr hopped off the rail wearing an arrogant smirk. In one move, two challenges had been overcome: the Balloon's crash was prevented, and his most difficult enemy had been burned to death. He leapt at the children, smacking Gollyplox out of his way.

The boys huddled in the corner of the gondola, staring in horror. Xylykynyxytyr coiled his throat muscles, but just before he could fire he felt a strong hand around the back of his scrawny gray neck.

Albert howled victoriously. "Leo! The Hair Shirt!"

Leo twisted the gray Cheevilnid around and with his right fist he began to pound the creature's face, causing the double 33.3's to rock back and forth repeatedly. After a dozen punches, he hurled the weakly wriggling body to the gondola floor.

"Wilwell," said Leo firmly, "Take the wheel, fast. That other Balloon is coming after us." He tried giving Oddo some instructions, as well, but the boy was over stimulated. With a continuous stream of nasal war cries, he pounced on Xylykynyxytyr and began pelting his lips and cheeks with his knobby knuckles.

Wilwell walked up calmly beside him and released the catch on the steering wheel to begin guiding the vessel. "Oddo, I think we got him already."

Oddo kept swinging.

"You're not really doing anything," Wilwell placidly insisted. "It's like you're punching a baby…"

Slowly, Oddo's spindly arms stopped falling upon the gray Cheevilnid, and the boy sat back with his small chest heaving and plump tears wobbling in his eyes. Xylykynyxytyr wheezed pitifully and made the mistake of shifting one arm, startling Oddo, who cried out in rage and fear and promptly punched the Cheevilnid in the chest. Having thus deepened in wisdom, Xylykynyxytyr's new policy became one of passive motionlessness.

"Albert…Gollyplox," said Leo, "take some of that rope and tie down that Cheevilnid. And be careful, he's tricky."

Seventeen

The Lincoln-green Balloon had gone up and down with so much rapidity and unpredictability that it's rust-red partner had not been able to close the gap between them. Mealworm steered clumsily, and Bludgeon tried to keep Ms. Winnipeg still with one hand while, with the other two, he struggled to understand how to increase their burner's flame. Even so, they still found themselves a hundred yards below their prey.

"Nevermind it," said Mealworm at last, his gargantuan eyes staring out aimlessly across the island. His voice sounded sleepy. "They have Thylykynyxthytyr. They're about to tie him up. We're moving north, Monsthieur Bludgeon…"

····✦·✦·✦·✦·✦·✦

From a Dark Wayover

Standing on his tiptoes and gazing below them, Albert was the first to notice the other Balloon beginning to turn away. "I think they're leaving! Yes, they are! They're not rising toward us anymore! They're turning!"

Wilwell's face drew up tightly. "Oh no! Ms. Winnipeg! We can't let them take her, Leo!"

"We won't, Wilwell…" Leo's voice trailed off as he tried to think of a plan.

"I'll keep following them!" Wilwell said. "They have to land somewhere…"

"We can't!" shouted Albert. "Look! Our torchtruffles are almost burnt out!"

Inside the clay cistern, all that remained of the store of plump red and silver mushrooms was a black, glowing mound.

"You have to keep them on medium heat," said Wilwell despairingly over his shoulder. "We turned them on full so many times now that it's burnt them out twice as fast! If we don't land soon we're going to drop!"

Xylykynyxytyr had been listening all along. With Gollyplox still gathering rope to bind him, and the others distracted by the fuel problem, he was able to suddenly turn on all fours and hop on to the rail.

"He's trying to escape!" squealed Oddo, clasping his arms around the Cheevilnid's torso and pulling him back down. Albert yelled and ran over to assist, and the two boys managed to overpower the creature and force him to the floor.

Xylykynyxytyr hissed with fury. His tongue lashed out and struck the wooden tab at the base of the burner. The flame was doused and the gondola pitched violently. The gray Cheevilnid was almost able to break free, but the boys held on tightly and Wilwell threw his own weight on, as well.

From a Dark Wayover

Gollyplox deftly batted the tab to reopen the slats. The flames shot out again, halting them with a bone-rattling tremor, fifty yards above the other Balloon.

Xylykynyxytyr used the tumult to break loose again from his captors' grip. With his legs bent and his flat webbed feet planted firmly, his powerful thighs let loose an explosion of energy that propelled his skinny frog body upwards like a gray missile.

Wilwell and Albert were thrown aside, but Oddo kept his hands around the Cheevilnid's torso. He now found himself being carried as if he was at Seaworld, riding a wicked dolphin. He let go instinctively, but by the time he did he was already out of the gondola and high over the valley.

Everyone wailed Oddo's name as they watched the boy fall.

The fifty yards that separated Xylykynyxytyr from Mealworm's Balloon went by quickly and, as he had intended, he hit the rust-red fabric on all fours and stuck there like a gray fly landing on a fruit.

Oddo came down a second later. He fell feet first onto the balloon and it received him like a pillow, creating a recess that, just for a second or two, looked like a navel on a giant's belly. Then the fabric of the balloon recoiled and threw Oddo right back into the sky.

Leo watched as the boy hurtled back up towards their gondola, with arms and legs flapping and his mouth open wide in a hysterical scream. His flight carried him closer and closer to Leo and the others, and his screams quickly grew louder and louder, and everyone hung over the side to scoop him up. As he reached the apex of his bounce, his arms stretched out wildly for his friends, even as their arms shot out to grab him; their forearms rubbed together, their fingers tore past each other, but somehow no one was able to get a firm grip. Oddo fell again.

From a Dark Wayover

His scream went from loud, to less loud, to less loud, to a tiny squeal as Oddo plummeted through the same fifty yards of air back down to Mealworm's Balloon. Once more he hit the fabric, feet first, and disappeared into another deep navel. Xylykynyxtyr was already gone; he had scurried to the underside of the balloon to reunite with Mealworm and Bludgeon.

The balloon spit Oddo back out. Wilwell had tried to stay right above the rust-colored Balloon so they would have a better chance of nabbing him, but now Mealworm was changing course. This time, when Oddo, limbs flailing, reached his apogee, he was ten yards away from Leo and the others. They reached out, but were nowhere near close enough. Oddo fell again, and his screams toppled after him.

"Wilwell!" Leo shouted, gesturing southeast. "TURN! *That* way!" Wilwell spun the wheel.

From a Dark Wayover

Oddo hit Mealworm's Balloon for the third time. He managed to keep his legs pointed basically downwards, and, after he sunk into the fabric, watching the sun and the sky wink out for a second and feeling the thick material of the balloon closing around him, he used every ounce of energy in his little body to propel himself at Leo's gondola. It didn't feel right, though; the trajectory seemed off, he thought he had shot himself in the wrong direction. He watched Mealworm's Balloon sweep away below and, when he glanced up, the other Balloon rushed at him. Wilwell spun the wheel and it hummed; Leo, Albert and Gollyplox nearly fell over the side of the gondola as they reached out, their fingers stretching. Everybody was shouting and crying.

Then, all at once, they had him. It seemed as if everyone's arms were intertwined, clinging so tightly that it hurt. With a chorus of snarls they hauled Oddo up and over.

From a Dark Wayover

They sprawled on the floor of the gondola, panting. Oddo lay across Leo's chest, gripping his shirt and weeping pathetically, until his emotions took a wild turn and he let out a shriek of anger.

Leo held him close. "It's O.K., Oddo, it's O.K. You're alright..." Leo couldn't quite make himself stand up again. He felt depleted.

"Leo!" shouted Albert. "The torchtruffles! What do we do?"

Leo almost responded, but could only let out a huge gasp before moaning, "Give me a second..." He held Oddo by the cheeks and looked into his green eyes. "You O.K.?" The boy puffed loudly a couple of times to get his breath back, and then nodded. Leo patted him on the head and they both shakily stood back up.

"Ms. Winnipeg!" said Wilwell, "Leo, we have to get her back!"

From a Dark Wayover

"I know, I know," said Leo, "We will…" He ground a fist into the palm of his other hand. "If only Mealworm hadn't taken my backpack! It has the *Smallsteam* inside."

He paced around the burner, rubbing the back of his head as if it might coax schemes out of his brain. "If we got on board their Balloon, do you suppose I could get to my pack before anyone stopped me, get the *Smallsteam* and use it to shrink Bludgeon? Ughh, no that's stupid. I'll get killed five different times before I ever open the bottle."

Albert gingerly pulled the material of Leo's trouser leg. "What about the *Snowball*? Could you use that for something?"

"No, it can't help us. That's in my pack, too."

Albert, looking pained and abashed, reached into his pocket and pulled out the *Snowball*.

Thunderstruck, Leo gawked at the boy.

From a Dark Wayover

"I sneaked it out of your pack while you were in the Pool," Albert explained. "When Mealworm showed up, he never checked our pockets…"

Leo's flabbergasted expression lasted for only another second before it melted into elation. He grabbed the boy by the head and kissed his scalp. "You're a genius!"

"Ah HA!" Albert blurted. "I knew we would need it! I knew it!"

Leo took the bottle and, as the silver-white paint on the bottle glittered in the sunlight, he declared, "I've got it! I know what to do…Wilwell, I want you to get our Balloon closer to Ms. Winnipeg's…come down on top of them, but don't let them see us…just get low enough for me to get to their gondola by rope…Gollyplox, you come with me…I'm really going to need your help…"

Gollyplox skipped on to Leo's shoulders and clung there like a lime-green backpack, his round little head peeking out beside Leo's ear. Leo climbed onto the rail and took hold of the long rope still hanging from their gondola.

He almost began to climb down, but then hesitated. He stared at the boys with a flash of love and fear: "I don't know what's going to happen here, fellas….just meet us back in Relm, O.K.? I love you…"

Albert ran to him. "Let me go with you, Leo! I can help!"

"No, Albert! Good gosh, no! Stay with Oddo and Wilwell…"

The burner sputtered. The gondola shook. "Leo," said Wilwell, "We have to do this right now…"

Leo and Wilwell looked into each other's eyes gravely for a second, and Leo nodded and began to climb down the rope.

"Leo, wait!" Albert cried.

From a Dark Wayover

"No, Albert!" shouted Oddo, grabbing the younger boy.

"Hold him!" said Leo as he disappeared over the side. "Don't let him go!"

Albert growled and fought hard to escape. "I can help! Leo! Let me go with you!"

Leo was forced to ignore him. With the rope looped around one leg, he lowered himself hand over hand as quickly as he dared. His first adventure on Zechariah's Island had almost cured him of his acrophobia, and his various exploits with the Charleston Fire Department had helped, as well, but even the boldest man feels his guts thaw at least a bit when hanging from a rope thousands of feet in the air. Worse, this wasn't some lark dreamed up by a sports enthusiast…lives were depending on he and Gollyplox, and there were only a few fleeting minutes to do the impossible…

From a Dark Wayover

As Wilwell descended, they drew closer to the second Balloon sailing along beneath them. Leo had no idea what was happening in the other gondola; did Mealworm know they were coming? Would Xylykynyxytyr and Bludgeon be lying in wait? The worse thought of all: was Ms. Winnipeg even alive anymore?

The air was freezing. Wind blew past Leo's ears in alternating deep and high strains. The rope swung erratically as Leo neared the end of it, and he began to despair of being able to get anywhere near Mealworm's gondola.

All at once his shoes touched the red material of the balloon. Though pliant, it was oddly comforting just because it was, at least, a surface. Still clinging to the rope, he trotted clumsily down the balloon's slope, all the while relying on Wilwell to lower him as far as possible.

With Gollyplox clinging tightly to his back, he was now low enough to step off the red balloon and into the air above Mealworm's gondola. Just below, he could see Mealworm himself, manning the steering wheel, gazing out across the valley. Xylykynyxytyr crouched in a corner, bitterly rubbing his bloody lips. Bludgeon, impassive and fearsome, held Ms. Winnipeg, who stared down with eyes dripping tears, her thin, pale body trembling in the cold…

···✦··✦··✦··✦··✦··✦·✦

"I can help!" cried Albert again.

Oddo hung on to the writhing, furious boy, his face bright red from exertion. "Albert, just stop, will you?"

"Hold him, Oddo," shouted Wilwell, but he had very little focus to give to anything other than carefully, steadily lowering their balloon while keeping just the right speed to keep up with their enemies.

"No!" shouted Albert. "*I've got to help my dad!*" He convulsed and twisted in a way that was too much for Oddo. Breaking free, he ran for the rope.

Oddo chased him with arms outstretched. "Albert! Stop!"

But the younger boy was already up and over the rail of the gondola, scuttling as quickly as a squirrel.

···✦·✦·✦·✦·✦·✦·✦

Leo hung from the end of the rope, shoes braced against Mealworm's balloon as if he was repelling down a wall. He kicked out once as Wilwell lowered him…this was it…he knew it, and Gollyplox knew it…together they swung out into space, and on the return swing Leo would leap feet-first into Mealworm's gondola…

As his swing reached its zenith, Leo's eyes caught movement from above. *Albert…*

It was not possible to do anything about the boy…to shout at the boy and tell him to go back would be to alert Mealworm and the others…there was nothing to be done other than to swing, and leap…

He let go of the rope. He was conscious of Mealworm looking up at him with wide-eyed shock. Cold winds drove through his hair and against the skin of his cheeks, and he watched his own shoes beneath him, whisking through the air, flying down to the gondola…

He hit the floor running. Gollyplox, without leaving Leo's shoulders, fired his tongue like a laser into Bludgeon's left eye, causing the three-armed man to briefly relinquish his hold on Ms. Winnipeg. Leo rolled, carried by tremendous velocity, and tackled her. She squealed with surprise.

Ripping the *Snowball* bottle out of his pocket, he locked one arm around Ms. Winnipeg's waist and sprinted for the rail, while Gollyplox slapped Xylykynyxytyr in the face repeatedly with his tongue to keep the gray Cheevilnid from intercepting them.

From a Dark Wayover

In those rapid-fire seconds, a frightening ballet of movements took place. Bludgeon whirled his weapons at Leo, missing by millimeters. His hammer came down like a pile driver, but it was far off-target and, instead, crashed into the burner and sent crackling torchtruffles and chunks of wood and clay spraying in all directions. He kept striking at Leo but, inexplicably, preposterously, he missed every time. After five separate swings from either the sword in his right hand or the hammer in his third arm, it was with his unarmed left hand that he finally caught hold of his prey's leg. Leo had been in mid-spring over the rail, but now he was stuck there, unable to get out of Bludgeon's grip, hanging halfway out into the sky, with Gollyplox still pasted to his back. Worse, Ms. Winnipeg tumbled all the way over. She dangled helplessly, screaming, her hand in his. Bludgeon, holding Leo's leg tightly, marched forward to smash the man's head in with his hammer…

Then came Albert, swinging in from the rope he was never supposed to be on in the first place. He dropped and, with amazing accuracy, his little shoes made hard contact with the back of Bludgeon's head. The three-armed man flinched, inadvertently letting go of Leo, who pitched the rest of the way over the rail with Ms. Winnipeg.

Albert followed, yelling and grasping for the material of his foster-father's trouser legs, but never obtaining it. They all fell, and they watched Mealworm's Balloon sail away and the valley rise towards them.

Ms. Winnipeg screamed again, clinging tightly to Leo, completely without hope, because she didn't know about the *Snowball*. Leo, however, refused to open the bottle: Albert was too far away—by twenty feet, at this point. If he opened the *Snowball* now, he, Winnipeg and Gollyplox would be safe, but the boy would be shoved away from the supersonic expansion of snow, and fall to his death.

It was Gollyplox who solved the problem. His tongue lashed out and pasted itself to Albert's arm with a wet snap. Flexing his neck muscles, the Cheevilnid reeled in the boy fast, bringing him crashing against Leo's back.

He croaked enthusiastically into Leo's ear: "*Snowballll!*"

Leo popped the cork out of the bottle.

⋯✦·✦·✦·✦·✦·✦·✦→

"They did it!" cried Oddo. "I see the *Snowball!*"

Wilwell spun the wheel hard and guided the Balloon in the direction of Relm. "What about Albert?!"

"He's fine! I saw him go over the side with the others. Gollyplox grabbed him!"

"Good!" said Wilwell. "Because we are going to run out of fire in seconds…"

Oddo's body went rigid. "Oh NO!"

"What's wrong now?"

"The *Snowball*! It's falling straight towards a lava river!"

Wilwell gasped. He shoved some small levers as far as they would go, tilting the Balloon at a steep downward angle and partially squelching what was left of the burner's flames, then locked the steering wheel in place.

He ran to Oddo's side. They watched the huge, white *Snowball*, far below, as big as a blue whale, silently plummeting. Farther down was the spring-green of the north end of the valley, slashed down the middle by an angry orange flow of lava.

"They're going to fall right in!"

Wilwell shook his head weakly. "No…I don't think so…they're going to miss it…I can't tell from this angle…"

From a Dark Wayover

Oddo gripped the rail. "No, Wilwell, they are headed right for it! Leo will be alright, because he has the Coat on…but Gollyplox, Ms. Winnipeg, Albert…"

Wilwell shot a look at the burner. "Our fire is almost out! Look! Our balloon is beginning to collapse! I need to steer…keep watching, Oddo, tell me what's happening!"

Wilwell ran and pulled back on the wheel, turning the rotors, anything to keep their Balloon moving downward at something like an angle rather than simply falling.

"They're going to go in, I know it!" cried Oddo. "Any second now! They're rushing right at the lava!"

The Balloon was speeding downwards now. There was a choking sound from the torchtruffle cistern, and the flames finally went dead. The gondola lurched roughly and then sped straight down. It hit the grass with a splintering crunch; Wilwell and Oddo were thrown to the floor, and the deflated balloon tumbled over them, blocking out the sunlight.

The two boys scrambled out of the gondola wreckage and burrowed like moles beneath the balloon material. They surfaced, shouting and kicking, desperate to know what happened to the others. They stood in the direction the *Snowball* had been falling; the river of lava rumbled and crackled and hissed on this side of Hollowchest, passing so closely that the boys could smell it.

"Where are they?" said Oddo. "I don't see them!"

Wilwell let out a sigh and punched Oddo in the shoulder. "There they are. I told you they would miss it."

Over a hundred yards away, the *Snowball* lay upon the lava riverbank, a strange, stark contrast of colors, shapes and temperatures.

There were messy puffs of snow as Albert slugged his way free. His skin, nearly blue from being inside the *Snowball*, now began a slow bake as soon as he emerged upon the rocky edges of the gurgling lava river.

Gollyplox soon followed him. The *Snowball*, now squashed into a half-a-globe, was rapidly converting to warm water and wavy steam.

Albert expected Leo and Ms. Winnipeg to be right behind Gollyplox, but they were still inside. He called out their names to the *Snowball*, but there was no reply. *They're hurt!*

He returned to the snowy mound and gazed into the narrow exit tunnel he had made, but he could not see Leo or Ms. Winnipeg.

He stepped back and called their names again. Still no answer. The *Snowball* was melting quickly, but he thought he should start clearing away what was left—what if a protruding chunk of rock had pierced the *Snowball* when it landed and stabbed into Leo and Ms.

Winnipeg? They could be injured badly! Bleeding, even, maybe to death…!

    Albert charged at the *Snowball*, ready to start an emergency excavation, but he stopped when the white hill melted to reveal Leo and Ms. Winnipeg's heads. Steam drifted off of their damp hair and their flushed red cheeks. The snow ran down from their necks and shoulders in clean rivulets, lightly whispering as it turned to vapor. All the while, neither the man nor the woman paid any attention whatsoever to the crumbling *Snowball* or the crackling lava or even to Albert, because their eyes were shut tightly and their lips were stuck together in a long, delirious kiss.

    "Disgusting!" Albert shouted.

From a Dark Wayover

Eighteen

They had ended up well past the uppermost end of the valley, northwest of Mount Hollowchest. The Balloon was irreparably shattered. Not far from its remains, Leo sat contentedly on cool grass, with Ms. Winnipeg under one arm. The two of them occasionally gazed at one another, and Albert, horror-struck, could almost see little red hearts floating around their heads.

About such things the other boys were less concerned than they were about the tidal wave of rollicking events and menacing persons they had just experienced. They showered Leo with questions for which he had no answer: why did Mealworm, Bludgeon, and Xylykynyxytyr want so badly to kill Leo? Why did they call themselves 'the Living Ones'? Why had the Island become volcanic? Who was Jean Dieu?

Ms. Winnipeg sniffed. "Pretentious fellow, whoever he is." She immediately had to define 'pretentious' for Albert and Oddo, who then demanded to know why the mysterious man fit such a description. "It's French. It means 'John God.' I doubt his mother named him *that*."

"She didn't," remarked Leo. "He was originally named Stephen—that's what Mealworm said, remember? The leader of the other Children's Crusade, the one from France. My forefather, Nicholas, led the one from Germany, but Stephen led the other. I kind of recall some of that from college history classes, but I'll never forget what Kak told me about him, back when I was his prisoner, during my first trip to the Island. Kak told me that Stephen—Jean Dieu—was the Corpse's 'ace in the hole'. Those were his exact words. A man who had not just been fooled by the Corpse, but who cooperated willingly with him! Together, the Corpse and Jean Dieu could be a kind of evil version of Zechariah and the boys: working together to make new creatures…"

"Like the Glusskreep…" said Wilwell.

"…Or change people into things like Bludgeon, or Mealworm, or Chog."

Oddo's eyes had grown wide as he listened. "While Kak was bribing Nicholas, Stephen was joining forces with the Corpse himself!"

"All those poor children," Ms. Winnipeg said with a shudder. "Stephen just left them. Thousands of children…"

"And he didn't regret it," said Leo, "the way Nicholas regretted selling out to Kak. In fact, it doesn't sound like Jean Dieu ever *died*. He's still alive, directing the only two followers who joined the Corpse, as well: Mealworm and Bludgeon."

In wonderment, Ms. Winnipeg made a clucking sound. "And the three of them have survived for eight centuries and are now trying to bring about some kind of…master plan?"

"What about Zechariah?" exclaimed Wilwell. "You talked to him, didn't you, Dad? He probably knew all about this, didn't he? Is he alright? What did he say?"

"He said he had been expecting me to contact him. He's close, he said…we'll see him soon."

The boys chattered with excitement at the news of Zechariah's imminent arrival, and they wondered exactly when and where he would appear.

Leo's thoughts had drifted to other things. "He told me the Corpse wants to kill me. That's why Mealworm and the others are after me. The Corpse, he said, is my real enemy."

Winnipeg made a small, fretful humming noise. "Why you, Leo?"

"I don't know. Mealworm interrupted us before I could get Zechariah to explain. 'I was chosen,' he told me, 'for an important mission in the war against the Corpse.' And the Corpse knows it. That's why I'm at the top of his Most Wanted List." Leo stared away again, frowning. "Zechariah also said I needed to get a sword."

"A sword!" cried Albert, embracing Leo tightly. "Finally! Can I have one?"

Leo gently shook his head. "No, it's some special sword I'm supposed to get. He seemed a little surprised that I hadn't already gotten it."

Ms. Winnipeg couldn't suppress a laugh. "A sword? An actual sword? Where is it?"

"He gave me a few clues—it's definitely a real sword, just not here on the Island."

Oddo clasped his thin white hands behind his back and thought deeply. "Somewhere in the Rest-of-the-World?"

From a Dark Wayover

Leo nodded. "We'll need to get back home and do some research, I think. Ms. Winnipeg, we'll need to borrow your brain."

She grinned. "Of course! I love mysteries…"

Albert cinched up his trousers and began stomping off towards Mount Hollowchest. "Finally! A sword! Will I be able to use it, too, Dad? Sometimes? Come on, everybody, back to the Wayover…"

"Wait, Albert," said Leo, slowly getting to his feet. "We can't go back."

Ms. Winnipeg rose, too. "Why not?"

"Mealworm still has my pack with him. It has the Flute in it."

Oddo's knobby shoulders became rigid. "Oh no! But he's long gone! They could be anywhere! We'll never get the Flute back!"

Albert balled up his fists. "We're stuck on the Island *forever*?"

Leo put his hands up to calm the boys. "No, no…not necessarily. We just have to go get the Flute back."

"But, love bug," said Ms. Winnipeg, "They're in a Balloon…"

Albert stared around in disbelief, wondering why no one was as repulsed as he was. "'Love bug'?!"

"You didn't see it," Leo continued, "but Bludgeon accidentally destroyed their Torchtruffle cistern. Smashed it to bits. Their Balloon must have crashed by now."

Oddo's eyes twinkled. "They could be dead!" He, Wilwell and Albert let out a collective "yayyyy."

"Look over there…" Everyone followed Leo's pointing finger. A few miles to the north, past thin woods from which hills rose like castles, was a plume of feathery black smoke. "That's where they went down."

Leo strode in the smoke's direction, and everyone followed except Ms. Winnipeg. "Wait, Leo! Shouldn't we get the boys back to the village? So that they will be safe?"

"There's nowhere safe. Let's just get to that crash site quick. Whatever happens, we'll face it together." He smiled tenderly at Wilwell, Oddo, and Albert. "Right, boys?"

⋯▸⋅▸⋅▸⋅▸⋅▸⋅▸

The region they journeyed through was made of green, grassy hills lightly garnished with lush palms or the boys' own Stikkins, those huge trees with avocado-colored leaves and the branches that looped out and downward and buried into the ground, making numerous hoop shapes. Beneath their elegant, monumental arches and around smooth boulders encircled by clover and wildflowers, Leo and Gollyplox guided everyone up a long and steady slope.

The sky was a clear blue, except for some white and gray thunderheads far to the east over the sea, reaching up like nebulous mountains. Light, fresh winds were whispering in from the northwest and, since Hollowchest was now behind the travellers, it was one of the few times since they had arrived on the Island that they couldn't smell ash in the air.

Almost as soon as the group reached the top of the first hill, they spotted the wreckage of the rust-red Balloon farther down the slope on the opposite side.

"Look!" Oddo shouted, pointing to three unmistakable figures at the top of the next hill. "It's them!"

"We'll just follow along," said Leo. "Not try to catch up. We just want to know where they're going. Then we can figure out how to get our Flute away from them."

Wilwell chewed his bottom lip nervously as they all began to descend the hill. "I hope they don't see us…"

When they came to the smoking ruins of Mealworm's Balloon, they were surprised to find that most of the gondola was intact. All three of the boys' packs had been left on the floor, which the boys, at least, found encouraging. They happily strapped them back on. Leo's was missing, which did not surprise anyone, since it was presumed that Mealworm had taken it with him. They began their climb up the next hill.

The new slope was less polite than the first. Sometimes it became so steep that, to haul themselves up, they had to grab exposed roots or bunches of grass to make progress. Regardless, Leo found that his spirits were light. One reason for it was that the villains they were pursuing were slow-moving, thanks to Mealworm, who was physically unsuited to travel on foot. But it was much more than that: the giddiness of escaping death; the powerful sweetness of this unexpected new romance with Ms. Winnipeg; the satisfaction of cooperating so harmoniously with his boys even in dire situations. Leo felt happy, and free of the dread that had been haunting him for so long. Strange that it had taken so much danger and strife to bring about this change in his soul!

Reaching over to help Albert wriggle past a steep, sandy incline, Leo saw that the stocky little troublemaker seemed to be sharing his exuberance. As they travelled along side by side, Leo patted the boy's head. "I want you to know something. What you did up there in the sky, coming after me down the rope and helping rescue Ms. Winnipeg—never in a million years was that something I would have wanted you to do. But you did it…and it was really brave. And really good. You were great. I'm proud of you."

Albert smiled sheepishly. "Thanks."

"Hey…and I couldn't help but notice something. You called me 'Dad' back there. Is that a new thing you're doing?"

Albert held Leo's hand. "Is that alright?"

Leo squeezed the boy's hand and lightly shook his small, stout arm. " 'Alright'? It's a lot better than 'alright'…"

He paused when he felt a low rumble under his feet. At first, he thought it was Hollowchest again, but it continued steadily and grew louder. Leo kept climbing towards the top of the hill and, no sooner had he reached it, a huge herd of pecan-colored animals ambled up from the other side.

They were bigger than oxen, with furry, almost rectangular bodies, and six very short, squat legs ending in hooves. Their heads were broad and flat, with gentle brown eyes situated exactly in the middle, like the two holes of button. From each of their foreheads protruded a single, stubby horn.

"Chellacorns!" Wilwell exclaimed.

"They were supposed to be cows, originally," Oddo remarked. "We gave Zechariah some cowhide boots to work from, and one of us—I think it was Frederick—described for him what a cow looks like, but I guess he didn't do a very good job. But, anyway, I love 'em."

"I love 'em, too," said Wilwell.

All three boys reached out and stroked the soft fur of the Chellies as they lumbered over the slopes. The creatures responded with short, high-pitched hoots, each of which sounded, almost precisely, like the word 'moo' (because that is what the boys had told Zechariah cows were supposed to say).

Leo gazed down into the next vale. A narrow stream ran through it, and Mealworm was clumsily trying to ford it. Bludgeon was assisting him, and Leo could see his own gray, polyester backpack in one of the big man's hands.

Not wanting to risk being spotted by them, Leo kept everyone in prone positions, chests to the ground, until Mealworm and his cohorts cleared the next peak.

The slow trek continued for hours. It might have been grueling, except the weather was lovely, and the Island was so beautiful. Passing more Chellies, Ms. Winnipeg finally found the courage to pet one. Everyone took a few moments to marvel at green and pink birds soaring by close to the ground, with long, floppy ears and bright red tufts trailing from the tops of their heads like party streamers. Around them, Island hedgehogs called Publugs scurried in and out of burrows and showed off their ability to suddenly extend their legs to six feet long, so that they could wade through ponds or grab caterpillars from Stikkin boughs. It was easy to believe, for short periods, that they were all on vacation at a spectacular new theme park.

As the sun began to fade in the western sky, so, too, did their enthusiasm. Leo looked across another shallow valley at the three silhouettes on the next hilltop and exhaled loudly. "Where can they be going? I don't know this part of the Island. What's this way, Wilwell?"

Wilwell shrugged. Most of the Island was wild but, in centuries past, Zechariah's Oblates had built a few structures for the boys at certain points. "I don't remember anything this way, though."

"I think they're stopping," said Ms. Winnipeg. "They haven't moved off the top of that hill."

All they could do was wait. The sky became a windswept dome of gray and dark purple as the sun left it behind. The silhouettes, still hesitating on the other side of the valley, began to become invisible in the fading light, and Leo worried that they might lose track of them.

He was right on the verge of risking a quick solo reconnaissance mission, when an orange light flickered on the other hilltop.

He pointed it out to the others. "A campfire. They're stopping for awhile."

The boys all breathed a sigh of relief, and everybody admitted to being famished. They decided to build their own fire, farther down the slope in the direction from which they had come, so that Mealworm wouldn't spy it. Various snacks and water bottles were collected from the boys' packs, and it all amounted to an acceptable meal for everyone, except for Gollyplox, who insisted on hunting down several insects and a live field mouse.

Watch duties were assigned in shifts for the adults and for the Cheevilnid, with a makeshift post established at the top of their hill. Gollyplox volunteered to watch first. Everyone else huddled around the small fire. The evening air had turned cool enough to be uncomfortable, but there were no blankets, so Leo became a kind of axis around which bodies piled for warmth and security.

"Do you think Mealworm knows we're here?" Oddo asked, his head against Leo's side. "He has those big eyes, and he can read minds…"

"I don't know," said Leo. "Maybe."

"Why did he let us follow him, then?" Wilwell said. "He would have just sent Bludgeon and the Evilnid after us, wouldn't he have?"

Oddo sat up nervously. "Maybe he's going to, and he's just waiting for us to go to sleep so they can sneak up on us!"

"Easy, man," Leo said, patting the boy's shoulder. "Gollyplox is watching. Nobody's going to sneak up on us. Besides, if Gollyplox sees Bludgeon and Xylykynyxytyr coming, we'll use the opportunity to slip around and catch Mealworm alone and stuff him in that net bag!"

The boys were comforted by this idea. "And remember," Leo continued. "This place doesn't belong to Mealworm and those others. They're intruders. They have no right to be here. Eventually, one way or the other, they will get kicked off this Island."

⋯⋅✦⋅✦⋅✦⋅✦⋅✦⋅✦⋅✦

No attack ever came. The boys slept in relative peace, except for two or three sudden awakenings, caused by animal noises in the night. Leo, who had taken the last watch, spotted another fire flare up in the dark on the far hill, and he waited while the dawn lay a blanket of hushed morning light upon Mealworm, Bludgeon and Xylykynyxytyr as they cooked and ate a somber breakfast.

Leo roused Ms. Winnipeg and the others, and they all managed to eat quickly and splash pond water on their faces just in time to resume their odd, plodding pursuit.

Their quarry did not make any changes to the generally northward course they had followed the day before. Hills became larger and higher, and instead of climbing them, they followed narrow, rocky passes or shallow creek beds. Furry, black and yellow caterpillars the size of weasels clung to the sides of the hills around them, eating the green lichens and grayish moss that grew there.

The weather had grown hot as the morning dragged on. Leo was tired and sore, and his head hurt, because he had not gotten his daily dose of coffee. Everyone felt more or less the same. The emotional effervescence that had previously accompanied them had fizzled out, and what had felt like a jaunt yesterday seemed like a slog today.

"Where are they *going*?" Oddo whined.

"It won't be much longer before we reach the ocean," said Wilwell. "Why are they going this way?"

"Maybe," said Albert, "There's a boat waiting for them!"

"Boats can't find the Island," Wilwell grumbled. "You know that, Albert."

A few handfuls of trail mix were all that was left for lunch, and they ate as they walked. Albert still had the Ritz crackers he had packed for himself and, although they had turned stale, he cheerfully offered to share them with the others, who declined. Next he pulled out the bag of ham he'd brought along, which was looking greenish. He was going to take a bite anyway, until Ms. Winnipeg shrieked in horror and grabbed it out of his hands. She gave it a sniff, winced, and tossed it into a patch of vegetation. "Fico, Albert! Don't you remember <u>anything</u> about last semester's class on *Salmonella* serotype Typhimurium and other food-contaminating bacteria!?"

From a Dark Wayover

The pass they were following ended, becoming a steep slope of bare, contoured rock that Mealworm, Bludgeon and Xylykynyxytr had used as natural stairs. Leo led the way up, and it became the longest, most tiresome climb yet. They were all hungry and their mouths were dry and gluey. Ms. Winnipeg, so averse to this kind of sustained physical activity, had turned pale and her limbs sagged. She smiled weakly when Leo put one of her slender arms over his shoulder, and together they finished the climb.

At the top, the ground opened onto a grassy, treeless plateau. The sounds of crashing waves carried on relentlessly somewhere ahead. Steady winds blew, heavy with the taste of salt.

The plateau sat on the top of a steep cliff that overlooked the ocean. Wilwell and Oddo jogged up to the edge, but suddenly dropped to their bellies, shooting wide-eyed glances at Leo and pointing out towards the sea.

Leo and the others assumed crawling positions as well and wriggled up beside them. Below was a long beach that seemed literally under attack by the ocean waves. The wind blew furiously, and endless mounds of white froth tumbled along the wet, brown sands.

Rising from the water were many hundreds of dark rocks shaped roughly like crude, misshapen pillars. They were of varying heights: the shorter ones were closest to shore; the ones farther out were as high as thirty feet. They pressed in closely to each other, like stony trees in an ugly forest.

"These are the Teeth," said Oddo. "That's just what we call them. We didn't make these. They're here naturally."

"Shh!" whispered Wilwell. "See? There they go!" He pointed at a Tooth that stood towards the center. It was flatter at the top and broader than the others. Mealworm, Bludgeon and Xylykynyxytyr were making their way towards it by a singularly bizarre method: Bludgeon rested his feet upon one Tooth, then fell over and grabbed the edge of another with his third arm, making a bridge out of himself. Mealworm and Xylykynyxytr then simply crossed over. The three repeated this process until they reached the broad Tooth in the center.

"Those guys are weird," muttered Albert. The words had hardly finished leaving his mouth when they all gasped in surprise.

Mealworm had disappeared.

Leo blinked, thinking the pudgy little man must have simply walked (or fallen) over the edge.

Then Bludgeon disappeared, as well. And the gray Cheevilnid after that.

"Where'd they go?" Oddo said.

"They were standing right there," Wilwell grunted. "Right in the middle of that Tooth. Then they were just…gone!"

"There must be a trap door or something," grumbled Leo. "They have a hiding place out there, inside that rock."

Oddo whistled. "I didn't see a trap door."

"Neither did I," said Ms. Winnipeg.

Leo sat up and crossed his legs. "Well, that's the way they went, anyhow. So that's the way we'll have to go, too."

Albert scampered to his feet. "I'll look for a way down…"

"No, my man," Leo said, grabbing the boy by his head and giving his coppery blond hair an affectionate rub. "You all need to stay here. Just Gollyplox and I will go."

"Oh, no…" Albert protested, but not strongly. The boys remembered the Teeth well: the riotous wind and waves of the ocean here and the strange shape of the rocks had always made this an area that was impossible for the boys to explore.

"But how will you get all the way out there, Dad?" Oddo said. "Gollyplox could make it by jumping, I guess, but what about you? I don't want you to get hurt…"

"I won't," Leo said with a warm smile. "We'll figure it out. You just stay here and make yourselves comfortable until we get back."

He wandered closer to the edge of the cliff and began looking for the easiest route down. A bulky shape moving along the beach drew his eyes. It was large and round, with what appeared to be multiple feet or claws. As Leo squinted down at it, he spotted another one close by the first, and then several more a few yards farther past.

"What are those?"

Wilwell followed Leo's pointing finger. "Oh. Those are crabs."

Ms. Winnipeg pursed her lips and made her "hm" sound. " 'Crabs'. Outer space crabs, perhaps. Why are they so very, very prodigious?"

Oddo placed his fists proudly on his hips. "That I don't know, but I *can* tell you why they're so big! At first they were just ordinary hermit crabs who lived on the beach, but we felt sorry for them because seagulls kept eating them. So we asked Zechariah, and he let us make some of them giant-sized—as big as hippos! We called them 'Bouldergongs', or sometimes 'Bolgongs'…we could never really make up our minds. Just 'Bolgongs', I guess. Aren't they amazing?"

From a Dark Wayover

Leo frowned at the crabs' motorcycle-sized claws. "They aren't going to try and eat us, are they?"

Oddo made a raspberry sound. "They eat Blobfruit!" The boy gestured below them. Curtains of green-and-yellow striped vines with thick, pulpy orange leaves hung everywhere upon the rocky sides of the cliff, and from them grew bumper crops of spherical blue melons.

Oddo reached down and deftly picked one of the fruits. "Try one, Ms. Winnipeg! There's no rind or peel—it's soft!"

Ms. Winnipeg took the Blobfruit in her hands and observed quizzically the way it wiggled in her grasp like Jell-O.

Wilwell smiled. "We wanted a fruit that was really, really easy to eat, so you wouldn't have to waste time peeling it, like an apple."

"Dumb apples," scoffed Oddo, shaking his head sympathetically.

Ms. Winnipeg took a bite. The whole melon bent and curved around her cheeks; it looked as if it must certainly break apart, and yet it didn't. She chewed thoughtfully. "It's very good! It feels like trying to eat a water balloon, but I'm so hungry that I don't care!"

They all took a few minutes to gorge. When they finished, not only did their bellies feel fuller, but the excessive levels of juice had slaked their thirst, as well.

"And now you can see why Bolgongs *love* Blobfruit," said Wilwell.

Leo smacked his lips. "Yep. Another fine invention, boys." He pulled Wilwell, Oddo, and Albert close to him, laying his arms over their shoulders. "Now, look—should I even bother saying it? Don't follow us." He gave a look of faux chastisement to Albert, who smirked uncomfortably. "Not this time. I'm serious.

From a Dark Wayover

There could be anything inside that rock. <u>Nobody</u> except Gollyplox and I are going in there."

Ms. Winnipeg clutched his arm. "Sweetheart, I don't want you going in, either…"

Albert gasped. " 'Sweetheart'?"

Leo held her by the hand. "I have to, dear. They have the Flute. Without it, there just isn't any other way for us to get back home."

Wilwell stood motionless, but his eyes had grown damp. "How long will it take until you come back?"

With pursed lips Leo reached out and rubbed the boy's head affectionately. "Don't worry. Not long."

It occurred to him that he would probably need a flashlight, and Oddo happily volunteered the blue plastic one from his backpack. Afterwards, he walked with Ms. Winnipeg a few feet away until they were out of earshot.

"Keep the boys safe. I mean: you know that…I don't know why I'm telling you that. And, look, I don't mean to sound melodramatic here, but…if we don't come back soon, just take the kids and get back to Relm, O.K.? Give us…two hours, let's say."

Ms. Winnipeg held on tightly to his wrist. She chewed her bottom lip anxiously, but nodded.

"And keep the boys busy, O.K.? Don't stay here and watch us. Go into the woods a little ways. Have them make a camp, collect firewood. Tell them stories, or something. Anything to keep them from just sitting around and worrying."

She squeezed his hand, and made a peculiar expression that combined a brave smile with utter dread. "Who's going to keep *me* from worrying?"

Leo sighed. He clasped her soft, round shoulders and stared into her eyes. "Gollyplox and I will get that Flute back. You'll see. Just stay safe, alright?" He kissed her once on the lips, and once on the forehead. Albert made a vomiting sound, until Oddo punched him in the back.

From a Dark Wayover

Nineteen

It did not take long for Leo and Gollyplox to find their way down from the top of the plateau, using the many rocky shoulders and grassy creases of the cliff walls. Seagulls cried out around them, hovering upon the air currents or soaring past like kites.

Upon the shore, shells were flung in long, narrow carpets. Leo privately noted the incongruity in the fact that humans with even the most sensitive tracking equipment on the most sophisticated sailing vessels could not discover this island, but everyday humble little creeping crabs and bivalves of any sort bumbled on or off the beach as they pleased, leaving behind their shelly homes as calling cards.

The boys' gigantic hermit crabs, the Bolgongs, shuffled slowly along the brown sands of the beach like spherical delivery trucks. The beige whorls of their magnificent shells were lined with a series of sky blue or tangerine-colored dots spiraling all the way to the centers.

Many of them wandered along the base of the high cliffs, their black eyestalks longingly scanning the orange leaves and thick vines in search of their favorite food, the blue Blobfruit. The sad thing, Leo realized, was that there was nothing left. Whatever fruit within reach had already been picked. There were plenty still hanging along the upper half of the cliffs, but the Bolgongs, although they were capable of climbing, were too heavy to go that high. With pity, Leo watched the strongest, more intrepid Bolgongs reach heights of fifteen or twenty feet and stretch out with their big, clumsy claws and almost snare a bouquet of Blobfruit, only to suddenly lose their footing, tumble down the cliffside, and land upon the beach with a thud and a burst of sand. They would just shuffle away afterwards, looking as if they were actually sad and even a bit embarrassed.

As Leo surveyed the Teeth, he saw now how badly he had underestimated the power of the surf on this end of the Island. Waves fell upon the shoreline in a series of never-ending avalanches, hurling frigid spray and causing explosions of vanilla-colored foam. The biggest Tooth, though distinctively shaped and wider than the others (and thus easy to spot), was simply impossible to swim to. The sea would force back anyone who dared with all the inexorable savagery of a troop of African gorillas. The trick would be to do what Mealworm and his accomplices did: start with a short Tooth near the beach, climb on top, and then go from rock to rock.

Leo sloshed through the cold breakers until he had his arms around a stubby pillar. Besides slipping twice, getting to the top was not challenging. From there, he hopped over to a second Tooth less than five feet away.

Conveniently, another pillar stood two feet from there. Leo pounced, catching the top, and he pulled himself up.

An assortment of even taller Teeth rose up around him, only now the distance between them and himself was more formidable. Waves roared and pounded the sides of the pillar upon which he crouched, as if daring him to continue.

There was just enough room for him to take a couple of steps and then fling his body into open air. The tips of his fingers clawed the peak of the next pillar, but the wet surface betrayed him and gravity steadily dragged him down the side. Somehow the toe of his shoe found a lip of stone, and for a few seconds he just clung to the pillar, panting, certain he would have to let go and fall into the roiling waters. Refusing to give in, he reached up, found a hold, and clambered to the top, inch by slow inch.

He sat cross-legged there upon the Tooth, evaluating the bloody wounds on his palms and forearms. Nothing serious, he could tell, but they stung sharply.

The central Tooth was now a little closer, but it may as well have been protruding from the surface of the moon, because before Leo could reach it he would have to make a nearly ten-foot leap to another, and even taller, pillar.

He turned back to the beach. Gollyplox, waiting on the sands, waved sanguinely with one spindly green arm. Leo spread his arms and shook his head to indicate that he had reached an impasse.

The Cheevilnid took it as his cue to spring into action. With a series of effortless bounds, he followed Leo's trail: to the first stubby pillar; then the second one; then the taller third, and at last to Leo's position on the fourth, all in a few short seconds and with no quantifiable expenditure of Gollyplox's energy.

"I wish I was a Cheevilnid, sometimes," Leo grumbled. It was clear that the stunningly agile Gollyplox would easily be able to continue to the central Tooth, but not Leo. Bludgeon had made himself a living bridge for his fellow villains, but there was no such arrangement for Leo.

Gollyplox leapt the ten feet to the next pillar. He stood and faced Leo, stretching out his arms. "*Cheeeeepcrikcrik!* I catch!"

"There's no way!" Leo shook his head, shouting to be heard over the bawling winds. "I'm too heavy for you! Even if I could make it that far, I would just pull both of us over!"

Gollyplox hunkered down, bracing his webbed feet against the rock, and reached out to his friend. "I catch! You jump!"

Leo moved back as far he could and pressed the ball of his right foot against the surface of his pillar. He exhaled purposefully. With a burst of energy, he ran forward and propelled himself off the edge and through the howling sea air. His legs crashed against the side of the next pillar and his fingers caught Gollyplox's noded digits.

Struggling to keep Leo from falling, the Cheevilnid's eyes bulged even more than they normally did. A croak of fear escaped his toad-ish mouth as one foot slipped out from under him, and he toppled over the side with Leo. The two of them crashed into the gray, pounding waves.

The water was only up to Leo's abdomen, but the relentless waves smashed the back of his head and rudely thrust him forward, as if they were guards teaching some new prisoner a lesson in obedience.

From a Dark Wayover

If moving towards the beach was difficult for him, it was completely impossible for little Gollyplox. The Cheevilnid, choking and spluttering, affixed himself to his human friend's back, and waited for him to get them both to safety.

When they finally stumbled onto the wet sand of the beach, they collapsed. Leo lay coughing, gasping for air and suffering throbbing stings from the sea salt that saturated the cuts on his arms. Worse, his mind had begun to torture him with visions of Wilwell, Oddo and Albert trapped on a volcanic island, never to escape, and of all the other boys back home, waiting in vain for Leo to return and defend them and teach them to be men and not abandon them like so many others had done…

"*This is stupid!*" Leo shouted to the sky. "There's no way to do this!"

He sat up, and looked at Gollyplox, who was rubbing seawater out of his grapefruit-sized eyeballs.

"How in the world are we going to get the Flute back?"

Gollyplox stared at him. "*Cheepreeekcrikcrik.* Just me go. I go, you stayyy."

"No!" said Leo sternly. "That's too dangerous. We need to go together."

He gazed calculatingly at the Teeth. "There has to be a way."

After a few seconds, a smile began to creep over his face. "I have an idea, Gollyplox. But I can't do it without you, old pal…"

⋯✦·✦·✦·✦·✦·✦

Within the next ten minutes, Leo searched for long branches, testing them for sturdiness. By the time he located one, Gollyplox came scampering back down from the vine-draped cliffs carrying a cluster of Blobfruit in his scrawny hands.

From a Dark Wayover

This did not go unnoticed by four Bolgongs wandering within Gollyplox's vicinity. They shuffled clumsily but eagerly over the sands towards him, the globular black eyes upon their eyestalks practically twinkling.

Leo gave Gollyplox the branch he'd found, exchanging it for the blue melons. He held them high, walking slowly towards the shoreline. The nearest Bolgong shifted direction towards him.

He felt a slow boil of dread. Until this point, he had regarded the Bolgongs as not much different than larger-than-average cattle: impressive in size, but passive. Now that one was bearing down upon him, he was shocked by how huge it really was, and unnerved by the brownish, hulking claws opening and closing with anticipation. He stopped, feeling water lap against his ankles, and he bent his knees, ready to drop the Blobfruit and leap for his life.

"Get ready, Gollyplox…"

The Cheevilnid scuttled several yards away from the surf and out of the Bolgong's trajectory.

Leo could hear the scrape of the crab's thick red-tipped legs plowing shallow trenches through the wet beach. Its antennae, longer than bullwhips, wiggled inquiringly, and smaller appendages around its mouth clicked hungrily. The black eyes were fixated on the Blobfruits in Leo's hands.

Leo began walking backwards. "Now, Gollyplox!"

The Cheevilnid leapfrogged lightly onto the back of the Bolgong's mammoth shell. He padded to the front, near the carapace, but the trundling creature either did not notice or did not care.

With a grunt, Leo tossed the Blobfruits into the air, and plunged out of the way just as the Bolgong shambled upon where he had been standing.

Simultaneously, Gollyplox thrust out one end of his branch like a spear and snagged the Blobfruits, holding them in mid-air.

"That's perfect!" Leo ran to the back of the Bolgong. "Just hold 'em there, Gollyplox!"

The perplexed hermit crab stood in place and stared up at the dangling fruit, but its claws were not made to be elevated that high.

Leo ran up the steep slope of the mighty shell and huddled beside Gollyplox. "Great! Now, just turn the branch that way a little, towards the big Tooth!"

The Bolgong turned with Gollyplox. As the Cheevilnid leaned forward slightly, the Bolgong took a few steps, straining up with its claws.

Leo kept encouraging the whole process, like a soccer coach. "That's it…good…lower it a little, so he really thinks he can get it…"

From a Dark Wayover

Gollyplox leaned out as far as possible, extending the branch in the direction of the sea, and the Bolgong shuffled into the foamy waves, reaching for the Blobfruit, never quite getting it, but unwilling to give up. Soon the creature had moved past the first, shortest Teeth and was well on its way to the taller ones, slowly following the Blobfruit like a fish after a fat, blue worm at the end of a fishing pole. Leo found himself laughing out loud.

Cold seawater rolled and smashed around Leo's shoes, but still only two-thirds of the big beige mound of a shell was underwater. The Bolgong's black eyeballs and the tip of its larger claw stretched above the waves.

All at once, Leo realized they had reached the base of the big stone pillar where Mealworm had disappeared. It was not a minute too soon: Gollyplox's arms were quivering with fatigue.

"We're here, Gollyplox! On to the rock!"

From a Dark Wayover

The Cheevilnid gratefully tossed away the branch, catching the cluster of Blobfruits in his own hands. With a spry hop, he stuck to the side of the dark rock.

Leo held on tightly as the Bolgong dug its limbs into the stone and began an arduous climb up the nearly seventy-degree angle of the Tooth's side. Gollyplox retreated upwards, holding the fruit down to entice the giant crab. Seawater gushed from the back of the creature as it left the waterline, and the dying light of the setting sun glowed upon the blue and orange dots that lined the whorls of its shell. Leo clung to the lip of the carapace near the crab's head, desperate not to be dislodged by the jolts and heaving of the Bolgong as it made its awkward climb.

They travelled fifteen feet…Leo's transport paused, unsure of itself, then kept going. They made it another arduous ten feet…the top was almost within reach…

From a Dark Wayover

The Bolgong lost its grip.

It scrabbled against the sides of the rock with its smaller legs, but it was too heavy an animal for this kind of near-vertical travel. Foot by foot, it slowly sank back down the Tooth.

With a defiant shout, Leo kicked up and grabbed the edge of the huge pillar. For a breathless second he hung there, and he was certain that he did not have the strength to pull himself up and would plummet into the ocean, having made all of this effort in vain.

Then, somehow, with a final pull and all of his back muscles as tense as piano wire, he was on top of the Tooth. Gasping, he rolled to the side.

"O.K. Gollyplox! It's done! Let him have it!"

Gollyplox stretched down and put the Blobfruits within genuine reach of the Bolgong. The big crab hung upon the side of the rock, its stalk-mounted eyeballs expressing a dumb amazement that its grueling quest had finally ended. Delicately, it plucked the blue melons from Gollyplox's hand and transported them into its small, clicking mouth. Its whole body seemed to relax, and gravity dragged it down to the base of the Tooth, where it happily sat halfway in the surf and contentedly chomped its prize.

    Leo, still trying to regain his breath, smiled down gratefully at what had been their crustaceous vessel. "You earned it, Mr. Bolgong. Thanks!"

From a Dark Wayover

Twenty

  High above, the moon had already risen, and was beginning to glow as dusk settled. Nonetheless, there was enough sunlight left to inspect the surface of the Tooth: it was black and porous, dotted by gull droppings, and seawater rested in tiny puddles here and there. There was nothing else to see. If Mealworm had a lair here, there was no sign of it whatsoever.

  Leo suspected there was some kind of camouflaged trap door. He stooped and inched forward, feeling the rock with his hand. He muttered in surprise when, within a few feet, the ends of his fingers slipped through the rugged surface as if the stone was nothing more than dense fog.

  He moved his hand around beneath the illusory veneer, feeling nothing but empty space. As he was about to insert his entire arm, he felt Gollyplox's long, froggy fingers clutch his shoulder. Exchanging a cautious glance with him, the Cheevilnid murmured, "*crikcreeeklln-chirrrpcrik.*" Leo was not sure what it translated to in English, but it was something like, "People who stick their arms down holes they can't see into often wind up armless," the logic of which was inescapable.

Leo sat back. "Well, is there a stick or a root somewhere…?"

He looked around, but the only trace of vegetation on the high, misshapen pillar were a few patches of flat, gray-green fungus.

He looked at Gollyplox and sighed. "We have to go in…" He bent down again, and brought his face against the surface of the stone until he could nearly touch it with the end of his nose. He squinted, and craned his neck. His head passed below the surface.

From a Dark Wayover

Gollyplox croaked uncomfortably, waiting for his headless friend. At last Leo reappeared.

"There's a tunnel going straight down, but not far…not more than ten feet, then it looks like it just stops. But that can't be right. I don't know—it's too dark to tell for sure." He shook his head and frowned. "Maybe there's another fake illusion-door at the bottom, and the tunnel just keeps going. Anyway, time to find out. We've got to get our Flute back and get everybody home."

Leo lowered his legs through the opening. Gollyplox held him by the wrists, although they both knew the little Cheevilnid didn't possess the sheer power to help Leo climb down.

Leo's shoes found the walls of the tunnel. He was submerged up to his waist when he realized that something was wrong: the tunnel walls had no natural protrusions of rock; the surface seemed completely smooth. He tried to shift his weight, and his foot slipped.

In the same moment, the stone that his left hand was clinging to broke loose. His arm tore out of Gollyplox's grasp and he fell backwards.

The floor of the tunnel received him like a waterbed. After the initial impact, he rose and fell gently two or three more times before his body finally settled into the surface, like a paperweight on a soft cushion. When he opened his eyes he could see the portal above him, glowing with evening sunlight, and Gollyplox's round, green head plunged into it. "Leo's okay? *Criiiieek.*"

"I'm fine…" Leo struggled clumsily to his feet, constantly having to adjust his footing upon the squashy floor. He took a cautious step; he reached out to steady himself and discovered that the walls were made of the same material—and they were warm to the touch. It all reminded him of…

"A Wayover! Gollyplox, come down! This is a Wayover!"

From a Dark Wayover

Gollyplox was by his side in a single deft leap. They quickly realized that, from where they stood, another tunnel ran horizontally in a northwards direction. They could not see more than a few feet inside it, but it was clear that it went well beyond where the edge of the Tooth should have been, proving that they truly had discovered another Wayover, metaphysically apart from the Island, just like the one over Mount Hollowchest.

Yet there were differences, too. The colors were not gentle, pastel pinks and yellows, but were gray, instead, mottled with black.

"It stinks here," said Leo, wrinkling up his nose. "What is that stench? I think it gets stronger, farther in…"

Taking a long sniff, Gollyplox expressed agreement with a series of throaty burbles. He gazed around thoughtfully, and then abruptly closed his eyes.

He began to make a humming noise, as if something important had begun to occur to him.

Leo squatted beside him. "What is it?"

"AmoAhsh'Qaya. We in AmoAhsh'Qaya."

" 'AmoAhsh'Qaya'. You said that once before, at the funeral…Strum's Upaway. What does it mean?"

"Way-over. AmoAhsh'Qaya many parts. Parts allll over…" Gollyplox made a wide circular motion with his arms. "Over sea. Over sky. Over sun. Over stars. Parts allll over."

"And they're all connected. That's right…I remember the Watchdog saying something about that. 'The universe is honeycombed with Wayovers.' Weird…like a subway system." Seeing Gollyplox's blank stare, Leo hurriedly added, "Sorry. You don't know what a subway is." He thought for a moment. "Like tunnels, is all I mean. Tunnels made for people to go from one place to another place much farther away, but very quickly. Right?"

Gollyplox made a sound of understanding, but then shook his head slightly, indicating that Leo was still off the mark. Rising to his full three-foot height, he waddled over to Leo. He gently grabbed Leo's right hand and placed it upon the wall. With Gollyplox's green node-tipped fingers pressed against the back of his hand, Leo felt the warmth of the Wayover's wall radiating through it's soft, tender surface.

"She *alive*. We *inside*."

It took a few more minutes of Gollyplox's laborious efforts to put it all into *criks*, *creeks*, croaks, and broken English before the truth really began to settle in. The Wayover was a living creature, and the various parts of her were, as with any body, connected and interrelated, but with this unique difference: they were not all together in one place.

From a Dark Wayover

The Cheevilnids, particularly Gollyplox, had discovered this as a result of numerous investigations of the Wayover above Mount Hollowchest. AmoAhsh'Qaya had spoken with them many times, by some kind of interior locution, and the result was that they had become friends. The Cheevilnids now had a love and respect for her that approached veneration: "O tank you AmoAhsh'Qaya! Frogs come down by AmoAhsh'Qaya, and then up, up, up to be not frogs…become pee-pul." Gollyplox stretched his arms out as if inviting Leo to appreciate him and, by extension, all of his kind. "Chee-vil-nids!"

Leo stared around, and he suddenly felt self-conscious about touching the walls and floor. "I wonder how she *looks*? What do you suppose her face looks like?"

Gollyplox hummed. "No face. No hands, no legs, no skin. AmoAhsh'Qaya all *inside*. No outside."

From a Dark Wayover

The insides of a trans-physical being, spread by parts throughout the world—throughout the cosmos, in fact. It was quickly becoming too toilsome to conceptualize. More than that: it was becoming highly disconcerting. For instance, according to Gollyplox's descriptions, the Wayover above Mount Hollowchest was part of AmoAhsh'Qaya's reproductive organs. It helped explain the Cheevilnids' affinity for her—they thought of themselves as her children, in a way, "delivered" as frogs in the crusader boys' tattered pockets, only to mature, thanks to the creative collaboration of the boys with Zechariah, into Cheevilnids.

Leo looked around at the mottled gray walls and grimaced at the unpleasant odors surrounding them. "So what's wrong with this part of her? Is she sick or something?"

Gollyplox could not answer that. No Cheevilnid had ever been to any Wayover other than the one above

From a Dark Wayover

Mount Hollowchest. They knew of the other parts only by what AmoAhsh'Qaya had told them.

Gollyplox reached into his side pack. He withdrew the smooth white and black stones and, closing his eyes, he began to slowly roll them around in the palm of his hand. His breathing became slow and regular, with a slight gurgle.

He's talking to her, Leo abruptly realized.

Minutes crawled by. The only sounds were the calm warbles of the Cheevilnid's breathing and the clicking of the white and black stones as they gently rolled in his bony fist. Leo gingerly approached.

Suddenly, Gollyplox's bulbous eyes opened and the stones stopped moving. "Guts," he announced.

Leo blinked. "Guts?"

Gollyplox pointed to his own skinny lower belly, below where the navel would be if Cheevilnids had them, and he traced a little circle. "Guts."

From a Dark Wayover

Leo cringed slightly. He gazed down the dark, northwards tunnel. *Guts. He means the lower intestines.* To get the Flute back, they would have to travel into AmoAhsh'Qaya's lower digestive tract.

Leo and Gollyplox looked at each other for a moment, as if each was trying to mentally help the other gather courage. From his pocket, Leo dug out the blue plastic flashlight that Oddo had given him. He guessed that it wouldn't work, after its dunk in the ocean, but it clicked on without hesitation and shined light into the tunnel ahead.

An unbidden thought came to Leo's mind as they ventured farther in: *what does a creature like AmoAhsh'Qaya eat?* He imagined a colossal woman at the center of the galaxy, slowly devouring entire planets like they were cupcakes, but he knew right away that could not be accurate. If she possessed no exterior, but only an interior that apparently existed only between dimensions, then food had to be something radically different…

He stopped. Gollyplox looked at him quizzically.

Leo now realized, from the first moment his nose had registered the presence of the tunnel's ghastly odor, that it was familiar. He had not been able to place it…something from his childhood, he thought initially, but that wasn't it. What was it? Acrid, ugly…not nauseating, but pervasive, almost like rotting vegetables…

Throtrex.

From a Dark Wayover

Twenty-One

The stinking tunnel—AmoAhsh'Qaya's *intestine*, Leo reminded himself—led them in a direction that one would expect of a gut: down and around, going one way for many yards and then making hairpin turns, or falling sharply without warning. Leo pulled the front of his shirt over his mouth and nose to filter the awful smell, but it did not help very much; Gollyplox was not overly bothered, because Cheevilnids do not have a well-developed sense of smell.

Leo suddenly put his hand up, silently indicating to his friend the need to halt, and he turned off his flashlight. Far ahead, firelight shivered in the darkness.

They slowly approached it, their hands sliding along the smooth walls as they went. They sensed a widening of the space they were in, as if they had just walked into a large hall. The fetor of Throtrex had reached a new intensity.

They now heard a murmuring—not Throtrex blather, but the conversation of humans. The firelight was from lanterns: one was carried by Mealworm, and Bludgeon held another and much larger one in his oversized third hand. Xylykynyxytyr skulked between them. The three of them stood in a narrow tunnel branching off from the main hall, their bodies pulsing in the trembling light.

A fourth individual was present with them; they seemed riveted to every word that the person was saying. Leo squinted hard but, from this angle and distance, he could only perceive that the dark figure was short, and had a male voice.

As he stared, he spied his pack, lying on the floor close to Bludgeon.

From a Dark Wayover

He felt a jet of panic and elation. This opportunity to steal back the Flute would surely not have a lifespan of more than twenty or thirty seconds.

Hastily, he and Gollyplox stole along the wall towards the pack. The conversation that Mealworm was having with the anonymous person in the corridor might end at any moment. The pack grew closer. The murmuring of the malefactors grew more audible. *This is actually possible*, Leo thought with a wild thrill. *I can grab the pack and we can be out of here before they even realize.*

Or it could all be for nothing... Leo did not know if his pack had been plundered. Perhaps his Flute was no longer inside of it.

As they slid along the wall, mashing the pliant floor with every step, Leo analyzed his pack. It did not look as if it had been emptied. There was no way to be sure, though, and there certainly would be no time to check. *Just grab it and go...almost there...*

From a Dark Wayover

Sweat beaded along his forehead. The stench of the place was awful, and there was almost no movement of air, as if they were at the bottom of a closed dumpster.

Almost there…

When he had nearly reached the pack, there was a change in the meter and tone of the murmurs in the corridor that made him think the conversation was drawing to a close. His peripheral vision perceived Bludgeon's muscular back and the heavy steel lantern clutched in that oversized third hand, but for now everybody's focus was still safely in the opposite direction.

Leo reached down and curled his sweat-glazed fingers around the pack's strap. The unknown fourth person said something like "next time," and this was followed by the sound of a flute.

For a half of a second Leo despaired, because he thought the mysterious man must have taken the Flute

From a Dark Wayover

from his pack after all, and was now putting it to use. It could not be the same instrument, though. It had a completely different timbre—not bright and cheerful like his Flute, but lower, like an oboe, or even a bassoon. An exotic, foreboding melody sounded throughout the Wayover; it sounded Turkish to Leo, or like medieval gypsies.

A blast of fresh air suddenly blew past Leo, and blazing sunlight tumbled into the corridor. Someone had opened the Wayover and was going back into the Rest-of-the-World, somewhere far away where the sun was up.

Time had run out: Leo snatched up his pack and turned to go the way he had come, hustling Gollyplox along before him.

He stopped again, and recoiled against the fleshy wall, staring out across the wide space of what he had previously perceived as a hall. It had been pitch black, but now, as all became illuminated by the sunlight pouring

From a Dark Wayover

through the newly opened portal, Leo could see where he was. Before he had only been able to smell Throtrex. Now he could see them.

An area reminiscent of a gigantic cavern lay before him, sloping slowly downwards by a series of broad terraces, like a stadium, to a vast center that plunged into absolute darkness. Everywhere upon the terraces were Throtrex. Their oil-black bodies covered the slopes in twisted heaps, lining even the farthest reaches like a dark mold, from the highest terraces down to the very edge of the stygian center. They seemed to be sleeping: they lay crushed up against one another, rhythmically sucking air into their gaping, stinking, drooling mouths, their sharp, spidery talons occasionally twitching, jutting out in every direction like a huge field of jagged black weeds.

Leo snapped out of his momentary paralysis. He and Gollyplox hurried out of the cavernous space even as

From a Dark Wayover

the opening to the Wayover closed behind them with its familiar suction sound and a smothering of sunlight.

Bludgeon broke the silence with a snarl of surprise. Leo glanced over his shoulder to see the triple-armed mutant scanning with his lantern the space where Leo's backpack had been. *It's not too late*, Leo thought. *In two seconds we can be back inside the passages leading back up to the Island…*

"It'sth them!" Mealworm's whiny, effete voice cast echoes throughout the Wayover. "Von Koppersthmith and histh Cheevilnid! *Get them!*"

Leo exhaled angrily, and he and Gollyplox darted into the black, airless confines of the upwards-bound passages. They stumbled along through the dark, their hands skidding over the walls. The fear of Bludgeon and Xylykynyxytyr propelled them, but more so the thought of all those Throtrex—countless hundreds of thousands of them—awakening from their strange slumber and stampeding after them from out of that deep, terraced cavern…

They could feel only the scrunching of the blubbery floor; hear only the sounds of their own distraught panting. Steadily they travelled around and around and up, mentally bracing for the maniacal howling and screeching of Throtrex that must surely rise up behind them at any second.

Leo wanted to run faster, but it was impossible: a medium pace was the only speed possible in a tunnel with such a doughy floor. His thighs ached with the effort. The odor of Throtrex raced in and out of his nostrils, but he still heard nothing behind him.

The dimmest of light invaded the darkness ahead. They emerged from the passage and into the vertical tunnel where they had started, and when they looked up they could see the moon almost directly above.

From a Dark Wayover

Gollyplox scrambled to the top in seconds. Leo, far less nimble, nonetheless shimmied up ably, assisted at last by his Cheevilnid friend until they both were standing atop the bare, dark windswept pillar of rock, staring down at the moonlit froth of the waves crashing around them.

Leo glanced at Gollyplox. "Did you see anyone coming after us?" He turned back to the spot where lay the opening to the Wayover, now rendered invisible by illusory stone. "I don't think they followed us…"

Leo crouched down and put his head through the intangible covering. He barely had the time to perceive that the bottom of the tunnel was empty before it suddenly, jarringly, ceased to be a fact: Bludgeon's three pale yellow arms stabbed in from the horizontal passage like the limbs of a huge mantis, followed by his round bald head and his sinewy torso.

From a Dark Wayover

Leo dodged away from the opening. "Use the rocks, Gollyplox…get back to the beach! I'll just have to try and swim…go, quick!"

He leapt off the edge of the great rock, plunging feet first into the wild waves below.

The sea was as relentless as always. No sooner did Leo surface, a thundering breaker tumbled down on top of him and rolled him like he was a toy. The tips of his shoes made contact with solid ground, but as he tried to hold his position another pile driver of ocean water crashed against him.

Digging his shoe against the ground again, he caught a glimpse of a small dark figure plummeting into the waters beside him. Certain that it was Xylykynyxytyr, Leo fought to twist and face his attacker. He let out a cry when it was Gollyplox who resurfaced.

Right away, the Cheevilnid was pummeled by breakers, and his rubbery green arms flailed uselessly.

From a Dark Wayover

Leo dove for him. Somehow, the Cheevilnid's fingers found his outstretched arm, and before another wave could blast them Gollyplox had scampered onto Leo's shoulders.

Leo took a short step in the direction of the beach, and it felt like a victory, in spite of more waves that roared like black lions and pounced upon him one after another. Gollyplox did not let go; by tumbling, rolling, tiptoeing a few steps, and tumbling some more, the two friends inched towards the beach.

Without knowing exactly when it happened, Leo found himself submerged only up to the waist. He forced his way on, panting, until just his shoes were dragging through the water, and then he was falling to his knees on the wet shore. Gollyplox slid off of his shoulders and rested on all fours in the shelly sands.

From a Dark Wayover

"Why did you dive into the water with me?" Leo said, still trying to get his breath back. "You easily could have just gone from rock to rock!"

Wearily, Gollyplox pulled himself into a cross-legged sitting position. "I help Leo, *wzzncrkkll*. Maybe I not next time? I not good ocean swim."

Leo smiled and gave him a fond, fake punch in the shoulder.

They looked back at the big Tooth from which they had come, searching for pursuers. Movements drew their eyes to the other rocks that rose like a grove of misshapen trees amidst the chaotic surf, and they caught sight of three familiar silhouettes: Bludgeon, again making of himself a bridge between pillars, with Mealworm and Xylykynyxytyr scuttling over his back.

Leo and Gollyplox stood on wobbling legs and ran as fast as they were able to the high cliffs. Leo, of course, had the tougher time scaling them, and when he

From a Dark Wayover

reached the top Gollyplox had already been there long enough to retrieve Ms. Winnipeg and the boys.

"You're not supposed to be here," Leo said to her, as he wheezed upon the cliff's edge. "It's been more than two hours. You were supposed to leave!"

Ms. Winnipeg helped him to his feet and kissed his cheek. "You're very stupid if you thought I was actually going to comply with that directive."

"Did you get the Flute, Dad?" Oddo said. His and all the boys' eyes glittered hopefully in the moonlight.

Leo did not answer, because he did not know. Holding his breath, he opened his pack and reached inside.

With a weary smile, he pulled out the silver Flute. Everyone cheered.

···✦·✦·✦·✦·✦·✦·✦

Mealworm stood upon the shore and stared in all directions, but he could not see his prey, because night had fallen, and there was too much salt and spray in the air. He, Bludgeon and Xylykynyxytyr began searching the beach. Even with constant briny winds scattering sand, it was Mealworm's gigantic eyes that quickly locked upon footprints: those of a man and a Cheevilnid, leading to the Blobfruit-laden cliffs, and from there towards the glowing orange veins of Mount Hollowchest.

From a Dark Wayover

Twenty-Two

The return journey to Relm took less time, since they weren't following the slow-moving Mealworm and because, on average, they were moving downhill more than uphill. They could not risk stopping for very long anywhere, nor did they much want to, feeling a renewed sense of vigor now that they had the Flute back and could go home. The exception was little Albert, who spent much of the time on Leo's shoulders, asleep, with his head resting heavily in Leo's hair.

They travelled all night. The sun rose, but remained hidden behind a gray, overcast sky. They regularly used the hilltops to look back and scan for their pursuers, but they saw only Chellacorns, and more Publugs.

From a Dark Wayover

It was late afternoon when they came to the northern end of Relm valley, but so much lava had pooled up in recent days that to circumnavigate it required almost two miles of extra travel. Leo and Ms. Winnipeg avoided discussing it in front of the children, but they both knew that Relm was in mortal danger.

As they reached the green lawns of the little village, the Cheevilnids, croaking cheerfully, rushed out to greet them. The boys were in so much need of sleep that their chins were drooping on to their chests, and it was the Cheevilnids who picked them up and carried them to the beehive-shaped meeting hall for food, water and rest.

Leo and Ms. Winnipeg felt anxious to depart for the Wayover, and as they discussed with Gollyplox the many dangers bearing down upon them, they both began to realize that the Cheevilnids did not share their anxieties. Gollyplox stared blankly at them as they assessed Hollowchest's ever-increasing tremors and the mounting lava floes at the head of the valley.

"Do you suppose," said Ms. Winnipeg, "That they don't understand what a live volcano next to their village means for them?"

Leo's face lit up. "Of course! That must be it. Cheevilnids are a brand new race of people. They've never heard of a volcano. They don't see the danger they're in."

Gollyplox listened patiently while Leo tried to explain it to him. "All that hot, melted rock you saw inside Hollowchest," he said, "It's going to just keep flowing out, and any time now it will come right into the village and destroy everybody. You're the leader, Gollyplox. You have to make them understand. Besides: Mealworm, Bludgeon, Xylykynyxytyr—it won't be long before they get here, too. But it's worse than that. You saw those Throtrex. Hundreds of thousands of them, right there off the coast. I don't know why they're all asleep that way, but you can bet this all has to do with the Corpse. At some point he's going to wake up those Throtrex and overrun this Island, if there's anything left to overrun."

Gollyplox looked down sadly. "*Creeee*, we must leave village? *Criiik*."

"Yes, Gollyplox," replied Ms. Winnipeg, touching his green shoulder blade. "I'm sorry. But Leo's right. You have to get Igwish and your nidlings, and all your people, to a safe place."

Leo rested his hand upon the Cheevilnid's other shoulder. "Why don't you all just come back and live with us? That was Oddo's suggestion, now that I think about it! I don't know how we would make it work, but we would, I'm telling you, and you'll be safe…"

"No, Leo." Gollyplox patted his friend's arm. "Cheevilnids stay home, on Island."

"But what about the volcano? What if the Island is about to blow up, or sink?"

Gollyplox shook his head. "It isn't."

The way he said it made Leo pause for a few moments before speaking again. "It's AmoAhsh'Qaya, isn't it? She told you that?"

The frogman puffed his yellow chest out proudly.

"But you need to escape the lava, anyway. You could return to your old cave homes under the river, maybe?"

Gollyplox sighed as he considered the idea. "No go back down in the river. We go up now." He nodded towards Zechariah's mountain.

"The palace! Right—that's a good idea. And Throtrex can't go there. But Mealworm can."

The Cheevilnid nodded again. They looked at each other, and they both knew they had arrived at the best plan either could devise.

From a Dark Wayover

"Well, you have to get your people going right now. And we have to go, too—there are no Balloons left, so we're just going to have to take our chances with going back up through Hollowchest, assuming the elevator hasn't fallen apart yet."

Within fifteen minutes so many Cheevilnids began flowing out of houses and hopping through the streets that, from a distance, Relm resembled a boiling pot of green peas. The humans helped retrieve wriggling podnids from their underground ponds and into water-filled barrels that could be carried on the males' backs; the older nidlings could travel well enough on their own, though their mothers insisted on keeping them close.

Leo was struck by how free of fear the Cheevilnids were. They weren't unaffected, but there was no panic or despair at work on their faces or in the way they interacted.

From a Dark Wayover

Part of the reason was surely Gollyplox's leadership. He stood upon a tall lump of brown and white stone, calling pleasantly to his fellow villagers. He carried his black and white stones in one hand, and had donned his robe; its big gems sparkled hopefully. His nidlings bounced excitedly at his feet. The Cheevilnids ambled confidently past him and towards the green hills that formed the base of Mount Highpalace. It was there that they would leave their great flocks of Waywobs to roam freely, while they continued towards the ancient, soaring peak.

"They're just going to *climb up*," said Leo with wonder in his voice. "I wouldn't have thought that was even possible."

Wilwell had been watching Gollyplox. "They aren't like us. They can make the climb."

Leo shrugged. "They're fifty times more agile than we are, that's for sure…"

Wilwell thought carefully for a few seconds. "Well, yes. But it's more than that. We have too many things wrong with us—too much weight. Cheevilnids don't have that, see? They're lighter than we are. They can make the climb."

Leo opened his mouth to respond, and then shut it again. Wilwell had a tendency to talk this way sometimes—the boy had a mystical streak. But he was right; as the Cheevilnids bent their gangly, powerful legs and leapt from rock to rock, Leo noted for the first time how nearly effortless it was for them.

"I don't know what it all means," Wilwell mused aloud. "But I think right now they are doing exactly what they are supposed to be doing."

For a little longer the two of them watched the Cheevilnids ascending the slopes of Zechariah's mountain, like green and yellow raindrops falling upwards, until a low, menacing rumble made its way across the valley from Hollowchest.

In response, Leo straightened up and took a deep breath. "Well, I definitely know what *we* are supposed to be doing right now. C'mon, my boy." They both managed to catch Gollyplox's eye, and the three of them exchanged long distance salutes. "We'll see him again," said Leo, patting Wilwell's back. "Don't worry."

"I'm not worried." Fondly, he took Leo's hand and together they went to find Ms. Winnipeg and the other boys.

⋯✦⋅✦⋅✦⋅✦⋅✦⋅✦

They left the valley and descended into the secret tunnel that led inside Hollowchest. The whole way Leo was nagged by the conjecture that they would find the elevator in ruins, under a pile of freshly strewn rubble.

Lampflowers lit the way for them into the lower caves, but after that there was more than enough light given off by flowing cascades of burning lava. The heat was all but intolerable, but they had no choice other than to squint their eyes and hurry as fast as they could to the center of the mountain.

When they reached the bridge that spanned the Fillwishing, Oddo stopped and pointed.

"Look!" he cried. "There it is! The elevator's fine!"

Leo's fists clenched in triumph, and he led them over the river at a brisk jog. As they went, they were all too focused on getting to the Wayover to notice Xylykynyxytyr, like a gray spider, crawling from beneath the bridge.

When they were nearly to the elevator's platform, the Evilnid let out a long, strange, wailing hiss that grabbed their attention and held it fast. As they stared in horror, Bludgeon leapt out from behind a mound of fallen boulders.

From a Dark Wayover

The huge man's hammer smashed into Leo's chest and sent him hurtling over the cavern floor. Ms. Winnipeg and the children screamed with anguish as they watched their Leo plunge backwards into an oozing cataract of lava and disappear beneath the fiery sludge.

Mealworm stepped casually from behind another pile of stones, pausing to adjust the net of birds across his shoulder, and he began to speak as if privately chatting with himself.

"Oh, now that isth stho pitiful. He went stho far to get that Flute back…allllll the way to the very Brim of the Hateful Deep itsthelf, where the World King rulesth, down there with the sthtink and our sthleeping Throtrexth, and alllll the way back again, and justht about to esthcape, and then…"

He stuck his tongue out and made an obnoxious squirting sound.

From a Dark Wayover

"Well, anyway: checkmate. Now let'sth finish thisth up, Monsthieur Bludgeon. You don't have to sthquash the boysth, or any of that. Justht tossth them into the lava—you can closeth your eyesth while you do it. Monsthiuer Cheevilnid, give him a helping hand, will you, pleaseth? But do leave that pretty golden-haired bird for me—oh, don't harm a sthingle sthell of her transthluscthent sthkin…!"

Ms. Winnipeg grabbed the three boys and pulled them close to her. She glanced around, looking for a direction in which to flee, but there were wide lava floes behind and to the sides.

Bludgeon started to approach them, but stopped. His round, staring eyes seemed emotionless, but behind them stinging words scrolled across his mind: *They are just little children…I do not want to do this…*

He shook the thoughts away, grunting with disgust at himself and this poorly timed gush of sentimentality. Resolving to finish once and for all this important work for which he had been given responsibility, he advanced without remorse.

Xylykynyxytyr crept along beside him, prepared to strike down with his tongue spikes anyone who attempted to dart past...

Ms. Winnipeg shrieked. The boys held on to her tightly. Albert began to cry.

To Bludgeon's left, out of his line of sight, the surface of the lava began to swell. Leo rose from the angry, orange, molten rock, with heavy, fiery chunks falling off of his shoulders. Before Mealworm could shout a warning, Leo hurled his green bottle of *Smallsteam* at Bludgeon's feet.

Hissing steam enveloped the towering three-armed man and the malicious gray-skinned Cheevilnid, and a moment later the two of them were the size of gerbils.

Leo hopped out of the lava river and scooped them up, one in each hand.

Mealworm gasped. He turned on one heel and shuffled off into the darkness of a tunnel as fast as he could, his net bag of birds smacking against his back.

Leo glared down furiously at his tiny captives as they squealed and wiggled in his hands, hating them for threatening the ones he loved. His heart became flooded with a nearly overpowering temptation to crush them, using every drop of strength in his hands.

Ms. Winnipeg, Gollyplox and the boys cheered and gathered close, hugging Leo, clapping him on the back, giving joyful thanks for the Hair Shirt that had once again protected him from a fiery death. Leo barely noticed them through the haze of his desire for revenge, but he knew, at least, that they shouldn't have to endure the sheer brutality of watching him squash his enemies until their guts and eyeballs popped out. Instead, he turned towards the crackling, steaming river of lava…

Just a flick of the wrist…they would simply melt and be gone forever…

He glanced at the boys, who were marveling at the diminutive monsters writhing in his grasp. Xylykynyxytyr chewed on Leo's forefinger, but it only felt like the toothless nibble of one of the little lizards that the boys often brought in from the shrubbery back home. Albert laughed, with all the innocence of a good child who perceives the humor in evil made impotent.

Leo looked at Ms. Winnipeg, then at the lava, and back again. She searched his eyes; she knew exactly what he was thinking, but she could not decide if she wanted to protest or not.

Leo mumbled under his breath and tossed his two shrunken foes. They sailed high over the molten rock and landed on a wide plateau of dry stone near the far

From a Dark Wayover

end of the cavern. They hopped to their feet, waving their stick-bug-sized arms at Leo and squealing with indignation.

Leo hustled Ms. Winnipeg and the boys on to the elevator and threw the switch. The mountain shook and clamored around them. From the vent below there came a renewed gush of magma.

When they arrived at the wooden platforms high above and ran for the stairs, Ms. Winnipeg shouted, "Are we going to make it?" The mountain bellowed in response.

The evening sky was a glowing gray, made darker by the rushing of ash and smoke from Hollowchest. Ms. Winnipeg and the boys followed Leo up the shaking, winding stone stairs, as wind whipped their faces and rocks cracked and splintered along the mountain's sides.

No sooner had they reached the top, they let out a chorus of screams as a geyser of lava spit through a fissure in the peak's surface. Leo shoved everybody to the metal ladder and sent them up: first Albert, then Oddo, then Wilwell and Ms. Winnipeg, with himself going last. The ladder vibrated like a tuning fork.

One by one they all disappeared through the sky portal, and, as Leo's shoe left the top rung of the ladder and he pulled himself into the Wayover, there was a sound like an array of exploding bombs.

In the warm darkness of the Wayover, they gathered around the opening and stared down. The ladder tumbled away, along with Hollowchest's summit. Massive pieces of rock tore apart, sinking into a blazing, mile-high fountain of lava and poison gas, heaving and pulsating, then collapsing, toppling over until the entire mountain had disappeared into a lake of raging, melted stone. Relm Valley was completely buried.

From a Dark Wayover

No one spoke, at first. Fredlegs, hanging halfway out of Oddo's pocket, let Cap see the dreadful sight, and then held him close and shivered.

Finally, everyone turned and trudged towards the other end of the Wayover, feeling frightened and relieved, exhausted and panicked all at the same time. As Leo opened his pack to retrieve his Flute, Albert mumbled, "At least Mealworm and Bludgeon and that Evilnid are gone for good."

Leo said nothing in response. He played the Flute, and they went home.

···✦·✦·✦·✦·✦·✦·✦

The Von Koppersmith mansion had been still, as was typical for a Sunday evening, but when the five missing Island adventurers suddenly shuffled wearily into a parlor where some of the other boys were playing a board game, the sounds that would build into a wild uproar began their crescendo. From everywhere, the entire populace of the estate began to assemble, including old Anselm and some of the recently hired security guards. At last came Mrs. Von Koppersmith; the parts of her face were drawn together as if being dragged into a black hole of dread, but once she saw Wilwell, Oddo (with Fredlegs waving from his trouser pocket), and Albert, followed by Leo and Ms. Winnipeg, arm in arm, she quivered, began to cry, and embraced them all.

  Everybody wanted to know what happened, why they were so dirty and spangled with so many bloody cuts and purple bruises, why it had taken them so long to return, and (perhaps most importantly) why Leo and Ms. Winnipeg were now holding hands. Partial responses were attempted, and repeated, but Mrs. Von Koppersmith and Anselm soon steered them all to a small dining room where they could be served hot vegetable soup and rolls. Afterwards, Wilwell, Oddo and

Albert were escorted off to where they could be plunged into a soapy bath, and then given fresh clothes.

Leo gently asked Ms. Winnipeg to stay the night rather than drive herself home, and she accepted with sweet awkwardness; with more of the same she kissed Leo goodnight, and from the few children who happened to be in attendance there were mixed reactions: laughter, cheers, horror.

Leo eventually found himself leaning against the cool tiles of his shower, letting hot, rainy water flow over his head and down his back to wash away three days' worth of accumulated mud, ash, leaves, sea salt, and sweat. Once finished, he had just enough strength left to roll on some underarm deodorant, brush his teeth and drag on some fresh, loose clothes before turning out the lights and dragging himself oafishly into bed. He fell asleep almost instantaneously.

From a Dark Wayover

Part 3 – Ms. Winnipeg's Sword Search. Darkshot Is Born. Max and Walter Hatch A Plan, and Leo Hatches A Borrowing, But None of It Goes Very Well.

From a Dark Wayover

Twenty-Three

It was the Monday before Leo, Wilwell, and Oddo (and Albert and Ms. Winnipeg) departed for the Island, that Maximilian Bosco made his decision to follow Mel Keystack's advice and become a vigilante.

The last straw, for him, had been on his way to work that morning. Coming up the street, he passed Miss June's, a tiny florist shop. Miss June was a small, kind woman in her fifties with a light Irish accent. Her two daughters helped her arrange flowers, take care of deliveries, and attend to all the other matters of the shop. The place was decades-old, and a charming burst of color and sweet scents on an otherwise dirty, gray and brown Cincinnati street. This morning, though, the windows of the shop were shattered. Wooden carts were overturned. Broken flowers of all shades and varieties lay scattered up and down the sidewalk like a mass grave of dead fairies. Over the bright green awning was spray painted the Hitback motto: **"When Life Hits You, Hit Back Harder!"**

Max could barely unlock the front doors of Keystack's, his hands were so quivery with indignation. Though busy with the duties of getting the store opened and ready for business, he was preoccupied with what he would do to combat crime in the city.

"...Think about what weapon you would use," Keystack had said. "That's important."

Max knew he didn't want a gun, because that would only increase the danger of accidentally killing someone, and he had already decided that taking life should be an absolute last resort. Sharp-edged weapons had the same lethal potential—even throwing stars seemed like too much of a risk, and, frankly, he couldn't get the hang of them. In practice, most of them just rattled off the walls, wildly off target. If he needed, for instance, to break a light bulb from a remote position, it would take him several shots before he succeeded and by then everybody would know he was there.

He considered a baton of some kind, like the one from Marvel Comics' *Daredevil*, but he thought it best to have a weapon that could disable criminals from a distance. In the end, a slingshot, similar to the kind he had used to subdue the Hitbacks during their raid on the surplus store, seemed ideal.

And slingshots were cheap. A high-quality Force Elite brand sports slingshot was less than twenty dollars, which he ordered through Keystack's. It arrived the next day.

It was all black (his signature color, he had decided). It had a grip like a handgun's, a sturdy wrist brace, and an adjustable sight. The handle had an integrated magazine, which could hold up to thirty 3/8-

inch ball bearings; a switch at the bottom allowed him to swiftly dispense one at a time. It did not take long for him to get the feel for it: he could load one shot into the leather pouch with his right hand, fire, reach down and catch the next bb as it dispensed from the handle, load it, aim, and fire again—all within two or three seconds.

The more he thought about what an average encounter with criminals would look like, the more he realized that it would also be wise to carry a secondary weapon. His thoughts returned to the baton idea, and he ended up choosing the very same billy club that Gray Hood had tried to use on him. As Max envisioned it, he could stun an enemy from a distance with the slingshot, then run close and knock him out with the club.

For clothing, he chose a pair of flexible, featherweight OCP Army Combat Uniform boots, a set of nylon/cotton blend tactical response trousers and shirt, and skin-tight gloves—all black. The shirt had reinforced elbows and shoulders and a mandarin collar. The trousers had a utility pocket that was the perfect size for his billy club.

For defense, he added a bulletproof vest, elbow and kneepads, shin guards, and forearm guards, also all in black.

He would need headgear, too. He found a matching combat hood online, the kind that leaves exposed only the area around the eyes, but he hesitated to purchase it because he thought it would make people think he was a ninja. Upon further review, he decided it was the best way to protect his identity without resorting to something flamboyant. *Like a gold helmet*, he heard Walter say in his mind.

All the pieces had arrived at the store by Thursday morning. He examined them to make sure everything he had ordered was present, accounted for, and intact, and then stowed it in a bin in the break room.

Tonight, after the store closed, his crime-fighting career would officially begin.

⸻✦✦✦✦✦✦✦

Before leaving for the day, Mel Keystack wished Max luck. He told him to use caution and wisdom, not just brute force, and advised him to keep his first outing limited in scope. It should be experimental, to 'test the waters'. Max agreed.

Now that the surplus store was locked and half-lit, Max put on his suit. He stood looking at himself in the surplus store bathroom mirror, in the black tactical response clothes and body armor, boots and gloves and hood, the club in his utility pocket and his slingshot in hand. He'd done a good job; everything looked right.

His heart rate was elevated, but not excessively so. He felt a unique excitement that seemed to wend through his arteries and veins and spray into every cell of his body. He thought, for a second, that this seemed inappropriate for what he was about to attempt. Shouldn't he feel angry? Bitterly determined? More sober, at least, surely? He did not feel those things. In contrast, he felt mildly intoxicated.

He switched off the bathroom lights and strode confidently but unhurriedly to the surplus store's front doors, unplugging lights and turning off switches as he went. He armed the security system, and stepped out into the cool April night.

The temperature was a comfortable sixty-five degrees, and the sky was clear. He locked the doors, and set the heavy chain around the door handles.

He stepped out of the purple floodlight and into the dark. Stretching out his arms and legs, he bent from the waist and tapped the sidewalk a few times to loosen up.

A car horn honked somewhere a few blocks away. A breeze blew a piece of papery trash across the street. Max began a relaxed jog down Buckeye Street until he reached the alley that would take him over to Lincoln Avenue, and then he broke into an elated sprint.

···✦··✦··✦··✦··✦··✦··✦

At 8:53 the next morning, Melvin Keystack found the door to his surplus store still chained and locked. Maximilian had obviously not yet arrived. Keystack went in, turned on the lights, and put bills in the cash register.

By 10:30, three men planning a hiking trip had come in to shop for last-minute camping paraphernalia, a hunter bought a box of buckshot, and an area manager for a blinds company came in to ask for directions to a restaurant. As Keystack changed the paper roll on the receipt machine, he wondered if he should call and check on Max. When at last he did, it went straight to voice mail.

Lunchtime came and went. The afternoon dragged by. Keystack tried calling Max again, but still received no answer. He did not leave a message—he never left messages, because the box didn't project well over a phone.

At 4:30, Keystack locked up the store and went home.

・・・✦・✦・✦・✦・✦・✦・✦

The next morning was Saturday. It was 8:28 when Keystack limped down the sidewalk to the front doors of the surplus store, and this time he found them unlocked.

He went inside. The lights were on, but the store was noiseless. Keystack locked the doors back and ambled to the front counter. He leaned against it and listened.

There was a cough, followed by a muffled sound that might have been a grunt of pain. His heavier shoe thumping awkwardly upon the linoleum floor, Keystack made his way around to the back room. The bathroom door was shut, and there were sounds of movement behind it.

Keystack knocked twice. He typed on his box: "**Mr. Bosco?**"

The sounds ceased. Keystack waited, and was just about to knock again when the deadbolt was drawn back. The door opened.

What Keystack saw made his round head flinch, as if a passing wasp had accidentally collided with the end of his nose. "**Mr. Bosco. You appear in need of medical attention.**"

The left side of Max's face was a swollen mash-up of ugly purples, blacks, and blue-greens. His lower lip was cut. His right eye was clumsily dressed with gauze and cotton. A long, one-inch wide abrasion glared red and angry on his upper forehead, near the hairline. His bulletproof vest lay upon the floor, and in its chest region were two small round gouges and a tear.

From a Dark Wayover

"Medical attention?" For a second, Max stared at Keystack with the confusion of a child. Then, he smiled broadly. Fresh blood gleamed thinly upon his teeth, and thickly in the seams where they met the gums. "Oh, no. I don't need medical attention. I feel *good*. I feel *really, really good*."

⋯✦✦✦✦✦✦✦→

Max described for Keystack how, on his initial foray the first night, he ended up staying out until four o'clock in the morning.

"What about keeping things limited in scope, Max? You were supposed to just experiment with all of this at first, to 'test the waters.'"

Max squinted one eye in embarrassment. "Yes, I didn't do that. But you wouldn't have either, Mr. Keystack! You should have been there…it was amazing!

From a Dark Wayover

The first hour I stopped a mugging in progress and broke up a drug deal. The dealers took a shot at me, but they completely missed—I was on a rooftop, in the dark."

"But, judging from your appearance, someone somewhere did not miss."

"Right. I took a few hits from some gang members I came across along West Liberty Street near the Music College. They had cornered a student—who knows what they were about to do to her. I took out three of them before the other six got to me and piled on. But I got away, grabbed the girl and we ran until we got her to her car! She drove off, and I headed for the shadows, because I remembered what you said, Mr. Keystack! 'Caution and wisdom'! I didn't forget! They found me anyway, though, and I got hit a few more times. But I gave it back as good as I got it, I can tell you! Anyway, by then it was 2:30 in the morning, so I decided that I might as well stay out a little longer. And it was a good thing I did! There was a home invasion on Chalmer Street. Three guys with knives and tire irons. The family was terrified…a mom and three little kids…the dad wasn't there…I did a good job and took them out first with some clean shots, then tied them up with more zip ties while the mom called the cops…"

    Almost breathless with excitement, Max continued to describe how, at the end of his long night, he went home and slept so deeply that, when he awoke again, it was past four the next day. He had thirty different wounds and was agonizingly sore but, after he took a shower and began to fully awaken, he decided he might as well go out again, which he did. That second night he prevented an appliance parts robbery and two muggings, apprehended the perpetrator of a hit-and-run, and disrupted what ended up being a sizable Hitback illegal arms deal not far from Findlay Market.

"After that, it was almost dawn. Since I was so close to the surplus store anyway, I came straight to work to clean myself up."

⋯╼╾⋯╼╾⋯╼╾⋯╼╾

While Keystack made a pot of strong coffee, he urged Max to elaborate on the Hitback arms dealers: how many there were, how many weapons were involved, and the outcome (which was not very good: Max knocked out two Hitbacks and clubbed three more, but then he was almost stabbed to death, and pursued by an uzi-wielding throng for two blocks.

"And those gang members," said Max, "from the first night? The ones who were about to attack the college student? They were Hitbacks, too. At least some were."

Keystack nodded somberly and typed upon his gray box, and the words `"Are you sure?"` buzzed electronically from the speaker.

"Oh, definitely. The leader had the green fingertips. Besides, he kept telling me he was a Hitback. I think he expected that it would drive me off. He was pretty surprised that I wouldn't back down."

Mel paused, looking away, then typed again. "They are really the main motor of crime in the city of Cincinnati, aren't they?"

Max nodded. "You think I should focus on them, don't you?"

"Strategically speaking, it would be the logical way to proceed, rather than wearing yourself out on a never-ending stream of petty villains."

"Somehow, I need to locate the center of the hive, I guess."

"That would be extraordinarily dangerous. I would not advise a man to do such a thing by himself. But it is the most effective strategy, if the goal is to drive back crime."

"Where do I start? I don't even know how to look. I don't have access to police files. I would just be shooting in the dark."

"Perhaps you could find a bona fide Hitback, and then follow him for awhile."

"Oh, right! Track him. Let him lead me to some kind of a headquarters or something. Good idea. I can try the area around Findlay Market again tonight."

Keystack nodded gravely, and, with a groan of discomfort, he rose to his feet. Hobbling to the store window, he looked out upon the wagging legs of passersby. "As long as we are talking about hives and headquarters, then strategic thinking leads to even bolder possibilities than what we are discussing here."

"Bolder?" Max got to his feet. "O.K., what?"

Keystack typed steadily. "You could defeat all the top agents of the Hit Back Harder Society here in the city of Cincinnati, and eventually they would simply be replaced, by new recruits within the city, or from outside of it. The Hitbacks are an epidemic, Mr. Bosco, and the heart of the sickness is not in Cincinnati."

Max took an eager step forward. "It's in New York." Everyone knew it; the statistics demonstrated it: of all the known areas of Hitback activity in the world, roughly forty percent took place in the Big Apple.

Keystack turned to look at Max. "I am speaking theoretically only, at this point,

Mr. Bosco. If one were serious about cutting out the disease, the place to do the work is New York City."

Max laughed. "But you're not just being theoretical, are you? That's where you think I should go."

"It has to be your choice. It cannot simply be: 'that is what Mel Keystack told me to do.'"

Max turned and began to pace, rubbing the knuckles of his fists. "It's my choice." He began evaluating plans in his mind, and it wasn't long before a frown clouded his face. "I can't afford this! My rent…"

"It would be paid."

Max froze, looking at Keystack with wonder. "What?"

"It would be paid. If you are truly going to attempt an assault on the Hitback world stronghold, then how can I do less than to give you what support I can?"

Max's arms dropped to his side. Across his features played an expression that was not usually found there: one made of suspicion and irony. "Oh, come on! Why?" He folded his arms. "Why are you doing all this?"

"You think I am manipulating you? For some nefarious purpose?"

"Oh, well…no. Sorry. I didn't mean to offend you. It's just that…this is all pretty weird, don't you think? You're doing a lot to keep me on this track—who else would do this? Most people—practically everybody—would just tell me to stop what I was doing. They would tell me I was crazy."

"I won't tell you that you are crazy. Neither will I tell you why I am doing this.

It should suffice to say that I am opposed to evil. Aren't you? Isn't that enough?"

Max shifted uncomfortably. "Well, of course. But it isn't that simple, Mr. Keystack. People don't do things like this—not really, not in real life…"

Keystack began typing quickly. "I have not known you for very long, Mr. Bosco, but that way of talking does not seem in keeping with your personality. I do know that it isn't in keeping with my own."

"But what about the police? I'll be just another criminal to them…a vigilante. I'll get arrested and thrown in jail…"

Keystack glanced down at the floor and sighed, his fingers hovering lightly above his translator as he considered his reply. Finally he began to type again, and the electronic voice spoke from the box:

From a Dark Wayover

"Yes, that is how the world is, Mr. Bosco. Sometimes good things are punishable by law."

Max stared in shock. They were, almost verbatim, the same words his own father had said to him years ago after his high school reprimanded him for his defense of Suzilu Milligan, and before he was beaten senseless by Kurt Vank and his deranged cohort.

Max went to the desk behind the counter and began looking up the cost of a plane ticket to New York.

From a Dark Wayover

Twenty-Four

He departed the next day. Before leaving town, he overnighted a tightly packed box, which contained his black clothes, his body armor, two slingshots, and packages of various ball bearings and pellets. He could only hope that they would arrive at their destination on time.

Now, sitting back in his seat, listening to the hum of the airplane and the soft murmurs of passengers around him, he replayed Keystack's words in his mind:

"Your friend—the chubby, impertinent one. He lives in New York, correct? Stay with him. Confide in him—but in no one else, do you understand? Just him."

From a Dark Wayover

It was a good idea, but Max was never able to ascertain what it was that Keystack saw in Walter, having interacted with him only once, on that day the Hitbacks tried to rob the store. All Keystack would say was: "`He is your only true friend, isn't he? He will help you decide where to begin. Make sure you listen to him. Follow his advice.`"

Walter Wallace expressed only the briefest puzzlement at Max's sudden decision to visit New York, but he hastily followed it with enthusiastic encouragement. He wanted to pick him up at the airport, but Max refused the offer. "I don't want you to do that, Walter. It will be too late at night. Just stay home. I'll get a taxi out to your place."

By 9:30 that night, Max was trudging resolutely through the roaring of plane turbines and the blazing lights of LaGuardia Airport, with his army-green duffle bag over one shoulder. It was less than twenty minutes by cab from there to Mount Carmel College, to the row of small houses that were rented by the seminarians who attended the school.

Max had only knocked once upon the door of Walter's apartment when it flew open.

Walter's hair was disheveled, and his cheeks were burning red. His eyes were wide and almost hysteric.

The two old friends shook hands as they had done for years, but Walter's grip was electrified with nervous energy, communicating relief and terror at the same time.

Max frowned with concern. "What's wrong?"

Walter took a deep breath, clapping Max's shoulder as he pulled him inside and took his duffle bag for him. "Sorry…come on in, please…sit down. How was your flight? Nevermind, I don't care. Just sit down…"

From a Dark Wayover

Max fell back into a tattered dark green recliner, unable to take his eyes off Walter. He had never seen his friend behave this way.

Walter stared back at him, perceiving his confusion. "Sorry. We need to talk about something, though. Something important. Oh, hey! Do you want a beer, or some hot tea? No, forget it, you can't have hot tea, that would take too long. We need to talk now. You want a beer?"

Max nodded, and Walter hastily grabbed two glass bottles from the refrigerator. He popped off their caps so that they fell and rattled across the floor. He sat down across from Max, pressing one beer into his friend's hand as he took a gulp from the other.

"I fell asleep on the couch earlier. I had pasta for dinner, and that always makes me tired, so I laid here on the couch, and I thought I would watch some Andy Griffith, but I just passed out. And I had a dream."

From a Dark Wayover

Walter took another drink and stared at Max with wide, goggle eyes. "This crazy, crazy dream. Like no other dream I've ever had in my life. It was like I wasn't even asleep, like I was wide awake, but in some other dimension." He sat on the edge of the couch, his spine as straight as a telephone pole. "I saw the United Nations building. The one here in New York—I recognized the front of it and all the flags. The United Nations building, as clear as if I were standing right in front of it. I could even smell the air, man. Then, it was like I shot through a wormhole into the building. I saw people. Lots of people, and journalists, with cameras and microphones. Everybody was just staring, like mannequins, all smiling these weird, vacuous smiles. Grinning, like happy puppet people, and just staring up at this big stage, where there was a podium. Flying above the whole room was Invictus…" Walter stretched out his arms, moving his hands as he tried to describe to Max what he had seen.

"But he wasn't flying quickly. It was slow, and sort of soothing. In fact, he had a thick string coming out of the middle of his back…"

Max nodded, still disturbed by Walter's behavior, but wanting to commiserate with him as much as he could, for friendship's sake. "Like a…what do you call it? A mobile?"

Walter snapped. "Yes! That's it! Like a mobile, in a baby's crib. Invictus was just going around and around, and that seemed to be why the people were happy, but it wasn't real happiness, of course, it was that blank, hollow smiling and staring…" He paused, shaking his head with disgust. "Anyway, they weren't looking at him. He was just above them all, flying around. They were looking at someone else. The man behind the podium. And do you know who it was, Max? Do you know? I'll tell you who. It was Molding!"

Max grimaced. "Jondas Molding?"

"Yep! The very one! I knew that guy was bad news. Haven't I always said so?"

Max shrugged. "I don't get what you're telling me. What did he do in the dream?"

"Oh, right…well, he was staring back at everybody. But he wasn't smiling. He didn't have much of an expression at all, but his eyes, Max…you should have seen them. They were bloodshot and filled with malice. Molding himself was on mute, but he seemed right at the edge of an outburst of rage."

Max shifted in his chair. He still had not taken a drink from his bottle of beer. "Well, man, that sounds like a terrible dream, but…"

"No! Look, I know what you're about to say, but I'm trying to tell you, it wasn't just a dream. It was a warning. Molding is bad, I'm telling you! The dream proves it!"

From a Dark Wayover

Again, Walter described the elements of the dream to Max, shaking his head fearfully over the unsettling visions, which he could still see clearly with his mind's eye. Talking about it all slowly put him more at ease, and eventually he went back to the kitchen and began putting together ham and cheese sandwiches for the both of them. For this, Max was silently grateful, since he had not eaten for hours. As they ate and talked, Walter continued to calm down and, finally, he asked Max why he had come to New York.

Now it was Max's turn to tell a strange tale.

Walter, in typical Walter fashion, scoffed at first, then expressed astonishment and even mild outrage as Max told the same stories of his nocturnal crime fighting adventures that he had related to Keystack the day before. Several times, Walter felt tempted to doubt what he was hearing, but the cuts and bruises Max had suffered, still not fully healed, gave wordless, gruesome testimonials. Regardless, by the time they both began to drift to sleep, Walter's mood was troubled and contemplative.

"This all sounds pretty ridiculous to me, I have to be honest," he mumbled irritably as he settled back on to his couch.

"I know," Max replied, adjusting the sheets on the blowup mattress from Walter's closet. "But it's not. It's a good thing. And it's going to make a difference. People deserve justice, Walter."

Walter closed his eyes and turned over on his side. "And sleep…"

From a Dark Wayover

Twenty-five

The next morning,

The Von Koppersmith Mansion…

Leo awoke slowly. He shuffled drowsily to the kitchen to make himself a cup of coffee. As he was stirring in half-and-half, Ms. Winnipeg appeared at the kitchen door.

She was a different woman from the one Leo spoke with a few days ago, with the flamingo legs and the uncertain eyes and the giant book of rocket scientist-level crossword puzzles. She had a fresh set of clothes on, composed of her usual assortment of colors, but for the first time they did not look drab to Leo: the grays were the charcoal of a fine art sketch, and the yellows like buttercups at dawn. Her hair was damp and pulled into a loose bun, and the white skin of her face gleamed.

"Good morning," Leo said, smiling shyly. "You look clean!"

"I am! I just took a shower. I showered last night before bed, but it felt so good that I showered again just a bit ago."

"I can smell your shampoo from here. It's nice! How long have you been up? Looks like you already have some coffee…"

She lifted a teal green cup to confirm his deduction, but said nothing. Instead, she stood and grinned at him mischievously.

"What are you smiling about?"

"I've been doing research, my dear."

"Oh, yeah? On what?"

From a Dark Wayover

"I can't wait to show you! Come with me to the library. I have a theory about the sword! Bring your coffee—come see!"

As they walked together into the mansion's baronial, leather-scented library, Leo shook his head in amazement. "I can't believe you've already figured out what this sword is all about, based on those miniscule clues Zechariah gave us! How?"

She led him to a table where she had spread out her laptop, several books, and a tablet of paper cluttered with scribbled notes. She picked up the tablet, her hazel eyes burning with excitement. "I wrote down what you said he told you: that although the sword is 'a legend' to him, because he spent so much of human history stuck on the Island, yet he insisted that 'it is real; you will be able to find it. It is a sword of kings, a joyous sword!'"

She pushed an encyclopedia towards Leo and began turning pages for him. "A sword of kings…well, *that* sounds like a coronation sword. Many European nations have a tradition of using a special sword as part of the coronation of their kings." She eagerly pointed to several color photographs of various glossy, jeweled sabers. "But Zechariah said that it's a joyful one, correct? That's a very interesting adjective to use in reference to a sword, don't you think, dear?"

"Ummm…yes…that's interesting…"

"That's what I said!" She turned to another, slimmer book and began thumbing through it. "*Very* interesting…a joyful sword…a joyful sword…ah ha! Here we are. Read this, dear…"

She slid the book towards him, opened to a particular page. He pulled it closer, noting its title in the margins: *The Song of Roland.*

"Oh! I know about this…"

Ms. Winnipeg gasped and happily clapped her hands together. "You've read it, too?"

"Of course not, honey. But I know about it. Big epic story about medieval heroes fighting against some people somewhere…"

"The Saracens."

"Right. Them. And Roland dies, right? And Charlemagne is the king of France at the time? See? I know a few things…"

"I'll give you a C minus. But *read*. That part, there…"

Leo followed her pointing finger to a paragraph numbered CLXXXIII.

"I get fairly lost on Roman numerals after 'ten'. What number is this?"

Ms. Winnipeg cackled. "One hundred eighty three! Never mind that now, silly. Read!"

Leo cleared his throat and read the verses aloud:

> The Emperor has made his bed in a
>
> meadow. The brave King sets his massive

spear at his head, not wishing to lay aside his arms that night. He does not remove his shining gilt-varnished hauberk; his helmet, studded with jewels set in gold, is laced to his head, and his sword Joyeuse is girded to his side. There was never another like it. Its brilliance changes color thirty times a day. We have heard of the lance which wounded Our Lord, on the Cross: by the goodness of God the point of it has come into Charles' keeping and he has caused the point of it to be mounted in the golden pommel of his sword. And it is because of this honor and this grace in it that the sword was given the name Joyeuse.

From a Dark Wayover

Leo stopped reading and looked at Ms. Winnipeg. "King Charlemagne's sword? So, from—what—the ninth century? That's the sword that Zechariah was talking about?"

"By a process of elimination, I have concluded: yes, it must be! A real, historical sword of kings, known as a joyful sword: 'Joyeuse'. Even beyond its name, the *Song of Roland* describes the joyfulness of the king and everybody around him as it is used to vanquish their enemies!"

She directed his attention back to another picture in the encyclopedia. The caption read: **La Joyeuse or Sword of Charlemagne, Musée du Louvre, Paris.** The photo showed a golden-hilted broadsword in a glass display case.

Leo stared at her, while at the same time scanning the horizons of his own mind. "But why does Zechariah think we need it? I don't know the first thing about sword fighting. Maybe it's not for me...yes, that must be it. I'm supposed to give it to someone, do you think?"

"Maybe to Zechariah himself?"

Leo nodded. "That's plausible. He already has his Spear, of course, but maybe there's something special about Joyeuse. Maybe he has to have it to kill the Corpse."

"Perhaps, but from what you all have told me, this Corpse doesn't sound...corporeal, no pun intended. He's just a shadow-thing. What good are weapons?"

Together, they strolled to the tall, clean bay windows and looked out onto the lawn, ruminating over the mysteries of the sword and its purpose. "It might help if we knew what the Corpse is, after all," Ms. Winnipeg continued. "He's not one of these Throtrex creatures, but he directs them? Where did he come from?"

From a Dark Wayover

With a wave of one hand and a roll of the eyes, Leo indicated his inadequate qualifications with respect to such questions. "The kids tell me that he's been around longer than the human race, and that he's the most evil thing possible. Which is hard for me to imagine, since that Archthrotrex called Kak that you've heard about was the most horrible being I've ever come in to contact with. And the Corpse has a lot of power, of course…but he doesn't get to use it. Not fully. He calls himself the World King, but the truth is that he's trapped, and has to operate mostly through other people."

"The dark pit at the bottom of that other Wayover. The Hateful Deep. That's where he's trapped?"

"That's it. Mealworm called it 'the place where the World King rules'. I'd hate to slip and fall down that hole. Otherwise, as far as I can understand it, there isn't much he can do unless a person wants him to. Invites him. Once that happens, he's unleashed."

"How does one 'invite' a fiend like that?"

"Two ways. You can be partially tricked into it. Not completely tricked—you have to know on some level that you're seeking him and that it isn't good. That's how guys end up with these Double 333 marks."

"What's the other way?"

"To formally summon him. I've only seen that once: one night during my first time on the Island. Crawlsome Bentpin had captured us, and he was about to hand over Zechariah's body to the Corpse. It was a formula, I remember…like a magic spell, almost…I won't try to recreate it now, of course, but it was basically invoking the Corpse three times, calling him the World King, and using these big, lofty titles. Just before Bentpin finished saying it all, Kak showed up…" Leo stopped as the incident came more clearly into his mind, and he shuddered involuntarily. "Regardless, I don't see how a medieval sword is going to help against the Corpse, or why I'm the one who has to get it."

Ms. Winnipeg let out a gentle sigh. "Well, love, I think we don't have enough letters to guess the answer to that little crossword puzzle. For now, we only know that your Mr. Zechariah insisted that you have to obtain Joyeuse…that it's of great importance."

"You're right. He said there was danger coming. The entire world is in trouble."

"Exactly. So, what do we do now, dear?"

Leo laughed. "You ask me like I would know the answer to that."

"Of course…I'm sorry. It's going to take a lot of planning to pull this off!"

Leo leaned his head to the side, puzzled. "Pull what off?"

"Taking Joyeuse from the Louvre."

Leo dropped his face into his palms, exhaling loudly and laughing at the same time. "That's it, isn't it? That's what we'll have to do next. I guess if I thought there was even a slim chance we could bribe the French into letting us borrow it for a couple of days…"

Ms. Winnipeg giggled. "I don't think even *you* have that much money, sweetheart."

The two embraced each other gently in the warm light of the morning. "Fico! This is really beginning to hit me. How in the world will we take a priceless artifact from the Louvre without being caught?"

"I don't know, but we have to figure out a way. Zechariah wouldn't have asked me to do it if it was just impossible."

"But maybe, when he told you about it, he didn't realize where it was."

"No, he knew. He was about to tell me, but we were interrupted by Mealworm."

Ms. Winnipeg shuddered. "Ughh. Don't mention that name, please. It makes me nauseous."

Leo smiled. "Sorry. Don't get nauseous—it's breakfast time. I'm starving. After we eat and everybody wakes up, let's talk to Anselm and Mom, so we can start working on a plan."

"You don't want to take a day or two to recover, dear?"

"We better not. It only takes twelve hours for that shrink potion to wear off, and it's past that now…"

"Oh! But surely Bludgeon and Mealworm and that awful little Zilli-whatsit couldn't have survived the mountain's collapse?"

"I don't want to just assume it. Besides, like you said: Zechariah wanted us to get the sword as soon as possible."

Hand in hand they started to slowly leave the library, and as they went their feet softly tapped the tan and brown floor tiles. Leo suddenly stopped and turned. He held Ms. Winnipeg by her skinny shoulders, and his face had gone dark.

"I'm really bothered about something, and I need to tell you, because otherwise I won't tell anybody and it will slowly kill me."

She reached up with one soft hand and touched his face. "What is it? Tell me."

"Back on the Island, in that mountain cave, after I shrunk Bludgeon and Xylykynyxytyr, you knew what I was going to do next. You saw it on my face."

"You were going to throw them in the lava."

Leo, his eyes filled with a mist of conflict, nodded at her in silence.

"But you didn't."

"I should have. They wanted to kill us. What if they are still alive, and they catch up to us later and hurt the kids? Or you? I think not executing those two creeps was the stupidest thing I've ever done."

Ms. Winnipeg slipped her fingers into his hands, pulling them close to her. "I'd say that what *I* saw in that mountain cave was you at your best. Leo, you're a great father, and a great man. You have a rare quality, the same quality you showed those fiends, that same quality you show all these boys every day, and the whole reason you adopted them and took them into your home in the first place: mercy. You're merciful. I've never met anyone who was so willing and able to show mercy. There isn't anything regrettable about that."

Though still dissatisfied, Leo also felt relieved and grateful, nonetheless. He and Ms. Winnipeg left the library and went downstairs for breakfast.

From a Dark Wayover

Twenty-six

About midmorning, all of the boys were put in the care of various tutors, with the exception of Oddo, Wilwell, Albert, and timid young Rinchwick. Ms. Winnipeg escorted them to the library, where Leo, Mrs. Von Koppersmith and Anselm were already waiting.

Leo smiled. "Come on in boys! Have a seat. Anselm put some crackers and stuff on that tray there, so help yourselves. Hey—you have your backpacks on!" Wilwell, Oddo and Albert grinned proudly as they turned to more fully display the packs they had worn on the recent excursion to the Island.

"We figured that you called us here because it was time to go on the next adventure," Oddo exclaimed.

"To find the sword!" Albert cheered.

Rinchwick look mystified. "What sword?"

From a Dark Wayover

Neither Rinchwick nor any of the boys who had remained at the mansion had yet heard the full account of what had happened recently on the Island, so Leo took a few minutes to explain. As he described how Xylykynyxytyr had been shrunk and (at least temporarily) defeated, perhaps even destroyed, he watched Rinchwick's face carefully for some sign of relief. This was why he had invited him to the meeting this morning, since it was Rinchwick, more than the others, who had been so unsettled by the gray Cheevilnid's invasion. When Rinchwick asked, in a low voice, "But you aren't *sure* he's dead?" Leo was secretly crestfallen. He knew right then that Xylykynyxytyr would only continue to haunt the boy's imagination.

Nevertheless, by the time the tale came back to the subject of the sword alluded to by Zechariah, and how Ms. Winnipeg had solved the riddles surrounding it, all of the boys, including Rinchwick, were thrilled.

"Don't get too excited yet," Leo cautioned. "We have a huge challenge facing us. We need to get it out of the Louvre. We'll basically need to break in and steal it."

Oddo made a disapproving humming sound. "We're not supposed to steal."

Leo glanced at his mother and at Ms. Winnipeg uncomfortably, regretting his choice of words. "Well—not 'steal'. Just borrow. And even though I don't have the Louvre people's permission, I have Zechariah's. I'd say he has the greater authority. Besides, the sword doesn't ultimately belong to the Louvre; it belongs to King Charlemagne."

The boys seemed content with that response.

Mrs. Von Koppersmith still looked concerned. "How will you break into the Louvre? Their security systems must surely be impenetrable."

"The Flute will get me in. Remember: Flutes have the power to take you anywhere you've already physically been. I've been to the Louvre a couple of times, back when I hiked through Europe. I just have to go into the Wayover, let it close, then Flute from there to the Louvre."

"You're not going alone," said Anselm. "Right, Leo?"

"That's what we have to figure out. We need to talk about how this can be done, and that will determine who will go with me, and what each of our jobs will be."

Ms. Winnipeg rotated her laptop screen, displaying a map of the Louvre's different floors. "Leo and I have been talking it over. They have motion sensors that get turned on after hours. The glass display case that holds Joyeuse has its own alarm…"

"None of us have the equipment or skills for that sort of thing," grumbled Anselm. "That's James Bond stuff. I don't see where you are going with this, Leo. Do you really need the sword?"

"Zechariah was emphatic. There are a lot of big things happening that I don't understand, but Zechariah made it clear that my part included getting my hands on this sword. So, somehow, we have to figure out a way."

Laying his hands on the table and resting his weight, he stared at the computer screen. "I hate to say it, but I made a bad mistake leaving those potions behind on the Island. Gollyplox had a whole pile of them stored away, and now they're buried under lava. They could have given us an advantage, maybe. For now, all I have is the one bottle of *Fixmender*."

There was a sigh, and the clearing of a throat. They turned to see Albert opening his battered backpack. Inside were two bottles.

Leo stared for a moment before he realized what he was seeing, then gave Albert a frown. "You took these from Relm? How did I not notice?"

Albert shrugged. "It was when we got back from the Teeth, and you and Ms. Winnipeg were talking to Gollyplox, and we were in the beehive place, resting. I hid them in my backpack. There's an *Instant Jungle*, and a *Fishbreath*."

Leo continued frowning, as he turned over the bottles in his hand. At last, his eyebrows lifted, and he smiled and patted Albert on the head. "Good boy. Maybe there's a way we can put these to use."

Albert beamed with pride. Exhaling heavily with relief, Wilwell and Oddo took off their packs and opened them, revealing every single one of the other potions from Gollyplox's stockpile.

Leo's lower jaw dangled.

"We didn't want to tell you before," said Wilwell. "Because we thought you might get angry."

Leo exchanged smiles with his mother and Ms. Winnipeg.

From a Dark Wayover

"You may have saved the day, boys," said Anselm.

"Defintely," said Leo. "So, let's work this out. The Flute will get us in. We could go in late, after midnight…"

"The motion sensors, Leo," said Anselm. "The security system will be on. Can one of these potions help?"

Ms. Winnipeg stared upwards at nothing in particular. "Why not just go in during daytime hours, dear?"

"People will see us!" Oddo grumbled.

Leo paced, hands behind his back. "It's either: go in after hours and trip the alarm, or go in while the place is still open, and give tourists the shock of their lives when we come walking through a hole in midair."

"Can you go when there are only a few visitors, when there's a reasonable chance no one will see?" Mrs.

From a Dark Wayover

Von Koppersmith wondered. "The Louvre is popular, obviously, but…"

"Late, near closing time," said Ms. Winnipeg, tapping keys on her computer and examining the Louvre's website. "Or lunchtime. Those seem to be the least crowded times."

Anselm shook his head. "It would only take one tourist—just one—to observe you and go screaming to the nearest *garde de sécurité*."

No one could think of a resolution. Finally, they decided to delay their decision and move on to planning the next phase of the adventure: the actual removal of the sword from its case.

"There is a medieval area where they display Joyeuse," said Ms. Winnipeg. "On the second floor…"

"I've been to that floor," said Leo. "The Flute can put us right there."

"But, like I said before, the case itself also has alarms on it. They're controlled somewhere in the museum, but there is no way for amateurs like us to know where precisely. Just going by these photographs, I don't see any locks or hinges on the case—it's just a big glass box. So, I don't even know how you would pry it open. And I'm betting it's pretty thick glass, too, so it would be difficult to break through. Either way, dear, an alarm will sound."

Leo sighed and leaned back. "O.K. Let's take another look at our potions."

The boys had lined them up side by side on a long, rectangular table near by. There were sixteen remaining from the original store of eighteen, since the *Snowball* and the *Smallsteam* had been used. None of the potions were labeled, but by the various shapes and colors of the containers or the material of which they were made—glass, wood, or clay—the boys knew them well.

"*Fixmender, Fishbreath, Instant Jungle,*" chanted Oddo, tapping each one lightly as he went, "*Bigifier, Bigifier, Bigifier, Bigifier. Subtility, Niblung, Niblung…Vermiform, Concretis, Instant Food, Instant Food, Nonpondo.*"

"What about this last one, here?" said Leo. "This red one?"

"That's *Apple Juice.*"

"What does it do?"

Oddo looked confused. "It's apple juice."

"Oh." Leo picked up one of the *Anti-Smallsteam Bigifiers*. "And these don't actually make anything grow, right? They're just for bringing someone who's been shrunk by a *Smallsteam* back to their original size?"

The boys nodded.

"Hm. So, these are useless. What's this…what'd you call it? *Nonpondo*? What's it do?"

Oddo put his hands behind his back and replied with the usual cavalier, authoritative tone he used in these sorts of conversations: "Pour it on your feet, and you can walk on surfaces you would ordinarily fall through."

"Oh. So, you could use it on…?"

"Water, for instance. We used to stand on the Fillwishing and let it carry us along."

"Like a conveyor belt. Cool. How long does the effect last?"

"Three hours."

Leo put the bottle back down. "Interesting. But I don't see how it would do us any good at the Louvre."

"What about the *Subtility*?" Wilwell said, a glimmer in his eyes. "We can get through the glass display case with it!" The boy explained how *Subtility* worked: any surface upon which it is poured becomes permeable for a short amount of time.

"How long does it last?"

"About ten minutes." Wilwell shook the bottle. "Not much in here, though. You couldn't subtilize the whole case. But you could affect an area of, maybe, four or five inches or so. You could reach your arm in, at least!"

"Without setting off the alarm," piped in Oddo proudly, as if he had thought of the entire idea.

Leo affectionately punched both boys' shoulders. "That's good! O.K.! That's something we can use."

Ms. Winnipeg made a 'hm' noise, followed by, "Fico. A hole only four or five inches wouldn't be enough to get Joyeuse out."

Anselm leaned in and studied the sword's image on the laptop. "She's right. Look at that cross-guard. It must be at least seven inches."

From a Dark Wayover

In frustration, Leo sharply snapped his fingers. "Off by two inches! Too bad we don't have another *Smallsteam*. We could have used the *Subtility* to get into the case, then shrunk the sword down to pocket-size and Fluted home before anyone knew a thing."

Leo had the boys explain the functions of the other potions with which he was not familiar. *Fishbreath* allowed the user to breathe underwater; some kind of creature called a Niblung lived inside each of the bottles that bore that name.

"What about this one?" Leo held up a cream brown-colored beaker. "What did you call it?"

Wilwell looked askance at it. "The *Vermiform*?" He and Oddo smirked at each other the way they had back on the Island when they first found it among Gollyplox's other potions. "*Vermiform*," they said together, snorting and chuckling. "So dumb."

From a Dark Wayover

Mrs. Von Koppersmith looked mildly irritated. "What does it *do*, boys?"

"It's just kind of a joke potion," Oddo said. "Whatever you pour it on turns into an earthworm."

"For half an hour," Wilwell added. Albert and Rinchwick snickered.

"A worm?" Leo wrinkled up one side of his face. "That *is* dumb. Well, let's think about how we could use these others…"

"Eureka!" Ms. Winnipeg cried. Everyone turned to face her.

"The *Vermiform*, Leo! Use the *Subtility* to access the display case, and the *Vermiform* to change Joyeuse into a worm! Then you just pick up that worm and bring it right home. Half an hour later it will transform back into the sword!"

"I don't know, Dad." Oddo's little face was pinched with concern, and his voice had become profoundly professorial. "That's dangerous. Whatever happens to that worm will happen to Joyeuse—that's just how *Vermiform* works. What if, after you changed it into a worm and took it out of the display case, you were to accidentally squash it or pull it apart? Once the worm effect wore off, it would change back into a broken, ruined sword."

They all began voicing their opinions simultaneously, but Anselm put his hands up and shouted them all down. "Our Ms. Winnipeg is right! It's the perfect idea. Just put the worm in a small pocket-sixed box or case, and it will be safe."

Rinchwick looked distraught. "But what if the worm dies?"

"What do you mean, son?"

"He means that if the worm dies," said Wilwell, "Then it stays a dead worm permanently."

From a Dark Wayover

"I found a website!" Ms. Winnipeg was cheerfully tapping away on her laptop. "Wormlove.com. 'How to take care of your earthworm.' Oh, listen to this: earthworms can live for several weeks in a cup, as long as it has holes. But they need proper moisture. Fifty to seventy degrees is the ideal temperature for an earthworm—they *can* survive in less-than-ideal temperatures, but it is very, *very* risky. Ooh, look at this: peat moss is well suited for temporary storage, but it must have adequate moisture—but not too much—we will need to squeeze the wet peat moss; squeeze it! Ha! But not with the worms in it at the same time, obviously, hee hee hee! And listening for a sort of spongy, mushy sound, and only a drop or two of water should come out. BUT, if we want to continue to keep the worm, we should transfer it as soon as possible to a container with a fresh bed of compost, with proper light and oxygen, naturally, so that the worms don't…"

Leo patted her shoulder, interrupting her train of thought. "We get it, sweetheart."

"Well," remarked Anselm, shaking his head and half-smiling, "I don't want to be too hasty, but this is beginning to sound like a one-man mission, Leo. You, the Flute, and these two potions…"

"*Subtility* and *Vermiform*," Oddo specified.

"You could be in and out in a very short time," Anselm continued. "Assuming it's timed properly, and no one sees the Flute portal, you could do the job in under fifteen minutes."

Leo found himself beginning to feel genuinely eager. "Under fifteen minutes," he repeated. "Ten minutes, I bet!"

Anselm held up one finger. "But you can't be seen. That is, I suppose it would not be a total disaster if you *were* seen, but we really need to research more and nail down the optimum time, when that part of the Louvre will be deserted."

"You should take the *Instant Jungle* with you, too, Dad," said Wilwell. "If someone does chase after you, you can throw it down and make a big obstacle for them. It will definitely slow them down, and give you plenty of time to Flute out."

Leo nodded proudly at Wilwell, who smiled happily.

"Very good then!" Ms. Winnipeg adjusted her indigo-framed glasses, and the immense lenses reflected the text and images on her laptop screen as she typed. "I'll keep researching the best time to go, and I will let you know what I find."

There was little else to say or to plan. Everybody began to slowly disperse, until only Leo and Ms. Winnipeg were left in the library. She shifted her mouse and clicked and tapped and scribbled notes on her notepad until Leo became bored. He gave her a kiss on the forehead, which brought a smile to her face, and then he left to go rummage in the kitchen for snacks.

When he arrived, he found Anselm already there. He was helping Ruggero, one of the part-time cooks, replace the filter in the vent over the huge copper stove. The mounted television was on, and upon it two middle-aged newscasters were engaged in sedulous punditry. Leo listened with tepid interest as he cut a slice of pepper jack cheese from the refrigerator.

"So, Phil, the big story that is dominating headlines this morning is the sudden announcement by world-renowned Visionary, Jondas Molding, that he will be holding a press conference on Wednesday at the U.N. in New York. What do you make of all this, Phil? What's your read?"

From a Dark Wayover

"Well, Tom, I think it's caught everybody way off-guard, and just when I thought we'd already gotten enough surprises, ha ha ha!"

"Ha ha ha! You can say that again, Phil. First, the world gets rocked by the arrival of a bonafide superhero..."

"Invictus..."

"Yep, that's the one, then Jondas Molding holds a secret meeting with him in D.C. last month, and now Molding announces a press conference. Naturally, speculation is heavy that this press conference ties in with Invictus somehow. What do you make of that, Phil? What's your read?"

"Well, Tom, we have to remember, first, that at Molding's insistence, this isn't a 'press conference,' in the traditional sense of the word, as in: closed doors, press only, carefully monitored questions. Molding's people are calling it a "gathering"..."

"Ha ha! Right, a "gathering." That's a peculiar choice of words. What's your read on that, Phil?"

"It means everybody's invited, everybody from whoever happens to be doing some sightseeing, to top level international officials..."

"Or even some homeless guy who happens to wander over from the Lower East Side..."

"Ha ha ha! Exactly. All of which is very much in keeping with Jondas Molding's well-known love of democracy and equal opportunity for all—everybody's invited, first come, first serve, to meet in the General Assembly room at the U.N. for what Molding promises will be a "historic"—his word, not mine—a "historic" announcement..."

From a Dark Wayover

Leo, Anselm, and Ruggero had slowly paused what they had been doing, and were now gazing up at the television screen…

Twenty-seven

"I'll tell you, Phil, it can't have been too easy to arrange an event like this at the General Assembly room itself, in the United Nations, which, as you well know, Phil, is technically not U.S. soil, but international property, isn't that right, Phil? What do you make of that, Phil?"

"I think it shows the incredible influence that Jondas Molding has. I mean, what Lola wants, Lola gets, am I right? Ha ha ha ha!"

"Ha ha ha! But what does it all mean? For Mr. Molding to put this all together so hastily, and then announce it so suddenly...what's your read, Phil?"

"And, Tom, no advance notice on what this "gathering"—not my word—is really all about?"

From a Dark Wayover

"Clouded in secrecy. So, the question is: will it be bad news, or good news? Should we all be worried, Phil? Ha ha ha! What's your read?"

"Well, this is Jondas Molding, after all. He's done so much good for so many..."

"A genuine humanitarian..."

"And known for putting others first. I think whatever he's going to announce at this "gathering"..."

"Not Phil's word, folks..."

"I think it will be very, very interesting. I, for one, am very interested."

"That is definitely interesting, Phil..."

"And that *is* my word, Tom. Ha ha ha!"

"Ha ha ha!"

"Idiots," sneered Walter, watching the T.V. from his couch with a fresh cup of coffee and a red blanket over his shoulders. "That's *my* word."

Max, scrambling eggs in the kitchen, laughed.

Walter turned down the volume on the television. "So, how do you like me now, man? I dream Jondas Molding is at the U.N. in front of tons of people, and—behold!—it's going to happen in real life. Who's the real Visionary?"

"I don't understand it," Max said, spooning fluffy, steaming eggs onto two plates. "But I have to hand it to you. It must mean *something*, after all."

"It means I'm a prophet." Walter took a plate from Max and began shoveling breakfast into his mouth. He continued his thoughts on the matter while chewing: "I've been sent from God. I'm His favorite."

Max smirked, shook pepper on his eggs, and ate as ravenously as his friend.

Before he could finish, the doorbell rang. When they opened the door, they discovered, sitting upon the front porch, a brown and white package with a Cincinnati return address.

"My stuff," said Max eagerly, and he brought the box inside.

Walter's disposition was lighter than it had been the night before, as if the bright morning sun had coaxed open some new interior bloom of pleasant enthusiasm. He watched curiously as Max put the freshly arrived package on a coffee table, opened it up, removed the contents, and, without commentary, laid them out for him to see.

"Why the black hood? Are you a ninja?"

Max glowered.

Walter picked up the slingshot. "This thing really works?"

"Yep. It's effective, and easy to use."

"And you really are serious about this? You are now a Fighter of Crime? And you've decided to single-handedly wipe out the Hitbacks?"

"Well, not 'single-handedly.' I have Mel Keystack, and you."

Walter leaned back and looked sidelong at him, then laughed. "Yeah, Keystack is one in a million. He's eager to bankroll you for whatever you need, and he seems to have no end of cash to do so—partly because he doesn't spend anything on himself, I think. You know he can afford better speech assistance equipment than that lunar module-looking voice box! And what's going on with his ancient clothes?"

"He's thrifty. Like a monk. He only buys clothes donated to Goodwill."

"Donated by a wealthy librarian from 1963. Anyway, that's beside the point. It's cool that he's decided to help you, and I haven't seen you this happy since grade school. But I'm still suspicious of the whole idea. It's weird."

From a Dark Wayover

Max leaned forward excitedly. "No, it's *right*, Walter! You should have seen that college girl I rescued from the gang—I mean, she looked terrible, actually, like she was going to explode from fright. But when she was driving away, she looked back at me, crying, and she *waved*. A little wave of thanks. She was safe, Walter. And that family, in the home invasion…what would have happened to them if I hadn't intervened? What I'm doing is making a <u>difference</u>. Things are being put right, and the bad isn't being allowed to just <u>win</u>."

Walter stood, his red blanket still wrapped around his shoulders, and he meandered around his living room pensively.

Max sat back. He was beginning to think that it might have been a mistake to involve his friend in his new career choice. It wasn't Walter's fault if he couldn't embrace such an unorthodox idea…

"I have a theory about Jondas Molding," said Walter suddenly.

Max stared, waiting for him to expound.

"It's bizarre. But hear me out." He sighed heavily. "I think he's possessed."

Max waited for the next part of Walter's theory, until he suddenly realized that there was no next part. "That's it? You think he's possessed?"

"By an evil spirit. Yes."

"Well…why do you think that?"

"Two reasons. First: he receives messages in his living skin. That is one hundred percent creepy, and the only other time I've heard of such a thing are from real-live, documented cases of demonic possession."

"Really? That's a possession-thing?"

"It's atypical; super-atypical, probably. But it's happened."

"When?"

Walter's expression lost its confidence. "I don't know! I'd have to look it up. But it's happened. What are you, a paranormal investigator now?"

"O.K., don't be so sensitive! I don't doubt you. I'm just saying: it sounds like Hollywood stuff. What's Reason Number Two?"

"My dream."

"The dream!? It showed him at the U.N., and, yes, it's amazing that what you saw in your dream is really going to happen in two days, but it seems like a big, big stretch to go from that to: 'he's possessed'."

"You didn't see his eyes, Max. They were filled with utter evil. And that wasn't a normal dream. That was a message."

Max almost spoke, then didn't, and instead simply gave his friend a look of disapproval.

Walter guffawed. "Hey, look, you came to me and told me you've decided to become a comic book character, and all-in-all I've been very cool about that. You owe me some open-mindedness, man!"

"O.K., yeah, but evil spirits are not the kinds of things that I know the slightest thing about. You're the seminarian. Tell me more—explain to me how Jondas Molding could be possessed. He doesn't look possessed. Shouldn't he be screaming and tearing off his clothes and howling?"

"No, man. That's rare. Evil spirits want to stay hidden. They try to keep the people they possess functioning in regular life as much as possible; flying under the radar, so to speak. Real exorcists know that."

"Speaking of real exorcists, I'm not one. Why are you telling me this?"

"Because I think you need to focus your investigations on him. I think he's the real enemy."

From a Dark Wayover

"The real enemy? I'm here to fight against the Hitbacks—they're the real enemy. They're *my* real enemy, anyway."

Walter put up his hands, as if to slow down a passing taxi. "I didn't tell you about another part of my dream. I just remembered it a few minutes ago. You know how Invictus was attached to that mobile above the crowd? Well, it wasn't just him. There were others hanging from the mobile, too. Hitbacks. With their trademark green fingertips. There were a dozen, maybe, suspended from this mobile, slowly turning, with Invictus seemingly pursuing them around and around above the people as they smiled and gazed at Molding."

Max could not think of a response. He shrugged.

Walter frowned. "Get it? The Hitbacks are in league with Jondas Molding. Somehow. Don't look at me like that, I don't know how, I just know this dream was not a bunch of random images like most dreams. Like I said, it was a message. And that message is: Jondas Molding is possessed by an evil spirit, and he's behind the Hitbacks, and it's up to you to expose him."

Walter glared at Max, who returned it, though with less conviction. They stared at each other for several seconds before an involuntary snort escaped Max's throat; Walter tried to ignore it and maintain all seriousness, but could not suppress a chortle. Finally, he let a loud laugh come blasting out. Max could only sit and giggle helplessly as Walter lobbed pens and pillows and other objects at him. "Man, this isn't funny! You have to do something. Nobody else is going to do anything to Jondas Molding—they think he's the Wizard of Oz. *I can't do anything. I have the athletic ability of a sea cucumber. But you've chosen this moment, of all times, to become a genuine costumed crime-fighter. That fact, and my dream, all at the same time…you're meant to do something about Jondas Molding, Max. I know it. That's what's going on right now. Whatever Molding is up to, it must be the very definition of injustice, Max. If you, on the other hand, stand for justice, like you said, then doing something about Molding is your number one priority."

Max had quickly stopped chuckling as Walter spoke. As 'number one priority' drifted off through the air, a silence followed. Walter idly doodled on a piece of paper, and Max stared down at his hands and thought deeply. Melvin Keystack's words flowed through his mind, especially his stern recommendations regarding Walter Wallace: "He is your only true friend, isn't he? He will help you decide where to begin. Make sure you listen to him. Follow his advice." It was strange that he had said that, and now here was Walter, urgently pitching a very particular course of action…

He looked up, and saw Walter toying with one of the slingshots again, pulling back the leather pouch and testing the feel of its bands.

"So," said Walter, "What do you call yourself?"

"Max."

"Unfunny. You know what I mean. What's your superhero name?"

"I'm not a superhero."

"Right, I know, but you still need a name. Have you thought of one?"

Max looked at the floor, absently scratching his forearm.

"You have! Well, come on…what is it?"

Max mumbled.

"Whatcha say?"

Max sighed. "I was thinking…the Night Bullet."

Walter frowned as if he had just smelled a backed-up toilet. " 'The Night Bullet'?! That's awful. 'The Night Bullet'?"

A look of pain crossed Max's face. "I like that one. I fight crime at night, and I have this slingshot…"

"But you don't fire bullets, do you? You fire ball bearings. You might as well call yourself 'Night Balls'. Look, Max, you have no talent—*none*—for coming up with hero names. That's obvious. Leave it to me."

Not really invested in any name, Max found his mind returning to what he considered more important topics, and now it was his turn to stand and wander. "What am I supposed to do about Molding, Walter? I'm not smart like you. I can go pick a fight with ordinary thieves and muggers seven nights a week, if I wanted, but I don't know how in the world I'm supposed to—what did you say? 'Investigate' a guy like Jondas Molding? The whole idea is way out of my league."

Walter had opened the boxes of pellets, noting the different types. "These are all non-lethal, aren't they?" He took a bright purple one out and compressed it between his thumb and forefinger. "What's inside this? Feels like gelatin."

"Basically. With a purple dye. The pellets pop open on contact with whatever I'm firing at. I mostly use them for target practice. But these here…" Max pointed to a case of greenish pellets. "These are more dense, and they don't pop open. I can just about knock a guy out if I shoot him in the head."

Walter nodded, but went back to the purple ones. "But the stuff inside these. I bet with a little ingenuity, we could drain that purple fluid out of them and fill them with something else."

"Like what?"

Walter smiled. He stood up, and began slowly pacing. His smile grew bigger. "Like water. Water blessed by a priest."

Max's face wrinkled up. "Holy water?"

"Evil spirits hate that stuff, man. It drives them crazy. If you could get close enough, and just get one good shot…blast Molding with a little holy water—then we would see. We would know. The evil spirit inside Molding will freak out."

Walter clapped his hands once in excitement, but Max just shook his head. "But <u>then</u> what would I do?"

"Well…*nothing*. Your job after that would be to run away—you'll have an army of policemen and, probably, secret service guys after you."

"What's the point?!"

"The point is that Molding will be exposed! Think about it: you hit him during the press conference, the 'gathering'—there will be cameras all over him. The whole world will be watching! Everyone will see with his or her own eyes that he really isn't the benevolent oracle everybody thinks he is! They will know his intentions are evil!"

Max stood sharply, his arms open. "But…" His hands fell limply by his side, and he breathed out in exasperation. "You don't know that he has 'evil intentions'. That's just something you suspect. Just you! No one else in the world suspects that, but somehow you're smarter than everybody in the world. This sounds crazy, and desperate. We're just shooting in the dark!"

Walter had a needle out, and was experimenting with stabbing it into one of the purple dye-filled pellets. His eyes grew suddenly wide and a new grin lit up his face.

"That's it! That's perfect!"

"What? What is?"

"*That's* your name! '*Darkshot*'!"

From a Dark Wayover

Max stared at his old friend, but again found himself unable to think of a thing to say. With his hands in his pockets, he trudged out of the room and down a short hall to the back porch. He sat on the bare cement steps, listening to the sound of the night air playing in the branches of two sycamore trees that stood nearby.

He wasn't angry. Not at Walter, anyway. Only at the overall bizarre-ness of what he was advocating. Going up against the Hitbacks was radical enough, but to extend the fight to a benign old celebrity like Molding? And yet, however uncomfortable it made him, it included the fulfillment of deep desires that only a few weeks ago he would have barely been able to articulate.

Before another hour passed, he arrived at the conclusion that Walter's ideas were sound. He didn't get there by added pressure from his friend, or even by logical progression, exactly. He simply *arrived* and, suddenly, the waving of the sycamore branches seemed almost like arboreal cheering. Max stood, feeling his natural resolve snap into place like an engine part. All that remained now was to turn the ignition.

From a Dark Wayover

Twenty-eight

The day wore on, and Leo returned to the library. He found Rinchwick sitting by the tall bay windows, pensively watching heavy clouds crawl across the sky. Ms. Winnipeg's long, slender nose was inches away from her computer screen, like a soft pointer directing her squinting, hazel eyes, but, once Leo strode in, her face relaxed and brightened. She stretched her stiff arms like a sparrow waking up from a long nap.

She gleefully explained to Leo how she had researched many subjects related to the impending mission, topics other than earthworms, but including the French Revolution, feudalism, sword-fighting, and the molecular composition of floor wax. Leo patiently waited for her to reach a pause before saying, "That's very nice, dear. What about the Louvre? Were you able to find out the best time to go?"

"Oh, right! Wednesdays. On Wednesdays, the Louvre closes off the medieval wing an hour before closing time."

"So there won't be any tourists in that area, at all! At worst, there might be a wandering security guard?"

Ms. Winnipeg smiled. "It looks that way!"

Leo gave her a loud, enthusiastic kiss. As he continued scheming with her, his eye caught a framed black and white photograph standing on a side table. It showed his father, Theodore, on a fishing trip with Mama. It was the only photo in existence that Leo knew of in which his father was smiling. Seeing it gave him a fresh idea.

"Hey, Rinchwick!"

The boy turned in his seat, looking cordially at Leo.

From a Dark Wayover

"How would you like to come with me?"

Rinchwick stared. "To get the sword?"

Leo nodded.

"Me?"

Leo nodded again, grinning.

The boy rose half out of his seat as if he was about to applaud, but quickly sat again, his face foggy with concern. "That sounds dangerous…"

"Oh, Leo," said Ms. Winnipeg. "I don't know about this…"

"It'll be good for him!"

"But won't it be dangerous?"

"Exciting, not dangerous! The Louvre just isn't ready for intruders with space warp flutes and potions that let a person pass undetected through solid objects! We can Flute there on Wednesday when nobody's around, grab the sword, and be home again in <u>ten minutes</u>! And, look: I've learned a lot these last few days about not being overprotective with the boys. I'm trying to turn over a new leaf here. Rinch'll love it! Right, Rinch?"

The boy gazed uncertainly at the clouds again, until finally he stood. Breathily, with a brittle smile, he said, "Alright. I'm ready."

"Right on! So, help me do some calculations, man. The Louvre closes at eight—we don't want to be there after that or the security system will be on. The medieval area will be closed to visitors at seven, so we should get there at about seven-fifteen p.m., their time. Paris is six hours ahead of us. What time should we leave on Wednesday?"

Rinchwick searched his mind for a few seconds. "One-fifteen. After lunch."

A sudden tremor of fear crossed Ms. Winnipeg's face, like the flitting of a bird. "What if Mealworm shows up while you're gone? Of course, it has been two days, and I'm sure he didn't survive, but…the thought of seeing him again makes my blood run cold."

"Well, we'll only be gone a few minutes. And I'll make sure the security guys are on high alert. Besides, I'm hoping that as soon as we get the sword we'll get some badly needed answers about Mealworm, and what the Corpse is up to, and why I'm involved."

Leo saw there was lingering tension on her face, and he laughed gently. "Don't worry! Rinch and I will take care of business and get home fast."

From a Dark Wayover

Twenty-nine

The next day was Tuesday. Leo was preoccupied with matters that were (compared to what he had recently experienced and what he was preparing to do) laughably prosaic, yet necessary: an appointment with a CPA to discuss family investments, and a meeting with landscapers about improvements to the eastern part of the estate, near the mill wheel.

Max and Wallace, on the other hand, had to spend their time working quickly to make all the necessary preparations for their incursion into the United Nations headquarters.

After nightfall, they climbed to the top of the Robert Moses Playground rec center, with a tightly sealed bubble-wrapped package containing Max's slingshot, his bulletproof vest, and his entire Darkshot suit. They loaded the package onto a length of highly stretchable shock cord and fired it into the sky. Soundlessly, it sailed a hundred fifty yards over 42nd Street and onto the roof over the U.N. Security Council chamber.

Walter grinned. "Spectacular! Man, wouldn't it have been stupid if we had missed? We'd have to run across the street, pick the package up off the ground, run back over here, do it all again…"

Max was ignoring his friend's prattle, a skill he had mastered many years before. *Tomorrow night is it*, he thought. *Molding's gathering.* Max stood staring at the U.N. headquarters as if it were his opponent in an impending pistol duel.

"What if they catch me?" He asked the question without trepidation. He felt resolved at this point—more than resolved, really. He felt elated, like the day after his first engagements with the criminals back in Ohio. He felt intent and focused, and now only sought the practical direction he lacked, and had always lacked, and which, he realized, was why it was so important for him to have friends like Mel Keystack and Walter Wallace.

Walter nodded. "A couple of weeks ago I was watching this YouTube video—a montage of several occasions with some guy—I don't know who, just some guy—who had his friend film him while he went around throwing pies at people. He would just go up to random people, throw a pie in their face and then run away. It was kind of funny, at first, I guess, then I just thought it was stupid and obnoxious, and the guy probably needs to get punched in the face a few times, but my point is: just pretend you're one of those kinds of people. If you get caught, I mean. A harmless practical joker, trying to get famous by shooting people with pellets full of water. (And don't tell anybody it's holy water! They'll think you're a religious nut; maybe a terrorist.) Legally, they'll probably just give you a slap on the wrist; give you some community service hours, or something. They'll put you in jail that first night, of course, but I'll call Keystack and have him bail you out. In fact, we should call him as soon as possible just to have him on standby. Sound good?"

Max nodded. "That's a good plan. Better than I could have come up with. Thanks."

Walter patted his friend's shoulder. "But the best thing to do is just don't get caught. Take your shot and leave—run to the roof, and use that rope we put in the package to go over the side. It's not very long, of course, but it will lower you maybe a third of the way down. Then, just jump. But remember to land on all fours. Not just on your feet, O.K.? Land on all fours, like a cat. That distributes your weight, and takes some of the force out of your landing. I'll be waiting on 42nd Street to pick you up. Got it?"

Max nodded once. "Got it. Anything else?"

From a Dark Wayover

There wasn't. They climbed back down, taking note of a spray-painted green scrawl on one wall of the rec center: "**Hit Back Harder!**"

They returned to Walter's apartment. They ate dinner, watched an episode of *Person of Interest*, and went to bed early.

Walter fell asleep quickly, and was snoring softly when Max got back out of bed. He stepped gingerly to a back room and closed the door. He called his older sister in San Diego and chitchatted with her for a few minutes, asking how things were going, assuring her that he was doing well. Afterwards, he called his oldest sister in Hawaii and had a very similar exchange. He ended both conversations by telling them tenderly: "I love you."

···✦·✦·✦·✦·✦·✦·✦

On Wednesday morning, Leo woke early. Breakfast was the usual epic event, in the colossal dining hall that had been added to the mansion a year ago, and the amount of milk used for cereal could have filled a swimming pool. There was no school that day, so the boys spent their time fanning out across the estate, exploring, kicking soccer balls at each other, risking their lives, and all the other things that young boys do. About an hour before lunch, Rinchwick met Leo, as planned, in the upstairs den, carrying a small, pale green backpack.

None of the other boys were allowed to visit the den at this time. Anselm brought in sandwiches, on the highly polished silver tray he always insisted on using. Leo wore tan cargo trousers; in one of the big side pockets he put the *Subtility*; *Instant Jungle* in the other.

He and Rinchwick talked casually about Paris, and what people ate there, and what the weather was like this time of year. The boy looked excited, and Leo was pleased to see that. He loved him, he realized. Of course, he knew that already, but the feeling filled his heart anew.

He just wanted the boy to be at peace, and to know that Leo would always be his devoted Dad.

A clock on the mantle ticked like the marching of a toy soldier. As it neared 1:15 P.M. Eastern Standard Time, Leo gave Rinchwick a mischievous look, and the boy, grinning in response, whispered, "It's time!"

Leo took out his pennywhistle-shaped Flute, and began to play.

···✦·✦·✦·✦·✦·✦·✦

At roughly the same time, Walter dropped Max off near the corner of 1st Avenue and 45th Street, so he could purchase a U.N. pass.

"I was thinking," Max said as he got out of the car. "I don't want you to pick me up when I'm done. If they pursue me, they'll see the car, and they'll be able to catch us. We don't want to be in a car chase with the NYPD and the Secret Service and all those guys."

From a Dark Wayover

A guilty look crossed Walter's face. "I thought of that, actually, but I didn't want to say it. I didn't want you to have to do this whole thing alone."

Max smiled. "I know. You're a good friend. But I stand a better chance of getting away on my own, if I stick to the shadows and keep my head down."

Walter sighed and was about to say something, when a car behind them honked impatiently. He turned and made a troll-face at the driver through the window, shouting incoherently.

Turning back to Max, he said gravely, "So this is it, then. After this, you won't have any way of communicating with me. You'll be on your own."

"I know." Max shook his friend's hand. "I'm ready. Don't worry about me."

He turned to go, but Walter gave a low shout that made Max halt just before closing the car door.

"I'll say a prayer for you."

Max looked slightly surprised. "Thanks. I mean…I don't know how much I buy in to all that. And, as for this evil spirit stuff: I don't know how I feel about that, either. I don't really believe in the Devil."

The car waiting behind them honked again, with one long, furious blast. Walter grimaced. "Isn't this guy behind us proof enough?"

Max laughed. "Well, that's just it. Humans are bad enough without needing a devil to take credit."

"Why are you doing this, then?"

Max shrugged. "Because I believe in you."

Walter tilted his head to the side as if he was a teenage girl. "Awwww, that's beautiful, man. Big hug?" He leaned towards Max expectantly.

Max laughed and slammed the door, as the car waiting for them honked a third time, with extra fury. Walter drove off with a squeal of his tires, giving his best

From a Dark Wayover

friend a hammy yet sincere salute, and the driver behind them a cartoonish shake of his fist.

Thirty

By three o'clock the General Assembly Hall was filling up quickly. Molding had been clear that this event was not intended merely for journalists, but for all people: first come, first serve. Even so, the place was teeming with photographers and news cameramen. Some of the U.N.'s security personnel were plainly agitated: Jondas Molding's hasty "gathering" presented a challenge for them that was almost unmanageable.

The increased rush of human traffic made it easier for Max to dodge away from his tour group. He followed a flight of stairs to the top floor, and located an emergency exit. A sign on the wall read "rooftop access," which was exactly what Max wanted: his bubble-wrapped bag of clothing and equipment was waiting for him on the roof. The problem was that the door would, of course, set off alarms if opened.

He was prepared for that. In his left shoe were a couple of strips of thick, heavily adhesive duct tape. Thinking that a tiny trigger would be what would trip the alarm if the door were opened, Walter had told him: "Just slip the tape over the trigger. Stick it so it keeps the trigger held down. That way, once you open the door, the trigger stays depressed and the alarm won't go off. It's simple!"

Slipping the tape out of his shoe, Max closely scrutinized the point where the door met the trigger mechanism. He grunted. There was no trigger.

"If you don't see a trigger," he remembered Walter saying, "Then it's probably electromagnetic. Just stick your magnet onto the little metal assembly inside the doorjamb."

From a Dark Wayover

The magnet was in Max's other shoe, per Walter's instructions, inside the rubber lining and thus safe from security devices. It was something called a 'rare earth' magnet, Walter had explained, otherwise known as neodymium, and was significantly more powerful than the average refrigerator magnet. Walter had found out about them years ago and ordered a set online, but, until now, he had simply regarded them as novelties.

"Once you stick the magnet on, the door will always think it's shut, so to speak. It's simple!"

"What if," Max had asked cautiously, "the door doesn't have a trigger or a magnet?"

"It will have one or the other, you'll see. But if it doesn't, then…give it up. Walk out of there. We'll think of another way to expose Molding."

Max thought carefully about the third option, because he didn't see any magnets on the door. There was a small metal box on the doorjamb, painted the same as the rest of the door, but he could not be at all certain if it was electromagnetic. It just looked like a metal box.

He took the silvery, rectangular magnet out of his right shoe. He held it near the box inside the doorjamb, and it virtually launched from his hand and sealed itself to the metal with a ponderous clonk.

It isn't too late, Max could almost hear Walter saying. *Walk out of there. We'll think of another way to expose Molding.*

But how? When would another chance like this offer itself to an average joe like Max?

Max gritted his teeth and pushed against the door. It clicked loudly and swung open. The sounds of the city's nonstop bus hums and car noise fluttered into the stairwell on chilly breezes, but no alarm sounded.

He couldn't entirely discount the possibility that a silent alarm had been tripped, but the neodymium seemed to have been effective. Max held the door ajar with a thick, black chunk of loose roofing tar he found, and then went in search of his equipment.

He had an abrupt foreboding of a disastrous encounter with U.N. security trolling the rooftop, but he forced it out of his imagination. Lights glowed at him from across the East River as he followed the darkest shadows under the forbidding, glassy stare of the Secretariat Building.

His bubble-wrapped pack of equipment ended up being right where it had landed the night before. As he began to peel it apart, he glanced at his watch: 6:37. Twenty-three minutes until Molding's presentation began. He frowned; he was running behind schedule.

Grabbing the length of rope that he and Walter had stowed in the package, he tied it securely to an exposed pipe near the edge of the roof, so it would be ready for him to make a swift escape. Next, he quickly doffed his civilian clothes and shoved himself into his black Darkshot suit with its various pieces of armor, including the bulletproof vest. He pulled the hood on last. On his way back to the door he double-checked the pellets in his slingshot handle, just to make sure they had not ruptured. He was relieved to see that they were all intact.

He re-entered the stairwell, closing the door behind him. He snatched another look at his watch: 6:49.

He bounded lightly down the stairs and ran in the direction of the General Assembly, recalling Walter's words:

"A friend of mine and I toured the U.N. building a couple of years ago, and he showed me a spot where workers can access the light bulbs for the dome. It's not the main access; kind of an old back up from when they first built the place, back in 1949. It's just a little panel, covered by a metal grill, which is fastened down by screws. Four phillip's head screws—that's it! It's simple!"

With that in mind, they included a screwdriver with the equipment they had launched onto the roof, and Max brandished it now as he knelt beside the access panel.

He had only taken out two screws when he heard the buzz of a walkie-talkie.

A security officer. Around the nearest corner, somewhere down the hall. Coming closer.

Max couldn't be sure how rapidly the officer was approaching. He spun his screwdriver as fast and yet as quietly as he could. It turned stubbornly, and sweat began to ooze from Max's forehead.

"…Wow, that's a tough break, no doubt about it…"

The officer's voice was dull; he was just a working man making a round he had made many times before, chatting lazily on his walkie-talkie with a fellow officer somewhere else who was, no doubt, following the same kind of routine. He had not turned the corner yet, but by the sound of his voice Max knew that it wouldn't be more than a few seconds before he would appear.

The third screw tumbled out and Max went to work on the final one with a silent frenzy.

He could now hear the padding of the officer's shoes on the soft, clean, multicolored hallway carpet.

"…well, yeah, that's exactly what I told him, but he never listens to nobody, least of all me…"

The fourth screw stuck. Max twisted his screwdriver with all his strength and got it going again, but it was still only halfway out. He reached down and fumbled with his slingshot…*can't use what's loaded!* They're only filled with holy water, meant to pop open on contact…

A pouch against his hip held a few of his 3/8 inch lead ball bearings. *Too powerful! They'll kill him! No choice, out of time*…He snatched one out, just as the security officer rounded the corner.

He was a tall man, in his late forties, with thinning blond hair and pale skin, except for an unhealthy redness around his cheeks and nose. A heavy paunch lay over his belt. For a second he stared numbly at Max, holding his walkie-talkie near his chin. He dropped one hand to the grip of his pistol…

"Don't!" Max had the tubes of his slingshot stretched back and the round, silvery b.b. aimed at the man's head.

There was no way to explain, exactly, why the security officer did what he did next. He didn't simply surrender, nor did he draw his pistol. Instead, he turned clumsily and began trotting back in the direction he had come.

Max dashed forward, rolling like a gymnast, and put himself into a firing position just as the officer pushed the button on his walkie-talkie and began to say, "Hey, we got a problem here on 4th Floor—code red! Code red! White male in a black suit, armed with a slingshot. Request immediate backup!"

He did not actually say it, though. Only "Hey, we got…" escaped his mouth before a lead ball bearing glanced off the side of his head and sent him sprawling to the ground.

Max felt cold. His muscles were weak and rubbery. This was the first time he had ever attacked an innocent person before. He recognized that it had been necessary, but he despised the feeling.

Kneeling down, he anxiously felt the officer's neck for a pulse. When his fingers detected the slow rhythmic gush of blood, he breathed a sigh of relief. He had purposely aimed at the edge of the man's skull, intending only to stun him, but it was, after all, a lead ball bearing traveling over two hundred feet per second.

What if his aim had been off? One inch to the left could have killed the man, an innocent man, and the very kind of person Max had come here to defend against Hitback violence...

Max was jolted out of his self-chastisement when the walkie-talkie, lying on the floor in front of him, crackled and spit out words: "Paulson, you there? Didn't catch that last part. Say again?"

Max grabbed the device and pushed down the black button on the side. He was terrible at imitating people, but he knew that it wouldn't matter much on a walkie-talkie. He lowered his voice to sound more like Paulson, and said, "Sorry—disregard. Thought I saw something. All clear."

Suddenly Paulson groaned and moved his arm.

He's waking up! Max buried his face in his palm, desperately trying to think of how to incapacitate the unfortunate Mr. Paulson.

From a Dark Wayover

Seconds later, he was dragging him towards the wall. This part of the hallway was lit by a series of electric sconce lamps with smooth stems that looped like branches. Max took Paulson's handcuffs and fed them through one lamp's loop, locking them tightly around the big man's wrists.

Max ran, leaving Paulson in a sitting position against the wall with his arms stretched over his head and his mouth covered by duct tape. The man was still unconscious, more or less, but it would not be long before he woke up. The lamp would not hold him, surely; it would not be difficult for a man of his size to rip it out of the wall.

Removing the fourth and final screw with a few quick turns of his screwdriver, Max pulled off the metal grill at last and set it aside. The panel beneath it pulled loose easily, revealing a dark chute, into which he slipped like a black eel.

From a Dark Wayover

He pulled an elastic band around his hand that was fitted with a flashlight that sat comfortably on top of his knuckles. As he crawled forward through the dark passageway, the flashlight beam shone from his hand, but his fingers were free.

The air was dank. Webs brushed his eyelids. The walls and floor of the chute were metallic, allowing him to slide on his chest with relative ease, pushing aside bits of ancient construction materials and dead roaches.

Ahead of him, he discerned a yellowish glow. Careful to not let his limbs bang against the walls of the passageway, he slithered closer and closer towards the light. He could hear a voice: muffled, at first, but as it became clearer he realized that it belonged to Jondas Molding.

The ceiling suddenly dipped down, and Max had to push to squeeze himself past. The chute made a ninety-degree turn. He passed under some kind of rubbery flap and onto a ledge, very nearly crawling right off of it and into the middle of the General Assembly room.

His arms grabbed at the walls and he recoiled. With his heart racing, he peeked over the ledge. The huge, dark blue dome was above him, and the room's floor was over three stories below. Blazing golden light, with vibrant crimsons, taupes and the U.N.'s signature blue, and chilly currents of fresh air conditioning all formed a cold soup in which floated many hundreds of people of every race and profession.

They listened raptly to Jondas Molding, who stood at the podium on the stage. He wore a glossy blue and red khalat. Midnight-colored, death's head circles stained the bags and wrinkles beneath his eyes. His hair was thin but sat high upon his head, and it reminded Max of the white, feathery fungus that grows inside jack-o-lanterns that have been left outside too long. Behind the

From a Dark Wayover

Visionary, to his left and right, were two large television screens displaying him in gigantic proportions, with the result being a trinity of Moldings all speaking amplified words that captivated his audience:

"…though I am reclusive, it's true, I have always felt that my gifts ought to be at the service of you, the good people of the world, rather than for my own benefit, and I have acted accordingly…"

Crouching behind one of the huge spotlights that ran along the ledge of the dome like a crown of stars, Max stared at Molding. Such an old, old man, wrinkled and bent and white as a bone…

"…Yet I must admit that, these past months, I have been feeling the limits of my abilities. I am not the spry young eighty-two year old I used to be!"

Laughter bubbled out of his audience.

"Besides that, as you may have heard, I have been diagnosed with myeloma, a cancer of my blood's plasma cells. It's slowly breaking me down, and my immune system isn't much to speak of!" He held up his hands, showing his gray, padded gloves. "It's even gotten into my bone marrow. The pain it causes comes and goes, but it goes less often these days."

There were half-smiles at his play on words, mixed with looks of sympathy.

"On top of everything, we now have these new radical terrorists threatening our way of life—and nowhere more than right here in New York City, unfortunately!"

The crowd filling the General Assembly room broke out in low 'boos' and snarls.

"I see some of their more nefarious plots before they happen, but I certainly do not have the power to see them all! There are many of you here—or you have friends or family—that have been the victims of Hitback violence. Consider this Hit Back Harder Society: they call themselves a 'society,' and yet they are opposed to everything that has to do with a legitimate society. They are so consumed by selfishness, that I do not doubt that they will eventually bring about major calamities; fiery disasters in the world's great cities. Yes, including this one. We all seem helpless to stop it. Even me! But now, my good people, we have reached a turning point. We have a hero now…"

There was a smattering of applause as some of his listeners began to realize whom he was referring to.

"…From out of a storybook, it seems, he has flown! Invictus! When I see him in action, it seems to me as if the universe has brought us the singularly perfect response to the Hitbacks. That, as you may have suspected, is why I insisted on meeting him last month in Washington…"

Molding continued his oration, with no notes, and no teleprompter, speaking with such warmth and charm that every individual in the room had the sense that the Visionary was speaking intimately to them. The entire audience was now a pastiche of cheerful and optimistic faces, yet that very fact brought to Max's mind the disturbing images from Walter's dream. Indeed, everything had become as Walter had described: Jondas at the podium, the blissful audience, the dramatic statements about Invictus and the Hitbacks. More upsetting were Molding's frequent smiles. Max now saw in them what Walter had seen: there was something in them that had nothing to do with a smile, something warped and vicious.

No one in the room perceived it, at least no one seemed to. They displayed only untainted trust. This was Jondas Molding; he was better than them, special, gifted, wise, far-seeing. He had once foretold the assassination of the premier of Yemen, and it was prevented. Arnold Keck—the U.S. president in office prior to Holloway—

would have lost his twenty-one year old daughter to an avalanche in the Rockies, the weekend she was on a skiing trip; the avalanche happened, killing five people, but President Keck's daughter was not among the victims because he had made sure to keep her home that day. NASA had delayed the launch of the latest Juno mission to Jupiter because Molding told them that a faulty circuit would cause an explosion and kill everyone aboard. Engineers investigated and discovered that Molding's vision was completely accurate.

    These were some of the confirmed and internationally famous events. Besides them, unverified legends abounded about individuals who went to him for information on the rise or fall of stocks; with perfect precision, it was said, he gave them what they sought, and they grew fantastically wealthy overnight. Such stories also took less grand forms: a mother in Colorado claimed that Molding had personally called her late one night to warn her that her infant son was about to choke to death in his crib, and when she went to check on him, he had a wad of yarn lodged in his mouth and would indeed have died if not for her mother's immediate intervention. In another case, a teenage girl in Belgium assured all her friends that Molding had appeared to her in a dream, and that was how she knew not to let her best friend drive her to school. That same friend died in a car accident the next day.

Most everyone knew almost without a doubt that Jondas Molding was here on earth to guide them, to save them. Whatever he was about to reveal tonight, they knew they wanted to be a part of it.

Max felt their zeal from his dark, lofty perch on the platform behind the lights. And, somehow, he felt Molding drinking it all in, inhaling it the way an obese child breathes in the smell of cakes and pies. But did any of this mean that Walter was right? Was there really some kind of spiritual entity involved with Molding and, through him, bringing about a terrible evil?

Frowning, Max dispensed a pellet. He looked at it in the palm of his hand. He looked back down at Molding, feeling his confidence in Walter's plan beginning to vaporize.

Just an old man. Not a monster. A man, trying to make a difference in the world. Wasn't he, then, just like Max, really? Someone who wanted to defend people from undue harm? Look: there was his assistant, standing off to one side of the stage. Max had read about her. What was her name? Magán. Jyha Magán. Molding had found her in Asia somewhere, abandoned and alone, and he had adopted her. Now look at her: grown up, and completely loyal to her heroic foster-father. Could Molding do a thing like that and also be possessed by an evil spirit, like Walter had said?

From a Dark Wayover

"I have called this gathering to bring great news to all the world. For there is something coming. Something worse than the Hitbacks, and yet something the Hitbacks will no doubt look to with perverse excitement. I have seen it, my good people! It is coming. I have seen it with my sight that sees what my eyes never could. I will tell you what it is—in a moment! But first, I wish to say: do not be afraid! What I have seen is a great calamity…"

People grew agitated and began glancing back and forth at each other and murmuring.

"…a calamity that threatens our entire planet! But I have also seen our salvation! This story ends not in tears, my good people, but in triumph!"

He paused and let his words sink in. Everyone waited, concerned, curious, hopeful, and terrified all at the same time.

From a Dark Wayover

"I have already made known this newest vision to the president of the United States. He will make a televised announcement from Washington, D.C. immediately following my presentation here. He will talk of specifics and practical measures, and afterwards discuss the situation with other leaders of our world. But we decided that first it should be me—me, your Jondas Molding—who announces it. For you know that I would never lie to you. You know I only want what is best for you. So, when I tell you of my vision, you know it is real, and reliable, isn't that right, my good people?"

Everyone nodded earnestly, but their heads seemed almost ready to pop off of their necks, so enthralled were they with whatever Molding was going to announce.

Along with everyone else, including everybody watching via television and satellite, Max listened carefully...

From a Dark Wayover

A huge comet, hurtling through space, on a collision course with Earth. Two mysterious heroes would rise to stop it. The first would not succeed, but the second most certainly would. Molding had seen it all in his mind's eye, and it had manifested itself in the living tissue of his skin…

Messages in his skin…

Max recalled Walter, sternly insisting on the demonic implications of such phenomenon. Even before Max's visit to New York, back in Ohio, the skin visions had been one of the early warning signs for Walter that Molding's seeming benevolence was a false veneer.

Max loaded the holy water pellet in the pouch of his slingshot. He pulled back the tubes until they made a rubbery, straining sound.

He stared into the eyes of the Moldings on the two giant screens behind the podium. He thought again of Walter's dream, and of his friend's agitated descriptions of Molding's eyes…now Max could see it, too. From them something peeked out, like the glitter of liquid poison. It was as if murder was an electric charge closing a circuit through Molding along the dull copper irises of his eyes…

"You're meant to do something about Jondas Molding, Max," Walter had said. "I know it. That's what's going on right now. Whatever Molding is up to, it must be the very definition of injustice…"

"Why are you doing this?" He'd asked Max earlier. "Because I believe in you," Max had replied.

"He is your only true friend, isn't he? Make sure you listen to him. Follow his advice."

Max fired.

During the split second it took his bullet to travel down to the stage, it seemed as if all the air was sucked out of the space around Max. Upon impact, Molding winced sharply and snapped his eyes shut. A woman near the front of the stage screamed, and several other people gasped. Magán and some security guards hurried from the rear of the stage.

Max waited and watched. Molding gritted his snaggle teeth and rubbed water out of his thin, coarse eyebrows, but these were only what anyone would do after being blasted with a pellet of water. There was no sign of a supernatural effect.

Molding, without opening his eyes or looking up, raised his blue and red sleeved arm and pointed one cadaverous finger at the exact light behind which Max was crouched.

Not waiting for anyone to follow the seer's direction, Max lunged for the narrow passageway from which he had come and crawled as fast as he could.

Everyone shouted when Invictus suddenly emerged from behind a curtain, his golden helmet and cape glittering under the lights. He rushed forward to see what was the matter with Molding.

"I've been attacked, my good people," Molding announced blithely. "And, see? It has spoiled my surprise for you. Yes, Invictus is here! I just told you a comet will soon smash into the earth, but didn't I also promise salvation? And that salvation is Invictus! I asked him to come, and he graciously accepted my invitation…"

Everyone began cautiously cheering.

"For it is Invictus who will stop the comet! But, first, I think, there is a somewhat more trivial chore for him and all of you good security folk to attend to. There is a man running loose here, shooting small orbs of water at people—ha! Of all things! Invictus, my friend, would you be so good as to apprehend him? For safety's sake. You will find him on the uppermost floor…"

From a Dark Wayover

Invictus stepped off the edge of the stage and soared through the air towards the room's main exit, with a throng of security officers scrambling to catch up.

Thirty-one

When Max emerged from the passageway into the fourth floor hallway, he found that Paulson had fully awakened. As expected, he had torn the sconce lamp out of the wall, and was holding it in both hands, trying to unlock the handcuffs. Max hurtled past him, easily evading him when he screamed incoherently and tried to swipe at him, lamp and all.

Max loped up the stairs and threw open the rooftop door. Slamming it shut behind him, he looked around for something to prop against it, but found only two half empty tubs of old roofing tar. He hastily rolled them in front of the door and then sprinted for the spot at the edge of the roof where he had tied off his escape rope.

From a Dark Wayover

He heard the door open again behind him, but even without looking Max knew instantly that it wasn't security officers in pursuit. It sounded as if someone had driven a bullet train through the door; metal ripped off of hinges, bolts whirled, and the door itself skidded like a surfboard across the roof, off the edge, and into the East River.

Without slowing down, Max turned to see Invictus hovering in the air, his golden helmet swiveling side to side as he searched for Molding's attacker.

With his heart leaping inside his chest, Max ran for the edge of the building. He snatched up his rope, ready to charge down the wall like a spider on a web.

Before he could make another move, arms as hard as asphalt engulfed him. The rope whisked out of his grip as he felt himself carried high above 42nd Street.

Invictus halted in midflight, holding Max with one hand by the front of his bulletproof vest. Although

From a Dark Wayover

they were hidden behind a faintly luminescent visor, Max felt certain that the superhero's eyes were crackling with indignation.

"You're done," growled Invictus. He shook his head and smirked. "Another Hitback lowlife! And attacking Jondas Molding, of all people. Despicable…"

He swirled, about to return to the U.N., when Max cried, "Wait! I'm not a Hitback! I'm trying to *stop* the Hitbacks!"

Invictus paused, his stern expression betraying a faint curiosity.

"Conrad! Don't you recognize me? Look, it's me! It's me: Max!"

Invictus used his free hand to snatch off Max's black hood.

"Max…Bosco?! What are you doing…you're a Hitback?!"

From a Dark Wayover

"No, of course not! I told you: I'm trying to *stop* the Hitbacks!"

The sound of shouting and stomping shoes drew their attention. Security personnel of various kinds were spilling out of the smashed rooftop doorway. They had not yet spotted Invictus and Max floating in the sky over the rushing 42nd Street traffic.

Conrad looked back at Max, scowling, but undecided about what he ought to do next.

"Please, Conrad," Max implored. "Just hear me out!"

Frustrated, the helmeted champion spewed a breath of air. With Max in tow, he skimmed like a firework across the street to the rooftop of the Robert Moses rec center.

He set Max down with no more effort that a normal person would use to stand a broom against a wall. He rested his bare knuckles against his hips and stared impassively, his glistening cape shifting in the night breezes.

"Explain, Max. What are you doing? Why did you attack Jondas? And with a slingshot…?"

"But not using ball bearings! It was just a low-density pellet with a breakable casing. It was filled with…" He almost said 'holy water', but suddenly remembered Walter's staunch instructions not to tell anyone that. "With water. I have a strict policy against shooting non-criminals…"

"Tell that to the security officer I met in the hallway! He has a lump on his head the size of a golf ball."

"Yes, yes, but that was the first time I've ever had to do that! I normally go after Hitbacks…you know, like you do…" Max's voice quavered.

"Like I do? Max…are you telling me that you've become some kind of vigilante? With these elbow pads and dark clothes and a slingshot?"

Max suddenly felt a rush of embarrassment, but his fists balled up defensively. "It's just something I thought I should try. I wanted to make a difference…"

Conrad sneered. "Well, you're certainly making a big difference! Congratulations! Just to satisfy my curiosity, explain how you expected to make a difference by assaulting Jondas Molding?"

"He's the leader of the Hitbacks." Max said it almost without realizing it, but once the words were out he understood how preposterous they sounded. Conrad turned away, holding his face in his hands and groaning.

"I *think* so, anyway," Max continued. "Walter and I…"

"Walter?!" Conrad whirled to face him again. "Walter Wallace?! You two are in on this together?!"

From a Dark Wayover

Max stood straight, unwilling to admit a flaw in his position, yet inwardly mortified. "Walter had a dream about Molding, and in it…"

"A *dream*?!" Conrad sped at Max, crossing the distance between them in an instant. Pressing the gilded letter 'I' that was embossed over the visor of his helmet close to Max's forehead, it was clear that he had ceased being Conrad from high school and was now Invictus, the cold and noble demigod.

"Listen to me now: Jondas Molding is an extraordinarily gifted man. I, also, have received gifts…power like no man has ever had! Max, I don't know why he and I were blessed with such abilities and other people, people like you, were not. But get it into your head, Max: you are not a hero! You are a regular, ordinary nobody—and that's alright! Don't let that depress you! It's normal! Just live your life. Be happy. Stop wasting your time trying to be like me. Because that's really what this is all about, isn't it? You and Walter went to high school with me, watched me turn into what I am…and you just wanted a little piece of my life." He emphasized "little piece of my life" by holding up his gloved fingers and pinching his thumb and forefinger together as if he was crushing a moth. "And I understand. Most people want that. But it's just not possible, Max. Most people are not born to be great. I am. But you aren't. " He turned and walked away. "You need to go live your life. Put away these ridiculous conspiracy theories and leave the heroics to the ones destiny has chosen."

Max's fists stayed clenched, but now he stared down at his shoes.

Invictus turned towards him. His voice became softer. "That was harsh, I know. But it needed to be said. Look, Max: I'm not going to turn you into the authorities. I won't tell them about you, and I'll tell everybody to let this whole stupid incident go. But this has to end right now. You're still living in Cincinnati, right?"

Max nodded.

"Go back. Stay there. I don't ever want to see you in New York again, understand?"

Max said nothing. Invictus nearly spoke again, but dismissed his thoughts with a slight shake of his head. He launched into the night sky, making the air whisper around him, and was gone.

Cold air blew in eddies among the A.C. units and ventilation pipes of the rec center rooftop. Distant sirens blended with the city's usual traffic noises, as emergency vehicles reported to the U.N. building across the street. Max felt no concern for them; he knew that Conrad would be true to his word. Instead, he just stood there, with shame and disappointment filling up his heart.

From a Dark Wayover

The holy water had no effect on Molding. He wasn't possessed by the devil…of course not! What an idiotic theory! And the leader of the Hitbacks? How likely was that? How could he be the secret leader of an organization dedicated to disrupting society and at the same time be doing all in his power to save society from cosmic destruction? A comet! A comet flying right towards them, and here Max was shooting pellets at the only person on earth with a plan to save everybody!

Invictus was right. Max had no business fighting Hitbacks, for the simple reason that he had nothing to offer. No powers. No skills. He was just a delusional, pathetic vigilante, as dangerous, in many ways, as the very criminals who so offended him.

A flock of pigeons settled near Max with a singsong fluttering of wings. Max had not moved for some time, so they did not realize he was there. He watched them out of the corner of his eyes, as they bobbed their heads and pecked at the surface of the roof and clucked among themselves. *That's my life*, Max thought. *I'm just not meant to do anything different with my existence than what these flipping pigeons are doing.*

All of sudden, the birds took flight. They left in a frantic rush, dropping feathers as they went.

Max realized that they had reacted to movements on the far side of the rooftop. A dark orange-clad figure was slowly materializing out of the darkness.

Max almost fled, but an odd curiosity held him. "Who are you?"

The figure drew within twenty yards and stopped. Max recognized the flowing dress, and the glossy dark hair hanging about the shoulders like oil…

"Jyha Magán…" Max felt a rise of anxiety, thinking that his pursuers had tracked him down, or even perhaps that Conrad had changed his mind about not turning him in. He bent his knees, ready to spring away.

"Stay." Magán's voice was impassive, lilting, and compelling. "I am alone."

"What do you want?"

"Invictus and you were talking. I did not hear what you were discussing, but he left you here, without taking you into custody. I find that quite interesting. Are you the one called 'Leo'?"

"Who?"

"Is your name 'Leo'? 'Leopold Von Koppersmith' ?"

"Look, lady, I'm just a nobody. I'm no threat to Jondas or anyone else, and Invictus knows it. That's why he let me go. So, if it's all the same to you, I'd like to get going now…"

"But, if you are not the one called 'Leo', then why did you do what you did to Jondas Molding?"

Magán took a few steps closer.

Max exhaled. "I don't want to go over all that again. I had a theory, but it was wrong…"

"What theory?"

Max laughed bitterly, waving off the question, and he began to walk towards a fire escape.

"Please!" Magán's voice suddenly sounded pitiful, and it made Max hesitate. "Like Invictus, I have no intention of turning you over to the police. I just want…information."

Max relented. "It's stupid, but you asked for it: I thought Jondas might be involved with the Hitbacks. Maybe even their leader or something. Satisfied?" He continued walking.

"Why did you think that?" The temporary pitiful tone was absent again from Magán's voice. She began moving with long, confident strides towards a position that put her between Max and the fire escape.

Max was now beginning to feel irritated.

"Because it seemed right, to me and a friend of mine…"

"A friend? There are others who think this?"

Max snorted. "What…?"

"Do you belong to some sort of organization?"

"O.K. that's enough." Max chuckled and walked more briskly, but Magán only matched his movements, not closing the distance between them, but more fully blocking the fire escape.

"Jondas Molding will not tolerate your actions. All attacks will be met with uncompromising retaliation." Magán reached up from the folds of her tangerine-colored gown and revealed her white, synthetic hand. The tendril fingers reached out and snaked into her black tresses, while at the same time a rubbery lid opened up on her forearm, revealing a narrow compartment. Aghast, Max watched as the pale tentacles loosened and then removed Magán's hair and deftly stuffed it into her forearm compartment. With her other, human hand, she removed the top section of her orange gown, revealing thin, muscular arms, and giving the dress the look of a ceremonial garb belonging to an ancient Asian warrior.

Max could hardly believe what he was witnessing: Jhya Magán now had a smooth, round, tan head. More significantly, with the top of the dress gone, the front of Magán's neck showed a small lump of an Adam's apple.

Max stared in shock. "You're a man!"

Jyha Magán crouched slightly, like a wolf preparing to leap. "I am whatever Jondas Molding needs me to be."

There was a small, sinister ringing of metal as a five inch blade emerged from the palm of Magán's white hand.

Max found himself almost tearing at his hip pocket to grab a ball bearing and load it into the pouch of his slingshot, but Jyha was upon him before he could take aim.

Somehow he lifted his arm and managed to block Magán's blade with the slingshot's metal wrist brace. For an instant the two weapons were locked together, but Magán withdrew, leapt, and executed a perfect roundhouse kick to Max's chest, driving him several feet backwards across the gravelly rooftop.

Max's vest had protected him from most of the shock of the attack. He had even been able to keep his ball bearing loaded, so he stretched back the tubes and fired.

He had been unwilling to shoot with full force, but his accuracy was flawless. The projectile caught Magán on the cheek. Without waiting to gauge the amount of damage caused, Max ran, and at the same time dropped his magazine and filled it with the rest of his bullets. Clicking it back into its place in the slingshot's handle, he dispensed another ball bearing and loaded it.

As he turned to fire, Magán, bleeding from the mouth and overcome with silent fury, rushed upon him and jabbed him repeatedly with his blade—twice to the stomach, twice to the chest—before he realized that Max was wearing body armor.

The ball bearing he had loaded had fallen to the ground, so Max slammed his fist into Magán's side. The strange, slender man let out a grunt of pain, which quickly became a snarl of rage. He stabbed at Max's face, but Max caught the pliant, white wrist and held it firmly.

The two men stood in place, grappling, holding one another's arms, but it became clear that Max was the stronger one. Magán opened his mouth wide and let out a disturbing shriek, like a vulture's, and suddenly one of the serpentine appendages on his synthetic hand slithered towards Max's face and up one nostril. Max felt it wriggling deep into his nasal cavity, shoving it's way in as far as it could go. He howled and threw Jyha off of him.

All at once a blaze of light fell upon the rooftop, momentarily blinding Max. There was a tornado of whirling rotors, and an amplified voice commanded submission in the name of the NYPD. Max shielded his eyes from the roving spotlight and searched for his enemy, but he could see that he was now alone on the rooftop.

He sped to the fire escape. The police helicopter followed, trying to keep its light on him as he clambered to the ground. He managed to find some protective shadows for a few seconds, until the light found him again.

"Stay where you are," the voice shouted. "Stay where you are or you will be fired upon…"

From a Dark Wayover

Max rolled into another patch of shadows under a grove of trees. The light came looking again, but when it found him, he already had his slingshot aimed.

He fired, and the missile smashed into the spotlight, extinguishing it with a spray of sparks and shattered glass.

The helicopter retreated a few yards, then swept back again, but Max was now deep under the cover of darkness, running at top speed down trash-littered alleys, into tunnels, even onto the side of a passing sanitation truck. By the time patrol cars, searching for Jondas Molding's assailant, arrived at the Robert Moses playground, it was too late for them to do much of anything other than put out a general call for an unknown man in black, a man who could be anyone, and who seemed to have disappeared altogether.

From a Dark Wayover

Thirty-two

Paris, France, 7:17 PM CEST…

On the first floor of the Richelieu wing, the entrances to the Medieval Decorative arts area had thick, red velvet ropes blocking them. All was dark, except for a few soft track lights. Sometimes the murmur of a distant voice or a sneeze or a scuffing shoe rippled lightly down the corridors from Greek, Etruscan and Roman Antiquities or up from the ground floor halls that paralleled the great glass entrance pyramid, but otherwise this region of the Louvre was currently as quiet as a crypt.

Leo did not know why, but he had no clear memories of the Medieval section, much less of Joyeuse. He supposed it was simply because, back when he first visited the Louvre, he had little interest in the medieval period. Fortunately, the Renaissance section was just around the corner, and of that area his recollections were quite lucid.

So it was that, among lavish furniture and images of pudgy cherubs flitting along the sides of tall vases, and the scarlets, cobalts and golds of exquisite tapestries, a patch of open space quivered like a sheet of glass in a gale. Air spilled through a mid-air portal, which widened quickly until it was as big and round as a dining table. From the opening's dark interior, Leo cautiously stuck out his head.

Seeing no one, he stepped lightly into the museum, holding Rinchwick by the hand.

The portal closed behind them with its usual slurping sound, and Leo returned the Flute to his pack. He took a few seconds to get his bearings, looking closely at the map of the Richelieu wing that Ms. Winnipeg had drawn up for him:

From a Dark Wayover

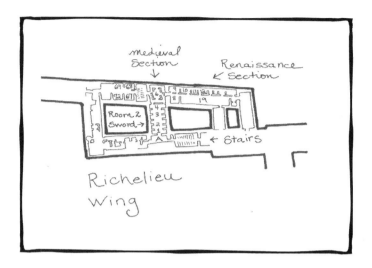

Figure 1. Ms. Winnipeg's Map of the Louvre.

Rinchwick, staring in wonder at the masterpieces surrounding them, gasped involuntarily.

Leo looked at him and smiled. "It's something, isn't it? Too bad we can't look around. I'll bring you back one day, O.K.? For now, we better get moving. The sword is this way. Are you ready to go get it?"

The boy's eyes glimmered and he nodded.

"O.K.! Come on, then! Stealing a priceless artifact has never been so fun…"

From a Dark Wayover

" 'Borrowing'…"

" 'Borrowing,' right…"

They left the Renaissance area and moved roughly west through a short, narrow hall. As if traveling through time itself, they immediately found themselves surrounded by the august craftwork of the Middle Ages. Turning south, they followed a series of open rooms, slipping past grim helmets that stared like iron skulls; past twisting coats of arms, French regalia and cold, gleaming jewelry.

Leo kept an eye on his map, looking for what was labeled as 'Room 2'. At the same time, glancing over his shoulder and to his right and left, he listened carefully for wandering Louvre officials. The only sounds he heard were his and Rinchwick's own whispery footfalls.

At last, they found what they had come for, where the walls were lined with ancient croziers, crowns and crucifixes. Joyeuse was displayed in the center of the

From a Dark Wayover

room, in the all-glass case Leo had, up to this point, only seen in photographs.

He was briefly mesmerized by its magnificence. The shining gold cross-guards were shaped like two winged dragons, and a diamond pattern covered the hilt until it reached a round, radish-sized pommel adorned with Nordic-looking swirls and wing shapes. The entire handle was raised on translucent plastic stems, so that the long, silvery white blade pointed downwards at an angle.

Leo and Rinchwick, blinking as they emerged from their brief captivation, silently retrieved the items they needed from their packs and pockets.

Subtility's container was smaller than most of the other potions. The boys had constructed it of a thick leather of some kind, so that it was squeezable, and the top was capped with a hollow bird bone. The clever result was that *Subtility* could be squirted onto any surface.

From a Dark Wayover

Leo had never tested the potion; there wasn't enough to spare. As to its effectiveness, he only had the boys' testimony, which he had not doubted in the slightest until this very moment.

He spritzed the side of Joyeuse's glass home, on a spot about halfway up, and all of the *Subtility* was used at once. An area of only a little over four inches (as Wilwell had predicted) was coated in an oily, golden-gray fluid, which shimmered softly for a second and then disappeared completely.

Leo touched the spot with his hand, and his fingers passed right through.

"Whew," he whispered to Rinchwick. "O.K.: *Vermiform!*"

Leo had allowed the boy to carry all the worm-related materials, as a special job meant to instill in him a thrill of honor and prestige. It was plainly successful;

From a Dark Wayover

Rinchwick was almost glowing with pride as he tugged the brown beaker from his little green pack. Leo took it and inserted it along with his entire right arm into the invisible hole in the glass case. He couldn't get in much farther than his elbow, but it was enough. With his thumb he popped the cork out of the beaker and let it clatter to the floor of the case. Its loss did not concern him. He intended to bring the beaker home with them, because he didn't want to leave anything behind with his fingerprints on it, but the cork wouldn't reveal anything to police, other than that this was truly the most puzzling case of theft they had ever investigated! Leo couldn't help but smile, thinking of how much the Walkchair back home would enjoy a detective story like that... *The Cork in the Case*, it might be titled...

Leo tipped the beaker, and a light, watery purple solution trickled onto Charlemagne's ancient weapon. In a blink, the blade dropped out of its holders and landed next to the cork as a fat, wriggling earthworm.

Leo reached down and gingerly grabbed the worm between his thumb and forefinger. He eased his arm out of the hole.

"Case," he whispered.

Rinchwick had it ready. Ms. Winnipeg had prepared a small, sturdy, translucent plastic food storage bowl, filling it with the perfectly damp peat moss she had researched so scrupulously. Leo dropped the worm in to the case, and Rinchwick closed it with a tiny pop and put it in his pack.

Joy shined in the boy's eyes. "We did it!"

Leo patted the side of his face. "Yes, we did! Let's go home…" He brought out his silvery Flute and held it near his face.

A loud, aqueous snap split the air, and the Flute was driven out of Leo's hands and sent spinning through the air. His eyes were barely able to follow a spike-covered cap on the end of a long Cheevilnid tongue retracting quickly back to its owner, who was perched on a nearby wall, blanketed in shadow.

Leo grabbed Rinchwick by the arm and they sprinted towards the Flute, which now lay against a far wall. They stopped with a jolt when Mealworm, grinning with self-satisfaction, waddled out in front of them.

Only a moment or two passed before Leo, his face contorting with rage, made up his mind to plow right over Mealworm, like a howling barbarian. He had only gone three steps when Bludgeon emerged from the darkness and stood beside his small, plump companion.

Forced to leave the Flute for now, Leo turned, sure that he and Rinchwick could flee past Xylykynyxytyr and find an exit on Richelieu's south side. Again, he managed only a few steps before he had to stop again, this time because Rinchwick was ripped away from him.

From a Dark Wayover

The boy was pinched tightly in the coils of Mealworm's rope, which extended like a tentacle from the hoary net bag full of bird bodies. It held Rinchwick in the air, displaying him like a trophy.

"You sthertainly do have an awful lot of theseth, Misthter Von Koppersthmith. You mustht be a collector, like I and my beautiful birdth!"

Leo stood paralyzed by shock and uncertainty. All he could think was: *How? How did they know we would be here?*

" 'How', Misthter Von Koppersthmith?" Mealworm chuckled. "Do you not yet comprehend the Ropemasthter? I told you: I sthee. I sthee you wherever you go. You can't esthcape!" He motioned with one hand, and the rope twisted around Rinchwick's waist even more tightly, making the boy squeal with pain. "Now: sthtop rathing around and sthurrender, or I'll cut your little boy here in half."

From a Dark Wayover

"Stop! Please! Let him go!"

"I will, if you sthurrender."

He's lying, Leo thought. *He'll kill him anyway.*

"I will not!" Mealworm seemed genuinely insulted. "I'll let him go!"

Leo was flustered by the apparent ease with which Mealworm was able to read his mind, especially since an idea was beginning to occur to him. He didn't want it to coalesce within his thoughts before Mealworm could discover it, so he decided to simply act. Its success or failure would depend entirely on if the invisible hole made by the *Subtility* potion was still present on the side of Joyeuse's glass display case or not. Had too many minutes elapsed, erasing *Subtility*'s effects?

In one lightning quick movement, from out of his cargo pocket Leo pulled the *Instant Jungle* that Wilwell had urged him to bring. He thrust it at the side of the glass case: the hole, fortunately, was still there, and Leo's hand passed through. He smashed the bottle to the floor of the case, releasing thick, yellow smoke, and quickly pulled his arm out again.

No sooner had the tips of his fingers withdrawn, a muted explosion of damp, pulpy, green branches and wide leaves filled the display case, making a cramped, cube-shaped rain forest. For a second, everyone stared dumbfounded, while tiny cracks threaded throughout the thick glass with a series of ticking sounds.

The display case burst. Jungle foliage and shards of glass filled the center of the room, and a riot of jangling alarms rang throughout the museum.

Bludgeon whirled towards Mealworm, and for the first time Leo heard the hulking yellow man speak. There continued to be no mouth, and yet pinched words that wobbled between a high and low pitch emanated as if from out of a helmet. "Make a portal, quickly! Guards are coming!"

From a Dark Wayover

Mealworm seemed to ignore his companion, keeping his gigantic eyes, aflame with fury, fixed on Leo. His coiling rope lifted Rinchwick another foot higher and squeezed. "Your *boy*, Misther Von Koppersthmith…"

From the south and north passages, they could all hear running footsteps and shouting Frenchmen.

An impatient, reedy growl escaped Bludgeon's mouth-less head. "Just put him down, Mealworm! You were never going to do anything to him, anyway."

Mealworm shot him with a look of intense rebuke, and then glared back at Leo. "Remember: I sthee you. Wherever you go. I'll sthee you again." He gestured sharply, and the rope threw Rinchwick to the floor. Leo ran to the boy and knelt beside him.

Mealworm hurriedly withdrew their brown, wooden Flute, his fingers pinching its skin-disease-like coating of stubby spikes, and he played a slithery melody.

From a Dark Wayover

A portal opened. Bludgeon entered first, and Mealworm followed.

Leo looked Rinchwick over, but the boy seemed basically unhurt. He lifted him to a sitting position.

"Come on, my boy. We need to get out of here fast..."

A screaming hiss fell upon them like lightning. Xylykynyxytyr, on his way to the portal, could not suppress his wrath and bitterness over Leo's newest triumph, and over Mealworm's sickening weakness in the very moment he held an advantage over Leo. He had let the boy go! Why? WHY? The question burned the Cheevilnid's insides like acid, and erupted from his wide, thin mouth in a stream of spit and more hissing. His thin arms flailed and his gray fists beat savagely upon Leo's head and on Rinchwick's chest.

At first Leo was off-balance and overwhelmed by the Cheevilnid's contemptuous ferocity, but he soon had a tight hold of the creature's wrists. Xylykynyxytyr only screamed louder, and jutted out the tip of his tongue. The vicious spiked cap was still on it. With a tight convulsion of his powerful throat muscles, he fired at Rinchwick. And fired again. And again. He HATED the boy, hated all those boys, hated, hated, hated...

With a berserk howl, Leo heaved himself to his feet and hurled the feral Cheevilnid at a display case against the wall, shattering the glass. More alarms went off. Leo had a frantic perception of dozens of jabbering security guards beginning to fill the area, and of his silver Flute gleaming at him from the same spot where it had originally fallen. He turned to grab Rinchwick.

His heart froze inside him.

The boy was not moving. Blood seeped out of multiple wounds on his chest and stomach, and parts of his face were mangled.

From a Dark Wayover

Leo made a desperate, incoherent sound and gathered Rinchwick into his arms. He ran to the Flute and picked it up.

The security guards were not paying attention to him. They were transfixed by Mealworm's portal hanging in the air before them, and by the ferocious, rawboned, gray-skinned little monster that sprung into it. They watched in astonishment as the frayed edges of the extra-spatial aperture steadily drew together, sucking in air loudly until it popped shut completely.

The high volume of its closing briefly drowned out the melody that Leo played upon his own Flute, so that no sooner did the first portal close, a second opened.

The guards were gripped by dread. Some fled. The ones who remained watched an anguished man carry a bloody, battered child into this second hovering doorway, disappearing into darkness.

From a Dark Wayover

The portal closed. Under the din of alarms, the *gardes de sécurité* stared at one another and for a while said absolutely nothing.

Thirty-three

Under the track lights of the mansion library, Mrs. Von Koppersmith let out a baleful groan when she saw Rinchwick's body, and Ms. Winnipeg began to cry.

Leo ran to a table covered with books and papers and, with one arm, wildly swept them on to the floor. He laid Rinchwick upon the table.

Anselm hurried to a closet to fetch cloths. With a weak and stammering voice, Mrs. Von Koppersmith said they should call an ambulance, but Leo shook his head vehemently. "Too late for that…" He pulled open the boy's shirt, exposing white skin that was punctured and torn.

He hurried to the table of potions. Wilwell already knew what was needed; his blue eyes brimming with tears, he reached for the opalescent bottle of *Fixmender* and gave it to Leo.

"Oh, Leo," whimpered Ms. Winnipeg, hovering over Rinchwick. "His skin is cold…"

Leo didn't respond. He ripped the cap off the *Fixmender* and poured its contents onto Rinchwick's small chest. The pure, clean liquid glittered like diamonds as it fell.

Everyone waited. No one spoke. *Fixmender* mingled with blood and trickled down Rinchwick's ribcage and onto the table.

Oddo chewed his thumbnail. With eyes wet and red, he mumbled, "It might be too late…I think it might be too late…"

Leo swallowed, unable to draw a full breath. He leaned in to Rinchwick's mouth and listened, but heard nothing. He lifted the bottle of *Fixmender* and shook it over the boy's face, causing a few last drops to plop out.

From a Dark Wayover

Rinchwick didn't move.

Leo's shoulders began to sag. He turned around, leaning heavily against the table, his eyes staring down at the floor, and through it, into a pit of utter misery.

Ms. Winnipeg began to cry again, and now Mrs. Von Koppersmith joined her.

Seconds crawled by.

Wilwell, who had been standing back, now approached the table. "Look! Look at him!"

Rinchwick's wounds were sealing up. Torn flesh twisted back into shape and black bruises melted away. The boy's face, so pale with the touch of death before, now grew warm and vigorous again. His eyes fluttered, and opened. He smiled up at Leo, who could only briefly smile back before he laid his head upon the boy's chest and wept.

Among them all, more crying, mixed with laughter, followed. The ladies helped get Rinchwick off the table and on to his feet, but the boy made it clear that he was in perfect health and needed no assistance. A light conversation began, about going to the kitchen and making food, but it was interrupted by a sudden burst of sound. Emotions were already so frayed that everyone involuntarily shrieked.

They turned towards the source of the noise. Upon the floor, Rinchwick's green pack lay where it had been hastily discarded, only now it was in pieces, along with chunks of plastic and peat moss. Atop this wreckage, Joyeuse glowed beautifully in the library's soft lights. The *Vermiform* had worn off; the earthworm had transformed back into King Charlemagne's famous weapon.

···◆··◆··◆··◆··◆··◆··→

On a northwards facing veranda on the third floor, under the moon, Leo sat nearly motionless in a teakwood rocking chair.

From a Dark Wayover

Only Fredlegs was with him. It was here that the Acorn Man lived, in a small house made of sticks and twigs, situated under the vines of a potted ivy plant. He preferred being outside and high above the ground, because it recalled sensations of when he was only an acorn, safe in the boughs of his mother oak tree years ago.

He sat comfortably in the soil of his potted ivy, breathing in the sweet night air, but he wasn't at peace. Leo was taciturn and brooding, and Fredlegs knew of no way to help the bearded giant, who looked down but did not see a "pleasant land of counterpane," unlike the sick boy in that story which the boys often practiced reading. The only thing Fredlegs could think of to do was to hold out Cap, in the hopes that his acorn friend with the floppy red arms and legs would draw a smile.

It didn't work. Leo didn't even notice. He was slowly sipping scotch and tonic on ice from a half-glass, staring numbly as a video on the glowing screen of his laptop relayed the story of the comet predicted by Jondas Molding.

"Ah, here you are," said Anselm, slipping through a sliding glass door. The housekeeper took a seat beside him. "I see you've heard about the big news."

" 'Big news' is one way to put it. 'Apocalypse' is another way. You think, maybe, it's a hoax?"

"Molding himself announced it on live television. Granted, he is the only reason we know, but he assures us that it's out there. And he is the Visionary, after all. There's never been such a prodigy." Anselm shook his head. "As I said before: the normal and the fantastic, becoming the same. I don't particularly like it."

"I can't believe how calmly most people are reacting. You always think, faced with something like this, that there would be worldwide panic."

"Because of Molding's vision. Two heroes will rise, and the second one will neutralize the comet, somehow or the other. Molding is convinced that the second hero is Invictus, and most people believe him."

"Do you?"

Anselm shrugged.

"Do the boys know?"

"Not yet. They're all asleep now—or in the process of falling asleep."

"How's Rinch?"

"Went to sleep with no trouble at all. He's alright, Leo. Don't beat yourself up."

Leo did not reply. He took another drink. He glanced up at the moon, and then gazed at the shadowy magnolia trees below.

"I can't stay."

From a Dark Wayover

"I thought you might be thinking something along those lines. Shall I make a half-hearted attempt to convince you otherwise?"

Leo looked at him. "Nope, I wouldn't bother."

"But why, son? Why do you have to leave?"

"Because I can't allow that to happen again. What happened to Rinchwick…that can't happen again. I don't know why Mealworm and the Corpse want me dead so badly, but it doesn't really matter. The bottom line is that wherever I am, the people I love are in terrible danger."

"But where will you go, son?"

"There's only one place, really: the Island."

"Why there? If what you say about Mealworm's abilities is accurate, then he'll find you there. You could go anywhere…"

"No, it has to be the Island. That's where Zechariah's Sleeping Pool is."

"The Sleeping Pool? Didn't you say it's…"

From a Dark Wayover

"Broken, yes. Bludgeon shattered it. But maybe I can repair it."

"But why…?"

"So I can contact Zechariah again. He was on the verge of telling me a lot of important things, about the sword, and what I'm supposed to do with it. Mainly, though, I just want to know why he isn't helping."

Anselm took note of a new bitterness in Leo's tone. "You're angry at Zechariah?"

"Of course! Where is he? He said he was close. Where? Monsters are breaking into our home, attacking us, chasing us all over the Island—his Island—Rinchwick was nearly beaten to death! I don't have the power to stop people like Mealworm and Bludgeon. But Zechariah does! Why isn't he doing something?

"Look, I do know a thing or two about military organization. The captain of an army will have a dozen

From a Dark Wayover

good reasons for not sharing the entire plan with his soldier..."

"Or maybe he's just a bad captain. Maybe there is no plan."

"Now you're letting fear and bitterness overcome your own experience! Has Zechariah ever seemed like a 'bad captain'?"

"O.K., no. But, for pete's sake, Anselm. Zechariah is the most powerful person I know. He can wipe out an entire army all by himself. He knows full well about these assassins after me, and he knows that the Corpse is behind it all. If Zechariah has a plan, it is far past the time when he might have shared it with us. What could he possibly be waiting for? And now a comet is headed towards earth. It's the end of the world, Anselm! WHERE IS ZECHARIAH?!"

Anselm placed one strong, timeworn hand on Leo's shoulder. "I can't answer that, of course. I'm

From a Dark Wayover

simply going to continue doing, as well as I can, what's been given to me to do, and if a comet falls on me tomorrow—well, that will hurt, won't it? For a second or two. But it won't take away my peace. As far as what you must do, I think you're right: go back to the Island. Fix the Pool; talk to Zechariah. Find out something that makes some kind of sense out of all this madness."

⸺✦✦✦✦✦✦

New York…

Walter opened two bottles of beer, gave one to Max, and the friends toasted their ambush with a cheerful clink of glass.

"So, thanks to you, now we know: Jondas Molding is not what he pretends to be. He's an enemy."

"I saw it, somehow, at the General Assembly…I could see it in his eyes. But, after my encounter with Conrad, I figured I had just been fooling myself. Then Magán showed up…"

From a Dark Wayover

"And that's what really proves it! What would the world say about their beloved Visionary if they knew his most trusted assistant was a cross-dressing psychopath? And all those paranoid questions Magán asked, trying to figure out what you're up to…"

"What do you think about Magán asking me if I was 'Leo'? 'Von Koppersmith'? Who in the world is 'Leo', do you think?"

"Well, whoever he is, he's a threat to Molding."

Max thought about that, taking a sip of beer.

"Anyone who's a threat to Molding is a friend of mine."

"Amen, brother."

Walter stood and let out a long whoop, and he smacked Max on the shoulder, causing him to wince.

"Ow. Everything hurts…"

"Sorry, man. The price of justice! Anyway, you don't have time to hurt. By now Magán has reported back to Molding about you, and it won't take much for

Molding to get your name from Conrad. You need to find somewhere to lay low."

"What about you? Remember: I told Conrad you and I were a team."

Walter waved it away. "I'm not worried about it. I have plausible deniability: I'm just a slow-moving, slightly overweight seminarian. I'll tell them you stopped by to visit, but I didn't know a thing in the world about your penchant for vigilantism, and if I had, why, I would have reported you directly to the police, like the dutiful citizen I am. But you need to get going soon."

"Where should I go?"

"Catch the first flight back to Cinci. Talk to Keystack. He'll help us decide what to do next."

Nodding, Max immediately began packing his clothes. He bundled all of his Darkshot gear into another cardboard box, so that Walter could mail it home for

From a Dark Wayover

him. Within twenty minutes, they were in Walter's car on the way to La Guardia.

With amber streetlights flowing by one after another, casting wobbly reflections on the windshield, their initial elation began to fade, replaced by wordless contemplation. It was Walter who finally broke the silence.

"Why didn't the holy water work?"

Max frowned. "Man, I thought you were the smart one. Don't you get it? He's not possessed. There's a reason people don't believe in all that anymore—because it's baloney."

"It's not baloney. And consider this, Mr. Doubting Thomas: there are different levels of possession. Know what the worst level is? It's called 'perfect possession'."

"Never heard of it."

"Not many people have, especially because it's extremely rare. Almost unheard of. It's when the person wants to be possessed. They know exactly what they're getting into, and they willingly choose it, because they know it will give them power…for a little while, anyway."

"What does that have to do with the holy water?"

"It wouldn't work on a person who's perfectly possessed. Because they don't want it to."

Max screwed up his face in disgust, and he sat quietly, letting Walter continue.

"It's a theory, anyway. But maybe *you're* right— maybe he's not possessed at all. I need to think about it some more. Do some reading. Regardless, Jondas Molding has to be stopped, right?"

"But what about the comet? He's at least trying to help prevent that. Maybe we should just let him and Invictus work it out."

"Because somehow or the other Molding is using that comet to bring about his own evil scheme. I know it. My gosh: what if there is no comet? What if he's just making it all up?"

"Won't NASA and other people be able to verify it?"

"But they haven't yet, have they?"

Walter's car turned into the drop-off lane next to a set of glass doors and a sign that read 'baggage check-in'. Max turned to his friend and gave him a powerful handshake.

"You're the best. I can't thank you enough."

"For what?"

"For trusting me. For not thinking I was a freak for wanting to fight crime."

"Hey, well…you trusted me, too, when I told you Molding was a bad apple. Thank you. Now, go home! Stay safe. Give it a week, and then call me, O.K.?"

From a Dark Wayover

Max threw his army-green duffle bag over his shoulder, gave his friend a wave from the sidewalk, and went through the glass doors. Walter sped away, shouting triumphantly: "Darkshot!"

···+·+·+·+·+·+·+

Five days later, the telescope aboard the Russian space station *Zossima* spied it hurtling from out of the pit of space. Seven days after that, smaller terrestrial observatories saw it, too. Astronomers labeled it as a non-periodic, hyperbolic comet, drawn from unknown origins by the gravitational pull of the sun on a one-time passage through the solar system. Earth lay directly in its path. Popularly, it became known as "the Jondas Molding."

As news of it began to filter out into the world, people took to speaking of Molding's foreknowledge of it's coming in awe-inspired, nearly mythical terms, calling it "The Vision of the Two Heroes." It was observed, by

From a Dark Wayover

astute commentators on talk radio programs or in online essays, that this name expressed the underlying hope of people everywhere, since it was not being referred to as "The Vision of Total Doom" or "The Vision of Armageddon." People were, it was deduced, confident in the saving power of the mysterious Heroes from the vision, and of Jondas Molding's assurances.

"The first will fail, the second will prevail" began appearing in graffiti on the sides of train cars and subway stations, at first, then as part of federal and state-funded ad campaigns designed to mollify everyone's anxieties. The intelligence and spiritual leadership of Jondas Molding and the superpowers of Invictus, with the support of governments everywhere, would save the world. There was nothing to fear. The first will fail, the second will prevail.

···✦·✦·✦·✦·✦·✦

From a Dark Wayover

The day after his exploits in Paris, before dawn, Leo left the estate to purchase camping and hiking equipment, including a machete, but only because it came with a green canvas sheath that could be attached to his belt and used to house the sword of Charlemagne. After he returned home, he gathered the boys and told him of his intention to return to the Island and contact Zechariah.

"Security guards will still be here, just in case, but you don't need to worry about attacks, because it's me the assassins are after, and they'll know that I went to the Island."

Many of the boys protested loudly. Tears began to flow. Nobody wanted Leo to leave, and they were worried that he would be hurt.

"And what if you never come back?" said Benjamus in his drowsy, turtle voice, wiping his nose ponderously with the back of his hand.

From a Dark Wayover

"No, no, now, that's crazy talk. Of course I'm going to return. But I have to talk to Zechariah first. He has a plan." Leo glanced at Anselm, and they exchanged a sober look. "And," Leo continued, "He'll let us in on it when it's the right time…"

"But, Dad," exclaimed Wilwell, "How are you going to get to the Island from the sky portal? Mount Hollowchest is gone. There's no way to climb down anymore!"

"I thought about that already, and I have an idea. Don't worry about me, fellas. Just stay here and be good boys, like always. Be patient. Keep doing your schooling with Ms. Winnipeg, and help take care of things. Will you do that?"

Leo spent the next hour giving out hugs, encouragement, and good-byes. He took Wilwell aside and had the boy re-explain all the remaining potions.

"You're taking them with you?"

From a Dark Wayover

"Yep…well, not the *Bigifiers*. But all the others, yes. When I get to the Island, I want to be ready for anything."

Oddo joined them, breathing rapidly, holding a sheet of typing paper covered in minute black doodlings. "I made a map of the Island! I can't believe it—I just happened to have been working on it for about a week, just as a fun pastime, but once I heard your announcement I ran and made a copy for you!"

He and Wilwell gave Leo hasty descriptions of the various regions represented on the map, and what sort of flora, fauna, and Oblate-built structures could be expected.

"Be careful, Dad," they said, hugging him as tightly as their little arms could. "Come back soon."

Leo closed his eyes, feeling his heart about to break, smelling the spicy warmth of their hair. He almost, *almost* invited them to accompany him, but he knew he

From a Dark Wayover

couldn't, he just couldn't…the way to protect them now was by facing the danger on his own…

By that evening, Leo was ready to depart. For fear of Mealworm, he did not want to stay a minute longer than necessary. With his gray backpack full of supplies, he went to an abandoned corner room of the mansion, accompanied only by Ms. Winnipeg.

"Well, I don't like this, Mr. Von Koppersmith," she said, staring up at him plaintively. "I was given to understand that when a boy and a girl at last find each other, they are supposed to remain together."

Leo knew there was nothing to say in response, so for several minutes they simply held each other.

"Look after everybody," he said at last. "And don't be afraid."

" 'Don't be afraid'," she repeated. Her face was a tangle of conflicting emotions. "Such a stupid thing to say at a time like this, I think. 'Don't be afraid'. Stupid,

stupid. I _will_ be afraid, and I _will_ miss you, until you come back."

Leo looked at her pityingly, and his smile was bittersweet. "Alright, then. Be afraid; miss me."

They kissed. He played the Flute, opened the Wayover, and stepped inside. They exchanged one last wave goodbye before the aperture pulled shut, and a heavy silence followed.

⋯⇾⋅⇾⋅⇾⋅⇾⋅⇾⋅⇾⋅⇾

Leo made his way through the warm darkness until he reached the final chamber, where blue-ish daylight glowed from the round portal on the floor. The air below was clear. Thousands of feet down he could see the green of forests and hills, and the orange of lava or the black and brown rubble of fallen Hollowchest.

Leo sat, and waited. There was nothing else to do, since there was no ladder and no mountain to offer him passage.

From a Dark Wayover

Two hours passed. He retrieved an electric camping lantern from his pack and clicked it on, and then pulled out some water and trail mix. As he ate, he listened to the moaning winds of the Island sky as they blew past the portal. What he was waiting for had still not happened, but he was confident it would.

He lay back upon the cushiony floor and let his mind leisurely ruminate upon the concept of the extra-spatial being within whom he now rested. *Amo'Ahshqaya.* She was here, around him, sheltering him. Leo wondered if she knew what he was thinking. He almost spoke to her, but he felt uncomfortable about it. *What if she answered back?*

Finally, to his pleasant surprise, what he was waiting for began to happen, and much sooner than he had expected.

He packed up his lantern, along with his shoes and socks. He hung his bare feet over the edge of the portal, and frigid air bit at his toes. The bright light of day had diminished to a gray glow, but not because the sun was setting. Clouds had coasted in from the south, a wide, thick front full of rain, high above the Island, and only about three feet below the portal.

Leo poured a dose of *Nonpondo* on his bare feet. The liquid was amber, and filled with miniscule blue beads, and it dribbled sloppily.

"Pour it on your feet, and you can walk on surfaces you would ordinarily fall through," was how Oddo had described *Nonpondo*.

Clinging to the edge of the portal, he stretched his right leg down into the sky.

He was instinctively ready for the sensation of cold, wet fog upon his toes. Instead, his foot was softly bumped, as the clouds slowly drifted by.

Leo let himself drop.

From a Dark Wayover

He now stood upon a vast gray and white land of thunderclouds. Some areas reached up like piles of soapsuds, while others toppled away into smoky canyons where sheets of purple and white lightning flashed and flickered.

The surface of the clouds was slightly pliable to Leo's feet, like a rubber mat. He took a step forward, and another, but then stopped as a moment of terror overtook him. He could feel the entire cloud continent moving him. It all felt so unnatural that he wasn't sure he could continue.

He looked back. The sky portal was, of course, invisible, now that he had passed through it. Without the peak of Hollowchest as a marker, there was no way to know where it was anymore.

Leo looked west. Many miles in the distance, rising like a conical island, was the top of Mount

Highpalace. The Cheevilnids will all be there by now, he thought.

 He took a deep breath. He adjusted his pack so that it was snug upon his back, and he positioned Joyeuse so that it hung comfortably in its green canvas sheath upon his left leg.

 Sunlight shone far away to the north and west, and more lightning played within the billows somewhere deep beneath his feet.

 Leo gave a last poignant thought to Ms. Winnipeg and the boys and everyone back home, interiorly asking that they would remain safe, and then he began his journey across the clouds.

THE END

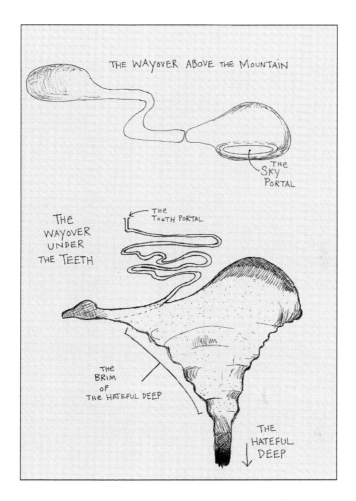

Figure 2. Wayover Maps, by Oddo, assisted by Leo.

From a Dark Wayover

By the Author

-The Von Koppersmith Saga:
    Book 1: *By the Downward Way*
    Book 2: *From A Dark Wayover*
    Book 3: *A Fantastic Confluence*
-*Choosing Joy*

Explore more of Dan Lord's work at

ThatStrangestofWars.com.

Figure 3. A sketch of the assassins, by Oddo.

Made in the USA
Middletown, DE
16 November 2021